——— BLOODSTAINED ARCHIVES ———
BOOK I

LIFEBLOOD

B.W. GREEN

DEDICATION

To Daddy, who taught me that stories are to be shared.
-Your forever monster movie buddy.

PART I
THE CAVE

1

The sun glowed warm on his face. Dr. Ethan Dalton turned back toward the building he'd just exited and had to shade his eyes against the sunlight glinting off the slate roof, making the rays scatter through his fingers.

At six stories high and extending over the whole block, the building had the architectural look of a palace more than that of a university. Presentations of scientific breakthroughs and cutting-edge research seemed to always take place in droll and hidden surroundings, like the last conference he'd attended in the basement of the 1970s office building in uptown New York City. The university in Bucharest, Romania seemed a much more fitting setting.

"Is that what you're wearing?" Dr. Jack Murray was jogging toward him, wearing a T-shirt, khaki hiking pants, and a suspiciously wide, dimpled grin.

Ethan glanced down at his own white dress shirt and black slacks. "Our presentation ended ten minutes ago. How are you changed already?"

Jack clapped his hands and extended them wide, "That's ten whole minutes we've been free to explore, man! C'mon, get your stuff from the hotel. We're burning daylight. I've got the rental car already."

"We have the whole weekend. What's your hurry to leave Bucharest? There's a lot to see in the city."

"I told you Alexi said we can't leave Romania without getting up to the mountains near Brasov. And we're going hiking so tell me you have different shoes."

Ethan eyed his dress shoes, thinking his friend and colleague was way too much of a jock for a genetics nerd. He should have known better than to agree to explore a foreign country with a man who spent his weekends escaping the city to hike to waterfalls and caves. Jack even looked more like an outdoorsman with his fit physique and stylishly spiked dark hair, while Ethan appeared more like the genetics professor they both were, with shoulders that were constantly stooped over something and hair that was forgotten for months at a time.

"You've got to get out of the lab more," Jack continued.

Ethan spun in a half circle and gestured at his surroundings. "I'm pretty far out of the lab right now, aren't I?"

"And would you even be *here* without me talking you into it?" Jack asked, his grin turning cocky.

Maybe not, but he wasn't conceding the point.

"But seriously, on the shoe thing."

Ethan gave his shoulder a casual push. "Yeah, I have tennis shoes all right? Let me go back to the hotel and pack up. There's no telling what you're going to get us into."

He got twenty minutes to change and pack before he was herded into the rental car with his overstuffed suitcase. Jack drove, and Ethan rested back against the passenger seat and watched the unfamiliar sights drift by. Having lived in New York City all his life, he'd seen a fair share of peoples and cultures, but he hadn't ventured far to explore them. Instead, he'd spent most of the last eight years of his life focused downward on the very tiny building blocks of life and their mysteries.

Jack, his research partner and fellow author on the research they were presenting at the conference, had somehow convinced him to come out of his lab and travel halfway across the world to share knowledge with other like-minded academics. But he wasn't going to admit that the trip had him embracing the idea. Not while they were busy getting lost in the back roads of Romania.

Views of architecturally varied buildings gave way to rolling hills draped with grass, its green tired from the long summer but not yet yellowed.

"Oh, did you see that road sign?" Jack cut into Ethan's reverie, jerking his attention back to the road but not in time to see the sign.

"No. What did it say?"

Jack's lips moved into several silent shapes before he said, "You know. Something in Romanian."

"Wow."

Jack's ever-present grin belayed concern.

Ethan reached for Jack's phone perched in a cup holder. "Why, where are we?"

"Well, I think I've lost service. The GPS is still pulled up…but it may have started having some trouble getting a lock on us."

"So we're lost."

"No, no, we're not lost. I'm just not sure it knows where we are."

"That's the definition of lost, Jack." Ethan set the phone down and retrieved his own to reveal the same lack of connection.

"We must be on this road here," Jack pointed to the screen. "I'll make the next left and see if I can get it back on track."

The rolling hills visible through the windshield grew as they approached them, until the tops were revealed to be naked rock reaching for the sky above, and the road degraded into a pothole-covered one lane.

"There's no way this is the road you're supposed to be on."

"No," Jack used a finger to scroll the map around, "And this doesn't have us on a road at all anymore."

"Just turn around and go back."

"Hold on, let me see if there's something up here…"

Ethan opened the glove compartment and pushed aside some rental papers to find a map. Unfolding it in his lap, he stared at it for almost a mile before looking back up with no further insight. It was pretty hard to use a map to figure out where he was going if he didn't know where he was to begin with.

Jack made another turn that took them down a narrow road with even more pot holes in it. "Seriously, there's no way this is going back to the highway," Ethan grew insistent. "Just turn around. We're only losing more daylight out here."

Jack's response was still, "It's an adventure!"

"Until you need food and a place to sleep."

"It's not even dark yet. We have time."

"If we turn around now." The GPS map had them in a blank field of green.

"Fine, fine," Jack sighed. "We'll turn around when I find a drive or turn off or something."

Five minutes after Ethan would have stopped and made a three-point turn—or however many points were necessary—Jack eased the car off the road next to an old post and rail fence. The ground momentarily evened out, but as Jack drove forward, the car bucked and threw Ethan forward to catch himself against the dash. Jack winced but kept cranking the wheel to get them back on the worn pavement facing the other direction. "Ok, here we go."

The bumping didn't stop as he started driving the way they had come.

"That can't be good," Ethan groaned quietly.

Jack stopped in the middle of the deserted road and opened his door to look. When he grunted without further explanation, Ethan got out to see for himself.

The back left tire was flat.

"Here's hoping that there's a spare in the trunk."

With no good options to pull off the road, they worked through changing it where they were. They each took a turn keeping a lookout for any traffic coming around the curve and scraping their knuckles on the pavement while trying to work the jack and the wrench.

As they finished, the sun dropped below the ridge of the mountain, and Ethan squinted in the twilight at the spare tire that looked little better than the flat one they had just wrestled off. "We're not going to get far on this."

"Well…" Jack's grin had mellowed a level. "We'll just–hey, look. A person."

Following Jack's wave to the field on the other side of the fence, Ethan spotted a figure approaching slowly over the old brown stalks. It was a wiry old man who had the look of a tree that had grown clinging to the rock of the mountain.

"What are the odds he speaks English?" Jack asked.

"Better than the odds that we speak Romanian," Ethan replied and started for the fence.

The old farmer met them there, and, after listening to Jack's eager questions and looking them over for a solid minute, he cracked a smile that showed several missing teeth. "American?"

"Yes, we are," Jack confirmed.

"Come! My village. Stay. Fix tire." His broken English was indeed infinitely better than their Romanian.

"Where?" Jack asked eagerly.

He gestured further down the road they were on, waving his hand in some vague directions, pointing up and then down with a few words that could have been instructions. Jack continued to nod as though he understood, although Ethan lost track after the first wave.

When he finished, Ethan asked, "You have new tires, out here?"

"I find, bring," the man waved, confidently dismissive. "You come. Visit. See," he opened his arms toward the mountains.

"Are there some trails back here? Hiking?" Jack pantomimed hiking with a walking stick.

"Yes, yes!" the man agreed. "Hike. Climb. Cave—beautiful!"

"Really? A cave?"

"Jack, I don't know about following this guy's random directions," Ethan tried to get his attention while keeping his voice low to avoid seeming disrespectful to the friendly farmer.

"C'mon," Jack turned to him. "You're right, it's getting dark. Let's just go to this guy's village, let him help us out with the tire, maybe spend the night and explore tomorrow. It's beautiful out here! Why not take advantage of where we ended up, even if we didn't mean to, huh?"

Ethan rubbed a hand over his face. *Next time I travel with you, I am doing the planning,* he thought. But he followed Jack back to the road. "Did you really understand his directions to the village?"

When Jack insisted that he did, Ethan helped direct him through a four-point turn to reverse their direction yet again before climbing back in the car himself.

It was completely dark by the time Jack took another turn onto a road that was barely paved but sloped down into a valley. "Here's that left turn he mentioned. See! We've got this!"

The minutes stretched out as Ethan peered forward until, out of the darkness, warmly lit windows appeared below and in front of them.

Jack drummed the steering wheel in victory, "Now we're talking!"

The town was nestled in the hollow of the dark mountains. As they drove onto a bumpy cobblestone road, the light from the house windows was enough to show pale colored walls, shadowy red tiled roofs, and wooden fences between them.

Jack stopped in front of a building that seemed noisier with people than a home would have been. "C'mon, adventure time."

"And the last four and half hours haven't counted, because...?" The car door squeaked as Ethan pried himself out of it.

At their approach, the painted wooden door of the building opened, and Jack greeted the first person they met with the whole story of their journey. The old man whose shoulders said he may have been a lumberjack when he was younger answered in curt Romanian and then waved over a younger man with a full beard who was able to greet them in English.

Ethan opted for a shorter version this time, "We're here from the States at a conference in Bucharest. We were driving and got a bit turned around."

Once they realized that Jack and Ethan needed a place to stay, the group of men became very hospitable. Before he knew what was happening, Ethan was seated at a table with a beer in his hand and some kind of sausage and potato dish in front of him.

Jack struck up a conversation with the bearded man, learning that his name was Nikolai. The others clustered around them as Nikolia told them that this was an old village that had been there in nearly the same form for centuries, and was definitely off the beaten track. They were nestled in the edge of the Carpathian Mountains, and Nikolai confirmed that there was much natural beauty to explore should they stay.

At that point in the conversation, the old lumberjack who they had first greeted started an angry sounding rant that seemed to be directed at them.

After their bearded host had argued back in Romanian, Ethan tentatively asked, "What's wrong?"

"Nothing wrong. He is—how you say—superstitious. Of the mountain."

"What about it?" Jack leaned forward.

Now we're in for it, Ethan thought. If there was some local legend to go with the great outdoors around them, Jack was definitely going to be hooked.

"Old stories," Nikolai continued. "Monsters steal children and take them back to their cave and thing like that."

"What's *strigoi?*" Ethan asked about a word the old man had said that rang some kind of bell in his memory.

One of the other men at the table got up and wandered away. Actually, the crowd had thinned considerably after the old man had started his rant.

"It is the evil, ah, demon. It eat blood and hide in the caves." Nikolai shrugged but looked away.

Ethan just nodded. Demons that drank blood. In Romania. He wasn't much into fairy tales, but even he had heard that one before.

Jack was grinning again.

Nikolai changed the subject and started asking them about lodging. When they finished eating, he led them down the cobbled street to a house he called an "Inn." With its stone walls, small wood lined windows, and vines growing over the arched doorway, it had an old-world cottage charm that was impossible to get at home in New York City. They hadn't seen the old farmer around anywhere yet, but Nikolai agreed that he could help them find a replacement tire tomorrow, so they prepared to spend the night.

An older, tidy-looking lady who seemed to speak exactly three words of English welcomed them and escorted them to a room upstairs with two single beds, a wooden chair, and a small table. She pointed down the hall to a room where Ethan could see a sink and toilet. Ethan thanked her repeatedly while Jack carried their two large suitcases up the very narrow staircase, bumping the walls despite his efforts.

Closed into their small room, Jack held out his arms. "Admit it. This is not an experience we were going to get locked up in the four-star hotel in Bucharest."

Despite the harrowing journey, Ethan acknowledged the uniqueness of their current situation. "Maybe not."

"You good if I hit the bathroom first?"

"Yeah, go ahead." Ethan sat cautiously onto the edge of one of the frilly dressed beds and pulled a scientific periodical out of the front of his suitcase.

"Seriously? Now? You're such a nerd."

Ethan shrugged, "I have a PhD in genetics. I think that's been established."

Jack gave an exaggerated gesture at himself, "But that clearly doesn't mean you can't also be cool."

Shaking his head at him, Ethan leaned back against the lacy pillow and opened the journal to the first article. As far as he was concerned, the greatest adventure was discovering something new. That could be accomplished in the pages he read just as easily as whatever crazy outside adventure Jack had in mind.

2

The wavy glass in the window in the front room of the small bed and breakfast gave an impressionistic perspective of the village outside. Ethan sat at a table covered with an intricate lace tablecloth eating breakfast and staring out at the mountains surrounding them. Despite his wariness at the unplanned adventure Jack had gotten them into, he had to admit that their surroundings were beautiful and the people were kindly hospitable.

Jack plopped down in the chair across from him, looking as though he had already taken a jog around the village. "Eat up. We're definitely hiking that as soon as you're done."

Ethan stopped with a bite of his pancake-like fried potato breakfast halfway to his mouth.

"You're telling me you don't want to go enjoy that beauty?" Jack pointed to the window.

"I'm enjoying it right now."

Jack dismissed that with a shake of his head and took a gulp of coffee from his dainty cup. "I ran into that old farmer dude while I was out. He said he's going to go find a tire—I gave him the specs—and he gave me directions to that cave he was talking about."

"Seriously?" Ethan took his own sip of coffee and coughed against the slap of bitterness.

"I know we didn't mean to come here, but you seriously don't want to go look around?" Jack asked with his mouth full. "You scared of that blood sucking demon thing?"

"That's not the point." Not believing the legend didn't mean he thought wandering into a cave alone was a good idea.

Jack just drank another swallow and urged him to hurry up.

⌐

An hour later, Ethan found himself in his tennis shoes tripping up a path behind Jack's hiking-booted feet.

"You coming?" Jack's voice came from around a bend.

"I'm trying to actually enjoy the view," Ethan tried to sound less out of breath than he was.

"C'mon!" Jack didn't stop moving up the hill.

Ethan resumed his pace but continued to lag behind because he stubbornly stopped to look out at the view a couple times. The deep green of the forest covered the hills like a blanket except where it was pierced in places by naked gray cliffs and peaks. In the valleys, fields of lighter green were dotted by white sheep.

By the time the morning cool had evaporated, leaving him sweating, Jack made some excited noises from somewhere in front of him. Ethan traipsed faster around a clump of trees to find Jack standing triumphantly in front of a rough cleft in the rocky cliff. Mist oozed from inside the cave to curl around the trunks of the tall fir trees. It was momentarily mesmerizing.

"You feel it!" Jack enthused. "It's inviting us to explore."

"I'm not sure that's what it's telling me," Ethan replied.

After strapping on his headlamp, Jack slung his small backpack back onto his shoulder. "Are you telling me you aren't the least bit curious?"

Ethan hesitated. He was…the least bit.

Apparently taking that as a "yes," Jack started toward the cave opening. "Let's go, fellow scientist. Explore."

"Just don't get too far ahead. The only light I've got is my phone."

"And whose fault is that?"

"Apparently I missed 'headlamp' on that packing list for presenting at a conference in Romania."

"You won't make that mistake again," Jack's voice echoed.

The instant Ethan stepped through the rock cleft, the air temperature dropped, sending a chill through his sweaty back. The gradually sloping floor of the cave was gritty, while the rock wall glistened with moisture. Mist glowed in Jack's headlamp beam. There was something inherently intriguing about caves, the way it was a completely different climate and ecosystem only steps away from the outside world.

"Look!" Jack's light pointed upward.

The rock above undulated and flowed like water, sparkling deeper into the darkness. "Ok, that is cool." They stared at the sight until Ethan's foot slipped off a rock, sending a sharp scuff echoing into the darkness.

"Woah–Hey!" Jack reached to grab at Ethan, who had only slipped a few inches. "Man! I thought you were a goner for a second," he started laughing.

"What, you think the demon had me already?" Ethan started picking his way down the slope littered with loose rocks.

"You never know about these legends," Jack followed, his hands-free light and better boots giving him the edge to quickly get back in front. "There had to be some origin."

"Stories people tell children so they'll behave," Ethan countered. He was a scientist. He believed what he could see and observe, not the supernatural. Although what he could see at the moment wasn't much, because as they walked further into the cave passage, the daylight was quickly blotted out.

The feeling of being cut off from the outside world settled over him like a blanket, but Jack was still moving and getting out of sight around the bend in the passage, so Ethan hurried to keep up. The relatively flat pathway wandered for a while between rough walls and ended in a stack of large rock slabs.

As Jack started exploring the area, Ethan's gaze compulsively followed the light of his headlamp to a very small opening near the floor.

"There's no way we're going in there." Exploring a cave he could walk into was one thing. Squeezing into a tight opening with possibly no way to get out again was quite another.

A moment later, Jack found another opening behind a rectangular boulder that would require some stooping and possible crawling to enter. "How about this one?"

"You don't know where that goes or if it narrows."

"That one?" The light was pointed up a sheer rock face.

"Do you have a death wish?"

"Ok, so option number two."

"Jack–"

"If it narrows, we just come back." He was calm in his logic and experience.

Ethan drew a deep breath. "We need to go back before we get completely turned around. I'm not getting stuck in here."

"We know the way back, it's right there," Jack countered. "We haven't gone that far. C'mon, let's just see where this goes, and we can come back." He bent over and waddled into the opening, brushing his backpack against the tunnel's top.

Ethan stooped to follow but then paused half in. Had that been a sound? A faint chirping or clicking? "Did you hear that?"

"What?" Jack's voice called back from down the tunnel, far enough that the light from his headlamp was already fading.

Alarmed at the idea of getting separated, Ethan plunged in, stooping further over to avoid ramming his forehead into a low hanging rock. "Slow down."

"I'm right here."

When he had to drop to his knees and hands, one of which still clutched his illuminated phone, Ethan stopped. "Ok, that's far enough."

"I hear you. But I think it opens up in a sec."

"I'm stopping right here."

"Yeah, just a second…" Jack's distracted voice echoed back.

Ethan scooted backward until he could sit up on his knees without ducking under the mountain of rock above him and tried to slow his breathing. There was no reason to panic. Jack was just up ahead. The way back out was right behind. He had a light, however inadequate, in his hand.

Everything was fine.

They were having fun.

Jack yelled—in fear, not glee.

"Jack?" Ethan leaned forward and shined his paltry light down the tunnel, but he didn't see anything except more rock. "Jack!"

Silence.

Or was that clicking sound back?

Icy fear snaked down his spine to grab something in his chest.

"Hey!" Jack's voice.

Ethan sagged in relief.

"Sorry, the ground dropped out in front of me there, startled me." Scuffling sounds preceded his light, then his face appearing out of the gloom.

"You scared me to death."

"Sorry. All good." But he wasn't urging him to keep going any more.

"Ready to go back?"

"Yeah, but take it slow. There's still plenty of cool stuff to see."

Less sure about that, Ethan squeezed around to face the way they'd come. The darkness sucked in the light only a few feet away. He shuffled forward more quickly, feeling an irrational urgency to escape the confined area. It seemed to take much too long until he ducked back out from under the flat boulder and stood up straight again.

Jack bumped into his back as he joined him and nodded confidently. "Take it easy. We're fine. Just go back the way we came."

But Ethan was looking the way he thought they had come, and it was not immediately obvious where the path back started. The blanket of claustrophobia tightened closer.

"It's not as bad as that," Jack addressed Ethan's tight expression, "We know it's right here. Just move that way."

A faint, high-pitched, repetitive clicking echoed through the darkness somewhere above. Ethan held his breath. "Do you hear that?"

"What?"

"It's like a clicking or something, listen."

Jack paused. "It's probably a bat."

That made sense, and Jack was the nature guy, but, "I don't remember seeing any near the front of the cave, did you?"

With a too-careless shrug, Jack adjusted his headlamp and continued shining it along the cave wall. "Here, the path is right there."

"Where?" Ethan squeezed around Jack, bumping into the boulder.

Pain pierced over his right shoulder blade.

"Ah!" His heart skipped a beat to launch into his throat. He was stuck, held tight, and couldn't get away.

"What?" Jack swung around, shining his headlamp straight into Ethan's eyes.

What's got me?

Nothing.

Nothing had him anywhere.

His shoulders and back were pressed against a slab of rock. The light that obscured Jack's face showed nothing but emptiness on Ethan's left and more rock on his right.

Ethan jerked away from it to stumble into Jack.

"What? What happened? You ok?"

Breathing was necessary for talking.

Inhale. "I…I don't know. I'm ok."

"Did you back into that rock?"

Had he? He could have sworn something had a hold of him. "Maybe."

Jack chuckled, "Wow, nothing like a dark hole to get you tense, huh?"

Embarrassment started creeping in, easing the fear. Ethan rubbed his face and looked from the bare flat rock to Jack.

There was something behind Jack, a shadow blacker than the darkness.

Reaching for him.

His heart plummeted. "Move!"

Even as Ethan grabbed for his arm, Jack was pulled away from his grip back toward the shadow. The light from his headlamp flickered like a strobe and gave the disorienting impression that the rocks around him were moving, until it went out with a crack and a scream.

"Jack!" Ethan lunged at him, but his hands closed around thin air. He swung around, phone light held out like a shield.

A shadow seemed to materialize at his other side.

Something seized his arm—something that was impossible to yank away from. It threw him to the side, smacking his hand—and phone—against the rock and plunging him into blackness.

Panic surged, pulling a yell from him that echoed high into the invisible cavern above.

Then he was free, able to move again. He ran, hands outstretched, into a wall of rock and edged along it blindly until a light momentarily lit again, behind him.

As soon as he turned around, it went out. Back into disorienting darkness.

Something grabbed him from behind.

He launched his fist at it and hit something solid.

"It's me!" Jack's voice gasped. "Move. Now. Go back!"

"I can't see!"

"Just move!"

Jack pushed him shuffling across the dirt floor until his heel caught on something hard and threw him elbows-first onto the ground.

Keep moving. He scrambled backward, following Jack's gasps until he could roll to his knees and stand again.

But we're trapped!

A small light flickered, illuminating Jack clutching his backpack and holding up a lighter with its single flame, his face smeared with blood and dirt and fear. "C'mon, this is the way we came—it has to be. Keep going."

They stumbled through the path in front of them.

Faint sunlight became visible once again, illuminating the whole rock-covered slope that led toward the entrance. Their panting and scraping steps echoed off the high cave roof as they strove for the light.

Only when he was out of the cave mouth did Ethan pause to look back into its yawning throat.

Nothing moved.

No sound but silence.

He was welcomed back into the daylight by a warm breeze, the smell of pine, bird chirps, and rustling leaves.

They collapsed at the base of a tree trunk, riveted on the dark cleft in the rock, waiting for something to follow, but only mist hovered on the other side of the opening as though it were a gateway.

"Ok," Jack wiped his brow with his wrist and then turned his hand over to examine the blood on it, "Do we believe in legends now?"

Pushing his hair off his sweaty neck, Ethan grasped for a realistic explanation, "Do you think one of the people from the town set us up? Tried to rob us or something?"

"I don't know, but I lost my phone."

"Me too." Eyes still on the darkness inside the cave, Ethan guzzled the water Jack handed him. "What made it let us go?"

"'It'? So, we are thinking—"

"He, she, it, whatever. I couldn't actually see anything. Did you get a look at who it was?" He wanted to question whether they were just jumping at shadows, but something had definitely grabbed him.

"No, I shined my phone light right at it, I thought, but nothing was there. That's when I got away."

Got away from what?

"Want to keep going?"

"Yes," Ethan answered before Jack finished his question and quickly stood, anxious to put more distance between them and whatever—*whoever*—had been in there. They hustled through the trees to the edge of the ridge where the village was visible in the valley.

"Want to see if we have a new tire yet?" Jack asked.

If Jack was thinking about getting out of the town, maybe he was more rattled than he'd let on. "That sounds like a great idea."

Without a path, they wandered over a carpet of moss and old brown leaves until the fear waned, making the whole ordeal seem less real, and they came to the edge of a field with another split log fence. By the time they once again approached the town from the hill above, Ethan started to question his perception of what had really happened in the cave.

"What do you think? Should we walk into town and find the pub like this," Jack held up his blood and dirt-streaked arm, "and see who's behind scaring us?"

"We don't know who it was. Maybe we shouldn't start accusing people." Considering he was growing less sure about what had actually happened, confrontation seemed even less ideal. "Besides, if someone was just trying to scare the foreigners, I feel like not admitting that it worked."

"Fair point. Inn first then."

The path morphed into old stone steps that led to the courtyard of the cottage, where no one seemed to be home but the back door was open. While Jack ducked into the small bathroom, Ethan started pulling off his dirty clothes in their room. His damp shirt was stuck to his skin on his back. Once he got it off, he found a large patch of sticky blood on the back.

After trying unsuccessfully to crane his neck to examine the back of his right shoulder, he gave up and perused the scrapes on his hands and elbows and one on his knee that corresponded to a new hole in his jeans. Tired of waiting on Jack and the shower, he trudged to the bathroom and tapped on the door. "You ok in there?"

The water cut off. "Yeah, I think so. It turns out I have kind of a deep cut on my arm. Could you grab the first aid kit out of my bag?"

Of course you have one of those. After rummaging in Jack's suitcase, Ethan returned with a clear bag full of bandages and ointments.

"Thanks," Jack opened the door and took it, holding up his right arm that bore an uneven gash on the side. At least one edge of the wound looked deep, like a puncture.

"There was blood on the back of my shirt, could you see what's there?" Ethan asked.

"Yeah, where?" He twirled his finger at Ethan.

Ethan twisted his shoulder in his direction.

"Oh." Jack picked up a washcloth and wet it at the sink. "There's actually a decent amount of blood there. Does it hurt?"

Ethan shrugged, "Yeah, but I'm sore everywhere now." He let Jack scrub the blood off, and it did hurt when he wiped right over the cut.

"Sorry," Jack grunted. "There's a couple of deep spots. Forget souvenirs. We'll take back matching scars to remember our trip by."

"Or to warn off anyone else who dares to travel with you."

Jack chuckled. "You want to shower too?"

"Yeah, I'd say so."

"Ok, go for it. Then I'm thinking it's time for a food quest."

"And tire."

"Yeah, that too."

3

Cleaner and hungrier, Ethan and Jack ventured down the cobbled street to locate the place they had eaten the night before. When they walked in, they were greeted by the old lumberjack. He seemed to eye them suspiciously but showed them to a table without objection. Since the place was primarily occupied by older men who didn't speak English, they weren't very successful at communication, including asking about tires. But they were given food and beers and discovered they were happy to sit and decompress for a while.

As the afternoon stretched on, more men appeared from out in the field or from whatever work had occupied them, and eventually Nikolai walked in.

Jack waved and darted a quick look over at Ethan.

Ethan shook his head. He could see no reason to admit what had happened to them. He'd rather just get out of the predicament. So, without mentioning the cave, they exchanged some greetings, relayed that they'd had a good day exploring the countryside, and asked about the tire.

While Nikolai was giving a vague answer about a place they could get one, Ethan noticed the wiry old farmer slink in. He hovered at the edge of the room and stared openly at them.

Since Nikolai apparently didn't have a tire or a concrete plan to get one, and Ethan was tired and buzzed enough that his attention was drifting, he nudged Jack and nodded at the farmer who was easing to the bar door. Catching his drift, Jack swallowed the last of his beer, set his heavy glass and some money on the table, and made some excuses for them.

Unwilling to let the first person who had promised to help them get out of the town out of his sight, Ethan hurried to the door after the farmer. They caught up to him in the street, and Jack stepped in front of him. "Hey, how's it going? Any luck finding a tire for us?"

"Ah, hello," he looked them both over. "I, er, not find one today. Next day, I find, yes? You enjoy the day?"

"Yeah, it's beautiful out here."

"We do need to get back to the city though," Ethan broke in.

"Yes, yes. Enjoy the night," the man turned slippery, backing up without meeting their eyes. "See tomorrow…" He ducked around the edge of the building, surprisingly quickly.

Ethan rubbed his face. "This is getting ridiculous."

Jack sighed, his expression lacking his earlier exuberance. "Maybe. Do you want to just go, see how far the spare gets us?"

Ethan studied the sky, where the sun was already touching the edge of the mountains that rimmed the town. If they left now, they may well end up in the exact scenario that had ended yesterday, but without a place to stay.

Jack followed his gaze. "Or spend the night, leave in the morning?"

Ethan nodded, "Yeah, that sounds better than getting lost with you in the dark *again.*"

Jack gave an exaggerated snort, "Fine. You want to go back inside?" He pointed his thumb at the pub.

Ethan's head was already spinning enough. "No, bed sounds good."

They started down the street toward their lodging, and he added, "Is it just me, or did that farmer guy seem a little surprised to see us?"

"I don't know," Jack stumbled over a stone. "You think he set us up or something?"

"I have no idea at this point. But I think I'm ready to be done with this adventure."

Once they made it back to their room, Ethan gingerly sat down onto the single bed with another journal in his hand. *Man, I'm sore.* Apparently he was not in shape for hiking, spelunking, and running from invisible assailants all morning. When he leaned back, the metal headboard squeaked uncomfortably against his back, so he reached for a blanket from the end of the bed and squished it behind his pillow, dropping his head back to blink slowly at the yellowed ceiling.

ꓶ

When Ethan blinked his eyes open again, the room was dark except for the bathroom light from the hall. He reached to rub his eyes and found the open magazine on his chest. *I must have been more tired than I thought.*

Jack stumbled into the room.

"You ok?" Ethan pushed himself up to his seat.

"Yeah. I think I must have had one too many beers."

Ethan rubbed his aching head. "Yeah, me too. Maybe the beer is as strong as their coffee."

Jack dropped onto his bed a few feet away.

"What time is it?" Ethan asked.

"Like two or something."

Moving his dry tongue around the inside of his mouth, Ethan stood up. "I'm gonna get some water," he mumbled on his way to the bathroom. After drinking from the tap, he rolled his shoulders against the stiffness in his back but stopped when the cut on his back pricked with pain.

Jack was already snoring when Ethan eased back into the bed to lay down with a groan and closed his eyes again.

The next time Ethan woke, sunlight was streaming in through the lace curtains over their window, stabbing at his eyes.

That must have been some beer. He squinted and shaded his eyes with his hand.

Jack wasn't in the other bed, but the sound of retching came from the bathroom. Steeling himself for the headache, he dropped his hand and pushed himself up, grimacing at the ache in his muscles. A fumble on the bedside table found his watch.

9:47 a.m.

Good grief. Their plan for an early start had already gone awry. He shuffled stiffly to the bathroom door and knocked. "You ok?"

"Peachy," came the reply, after a couple more coughs. The door swung open, and Ethan closed one eye against the light above the sink.

Jack was sitting on the floor against the wall. "You look like I feel," he croaked.

"Remind me to warn people from hiking *or* drinking with you."

Jack grunted and wiped his mouth on a towel.

"I'm going to see if I can find something to drink downstairs. You want anything?" Ethan asked.

"Definitely not."

The descent down the stairs went slowly. He felt kind of feverish, achy, and chilled. One day didn't seem long enough for infection to set in any of his cuts, but maybe he should check them.

As soon as he entered the front room, their hostess bustled a greeting in Romanian. From her look at the clock, he guessed she mentioned something about their sleeping in.

He tried to wave away her motions to the kitchen. "That's ok. We're not feeling too well this morning. I think we had too much to drink last night." He accompanied his explanation with some hand motions, and she seemed to get the gist.

She offered coffee, and he countered with, "Water?"

She pulled a container of water and a jug of juice from the refrigerator. When Ethan pointed at both with a grateful expression, she handed them to him with a smile and two glasses.

Using his chin to avoid dropping a glass during his ascent, he forced his legs of jelly up the last stair and into their room and set it all on the small table. Jack was slouched on the edge of his bed with his head in his hands.

"You should drink some water." Ethan poured a glass of water and pushed it into his hand.

He got a groan in response.

"Just drink it," Ethan prodded and followed his own advice before plopping into the little wooden chair next to the table. "Ready to get on the road?"

Jack propped chin on his hand and blew a breath through his lips. "Let's give it a couple hours, huh?"

"Yeah, ok." After a sip of juice, Ethan shuffled to the bathroom. He lifted his shirt and twisted to get a look at his back in the mirror but could still only get a sideways view of the wound there. Despite being more sore, it didn't look red or swollen or anything like he thought it would if it were infected, so he dropped his shirt and rubbed his temples. More liquids and rest became his plan, after a dig into his toiletry bag for some aspirin.

Since Jack was lying down with a pillow over his head when Ethan returned to the room, he laid down too and tried to read some more. But his eyes burned and his head throbbed, so he gave up, dropped the journal with a thwack to the floor, and closed his eyes again.

⌐

It started raining at some point. Ethan listened to the tapping of the drops against the window pane for a while as his head pounded even more intensely.

A thump made him open his eyes.

Jack staggered from one side of the door frame into the other.

"Jack." Ethan moved to stand but sharp pain in his legs made him stop with a gasp.

When Jack thudded louder in the hall, Ethan struggled to the door. "Hey," Ethan reached for him, down where he was on his knees, and grasped his shoulder right as Jack vomited onto the hall floor.

Ethan jerked back with a curse.

The vomit was red with blood.

Bad, bad, that has to be bad! Something more was going on than a hangover. "Hey, let's get in the car right now. We need to get you to a doctor."

Jack slumped.

"No, come on!" Ethan shook his shoulders hard, rousing him enough that he leaned against the wall and opened unfocused eyes.

"We need to drive back now. We need to find a hospital."

Sluggish head shake.

"Yes. I'll drive. Let's go now." It felt like there was an ice pick embedded behind his eyes, but Ethan was scared and not about to let his friend die in a small Romanian town. It was time to get out of there.

Light footsteps sounded on the stairs, and their hostess called something up. She appeared just as Jack vomited more blood onto the floor. She froze and stared with wide eyes.

"I need to get him to a doctor," Ethan rasped. "Do you think someone could help us to the car?"

Without taking her eyes off Jack and the blood, she scurried back down, yelling something.

Ethan straightened. His head throbbed hard enough to blur his vision, making him grab the wall for support.

You have to do this.

Clenching his teeth against the nausea from the pain in his head, he collected all of their things he could quickly lay hands on and shoved them into a suitcase. Leaving Jack momentarily, he grabbed both bags and the keys from the table, sucked in a breath, and dragged them down the stairs. He had them halfway to the door when he heard the old woman's voice again.

"I say no." A thick accent coated her English words. She gestured to the stairs and then out the window.

"What?" Ethan had to blink to focus his gaze on the mountain outside.

"No," she repeated and pointed up the stairs. "Die."

"No. He's not going to die. I just need to get him back to Bucharest." Ethan didn't understand, but her conviction was feeding his growing fear. He wiped at the sweat running into his eyes. "We're leaving. I'm sorry for any trouble."

She started motioning at him.

"I'm fine." He resumed pulling the bags to the car and braced himself against the trunk when he got there.

He wasn't fine. But he also wasn't vomiting blood, so there was that.

He managed to lift both bags into the back of the car and close the trunk. Out of breath, he plodded into the house where the woman was still standing, staring at him, jaw set.

Ethan shook his head. *He's not going to die.*

Back upstairs, he grabbed Jack by the upper arms. "Jack. I need you to walk, ok? I can't lift you."

He nodded slowly and with Ethan's help managed to get his feet under him. One stair at a time, with Ethan holding onto the wall himself, they got down the stairs.

It took much too long.

Ethan ignored the woman, still hovering in the front room, and concentrated on making it to the car.

After getting Jack into the front seat and slamming his door closed, Ethan almost collapsed. Grimacing, sweaty hair falling into his face, he supported himself with his arms on the hood to get around the car.

It had started drizzling again. His grip on the door handle slipped, making him grab for it twice. He fell into the driver's seat, pulled the door closed, and reached across Jack for the map, dripping water droplets onto it. It was in his hand when he remembered that he still didn't know exactly where they were.

Useless. He dropped it back on the floor. There was no going back into the house just to get told that they were going to die again. He would start by retracing the way they had come. At the first sign of someone else, he'd stop and ask for directions to Bucharest.

"Sure about this?" Jack slurred from the passenger seat. He was limp against the seat, eyes open but unfocused.

"No," Ethan shifted the car into drive. "But there's not another option." He aimed the car up the road they had taken into town.

Clouds obscured the late afternoon sun. *When did it get so late again?*

Fumbling around the sides of the steering wheel for the windshield wiper control to clear the drizzle from the windshield, he steered up several switchbacks to the ridge. From there the road started to dip down the other side.

Jack slumped against the door.

Ethan looked over at him. "You still with me?"

He almost didn't see the old truck pulled across his lane.

Ethan slammed on the breaks and yanked the steering wheel to the left, screeching the tires on the wet road. The front of the car slid into the low shoulder, stopping with a jerk against a fencepost.

"No, Come on!" Ethan slammed his palms into the steering wheel, jolting pain up both arms to explode in his head. Blinking hard, he saw a figure out the raindrop-distorted window. Maybe he could help Ethan call for the police or an ambulance. Surely there was some emergency help, even out in the middle of nowhere Romania?

Ethan opened the door but stopped before getting a leg out.

The wiry old farmer stood at the fence line.

He was staring across the car at the other side.

The passenger side door swung open. A figure in a dark hood loomed over Jack, something metal glinting in its hand.

Jack held a hand out, but the figure swiped at Jack faster than Ethan could blink.

Scarlet blood spilled from Jack's neck as he fell back against the seat.

"No!" Ethan yelled and reached across the seat for him.

There was blood everywhere.

Covering Jack's chest and arms.

Sticky on Ethan's hands.

Still pouring, pouring to fill the seat with a pool of it.

Jack's eyes implored Ethan for help for a moment, but then his body started to relax as color faded from his face.

"Jack." Ethan's plea was a whisper as he watched his friend breathe his last.

Something grabbed Ethan by the arm and dragged him from the car. Weak and spent, he barely even got his feet under him before the old man shoved him face first up against the car.

His mind wouldn't move. He could only wait to die the same way.

Rough hands tore at his wet shirt, pulling it against his throat and ripping it down the back. When the old man released him, Ethan gasped and slumped against the car.

The man pointed at him.

Was that fear in his face?

"Strigoi," he rasped.

The hooded figure appeared in front of him.

Was this the moment he died?

Instead, the figure grasped Ethan's face and raised it. Ice blue eyes stared out from the darkness under the hood.

Her voice was triumphant: *"Strigoi."*

4

Ethan's shoes slid on the wet leaves, landing him once again on his knees in the undergrowth. An iron grip on his arm pulled him upward, but he had no will to stand again. He didn't know where the woman in the black cloak was trying to take him, but he wished she had just finished it back at the car. With Jack.

Before he could finish the thought, her hands lifted him upward. His yell for help ended when he was hoisted over her shoulder, which punched the breath out of his chest.

His weight didn't seem to slow her ascent through the forest. Rain streamed into his eyes, turning the trees into phantoms in the dim wet world, and dizziness flooded his throbbing head. Unable to even tell which way was up, he gave up fighting.

When she eventually dropped him, he flopped heavily onto the mossy ground. It took a moment to bring the bare rock face of a cliff into focus. There was a black opening at its base.

Something was making a high-pitched clicking sound.

Panic injected strength back into his aching muscles. He pushed up to his hands and knees and scrambled backwards, away from the dark maw.

A second figure emerged from the cave mouth. A man.

The woman said something incomprehensible, including the word *"strigoi"* again. The man's lip curled, but whether in disgust or in a smile Ethan didn't have time to guess, because without warning he strode to him and yanked him by the arms and legs onto his shoulder.

Watching the dark opening approach was watching death descend, but no amount of struggle stopped it from swallowing them into blackness that was absolute within moments.

Apparently unhindered by the darkness, his captors moved fluidly forward, bouncing him against the man's back until the aching muscles in his arms spasmed into tight knots of fire. His mind refused to accept what was happening. His thoughts splintered. Could he be back in bed at the inn, feverish and dreaming? Or maybe he had never even left Bucharest. Or his home in New York.

Or maybe he had died next to Jack. Was this the dragging of a damned soul to hell? Perhaps he had been a fool not to believe in an afterlife.

In any case he was powerless.

Consumed by the growing pain, he closed his eyes against the darkness and didn't open them again until he was abruptly dropped. Gasping for the breath that was knocked out of him, he turned his head, felt a soft material under his cheek, and forced his eyes open.

He could see. The light was warm and flickering on the surrounding harsh walls of stone. Under him was something like a blanket. The cloaked woman stood in front of him, with her hood pushed back off her black hair. Dark eyes, not blue, caressed his face in a way that was not entirely severe.

"Am I dead?" he rasped.

Her pale pink lips parted to reveal white front teeth, then pulled back into a smile.

The points of her canines reached down to her lower lip.

Ethan stopped breathing. *Legends and demons and—*

"Strigoi," she purred. *"Etem Vampir."*

⌐

Ethan was left alone, but he didn't have long to consider entering the darkness beyond his open cell because the pain in his body and head continued to grow, crippling him. The dull ache that started deep in his bones blossomed to a burning fire that gradually expanded outwards, causing him to writhe on his pile of blankets until they were damp with his sweat.

There was only enough energy to concentrate on breathing one breath.

And then another.

Until even that was agony.

The screams that tore from his throat brought no relief or attention. When the burning lit his skin afire, he again waited for death, certain that the human body could not survive pain at this level for long. Surely something would burst if one more neuron fired.

Then the fire burned into his head, and smells and tastes erupted through his consciousness with fireworks that emblazoned his vision.

Only then, finally, did oblivion enfold him.

⅄

It wouldn't completely hold him, though. Unconsciousness repeatedly, partially released him into a fog of endless anguishes, again and again.

⅄

Until she was there again. Sandpaper seemed to line Ethan's eyes as he blinked slowly, forcing them open and closed and open again.

Her words meant nothing to him. His tongue was cemented to his palate, preventing him from opening his mouth.

She knelt next to him and lifted him. Unable to muster strength enough to tense a single muscle, his head fell back, until she rested it against her shoulder and brought a cup to his face. It smelled sweet, with a hint of something sharp, and he managed to look down as she tipped it.

The liquid was blood red.

He tried to pull away, but his body wouldn't cooperate, and she easily maintained her hold on him while bringing it to his lips, tipping it upward, and giving a one-word order.

The warm liquid coated his tongue and slid down his throat, rich and sweet. She stopped after the one sip and lowered him back down.

For the first time in untold days, he didn't immediately slip back into a semi-conscious fog. The taste still on his tongue, he was gradually able to think more clearly. Something in his chest felt…not pain.

⅄

The next time she entered, he could turn his head to look at her. She lifted him, but he was able to hold his head up. When she held the ornate silver chalice to his lips and gave him the same one-word order, he didn't fight her but swallowed twice. The richness coated his stomach, reliving an ache of hunger he hadn't identified until then. When she left, he lay still, feeling more intact.

The third time, he lifted his hand to grasp the cup. Smiling, she allowed him to empty it, and when she had gone again, he rolled over as calmness washed over him. His mind stilled but was also clearer. His body felt relaxed but stronger.

It was sleep, rather than unconsciousness, that embraced him when his eyes closed.

5

Ethan awoke before she came back. It was brighter than he remembered. The floor and walls appeared to be smooth stone, but the ceiling rippled in formations that glittered in the wavering light. His hands curled into the soft fur under him as he pushed himself to his seat. The ache in his bones was still there, but it was a faint memory of the fire that had been.

Closing his eyes, he tried to think, to remember what had happened over the past few…days? His mind seemed to skip and catch at vague memories. He had no idea how long he had been in the cave. He had no idea what had happened to him since the night in the rain.

But that night he could remember, clearer as seconds passed, and panic started to bubble up.

They'd been sick. Poisoned? Infected? It didn't matter so much because of what came after.

Jack. The car. Blood.

Jack was dead.

She had killed him.

She had taken Ethan.

Now he was…in the cave?

That part didn't make sense. He hadn't died. Had he?

She returned, interrupting his spiraling thoughts, and met his stare with a raise of her chin. Her black hair was braided back in several braids, she wore dark clothing but no cloak, and she carried more than a cup.

When she handed him the goblet, he hesitated. He comprehended more fully now what it was inside. It should have revolted him. Instead, it was as a cup of cool water to a man dying of thirst.

Closing his eyes, he took it, drank it, and relaxed at the taste and the satiety that it brought. When he opened his eyes, the panic had retreated.

She retrieved the goblet with something like amusement in her face and set down a bundle of what looked like clothing and a pewter pitcher of water next to it.

As if suddenly aware that he had a nose at all, Ethan noticed the stench emanating from himself and the area around him. She said something else to him, but seeming to anticipate that he wouldn't understand, then simplified her instructions into two words, one when pointing to the pitcher and another pointing to the clothes.

"I think I get it." The words croaked from his hoarse throat.

She didn't move.

He eyed the clothes and water, himself, her. She seemed content to sit and stare. Ethan ran a hand over his face, stopping when his fingers reached his jaw. There was minimal stubble there. It disputed the feeling that his agony had lasted a long time. The small observation threw reality back into question.

She stood abruptly and left.

Left alone with his tangled thoughts, Ethan started moving, mostly to see if he could. His reach was slow, testing, as he picked up the clothing on the ground. The material was black, a little rough, and the front of the pants and tunic style shirt laced up without buttons.

The water was cool, but it didn't chill his skin when he used the provided piece of cloth to clean off. Not sure standing was a good idea, he completed the task of changing seated on the edge of the fur as his mind started spinning again. Shirt half on, he reached a hand back over his shoulder. There was no wound there now, within reach of his fingertips.

The image of it, half glimpsed in the bathroom mirror, flashed in his mind followed by her smile.

Her teeth.

Had a rock cut him? Or had it been a bite?

What had really happened to him?

She had used the word "vampire." He'd heard that one clearly.

Was he really supposed to believe that he had been bitten by a myth and somehow changed into a supernatural creature?

What are you drinking?

Reality warped around him.

He pitched sideways and caught himself with his hands on the rock ground.

That felt real.

It was cool, rough, hard. It allowed him to click his analytical brain back on.

Stop! He gave himself the mental command.

Just stop. Start over.

If he was going to get through this, to figure out what had happened to him, he had to take it one step at a time.

So. How to start?

Ground rules.

First, he had to assume that what he could observe was real. If he was hallucinating or delusional or…well, then none of it mattered anyway.

Second?

Second, he had to suspend all previous understanding. If what he saw didn't fit his understanding of the world, he had to analyze it as something new instead.

Those decisions made, he finished pulling the shirt on and blew out a breath.

Wait.

First observation: Was he breathing?

He placed his fingers on his wrist. His whole premise tilted when he couldn't find a pulse, and he slapped his hand over his chest.

Thump.

A heartbeat below his palm.

Two seconds went by.

Another thump.

His brain told him his heart should have been racing, but it was…he counted. Without a watch or clock he couldn't be exact, but his pulse rate may have been about twenty-five beats a minute.

He inhaled and found it unnecessary to do so again for a count of twenty.

He was alive. His heart was beating; it was just slower. As was his breathing.

He touched the stubble on his face. He considered how little it seemed he'd had to eat or drink in the last few days he could remember, but felt no hunger now. If he put those things together, he could hypothesize that he had a lower metabolic rate overall.

Why? How?

Slow down.

She was back, with a piece of glass in her hand. A mirror.

It was as though she wanted to help him discover what he had become.

Ok, then.

He hesitated before taking the cracked square of reflective glass, and repeated the rules to himself again before he looked into it. *Assume what you see is real. Analyze it as something new.*

It was his face.

Dark straight hair, a little long for a clean-cut professor but about right for an absent minded one. Dark gray eyes. Light skin. A couple days' worth of stubble. His face was a touch thinner, perhaps, and a little paler, but there was plenty to explain that.

Teeth?

He pressed his lips together, hesitating again. With a quick head shake, he opened his lips. Crooked front teeth, the same as they had been since he was a teenager. He pulled his lips back further. Pointed canines, upper and lower, extended nearly to the opposite gum line when he closed his mouth—not extreme but definitely different.

What's your explanation for that? If he was to accept that something had changed certain things about his body, how did he explain how had it gone so far as to change teeth that had formed when he was a child?

One thing at a time.

She was reaching for him again, slowly at first, with eyes that bore into him. Eyes that turned instantaneously blue, and then her hand was at his throat.

Ethan jerked backwards.

But she let go easily and motioned to the mirror.

His own irises had turned the same shade of blue. The mirror dropped from his hand.

She tilted her head, and in the span of a blink, her eyes were brown again.

Ethan looked down at the mirror, now on the fur-lined ground under him with a crack on the edge, and watched his eyes fade back to brown.

It was a struggle to analyze rather than react.

Ok, so that's different.

It did explain why he remembered her on that night with blue eyes. They could change. Being scared had changed his. Maybe it was linked to an emotional or hormonal response.

She pointed to him and said something the inflection seemed to indicate was a question. The language sounded similar to Romanian, but more archaic. Although he wasn't a linguist, he recognized an ancient Latin base to it, but not enough to understand what she said.

"Caterina," she pointed to herself.

"Caterina," he repeated.

She pointed back at him.

Oh. "Ethan."

"Etan," she adapted.

"Sure."

She said another word, motioning with her hand for him to follow. *"Come,"* he mentally interpreted.

Could he?

He tentatively pushed himself to his feet.

Yes.

He took a step. There was no head-swimming dizziness or knee buckling.

So, another.

She led him out of the room and down a narrow passage. The floor was cool smooth rock under his bare feet. He passed a wrought iron lantern hung on the wall of the passage, where a warm flame burned a lump of something, and smoke wove into the crack in the cave ceiling above. A look backward showed that he had not passed any other source of light.

It didn't seem enough light to see by, but he could, clearly.

He swallowed and continued to follow Caterina as the path floor became steps upward, steep and uneven but smooth and easily climbed.

The passage opened, as though through a doorway, into an expansive cavern that stretched above and away from him. It was the size of a massive stadium, larger than any cave he had ever seen or imagined. The floor was relatively flat and smooth, and several passages extended out of the cavern, marked by a pair of flanking lanterns each. The roof undulated in curtain after curtain of stalactites hanging high up in the shadows.

He stopped to stare.

"Come."

Feeling adrift in a strange world, he obeyed and followed her across the open space, past an enormous table at one side, and into another tunnel. The walls were ornately carved, like stone pillars of an old castle, and it ended in a huge wooden door held by massive iron hinges.

Caterina grasped the hefty ring handle and pulled it open. Across a floor layered in furs, between two stalagmite pillars, was an ornate iron chair that could only be described as a throne. The man seated on it looked older than Caterina and was clearly a type of royalty. A thin circle of silver sat low like a crown on his gray-specked hair. His thick black robe pooled at his feet as he rose from his seat and greeted Caterina. She inclined her head to him and swept a hand in Ethan's direction.

Ethan stood rooted to the spot as the robed man approached him, circling around him as though inspecting a new specimen with piercing blue eyes. When he came to Ethan's face, his lips pulled back into a smile.

The elongated canines appeared even more prominent in his mouth.

Before Ethan could dare to guess at the meaning of the exchange, Caterina led him out again and partially across the central cavern. Approaching one wall of it, she leaped, in a single step, up to a stair approximately two stories above their heads.

Ethan stopped in his tracks and stared upward.

"Come," she repeated the word Ethan had interpreted and waited, looking down at him.

But that was, in all his previous experience of life, impossible. The rock shelf she stood on was far above his head on a smooth rock wall with no handholds. Unable to find adequate words, and aware they might not mean anything to her, Ethan just shook his head hopelessly.

She crouched and reached a hand down toward him. *"Come,"* her voice was confident.

There seemed to be only one answer. Suspending his disbelief, Ethan inhaled deeply, took one running step, and jumped toward her.

Somehow his shoulder collided with the second step above her feet, nearly ricocheting right off again before she grasped his arm. Her grip secured him and let him put both feet flat down on a step.

She met his baffled look with a knowing smile and continued ascending the steep staircase cut into the wall of the cavern.

Ethan's brain felt like it was going to overheat.

One at a time.

He focused on one step at a time and climbed up the uneven stairs. When the weakness he'd expected at his first step of the day caught up with him several stairs in, Caterina wrapped an arm around him and supported him the rest of the way to the opening in the rock wall at the top. The edges of the opening were carved, and it opened into a hall-like passage. She led him a few hundred feet down it, turned into an opening on the left, and left him next to a...bed?

Iron posts supported a kind of mattress which was layered in woven coverings and a soft animal skin. A small lantern sat on a rock shelf nearby, giving flickering light to the small space. With another one-word command and a gesture at the bed, Caterina left him there alone without a backward glance. Unable to stay upright, Ethan fell back onto the forgiving mattress and blinked hard.

His thoughts swirled but were overcome by fatigue, and he drifted back to sleep.

6

Voices echoed faintly, and a high chime rang somewhere from the other side of sleep. Ethan slit his eyes open to focus on the iron lantern on the rock shelf next to him. The flame had gone out, but enough ambient light seeped in through the doorway that he could make out his shadowed surroundings.

He pushed himself up and took one slow, slow breath as his mind filtered the events of the day before. His first inclination to panic, while tempting, had to be abandoned. As far as he could tell, he'd been kidnapped, physically altered somehow, and imprisoned. If he wanted to reverse any part of his current condition, he needed to think, not panic. So, he forced his mind only to observe and analyze.

There was still a weary and sore quality to his body, but he felt rested. With no way to measure time, he didn't know how long he had slept. He also felt thirsty, or hungry, maybe both. The bed and its coverings and the lamp were the only objects in the room. He eyed the open doorway, wondering what manner of imprisonment this was, exactly.

You might as well test the rules.

That was an unnatural thought for him, but since sitting still alone was unlikely to yield the answers he needed, he got up and obeyed it. Eyes roving, each step tentative, he followed muted sounds to the main passage that had led from the stairs and across it to a chamber on the other side where the light was strongest.

Inside, Caterina sat at a wooden table. Next to her sat a man—the one who had carried him into the cave.

Ethan stopped.

37

Caterina motioned him into the room as though not at all surprised to see him and introduced her companion simply as "Stefan." She took the ornate pitcher in front of her and poured thick red liquid into the third simple cup on the table and nodded at Ethan.

It was morning coffee with the roommates. Except he was in a hole in the rock lit by a flickering lantern and offered a cup of blood. And these weren't his friends. These were his captors.

I'm going crazy.

But who could blame him?

He sat down on the empty stool in front of him and took the cup.

It smelled different today. He took a sip and gave it a second look. It still had a sweetness but wasn't as rich as it had been before, and there was a metallic aftertaste.

Are you seriously critiquing how blood tastes? he questioned himself.

Then Stefan snickered.

Caterina flicked a wave at him and told Ethan to, *"Drink."* Another word he could interpret based on recent experience.

When he obeyed, she refilled his cup.

After Ethan had finished the second cupful, he was led down some of the stairs to a space that clearly functioned as a communal bathroom. Realizing that he hadn't needed to search for it since he'd changed his clothes yesterday, he got lost in wondering how his bodily functions had all seemed to become much slower and blindly followed Stefan until he found himself back in the room with the table. *The parlor,* he mentally called it, looking around again.

Definitely going crazy.

Caterina glided into the room and handed him a stack of clothing topped with a pair of leather shoes. The whole stack was black, as was the tunic she wore.

She held her palm out to Ethan with a single word, *"Stay,"* perhaps.

"Here?" Ethan pointed at his feet.

Her response was to repeat the *"stay"* word and gesture at the table and in the direction of the room where he had slept.

"Then what?"

His questions didn't matter. They left him standing there alone.

Did they trust him to just obey?

Such a strange imprisonment.

At first, he did stay. Stay and analyze his surroundings the best he could. The walls of the rooms were artificially straight, the floor nearly polished, while the ceiling was the roof of a cave. The style of his wrought iron bed frame and lamp, stuffed mattress, and stitching on his leather shoes seemed decades or centuries old, and yet nothing looked worn.

Unease coiled in his chest, like he was missing something. Of course he was missing something—he was captive in a cave in a changed body—but it felt more specific.

He wandered into the corridor, which led to the stairs in one direction and farther into the rock in the other. Before he could take a step either way, he realized something. Yesterday, after drinking the blood, he'd felt better. Less uneasy. Calm even, enough to find himself curious rather than only fearful about his surroundings. Today he might jump out of his skin at the next shadow.

Now uneasy about feeling uneasy, and anxious to not think about blood for a minute, he hastily chose to venture deeper into the rock. He wasn't just going to "stay." Even if they caught him, what else could they really do to him for disobeying, anyway?

There were more rooms, or small caverns. Two held little to prick his curiosity, but the third had a door. Feeling uncharacteristically impetuous, he pushed.

It opened. The chamber was much larger than the others and grander, in a cave-like way, with crystal stalactites along one wall. It held several trunks and a table and chair in addition to a bed draped with furs. What looked like a partially finished garment lay on the table, alongside needle and thread.

It must be Caterina's room. But it wasn't a way out.

He walked back the way he'd come and cautiously started down the stairs. About half way down the unease blossomed to outright fear. He could see the cavern floor below. It appeared empty, but it was huge and shadowy, so there was no way to be sure. He could also see how many passages appeared to lead out of it—a lot of them. He had no idea where any of them went or where to start.

His prison had no bars, but it was a maze. And he was still weak from whatever had altered his body. He needed more information, more strength before he just ran.

He retreated back to the relative familiarity of the parlor and found a bowl of fruit on a rock shelf.

Can I eat you? he almost asked the purple plum he picked from the bowl. But why not? He was alive. In a body that had different rules, but not a supernatural creature or ghost. It was reality, still. Surely.

The firm skin split under his bite and dripped tart juice onto his chin. It went down fine, and settled into his stomach without problem, although without adding much to his satiety.

Weary with wondering and striving to keep the fear at bay, he retreated to his room—if spending one night in a place could make it "his."

Spiraling thoughts…

One thing at a time.

Repeating it didn't keep the resolution from slipping through his fingers.

7

The next time Ethan ventured from his room, Caterina and Stefan were once again seated at the table in the parlor. At least 50% sure it was the next morning, he decided to interpret her greeting as, *"Good morning,"* or an equivalent and sat down and reached for a cup.

The sudden slap on his hand made him recoil in surprise.

"No." The meaning of that word was apparent. Caterina turned his cup upside down.

Stinging hand snatched back into a fist in his lap, Ethan watched her warily and wondered why the rules were different from yesterday.

"Stay," she gestured to the table and toward his room and paused. Then she pointed at him and up the corridor toward the other rooms during a speech that sounded disciplinary and included the word, *"No,"* again. Her last motion was back to the overturned empty cup.

Ah. Ethan understood. She knew he hadn't quite stayed yesterday, and here was the answer to his wonderings about repercussions. *Fine.* He stood to leave again.

"Stay."

He slumped back into his chair, pointedly avoiding Stefan's smug look and feeling like a petulant child, which irritated him.

Sometime later, when their cups were empty, Caterina stood to leave and waved at Ethan, *"Come."*

Now what? But he'd found few answers so far, even while disobeying. So, he followed.

She led him to the long staircase on the wall of the huge cavern, down a short way, and to another opening halfway down. Squeezing through a crack-like crevice in the massive rock wall brought them

41

through a tight passage to the base of a steep incline littered with small rocks and debris. Gaze darting around the space that appeared much more like a cave than the squarish rooms, Ethan stopped. There was no light in here, other than what shone through the opening behind them, yet he could see details of every stone. How different it was to take in the cave this way than it had been to see only a few feet at a time in a flashlight beam.

Pain stabbed in his chest, sharp enough that he grasped at his shirt to find what had impaled him. Finding it intact, he choked on the grief and met the gaze Caterina had turned back to him. "Why? Why did you kill him? We were both sick. How could you just kill him!"

Her smack to his mouth took his breath, and words, away with its sting.

Questions weren't allowed either? Or was it English that was off limits? Either way, he was forbidden answers. He was here, and Jack was not. Every second that passed he waited for that to change, but here he stood, at the bottom of an incline that Jack would have loved to explore, being urged forward by his killer.

I'm crazy.

C'mon! His friend's voice echoed in his mind.

How can I?

One step at a time.

Rocks and soil slid from under his feet as he tried to follow her up the incline, but when he used his hands to help, Caterina slapped them and knocked him to his knees on the jagged rocks.

Without giving him time to gasp and wince, she pointed to his feet. *"Use your feet,"* he guessed at the meaning.

Shaking his head, Ethan struggled to get his unsteady feet under him, flailing with an arm for balance.

She tapped his head and waved her hand away, *"Stop thinking. Come."*

Thinking that he wasn't one to just stop thinking, he watched her feet dart over the rocks, landing directly under her body with each footfall. He hadn't thought he could make that leap upwards to the stairs, but she had known. Maybe he could do this. Maybe he would need to do this, to get out.

He pushed himself up, stepped, slid, kept from reaching down, and tried again. He managed to reach the top of the incline and dropped to his hands and knees, panting. At least it felt like panting. The heartbeat pounding in his chest was still slower than once a second.

A flame flared suddenly, under Caterina's hand in a lamp on the rock wall. The space around them had gradually become darker as they climbed, but now, with the light from the flame, Ethan could actually see in front of him.

"Oh boy."

The cave opened up into an expansive passage that looked as though the roof had caved in at some point. Rock slabs the size of trucks lay toppled against each other, arrayed like a giant child's pillow fort. There were high points and crevices deep enough that the lamp light couldn't reach the bottoms even with his new vision.

Caterina leaped over black space to a large flat boulder that stood on end against another. *"Come."*

No way.

"Stop thinking. Come!"

If he didn't, would she punish him in some other way? Worse, if he didn't, would he have no hope of figuring out how to get out of here? Or if he did jump, and he did fall, and he died…would death be worse than living helpless in the cave, as this, in this world?

"Etan!"

Nah.

He jumped.

And landed on the sloped surface of the rock he'd been aiming for. His feet slipped from under him, but he caught the edge of it with one hand.

"Again." Caterina seemed to simply step across the wide void to the next one.

He followed, flailing his arms on the landing but staying on his feet.

They continued, landing on precarious footholds three more times across the boulder graveyard, until Ethan's tired legs gave out and dropped him to his hands and knees on a tilted boulder.

Caterina nodded and crouched into a more relaxed posture.

Relieved, Ethan sat on the top of the rock with a heavy sigh. *That was the craziest thing I have ever done.* But he'd done it. Those leaps should have sent him careening into the depths of the cave, but he'd landed every one, albeit gracelessly.

Caterina pulled a flask from a cord around her neck and extended it. Ethan accepted it and took a sip. It was water. He frowned at his disappointment. *What have I become?*

The rest she allowed was not long enough before she glided to another rock. *"Come."*

Ethan remained where he was. "What if we don't?"

Quicker than it took him to say it, she stepped back and struck him on the mouth again.

After blinking at the sting, he glared at her, infuriated to be denied any reply whatsoever.

When she leaped away, he tried one word in her language, *"No."*

Without addressing him, she took another leaping step back the way they had come.

He was still sitting in the middle of a rockfall, at least five jumps from the way back to familiar territory. What was he going to do? Just sit here?

It was a futile rebellion.

He meant to yell his frustration, but the sound that came from his throat was higher pitched and echoed about the cave and its crevices.

More evidence that his body had been altered. It was disorienting. And terrifying, but he couldn't think of that and keep moving.

When she'd disappeared, he debated options but ultimately admitted that he only had one. He didn't know enough to try to run off. He had to go back for now. To her.

It was harder to get back without her directly leading the way. More than once, the rock he decided to aim for proved a poor choice, threatening to dump him into the cave depths. Yet he clung on and made it back down the hill to the opening that led to the staircase.

Exhausted, he flopped onto his back.

Dread coiled in his gut.

He'd worked out very little regarding how he'd been changed and where they were, but he had learned that she had multiple ways of making him do what she wanted. And wasn't sure he wanted to know what was next on her agenda.

8

Dr. Garth Qualls propped his chin on his hand to close his gaping mouth. *There has to be more.* His fingers tapped his long, pointed nose. A month had passed since all contact had been lost with his colleagues Jack and Ethan, and they still knew absolutely nothing about what had happened.

Carol, the administrator for the Genetics Department at Columbia University in New York City, studied the small gathering over her purple rimmed glasses. "I'm sorry," she seemed to especially address the woman next to Garth. Lee and Ethan had recently started dating, and Garth had been cheering for Ethan to lose his status as one of the bachelors in their department. Carol continued, "The chairman has another phone call with our state department contact later this morning. Maybe someone can finally get their rear in gear and go in search of their rental car or something more useful."

Carol had unearthed an email from Jack's account which documented that he and Ethan were headed in the direction of the mountains for some hiking. That sounded about right for Jack, but Garth had trouble picturing Ethan doing much outdoors. Of course, Jack could be persuasive. It made him almost smile to think of Ethan hiking. The man was brilliant but not the outdoorsman Jack was.

Other than the email there was nothing from either of them—no calls, no emails, no contacts to say where they had gone or what they had done.

Even if they'd gotten hurt or lost or something, they should have been back much earlier, or at least called for help. Yet there had been nothing from them after they left their last meeting at the conference

45

in Bucharest.

It seemed plain to Garth that something nefarious had happened, but nothing seemed to move as fast as it should have in the Romanian authorities' investigation, at least from his point of view. In keeping with her usual tenacity, Carol had offered to go to Romania to speak to someone in person, but the chairman had made sure she remained at her post since the department probably would have ceased to operate without her. Instead, the chairman continued to pursue frequent virtual meetings with a counterpart at the Bucharest university and now someone with the US embassy.

Hope that the morning's meeting would yield answers had proved false hope once again.

Footfalls echoed starkly from her new vampire's quarters. He was up early today, undoubtedly due to an empty stomach. Depriving him was not something Caterina had planned to do, since at this stage of the turning he would still need more. Nevertheless, it would be a lesson he would not soon forget.

She retrieved the urn of blood from its place in her quarters and met Stefan in the middle room. Ethan entered only moments later, cautiously, with a posture reminiscent of a whipped animal. She welcomed them both and placed the urn and chalices on the table. She served herself, then Stefan, then Ethan, who did not hide his eagerness well.

"Are we performing the rite today?" Stefan asked her.

She knew Ethan heard but did not understand their words. She understood some of his, but he was that person no longer and could not be permitted to continue speaking his tongue. She pondered Stefan's question and studied Ethan before answering. *"I am not sure if he is ready. It will weaken him considerably."*

"He is too curious. And he has already tried to defy you. Should we not show him the truth now?"

"It is my decision."

"Yes, of course." Stefan returned to his cup.

Ethan was clearly trying to judge the timbre of the conversation and had placed his empty cup back on the table to see if he would get a double portion today.

Caterina leaned back with her cup in hand, deciding. *"Give it to him,"* she instructed Stefan. *"We will do it today. He will need it."*

Stefan leaned forward to obey with a derisive glare at his young companion. He was jealous, Caterina knew. It was perhaps not unwarranted. Etan was the first turned in half a century, and he was hers.

ㄱ

The second cup of blood that Ethan drank managed to temper the hunger gnawing at his gut. It was strange that two cups of blood would slake that large a void in his stomach, but at the moment he felt only relief. Although, there was still something missing that would have made him completely full.

Or ease the tension in his chest. When they had finished and Caterina again bid him, *"Come,"* both she and Stefan led the way wearing long cloaks. Left with no other option but to follow, the dread of the unknown seemed to turn the blood sour in his stomach.

They descended the entire tall staircase, and she completed the descent with a step off the two-story cliff to the cavern bottom, landing the drop as though only stepping off a curb.

Seriously?

Well, you jumped up here. Why not down?

Forbidden to speak, he'd apparently taken up arguing with himself in his thoughts.

Stefan's haughty presence behind him kept him from hesitating for long. Resisting the urge to close his eyes, Ethan obediently stopped thinking and stepped off. He landed evenly on both feet, feeling a smooth impact rather than a jarring one as his ankles, knees, and hips bent naturally to absorb the energy. He blew out the breath he'd held and continued after Caterina who strode toward an opening at the other edge of the cavern.

They followed one tunnel for what must have been miles. As they traveled further, the walls became rougher, more naturally cave-like, and the lamps were further apart. When there were no more lamps, Ethan was left to test the limits of his new sight with only the dimmest vestige of light coming from behind.

Until a new light became visible from up ahead—one that wasn't flickering.

Daylight!

His heart leaped hard but slowly against his ribs. He'd had no idea how to find the way out, but now they were leading him right to it.

The opening wasn't as close as he'd thought; the light continued to gradually brighten as they wound around several bends. When the small cave opening finally came into view, Ethan couldn't look at it. The bright rays piercing through the opening made his eyes water.

That was understandable. He hadn't seen anything brighter than a flame lantern in days, or more. Besides that, his eyes were clearly more sensitive now. When he paused in an attempt to let his eyes adjust gradually, Caterina pulled a crossbow from beneath her cloak, raised her hood, and urged him, *"Come."*

That couldn't be good. But anything that was out of the cave had to be better, had to give him a better chance to escape. Squinting eyes on the ground, he shuffled toward the wall of white light that was outside until a shove from behind propelled him abruptly out into it.

He cowered and held his arm up in front of his eyes, straining to make out separate hues amid the glare. His back was to the cave mouth in the side of a rocky hill—not the same entrance he'd come in—and the only thing in front of him was an open grassy slope on which grew a single tree. The sun was near the horizon to his right, or at least that was the area of the sky that blazed the brightest.

Go! Run! blared through his brain, and Ethan started into the grass but couldn't help a look back. It didn't make sense that they would just let him go. But the very earth seemed to glow with light, making it all seem unreal and scattering his thoughts. When the dark hole remained silent, he kept staggering down the slope. *Go first. Questions later.*

"Stay!" yelled from the cave, and a crossbow bolt appeared in the ground in front of him, where his next step would have landed.

Ethan gasped and spun toward the cliff. "What!" They brought him out here, yet he was commanded to just stay put? He inched half a pace further into the grass, torn between the promise of the field and the threat of a crossbow bolt to his back.

Freedom and death. Or life imprisoned.

His world had imploded.

"What do you want from me?"

No answer.

Just the overwhelming flood of sunlight that wouldn't fade into something endurable despite the minutes ticking by.

You can't stay. This is no life.

Before he could act on his strengthening conviction, a new sensation arrested his attention. There was a growing burning in his hand—the one stretched out as a feeble shade against the sun. He turned his back to the molten orb and examined his hand, turning it over and flexing his fingers. The skin felt tight, as though he had already obtained a light sunburn.

All at once, he noticed the same sensation in his neck, cheek, and other hand.

No. No, this can't be real.

He stood in the middle of the open sloped field in disbelief. The sun, as bright as it was, didn't feel abnormally hot, but his skin already felt as though he had been at the beach for hours without sunscreen.

This isn't happening.

But the teeth, the blood, why not this?

Reality skewed again, tipping the world.

He took a faltering step back toward the cool shade of the cave.

"Stay!" Another arrow slammed, quivering, into the ground in front of him.

Cringing against burning rays, he attempted to shield his face to see the two people inside, but he couldn't. As he stood there, baffled, even the skin under his shirt was starting to sting. Ethan remembered the tree and blindly took a step in its direction.

"Stay!"

Pain sliced through his left arm an instant before the bolt landed in the grass. Ethan grabbed his arm with a gasp and dropped to his knees.

What, then? He knelt in the center of the three arrow shafts embedded in the ground around him. To approach the cave, tree, or to run away was to take a likely deadly shot. What was their goal? To make him burn in the sun?

Each minute he remained crouched in the grass felt like an eternity.

Just go.

If the alternative was to burn to death, maybe a quick death was better anyway. He stood slowly, waiting for a response that didn't come, and started to walk down the hill again.

Pain stabbed his right leg, knocking it out from under him. His shriek echoed off the rocky outcrop as he caught himself with his hands in the grass and reached back for the shaft embedded in his thigh. His thigh spasmed around the bolt, doubling him over in pain and immobilizing his leg.

Maybe his fate *was* to burn.

Tired, so tired, of the pain.

How many ways could a man be damned to die and still live?

The coil of tension and hope broke, leaving him limp in the grass.

Without the will to wonder if it was what giving up felt like, he laid down and curled into a fetal position with his back to the sun.

9

The burning continued to intensify to a level Ethan wouldn't have imagined before the pain he'd already experienced in that cave. After an eternity, the sunlight vanished nearly all at once. The sun must have dipped below the mountain.

He opened his eyes again to a blurry sideways world of grass and a dark blue sky streaked with orange. Two cloaked figures were approaching him.

They weren't done with him yet.

Being lifted by the arms to be carried back into the cave pressed a hundred pins into his skin under their grip. He may have groaned but was too disoriented to know until they set him down a little later and Caterina pushed back her hood with a calm expression.

His swallow got stuck in his throat.

She pulled a leather flask from the cord around her neck and opened it. When she brought it to his lips, he drank the blood like a man dying of thirst.

After he'd emptied it, she put it back around her neck and reached for the bolt in his thigh.

"Don't—"

But Stefan wrested his arms away, pulsing more pain into his skin, and she yanked it from his body in one quick movement. He shrieked with breath he hadn't known he had left and sagged against the rock.

Caterina stood. If she expected him to follow again, she was going to be disappointed. His skin was one large open wound, his muscles were jelly, and he felt he might throw up what he had just drunk. And that was besides the hole in his thigh, which she hadn't bothered to further address.

He should have realized that she had anticipated everything and that bringing Stefan hadn't been for the fun of it. After a short order, Stefan hauled him over his shoulder and began walking. It was a nightmare Ethan had no desire to revisit, but again he wasn't given an option.

When he did vomit the blood up over Stefan's back, he was tossed head first onto the hard ground. Unable to do much else, Ethan looked up and hissed at Stefan, pulling his lips back behind his elongated teeth. It was not an expression he had ever made before, but it felt right, especially when Stefan hissed right back.

Caterina intervened, scolding Stefan, who argued in response, and after a shrill shriek Stefan disappeared into the shadows. Caterina leaned over him again. Ethan lifted a weak hand against her approach, but his skin split, spilling blood and fluid from the blisters that covered it. Unable to muster the energy to move anything else, Ethan dropped his hand and stared up at her, resigned.

Unexpectedly, Caterina sat down next to him and let him rest a while.

⇗

Caterina watched Etan's slow ragged breathing. She knew how much pain he was in, but she could not be remorseful. It was necessary.

He was stronger than she had thought. She remembered the last vampire who had been shown the truth of the sun, who had remained despondent for months. Reengaging her had been difficult. Etan had been remarkably resilient from the beginning, showing more curiosity than fear after the difficult turning. She had thought he might have despaired today, in the field, but his response to Stefan showed he still had fight in him.

He would be a great vampire. Even Stefan would see his value in time. He had become complacent in his position which he now felt threatened, but he would adjust. As would Etan. For the first time in a long while, the days ahead held cause for anticipation.

10

The delicate formations arranged like coral or flowers glittered in the firelight, making the section of the cave ceiling above his bed sparkle. Ethan had spent a lot of time staring up at them. Staying perfectly still had kept his skin from tearing open, even if it didn't temper the burning.

He had lain in the bed for over a week, if time was still kept by Caterina and Stefan's morning "coffee" in the parlor room. Caterina had carried him back through the tunnels herself and washed the wound she'd inflicted in his thigh, as well as the open sores and blisters all over his body. She had then brought him blood several times each day. Apparently, she knew that his misery was heightened by a new level of hunger that fought with the nausea.

For one whole day it had been the better blood. The first time she'd brought it to him in the silver chalice, he'd thought it was only intense hunger that made it sweeter, but then she'd given him a knowing smile. There was something different about it. It had filled that remaining craving, the uneasiness that lingered without it, and calmed the cramping in his gut. For one night, he had fallen asleep, grateful that his memory wasn't entirely unreliable.

After that it had been the other version, the blood that was in some way inferior, but at least she had kept it coming in multiple cups a day.

This morning, Caterina called his name and what sounded like an order without entering the tunnel to his room.

Ethan groaned. His skin still felt tight, and his face and hands were still raw, but he could move. He just didn't want to.

With plenty of time and nothing to do but think, he'd realized what they had done: they had shown him that there was no way out.

Not from what they had done to him.

He craved blood as food and burned in the sun—something had made him utterly different than he had been. Even if he found a way out of the cave, then what? How did he escape from himself? He wasn't dead, or undead, and was convinced there must be some physical explanation, but how could he find those answers here? And how could he leave without those answers?

Even if escaping was possible with the sun as a guard.

If he hadn't been hungry again, he might not have moved at all, but hunger had become a cruel taskmaster, so he stood up with a long sigh and shuffled down the hall-like tunnel to the parlor. He was able to without much difficulty since the hole in his thigh had healed faster than the burns.

His gaze didn't stray from the floor as he took a seat and picked up his cup. The tender flesh on his fingertips made holding the cup uncomfortable, and he gulped the contents quickly. He might have sat that way, uninterested in their incomprehensible conversation, for the whole routine if Stefan hadn't stood and started strapping a sword to his belt.

Abruptly more alert, he saw that Caterina already had a black leather belt around her waist, the silver hilt of a sword glinting at the top of the affixed scabbard.

There were two long black cloaks tossed across her chair.

Agony had burned fear of the sun deeply into him, and that fear propelled muscles that hadn't moved much in days to throw him from his chair toward the tunnel before Caterina interjected.

"Etan. Stay!"

But he'd rather die falling into some deep recess of the cave than be burned again. That much he knew.

"You stay," she repeated, pointing to the floor. Then to his room. *"We,"* she motioned to herself and Stefan before waving at a vague distant point, *"Go."*

He wasn't supposed to be going with them. Relief made his legs go limp, and he slid to the floor.

Where are you going?

But he found that didn't matter so long as he didn't have to follow, so he got back to his chair and sat watching Caterina lace long leather boots over her leggings, slide a knife in place, and pick up her cloak before sweeping out into the tunnel, leaving him alone.

At some point deeper into the day, sounds seeped down the tunnels into his room where Ethan sat listlessly on the bed. There were never any sounds. A dripping, a whisper of air current, maybe, but the sounds were something else, something intentional.

He tried to ignore it, but with the threat of new agony removed for now, curiosity eventually won out. Any answers had to be better than only questions. He crept to the top of the stairs and ventured only a few down, so that it still felt like he was obeying Caterina's command, but far enough that he could see down into the huge cavern.

There were others.

Men, women, all dark haired, pale skinned, and wearing dark clothing. There were fifteen or so on the smooth stadium-sized cavern floor engaged in different activities. At the end furthest from the long table, a pair sparred with glinting weapons while a few spectators urged them on and intermittently traded places with them. There was a small group engaged in conversation, and a few others playing music on some old-fashioned looking instruments.

After a while of watching, he felt a strange air of expectation coalesce. It drew everyone from their individual absorptions to a concentrated focus near one of the large tunnels. Ten people, vampires—there was no use ignoring that name anymore—entered in organized ranks at a dignified pace. They were all arrayed in cloaks, tall boots, and weaponry and carried lit torches or naked silver blades that reflected the flames. Stefan appeared in the center, and Caterina brought up the rear, cloak hood pushed back, head held high. As they entered, the gathered crowd exulted with piercing shrieks, undulating cries, and beats of the drum and tambourine, as though welcoming a parade of soldiers.

When Caterina peeled off from the gathering and leaped the distance to the first stair below him, Ethan hastily retreated to his room and stood nervously waiting.

He stood there for longer than he had expected. Even though he was waiting, straining to listen for anything new, he wouldn't have heard Caterina enter his room if not for a tinkle of the silver chain that graced her neck. Gone were the weapons and the leather. Now she wore a long dress that could rightly be called a gown with embroidery laced with silver thread. Wary of anything new, he retreated a step back.

Smiling softly at his gaping, she glided forward and extended her hand. It held a shirt. He reached for it tentatively. Like the one he was wearing, it was black, but there was black embroidery at the cuffs extending up the sleeves, giving it a more formal feel. She pointed at it and him and gave some instruction that might have been telling him to change and definitely ending in, *"Now."*

He pulled the shirt he was wearing off over his head and put the new one on. Her reach to fix the laces at the neck was accompanied by a look that seemed to be checking him out. Although, he could have had that wrong as he wasn't used to such a look being directed at him.

Then she turned and instructed him to, *"Come."*

Now what?

He followed her out to the stairs and down, all the way to the rim of the stadium-sized cavern, and over the edge. His heart was still in his throat when he stepped off the two story drop to the floor below, but he managed it with minimal hesitation.

Approaching the gathered others was a different story.

There were over twenty milling about now, all wearing dark decorated clothing. They also wore varying amounts of jewelry—gold, silver, and maybe copper. Some were more adorned than others, but all clearly dressed to impress.

All deferred to Caterina as she walked through the throng to the long table, and after a nod or curtsey, each stared at Ethan. Feeling like a specimen under a microscope, Ethan continued following Caterina, each step less sure.

A gong rang out a deep reverberating note that filled the hall, and everyone stopped their conversation or study of Ethan and turned toward the larger entrance at one end of the hall. The regal vampire emerged, once more grandly arrayed in furs, jewelry, and a small silver crown. Every head bowed toward him, and everyone murmured a phrase or title addressing the ruler. *"My lord,"* Ethan mentally interpreted, mostly because "king" sounded even more ludicrous. Lord Vasile, if he separated the name from the title correctly.

Once the lord was seated at the head of the long table of heavy dark wood, Caterina took a place at his right hand. Stefan sat next to her. From his nod, Ethan was clearly supposed to sit next to Stefan, so he slid into the smoothly worn seat.

With a slow scan of the rest of the table, he counted twenty-seven vampires seated around it. Twenty-eight, when he included himself in the count. There was a hierarchy to how they were seated, he thought. Several of the most richly decorated, like Caterina, sat close to the head of the table, their seats also flanked by their own underlings, as he assumed Stefan and he were to Caterina.

The table had been arrayed with pewter pitchers and wooden trays laden with pears and plums and greens of some kind. Each place, including his own, was set with two stemmed cups and a plate.

Lord Vasile made a greeting or announcement of some kind and then motioned to Ethan in an apparent introduction that ended with his name. Ethan sat as still as a statue under the stares from every set of eyes and the table-wide murmur. When the speech ended with a gesture that seemed to indicate, *"Dig in,"* several vampires stood and began serving.

Stefan's voice in his ear disrupted his study of the ceremony. He was pointing at a nearby pitcher and expecting some action from him. Ethan's second look around the table revealed a theme to the servers. They all seemed to be the lowest seated member of each group. His role, now.

With a sharp breath, he stood and picked up the nearest pitcher. The unexpected smell made him pause. It was wine, not blood.

A single piece of something "normal."

When pointed toward one of Caterina's stemmed goblets, Ethan poured her wine, trying to ignore the weight of eyes on him. It shouldn't have been a difficult task, but it wasn't as if he had a lot of experience. He was a New York City bachelor–his idea of wining and dining someone was taking them out to a restaurant and letting the waiter pour the wine.

The wine made it into the cup with minimal splashing. After serving Stefan and himself, he perched on the edge of his seat anxious to do well enough to avoid punishment while daunted by the answers he was getting to some of his questions. There was a lot more to their life than he'd imagined.

The rows upon rows of crystal stalactites draped across the primitive cave ceiling glimmered more beautifully than any ornately crafted chandelier could have. Lanternlight and candlelight reflected off each piece of jewelry and silver thread embroidered into the garments, causing everyone's movements to sparkle despite their dark clothing. The reflection of the polished serving vessels contrasted with the dark iron of the candlesticks.

It was a very ceremonial feast. At Stefan's ongoing prodding, he served him and Caterina a tray of fruit before retrieving a peach for himself. As cups and plates emptied, the atmosphere seemed to change. Conversations picked up all around, and people kept sneaking glances at the end of the cavern.

It was all immediately silenced when Lord Vasile stood again.

Addressing the vampire at his left as Alena, he gave her a signal that had her and her underlings standing and everyone else watching expectantly. Alena started across the cavernous room and met another vampire who had apparently slipped out earlier and now carried two large jars. They placed these on the table and, after arranging some silver vessels around them, Alena opened the lid of a jar.

The scent of the blood filled the room, causing a celebratory murmur to rise again.

This was what the pomp was about.

The scent said that this was the better blood, the one Ethan had so far only tasted while in pain but still desired to taste again.

Alena poured the crimson liquid into individual pitchers and then into an ornate silver chalice at the lord's hand.

Vasile raised the cup with both hands and made an announcement that sounded nearly like a prayer. Ethan picked out the word for blood, having heard it a few times, but there were other descriptors and a word that had a Latin base that could have been translated "*gift*." Stefan bypassed Ethan to reach for the nearest silver pitcher and poured it into the second silver cups of Caterina's, his own, and Ethan's.

Relieved not to have another task to flub and also just thankful that Stefan did pour blood into his cup, Ethan sat still and watched, wary of his own eagerness.

Everyone thus served, and each goblet raised, the Lord issued a proclamation that was repeated around the table before they all drank deeply. Ethan savored the rich taste and filling sensation, for a second tempted to enjoy the feast and celebration.

Once every drop was drained, and the gaiety around the table had splintered into groups and couples who left the table gradually, Ethan set his empty goblet back onto the table and followed Caterina and Stefan to their staircase. They disappeared down the hall together, and he was left by himself in his bedroom where he flopped down onto the bed and stared up.

Stomach full to bursting, and burns barely tender, the questions ventured back into his mind.

Not tonight, he begged them. *Tonight, pretend you're not scared or hurt and go to sleep. Tomorrow there will be plenty of time for fears and questions.*

11

This is where they get the blood.

Ethan was supposed to be holding on to the pig. Irini, the vampiress who was in charge of the pig, corrected his hold of it inside the narrow stall, then inserted a thin silver tube into its neck. Blood dribbled through into an earthenware jar she held underneath. Once the jar was half full, she removed the tube, held onto the pig's neck for a minute, then waved at Ethan to release the rope around its snout.

It was such a simple, almost normal answer to one of the questions that had been looming in his mind.

Since the night Ethan had attended the first feast, days had passed with rules and patterns that he was starting to grasp. For one, the way to keep track of time without a clock while living constantly in the dark: a small tenor gong rang three times a day. He'd heard it but hadn't put the pieces together until he saw a vampire light sequential candles, then ring the small gong in the main hall each time one burned down.

After the first gong each morning, Ethan got up, kept himself and his clothes clean, drank his cup of blood, and followed Caterina. By doing so he stayed alive, he stayed fed, and he learned a little more.

For fifteen days she had led him back into that crevice off the staircase, up that rocky slope, to leap and climb and try not to die in the obstacle course of rocks. Every seventh day there was a feast in the evening. However, at the last two feasts they'd only served wine, fruit, and the usual daily blood. There had been no swords, no parades, and no ceremonial blood.

Then yesterday Caterina had led him down a long serpentine tunnel and left him there with an eager dusty vampire. The vampire had attempted, with a lot of words Ethan didn't understand and some vigorous hand motions, to teach Ethan how to mine coal. Because they were mining coal in the deep roots of the mountain. It made sense, in a strange way, given that coal seemed to be the universal light source in the cave.

Ethan had not picked up on the instructions quickly. Swinging the heavy pickaxe was physically easier than he'd anticipated, but he still hadn't been any good at using it to hit the right things. Despite the vampire's admirable persistence, he'd ended their session by giving an apologetic sounding report to Caterina.

Today Caterina had led him miles down one of the larger passages shaped like a huge oval tube to the surprising sound of goats and pigs which were milling around in a hay strewn fenced off area of the cave.

When she'd left him with Irini, he'd felt a little lost without her, which messed with his head, and then Irini had expected him to know how to act around animals.

Irini couldn't have known better, but she should have.

"Yeah, well, I grew up in New York City. Do you know how many times I've even seen a pig? Including this one, twice," he muttered in response to her incomprehensible lecture.

They repeated the bleeding process a few times, with pigs and a goat, and she had to help him with every one, which clearly annoyed her.

Once they had finished that task, she picked up a slender branch and started clicking at the animals to herd them around the corner but stopped him when he moved to follow. Instead, he got pointed to a shovel and the manure strewn stalls.

Ethan picked up the shovel and ran a hand down the long wooden handle. Understanding what he was supposed to do was not the same as knowing how to do it. There was no way he was going to get the seemingly simple task right either.

The patterns to vampire life may have made more sense the more he learned, but the more he participated in their life, the more he felt he was losing hold of himself. He didn't want to become one of them, but every day it was harder to remember who it was he should have been, much less make a valid plan to escape.

ᚩ

Caterina listened stoically to Irini's report about Etan's

performance. It had taken some prodding to get past the first tentative explanation from the animal keeper, but it was now clear to her that Etan showed absolutely no aptitude for working with animals.

Rather than becoming angry, she wondered anew what he had done in his previous life. Whenever they welcomed a new vampire, they were placed in a position that suited them. Thus, she sought to find Etan's proficiencies. After such an abhorrent report for two very different trials, she knew that Stefan would suggest putting him to menial tasks. She would remind him that would not elevate their standing as a clan. No, Etan had been successful at something. He was smart and persistent and could certainly be skillful at some profession.

"What is your skill?" she asked him and watched his mind work behind his eyes. He did not understand her, but neither had he simply accepted that, but rather considered her words, her actions, her face to see if he could piece together their meaning.

She had seen enough of the outside world. She was not so naive as to think it had spun out over cycles of cycles and not changed. Likely she herself would not understand what he had done. Still, she would find something to suit her thinker.

"Come." For now, she would return to the task of making him a more competent vampire.

There was also punishment to be meted out. He had ceased speaking his native tongue in her presence but had been found to persist in it when he was with others. She would keep it simple. Once she was certain they were alone, she spun without warning and struck him in the mouth, then waited to see if he comprehended the meaning in her discipline.

Knocked back a single step, he worked his jaw, spit blood from his mouth onto the rock at his feet, and turned his eyes to her slowly.

She nodded confidently. His sober acceptance of the punishment indicated that he did understand. Good. He would understand also that he was never outside her reach or oversight.

Turning back to the task at hand, she glided over an intricate pathway along a small ravine and turned to wait for him. She could sense his ire as he worked his tongue along the inside of his injured lip and shifted on his feet where he was for a few moments, but he did follow.

He had started watching her steps and the manner in which she traversed the terrain. She approved as it led to improved proficiency when he attempted to follow. It was time to lead to more harrowing areas. She would yet expunge him of the fear of dark, closedness, and heights that plagued his former species.

But first they would try something else.

꙳

His own blood in his mouth tasted more like blood should: sharp, metallic, not sweet. Adding that to his endless mental list of strange observations, Ethan followed Caterina into a wide flat space to find Stefan and another vampire waiting.

That can't be a good sign. The stone of dread dropped into his stomach again.

"*Stefan, Luca,*" Caterina greeted them.

Stefan saluted with a fist to his chest before abruptly launching an attack on Luca. They both instantly produced long glinting knives. The weapons appeared as extensions of their arms as they danced across the smooth floor in a quick series of thrusts and dodges, the blades touching nothing but air.

When the duel had Stefan within a pace from the rock wall, he stepped up against it and turned his body into a roll in the air, parallel to the ground. He simultaneously slung his arms in a swipe that required Luca to bend his upper body back in an arc to avoid his blade. As soon as Stefan's foot touched back down onto the ground, he spun on it into another thrust that forced his opponent to parry, ringing out a sharp note.

Luca used the momentum to spin himself around and bring his blade toward Stefan's neck, but Stefan ducked into a forward tuck roll that landed him on his feet close to Luca's chest. Since Luca's blade was still wide with the force of a missed swing, Stefan thrusted upward with his knife while blocking the vampire's other arm with his forearm.

Luca's quick dodge backward was brought up short by the rock wall behind him.

Stefan's blade drew a drop of blood at his neck.

Instantly taking a step back, Stefan nodded to his opponent, and Luca disappeared after a quick bow to Caterina.

That left Stefan turning to Ethan.

Still blinking at the speed of the match that had lasted only a minute, Ethan grimaced as the dread in his gut grew heavier. Learning to get around in the cave was useful. It gave vague hope that he might one day be able to escape by himself. Weapons play was another matter. He'd just seen enough to grow an ardent desire to avoid it.

Stefan's silver blade disappeared even as it was replaced in his hand by the darker blade tossed to him by Caterina. The twin handed to Ethan was lighter than it looked, with a metal hilt that fit into his hand and a blunt blade that was shorter than his forearm by a couple inches.

Stefan barked an order at him and bent his knees into a ready stance with his blade extended forward.

Maybe this is how I die, Ethan mused and slowly took a similar stance.

He barely had time to see the strike that knocked the knife from his hand and jerked back a step, shaking the sting out of his fingers.

"Look," Stefan instructed and turned his hand so Ethan could see how he held the knife.

His own grip hadn't been correct, so it was easily knocked from his hand. *That's what happens when you've never held a weapon before.*

He obediently retrieved the knife from the other side of the room and slothfully stood back in front of Stefan, his vision sharpening slightly as he adjusted his hand on the knife hilt.

Stefan laughed and said something like, *"No need for that."*

His eyes must have turned blue. The others seemed to have more control, but the color change came unbidden to his eyes whenever he was feeling especially threatened or angry. He blinked, although that wouldn't change them back, and tensed as Stefan struck out again. Ethan saw the blow in time to flinch out of the way before it hit.

Since that wasn't the point of the exercise, he still got a reprimand from Stefan despite the appreciative tic of Caterina's mouth.

Ethan pushed down the useless timidity, resigned himself to getting hit, gripped his knife in his hand, and let Stefan strike it. The blow vibrated all the way to his shoulder, but he held on to it.

With a nod, Stefan moved on to show him a different grip and thrust motion.

12

"Hand me that." Ethan nudged Garth's elbow and pointed to the tray of test tubes in front of him.

"Oh, you think you can do it better?" Garth taunted, then turned to the students in stiff new lab coats, "Watch out y'all, the expert's going to give you a tutorial."

"Somebody remind Professor Qualls that he's not in Texas anymore," Ethan countered and took the test tube from him.

The students snickered but kept rapt attention on him.

Meanwhile, Ethan was promptly distracted by a beautiful woman of Chinese descent who took the seat next to him. "Lee. What brings you to our lab?"

"I heard you might need a hand." Her almond eyes sparkled.

"The more the merrier."

⅄

The clear note of the morning gong snatched Ethan from the dream.

Cold, stark reality settled onto him until it pressed him breathless into the bed. *This can't be what's real.* He squeezed his eyes against tears. *I'm supposed to be a professor in New York City, not a vampire in a Romanian cave.*

Had his friends and colleagues missed him? Were they looking for him? But what would they find if they tried?

Ethan did ultimately leave his room, in search of food and because he was supposed to. To sate hunger and avoid penalty. Vampire that

65

he apparently was, he picked up his cup of blood and drank. Caterina seemed to be studying him. Probably because he wasn't very good at being a vampire. He didn't seem to be much good at anything here, and there was no telling what she would demand of him today.

After breakfast, Caterina didn't lead him nearly as far as they had gone yesterday. He slumped as she nudged him to today's minder, a woman wearing a leather apron and tucking strands of dark hair back behind her ears.

"Nicoleta," she introduced herself and invited him to join her with a wave.

It was warm in the wide low chamber. Multiple iron cauldrons sat over fires, and there were other pans and vessels scattered about. Smoke wafted up into a funnel shaped hole in the ceiling. Nicoleta handed him a lump of rock and picked up a thin rod of shining silver metal. She gestured at the row of cauldrons and trays, then held up the rod.

"Huh." Was she smelting silver? He leaned closer to the row of fires. It was not a familiar process, but he was pretty sure that's exactly what she was doing. He took the small rod, turning it so it caught the firelight.

"Silver."

"Silver," he repeated her word for it. *Interesting.*

She approached the first cauldron and used some heavy tongs to reach into it. With mostly gestures, and a few single words, she walked him through the method by processing a small quantity of ore. She pointed out specifics: color of the flames, how many bubbles, texture of the metal.

It made sense.

Unfamiliar or not, it was a scientific process. If you kept the variables consistent, it worked the same way every time. *This* he could do.

A tension relaxed down the back of his head as he focused on her actions and started trying to ask questions with a word or point.

By the time Nicoleta had finished the whole process of refining a small lump of silver, he was thoroughly impressed. *"Neat, yes?"* She held it up with a pair of heavy clanking tongs and flashed a smile.

"Neat," he repeated her word and made note of its approximate meaning.

She pointed him to a hollowed out area of a rock ledge that was covered with an iron grate bearing ash and remnants of coal but currently cool. *"Fire."*

Well, we were bound to reach the impossible order phase at some point. He kept his words to himself and spread his hands with a shrug.

"Fire," she repeated with an explanatory gesture to the burning fire under the cauldron.

"Yes, fire. But…" *I have no earthly idea how to start one.*

"You don't know how to start a fire? How could you not?" her question must have meant. The object she pulled from her pocket looked like a rock and…maybe flint or ferrous? *"You have one?"*

Another shrug.

When she walked away, he wondered if she had given up on him that quickly, but she returned with another flat rock and small rod, handed it to him, and waved him over to watch her as she bent over the cold hearth. The gathered wood shavings and chips went at the bottom, and a piece of coal was placed directly over it resting on the iron grates. She struck the flint with a sharp motion, and the sparks ignited the wood shavings, which started gradually heating the coal above to a red glowing ember. She placed the flint and some wood shavings back into a pocket sewn into the side of her tunic.

That makes so much more sense. He realized it must be how Caterina had been lighting the cold lamps out of nowhere all along.

Nicoleta pointed to the next cold hearth, *"Your turn."*

After struggling for what was probably half an hour, he finally produced a spark that ignited the wood chips enough to start heating the coal and exulted with a "Ha!"

"Yes!" From across the room, Nicoleta gave a single clap of congratulations.

Blinking in surprise at her shared celebration, Ethan stepped over to her pile of coals to investigate what she had been working on. She had delicate tools arranged near a small anvil and used a lighter pair of tongs to retrieve a glowing rod of silver from under the coals. He watched her lengthen the rod and twist it into an intricate design before accepting a tool she handed him to help hold onto the delicate object.

Having had decent dexterity for precise tasks even before his body had been altered to be better at it, he found following her instructions refreshingly easy despite the language barrier. It was remarkable to watch the serpentine ring take shape in their hands.

It was the first time the day hadn't dragged on, unless Caterina arrived to retrieve him early. But, no, he'd heard the timekeeping gong echo faintly a few moments ago.

With the uncertainty of tomorrow looming, he was suddenly reluctant to leave, but he nodded a simple goodbye at Nicoleta, patted

the flint and tinder in his pocket appreciatively, and turned to follow
Caterina once again.

13

The basement door was stuck. Garth knew the key was the correct one, so he shoved harder until it popped open suddenly and sent him reeling into the apartment.

Into the middle of Ethan's apartment, next to his couch, by his bookcase buried in books and journals, in the light of a lamp that had never been turned off.

Garth turned in a small circle. "What now?"

It was Garth's building. He'd inherited the Brooklyn brownstone from his aunt, and he rented out five of the divided apartments and lived in one of them. The basement apartment was Ethan's. Ethan could have taken an apartment closer to the university, but he and Garth had been through a lot together during undergrad and then grad school. Ethan had finished his training first and had garnered the highly sought position of primary investigator of his own lab at Columbia while Garth continued to work on his post doctorate in the same department. They shared a lot of life.

Had shared.

Ethan was dead.

The chairman of the Genetics Department had shared an update that morning.

Local authorities had finally found Jack's rental car out in the middle of nowhere. At the bottom of a cliff. It had exploded, or fallen and then caught fire. Either way, fire and impact had destroyed the car and burned the cab to ashes. The human remains inside were not identifiable, or intact, but a bag from the trunk had apparently been more lucky. Inside they'd found two partially burned passports.

Jack's and Ethan's.

Oh, God, he wasn't ready…

Garth sank onto Ethan's couch and wiped at tears that he'd held back until now.

No one could explain why they were that far into the mountains on a one lane back road. It seemed a little far out there even for Jack, but the man loved his outdoor adventures.

Had loved.

No one seemed able to explain why it had taken so long to find them, and the chairman and Carol promised to continue the investigation. But Garth wasn't sure what else could be done.

Except figure out what to do with an apartment worth of stuff from his friend's life.

א

Ethan awoke to a still glowing coal ember in his iron lamp. Although it produced relatively dim light after burning overnight, it still gave the whole room a warm cast. An odd thing to take pride in, but it gave him a small sense of achievement to wake to it. He'd done one thing right, as a vampire.

Does that make me less human?

After breakfast, he followed Caterina down the same passage they had taken the day before. Ethan squashed the tinge of hope that he might get to spend another day at the forges instead of failing at another mystery task. There seemed less and less point in hope. Just wait and see.

But then she was handing him off to Nicoleta in her cavern of fires and ovens, and he let himself smile a, *"Good morning,"* to her.

She pointed him to the same line of fires from yesterday, one of which was already lit, and handed him a lump of rock. *"Refine to silver."*

There was nothing like a pop quiz to get an academic's mind spinning.

When he was finished, he held a small, slightly crooked bar of shining silver in his tongs.

"Yes," she clapped once and motioned for him to put it next to a couple others on another tray.

That felt like a passing grade to him, especially when she called to Mac to bring Ethan a heavy leather apron. Mac had been on the other side of the room at his own forge, hammering away on a large ax head.

For the rest of the morning Ethan helped her plate jewelry, a process he hadn't even realized could be done without electricity, but she was a regular chemist.

Again Caterina came to retrieve him too early for his liking, and he followed her feet mindlessly until they disappeared into a small hole near the cave floor. He groaned silently, as it did no good to groan aloud. Even though he knew from recent experience that he would fit through the tight space, he couldn't completely ignore the instinctual fear that rose from being hugged by a mountain's worth of rock on every side.

The passage emptied out into a long chamber of rough terrain he was not familiar with.

Whenever he thought he had become nearly good enough at navigating the terrain to keep up with Caterina, she started moving faster, showing that her previous pace had been purposefully slowed to compensate for him. Still, he didn't hesitate at the drop down from the ledge or the leap across a ravine to a pyramid of leaning boulders.

At least until she extinguished the only light.

She had told him to stay before retreating to the last mounted lantern, apparently to trick him into advancing past it before pitching the whole cavern into blackness.

He froze on the narrow boulder on which he was perched and slowly crouched so that his hands as well as his feet were in contact with the rock. His strained ears picked up multiple sources of faint drips and a distant heavier trickle of water, but he didn't hear her until her leather shoe made the softest caress of the rock he was crouched upon and her heart beat once, as though she could control even it.

He knew she would want him to move. She had tried it once before. But the utter darkness seemed to hold all the fears he had left.

"Listen," she whispered.

The high-pitched repeating click that emanated from her throat next to his ear created echoes of itself in the variegated chasms around him. It simultaneously dug out a pit of primal fear.

It was the sound. Not of a bat—there had never been any bats in the entrance to the cave he had first visited. It had been her. Always her.

Caterina hadn't just come to retrieve him and kill Jack that evening in the rain. She'd been in the cave as they'd explored, had attacked and bitten them. She'd let them go because there was no chance of true escape.

He had probably always known. He knew he had considered it at the beginning, when first trying to make sense of the new environment, but then there were twenty-seven other vampires and a whole world that didn't make sense.

But the sound, her sound, was undeniable.

He was under her authority because she had made him.

He felt rather than heard her move to face him. Some change in his breath or heartbeat must have divulged his realization.

Another click from her throat, long and clear.

Unable to move for fear of slipping into the unseen depths around him, Ethan remained still except to breathe faster into her invisible face in front of him. He wanted to rail against her, throw her off their narrow perch, sink his own fangs into her flesh for what she had done, but he was still as much at her mercy now as he had been the first moment he'd entered her domain. And she knew it.

She clicked again, her breath revealing that she'd tilted her head as though to study him, and her hand reached slowly to rest on his throat. *"Your turn,"* she breathed onto his cheek.

When he remained silent, she took his hand and placed it on her own throat to feel the vibrations when she made the clicking again. Then she grasped his throat a measure tighter.

His attempt felt like a betrayal of his humanity, perhaps as she intended, but wasn't quite the clear distinct clicking sound she made.

"Again."

He repeated the sound until it was at least sharp enough to echo through the cavern.

"Listen to see," she breathed again before retreating out of his reach.

He couldn't interpret the overlapping echoes into any information that would help him know where to jump or where not to step, and his anger and regret didn't make it easier to focus. He'd given up and begun wondering if she had left him when, with barely a whisper of warning, a hand connected with his face.

He was knocked backward with only an outstretched hand to catch himself. Fortunately, another boulder leaned against his, making his perch wider than he remembered, but he was in the dark, unable to navigate, and under attack. His only hope was that she valued him enough to catch him before he plunged to his death. Unfortunately, he knew from experience that her care did not extend to leaving him uninjured.

Listen, the rational part of his mind insisted.

She couldn't see either and so needed to create sound to navigate unless she was already close enough to reach him, and she couldn't stop her heart completely.

Abandoning his thoughts to narrow his focus completely to sound gave him what he was searching for: two clicks there, a single heartbeat closer, a whisper of air to the left—at least he got his arm up to block her blow and kept his footing.

A quick sweep of his hands along the rock told him the perimeter of his sanctuary and let him place his feet more securely but covered sounds of her movement, leaving him blind to her next jab to his temple.

He winced, dropped lower, and closed his useless eyes, tilting his head before hushing all movement, breathing, and even slowing his heartbeat. He was rewarded with enough warning to completely dodge her hand, and her high chirp seemed nearly a laugh.

"Now come."

"No."

"Come or stay."

He cursed silently. She would leave him here alone, he had no doubt.

When she clicked again, he realized that if he couldn't use the echo to tell him where rock was or wasn't, he at least could hear the direction she was in, and it wasn't likely that she was hovering in mid-air.

Before he could think too much about it, and bolstering his confidence by imagining he was aiming to hit her, he leapt in the direction of her clicks. Of course she moved out of the way easily, but he succeeded in slamming into a rock ledge. When he started to slide off, there was a stab of panic, but then her duplicitous grip secured him long enough for his foot to find purchase on a toe hold. He used it to propel himself after the light sound of her footfalls, feeling his way forward and cutting his hands against the draperies on the ceiling.

She stopped in the middle of the passage where the lamplight from beyond just started to touch the tunnel. A small smile played on her pale lips while she raised her chin and studied him.

He paused. *After everything, why does your approval matter to me?*

The look in her dark eyes grew intense and didn't leave his as she strode for him.

Backpedaling only ended with his back against the rough cave wall, and she didn't stop until she pinned his shoulders firmly against it and leaned in close. Though he was sure he was stronger than he had been before, struggling against her grip didn't move her at all.

Her eyes turned blue inches from his own.

Before he could dare to imagine a new torment, her mouth covered his in a pressured kiss.

When she broke contact, he gasped for air and searched her eyes, still blue, for any clue to her intentions. It seemed unlikely that his clumsy moves had turned her on. More likely it was another way to prove that he belonged to her.

She pressed closer.

He felt his flesh respond to her even as his mind spun.

Did he belong to her? She'd taken him, changed his body, burned it beyond recognition and nursed it back to health. Even his mind seemed under her rule. He was not allowed to speak except the language she allowed, not allowed the space to think of anything except surviving the challenges that she kept throwing him into. He wanted to hold on to some part of himself, at least some sliver of his humanity. But she slithered further and further in, somehow wooing him to seek her approval despite how he should hate her for all the parts of him she had already killed.

He wanted to resist her advance, but he also longed to feel something other than dread for even one moment.

She won't take everything, he promised even as the fight faded from his body and he stopped the futile efforts to push her away. He started walling off some deep part of himself, his soul he might have called it, if he'd believed he had one. He pushed it down, closed it in with layers of stone, and turned off its light so it couldn't see or feel his betrayal.

And he kissed her back.

14

Ethan's life settled into routine. Caterina had started telling him to report to the forge on his own. She still retrieved him at the second gong, because their afternoon lessons varied in location and theme, but the timing for those remained the same, excepting feast days.

The communal feast of fruit and wine and regular blood at the long table occurred on the night of every seventh day, and not only was the work morning abbreviated on those days, but he had no lessons with Caterina either.

Today would be his fifth feast. Last week on the empty afternoon of the feast day he had dared to venture a little wander by himself, and no one had stopped or punished him. He considered that as he relit the lantern in his room. He might try exploring alone again. The routine pressures and expectations of him did a fair job of occupying his mind and keeping him from questions, but these moments of stillness turned his thoughts treacherous.

Was that the distant whisper of a blade being drawn?

Four weeks—a lunar month—could be a ritualistic time frame. Maybe that first feast had not been a singular event. Or maybe it was something worse.

Dread returned in force. Wanting to stall but not enjoying the suspense, he rolled from the bed to his feet and walked to the parlor to find Caterina and Stefan in the process of strapping on weapons. When bracing himself for an answer that never came grew too uncomfortable, he attempted a question. *"Caterina, what do today?"*

"My lady," Stefan corrected haughtily.

Caterina only passed Ethan a look that said he'd gotten himself into that one and didn't bother to get involved.

Stefan looked him up and down critically before giving the terse order, *"You stay."*

Since that was the answer Ethan had been hoping for, he ignored the apparent insult and reached for his cup of blood.

Too bad it felt like a crucial question needing an answer. Only a moment after they left, curiosity won out, and he followed them at a distance. They dropped into the large main cavern to join four other vampires. Each was from an important clan, judging from their usual positions at the feast table, and all were similarly arrayed with weapons strapped onto leather belts under voluminous black cloaks.

He followed them down a long straight path until he felt he'd tempted fate long enough and turned into an intersecting path. He found a ledge up the wall to rest on and listen, but the sound of them meeting two others and walking away with some excited jeers did not provide him with much more information.

He caught himself anticipating tonight's feast with something other than dread, which disturbed him. To distract himself, he wandered about the nearby area of the cave, exploring an unfamiliar section, but not straying so far that he might miss some clue if the party returned the same way.

When the second timekeeping gong rang, he gave up and started back along the wide path to the cavern.

But there was a new sound.

A distant mewing.

It was strange, possibly the sound of an animal—plausible considering it was in the direction of the animal pens—but it sounded distressed. Wrong.

So, he followed the sound in that direction but turned down a tunnel before he reached the pens. When the sounds grew louder and the tunnel started to open up, he found another offshoot, high up on the wall that he could wriggle through. It seemed a better idea, if he wanted to stay out of sight, to approach the area from a roundabout way. His strategy was rewarded with an opening in the tight passage that showed him the view below.

Flickering firelight illuminated a large space with empty stall-like partitions. Three cloaked and weapon-clad vampires stood on the hay-strewn ground in front of one stall, where the yowling cries were coming from. When one moved aside, Ethan could see their source.

A young man cowered there under their watch, his hands and feet bound. His eyes were frantic with fear, but his open mouth cried only pathetic moans, unable to form words.

Not a vampire.

A human boy.

Apparently mentally handicapped and clearly terrified.

One of the vampires approached the boy, agitating him further. He grabbed the boy by the rope around his ankles and lifted his feet above his head to secure them on a hook in the wall. Another, Alena, head of the largest clan who sat across from Caterina at the banquet table, had a metal tube and vessel prepared.

The same tools they used to bleed the pigs.

What—

As soon as the first vampire had the boy held upside down and still, Alena pierced his neck.

The smell was unmistakable.

Icy horror shot from his chest through every artery in Ethan's body.

Blood flowed through the tube smoothly into the silver vessel, and the familiar fragrance permeated the room inciting hunger for an instant before twisting Ethan's gut with a sharp jerk.

It was the difference in the blood.

He'd been drinking—desiring—*human* blood.

He doubled over with a sudden dry retch but couldn't tear his eyes from the sight of the blood frothing as it filled the silver vessel below. Alena exchanged it for another and another. The boy's distressed expression gradually relaxed.

Once they had filled five containers and nothing more dripped from the pale, motionless body, Ethan backed away as if released. As soon as the tunnel allowed room to do so, he turned and ran, blindly following the narrow passage.

Away. Anywhere. Just away.

Tears blinding him, he nearly collided with a wall. He bent over at the waist, wishing his body would throw up to release the nausea gripping him. If only there were a way to vomit up everything he had ever swallowed.

He gasped and dropped to his knees, gripping his head in his hands. How did he live in a world that celebrated butchering a disabled teenager for a meal? A delicacy. A drug, even. He spat saliva from his mouth, and it mingled with tears in the dirt. Perhaps he should have guessed at that truth before, but he'd never dared imagine that part of the legend was true. It was too horrific.

He blinked with new understanding. The word they had used for the blood that first feast, it hadn't been *"gift."* It was *"sacrifice."*

The armed company went out once a month to retrieve a source of blood. A human source. The weapons only highlighted the lengths they may have been going to or threatening. The boy had been a sacrifice offered to the *strigoi*, the demons who haunted the night once a lunar cycle.

If the cave was hell, surely that boy had not deserved to befall the evil that lurked in its depths.

The reverberation of the deep gong echoed even into the passage Ethan still knelt in, but it didn't move him. He didn't care if he missed the feast. He didn't care if it was disobedience or if his punishment was never eating again, because he didn't care if he lived another day.

Enough was enough.

Eventually the sound of his name echoed through the rock passages. Somehow, despite his staying silently crouched on the cave floor, Stefan found him. When his barrage of irate, *"What are you doing here? Come on! Get up!"* had no effect, he reached down to grab Ethan.

Anger and agony surged through Ethan and restraint vanished. He slapped Stefan's hands away and slid back a pace with a hiss.

Undeterred, Stefan blocked Ethan's flailing blow with one arm and grasped his bicep with the other. He was strong, but not as strong as Caterina. Ethan got a foot planted against the wall and twisted away with a practiced full rotation to land flat-footed again. Perhaps the sparring lessons were not useless.

Stefan's eyes turned blue as he hissed at Ethan. In one fast motion he grabbed Ethan around the waist and lifted him, knocking his head against the tunnel wall.

Ethan ducked his head in and bit into Stefan's shoulder before getting thrown to the ground. The impact punched the breath from his lungs, leaving him to scoot breathlessly backward along the ground, glaring upward. His mouth dripped with Stefan's blood.

Stefan bared his fangs and shrieked.

The sound echoed around them.

Ethan stood up and waited for Stefan to try again, but despite shaking with clear fury, the vampire didn't move. It certainly wasn't fear or care for Ethan's life that held him at bay, so it must have been something else, some propriety or rule.

Something Ethan had just discarded.

Several vampires responded to Stefan's shrill cry, but no one stepped past Stefan's position until Caterina parted their ranks.

Regal in her long shimmering dress, she didn't speak, silencing Stefan's first word with a jerk of her head.

She didn't need to speak. Ethan knew he had disobeyed, and probably brought some shame to her by not appearing at the feast with everyone else.

But there had to be a line he wouldn't cross. He met her eyes and lifted his chin. *"I no drink."*

Her wave dismissed the others, and only after they left did *her* eyes change.

"You will."

Ethan crouched and waited. He had no hope against her, never had, but maybe she would end it.

LIFEBLOOD

15

She hadn't.

She seemed to know exactly how far to go to avoid it.

Ethan was dropped and smacked his head into the rock floor. The impact flooded his already blurred vision with pinpricks of light.

A gate clanged closed.

He started to roll over, but his right arm was only spasming with pain rather than moving as he instructed, so he stopped and let his face rest on the cool rough ground until the world's spinning slowed. Voices and footsteps were retreating, leaving him alone in near darkness.

Getting himself to his back didn't help with any of the pain, but it did let him confirm that he was in a small rough room barred by an iron gate, the only light seeping from somewhere down the now empty space beyond.

If she would deny him death, he wished she had at least hit him hard enough to knock him unconscious. Instead, pain pounded in his head, chest, and side, his left arm hung abnormally to the side, and sticky blood oozed from a gash in his thigh.

Still nothing eclipsed the agony in his chest at what he had become. He saw that boy's helpless face every time his eyes dropped closed.

Left for dead locked in a cell seemed an appropriate fate for drinking blood from such sacrifices.

꒳

Ethan had never known hunger that hurt before. Not like this. It gnawed in his stomach until it hurt worse than the pounding in his head, leaving him to curl up in silence on the ground. Even though the last of the light had been extinguished hours ago, he knew they would hear if he cried out, and he wasn't yet ready to give them that satisfaction.

↗

The smell pulled him from tormenting dreams and had him dragging his battered body halfway across the cell before he could stop, trembling, just out of arm's reach of the gate.

Caterina stood there holding a silver cup full of blood.

The boy's blood.

The only thing in this world that would ease his suffering.

He screamed at her. At the upside-down world. At himself.

He'd abandoned his silence ages ago, but his scream tore from the agony deep inside and erupted out his mouth, echoing into the recesses above and away.

She stood still, quiet, so very confident just outside and yet within his reach.

When she turned to walk away, he shrieked in despair, because he was starting to understand that she could simply wait until every cell in his body cried out for it and there wasn't one left to resist.

↗

He would never know how long he had managed to last, dying all too slowly in that rock cell.

It was ultimately meaningless.

The moment she stepped through the gate and placed the sweet viscous liquid under his nose, the last thread of rebellion snapped, and he was devouring it with a grip on the cup of a drowning man to his lifeline. As soon as the last drop was gone, he hurled the goblet to clang against the wall with a hiss in her face, simultaneously aching for more and hating her for giving it to him.

She stood and left, silent in her victory.

It left him to crumple back to the ground. He stared blankly up at the formless ceiling as if it were the broken barrier to his deeply walled off soul, now let out to see all he had utterly become.

16

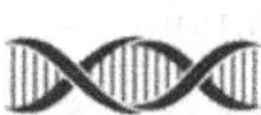

The next time she brought a full pitcher of blood, and he drank it because there was no other choice. The hands that had broken him became gentle as they eased him out of his bloody torn clothing, cleaned the deep wound through his thigh, and secured his torn left arm in a kind of sling.

Then the cell door was open, and she was beckoning him to *"Come,"* again.

The trek back to their quarters was its own kind of torture. Besides the simple fact that every movement hurt, he couldn't lift his left leg to step up–something deeper than the skin must have been sliced apart. Additionally, whether due to his arm being bound or the blow to his head, his balance was off, so he was left to limp slowly, nearly falling constantly, and leap the two-story first stair without aid.

The only mercy was that once he was finally to his room, she left him to collapse into the bed alone and didn't disturb him for one entire day.

ק

That was apparently all the mercy afforded to him. The next morning it was a vengeful Stefan who ordered, *"Get up, fool, it is time for duty."*

Ethan stared dully up at him for only a moment before Stefan yanked him from the bed by his injured arm. Stumbling quickly to his feet to reduce the force on that shoulder, Ethan hissed, *"Stop!"* but didn't fight back again.

It was pointless. All pointless. Somehow they would make him do it anyway.

Ethan on his feet seemed to complete Stefan's assignment, because he left as quickly as he'd appeared, leaving Ethan to take stock of his condition, if he'd cared to.

He didn't. Instead, he numbly searched for his shoes out of routine, wincing when he took a step but able to do it. He discarded the sling that had slipped off his arm and held that arm close to his body when it still didn't work correctly. The agonies had faded to aches, but the simple movements of bending to lace his shoes, found by the door, felt toilsome.

The morning proceeded as every morning did. He drank his cup of pig blood without looking up until Caterina ordered him to return to the forge for duty.

The walk took twice as long as it normally did, but report to the forge he did, dutifully donning his apron with his more functional left arm. He avoided making eye contact while awaiting instructions. He didn't know just how many of his wounds were obvious on his fully clothed body, but it was doubtful that his public display of rebellion was still a secret from anyone.

Ignoring the traitorous shame that rose in his belly, he moved to light the fires Nicoleta indicated. It wasn't easy, but it did go without incident until she requested a large heavy-bottomed pot on a rock shelf in the corner.

He was unable to lift his right arm from the shoulder–something simply did not work in it–and lifting the pot proved impossible. It fell, managing to bump against his sore ribs and his thigh before landing with a deep clang on the ground. Unable to suppress the grunt of pain, he leaned down against it, trying to even out his ragged breathing.

He heard Nicoleta take a step toward him before Mac stopped her with a quiet warning.

Ethan was not the only one subjugated to Caterina's rules. For their sakes, then, he started, noisily and slowly, dragging the large pot to the fire. Abandoning appearances, he lifted clumsily, one handed, using his body and the edge of the raised fireplace to brace the cauldron, pushed it into place, and collapsed to one knee as soon as it was done.

Banging from Mac's forge resumed as Ethan recollected himself before turning back to Nicoleta. If she had been instructed not to help him, she'd probably been told to work him hard as well.

The regret in her eyes was unexpected as she instructed him, *"More coal."*

"It's fine," he found himself trying to reassure her. He would rather feel the physical pain than the hole in his soul when he stopped moving.

⅄

Half a moon's cycle from the last grand feast, Caterina followed her young vampire to the forges. From the shadow of the low entrance, she observed his deliberate movements as he checked the consistency of the molten metal in the cauldron.

He had recovered physically from the discipline required, but his inquisitive spirit had not returned. He performed the duties of each day but with no more movement than necessary. He was obedient in her daily lessons but seemed to prefer loss to victory during sparring so that even Stefan held no joy in besting him any longer. He recoiled at her every touch.

Nicoleta, in her heavy apron with her hair ever falling out of place, joined him wordlessly at his fire and reached with a tool to cooperatively lift the pot to pour dross from the top of the gleaming silver. A glowing drop escaped the lip of the pot and dropped downwards. Only a quick slide of his foot let it land on the rock floor rather than the leather of Etan's shoe.

"Oh, you're getting faster—good thing!" Nicoleta exclaimed.

"I learned after last one," Etan replied clumsily but with a slight smirk.

In the forge he still lived. At that work he could even smile. It showed not all had been broken.

She watched them finish with the silver, performing a practiced choreography to complete it swiftly and with apparent ease.

Let it be, then. With patience, she would yet form him into a vampire.

17

Ethan had stopped keeping track of the months. Weeks were still marked by regular feasts, and every month culminated in a *"Great Feast,"* as he interpreted it, at which the sacrificial blood was served. On the first great feast after his futile rebellion, he had attended, albeit after waiting as long as possible to come to the central hall, and drank with disgusting desire before leaving as soon as possible. He had purposefully avoided as much exposure to what else had happened that day as he could, telling himself he had no options but to complete the acts he was forced to. It wasn't as though another show of useless protestation would prevent the death or sacrifice of whoever provided the blood.

At the next Great Feast, Caterina had made sure he attended some of the festivities. So he'd sat to one side, watched a storytelling reenactment of some vampire hero fighting off a snarling beast, and kept well away from the sparring ring until it was time to go through the motions again.

After that he'd stopped keeping track.

Still, somehow he knew today would hold more. Maybe he'd finally learned to read a pattern to things, or maybe he just figured it had been a couple weeks since a new torment had presented itself, but somehow he'd known.

When he walked into the parlor before the first gong, dressed, a knot in his chest, Caterina was still tightening the belt around her waist. As soon as she was finished, she extended him a short leather-wrapped weapon. The small sheath held a gleaming silver knife the length of his forearm from hilt to tip. There was barely a guard on the hilt which melded sleekly into the double-edged blade with only a notch to separate it. Clearly some of Mac's more intricate work, it mirrored the one she strapped on under her tunic. He took it and watched her with dead eyes until she told him to wrap the belt around his waist and pointed to a third long cloak resting over the back of his chair.

They had made it clear that he could not escape drinking human blood. Today, then, was the next step, the next test. Today he was required to participate.

Could he really hurt someone? He would have said no one could make him do that. Before.

His morning blood boiled like molten metal in his gut.

Minutes, or maybe an hour, fled away until he followed the black cloak in front of him in the flickering light of the torch held by one of Alena's clan members at the front of their procession. The packed silt wanted to crunch under his leather soles as he walked through the sinuous underground canyon.

Those in front of him started ascending the canyon wall. Ethan leaped to clear the outward bow of the wall, used a foothold to jump higher, and grasped the shelf of rock above. When he had quickly heaved his body up over it, tucking his chin to roll smoothly to his feet, he followed the torchlight to a large slope of rubble that met a ceiling that appeared to have caved in. He didn't see the hole to the outside until Stefan shoved aside a well-placed boulder to reveal the dimly glowing night.

It almost seemed like falling to stare up into the open dark blue sky, making Ethan gasp a breath as he slid from the opening onto the dry grass below. Even though the sun was obscured behind the mountain at his back, it was still the most light he had been in since being forced into the sunlight months ago, and he stood blinking at it while the others pulled up their hoods and continued walking.

"Come on." Stefan's urging pulled him from his shock to follow across the sloping field. Hooded figures in front of him faded into the twilight shadows at the edge of a tree line and turned along it until they reached an old stone wall.

The sound of a cough drew his attention to a new figure.

Caterina spoke, *"You have it?"*

A man with a gray beard, dressed in dirty pants and a plain coat, took a step back into the field and eyed them all warily. His response was in more modern Romanian, and Ethan didn't catch the meaning of most of his words, but he motioned at two large sacks that lay on the wall. After looking inside, Caterina produced a small black satchel from her cloak and held it out to him, making him step timorously forward to take it. Once he had shuffled back again, he opened the satchel and pulled out something that was silver and glittered in the fading light.

Could this be an exchange of goods? Ethan had known he couldn't have been simply making jewelry for those inside the cave, but it looked as though they had just traded some of it for sacks that smelled of grapes and something else. Of course, the fruit and candles and wine had to come from somewhere. There weren't any orchards or vineyards in their cave.

It was considerably less barbaric than he had been imagining.

But then Caterina chirped and began leading their group of eight into a copse of trees. The fun had only just begun for all but one vampire who returned to the cave with the sacks.

By the time they ducked through the old fir trees to crest the next hill, the vast host of stars stretched all the way across the dark bottomless sky to the horizon. Ethan looked back over his cloaked shoulder at the dark purple silhouette of the ridgeline of mountains and considered where they must have started walking from to have finally come out there.

Rather than head down into the valley, the cloaked wraiths in front of him continued silently through the trees. It felt strange to be trekking with so little effort over the rocky feet of the mountain. The branches above played with the starlight, and the cool breeze held the smell of woodsmoke and flowers. When he halted with the others just outside of the cover of the trees at the crest of a hill, enough dread had fallen away for him to feel somewhat foolish at creeping around in an imposing cloak that billowed in the wind.

The white walls, red roofs, and warm lights of the village visible below cracked the illusion and rekindled his fear. At first glance, it had appeared as the village he had found in the dark of another night, but it wasn't that one. It only bore the same old-style buildings, cobbled streets, and wooden fences, while sitting against a rockier cliff and spreading further into the flat field beyond.

Two clicks from Caterina's throat had Stefan breaking off to disappear into the trees at the edge of the town, and the next signal was a familiar trill of her tongue that she'd been using in training to signal Ethan to take up position at her back. When he hesitated a fraction, she followed it with an impatient hand motion, so he moved, as quietly as he could in the unfamiliar underbrush, close to her back at the side of a low stone wall.

After a few still moments, Stefan appeared at Caterina's right hand and breathed words into her ear so soft that Ethan could barely make them out despite being against Caterina's back. *There is no one to await us.*

Her dark eyes searched the quiet village. *"No,"* she answered, *"They have forgotten fear."* As Ethan pieced together the meaning of her words, a chill stole into him. He would have vowed to remember it for them if only he could turn back now.

Stefan waved a signal to two of their party, and they disappeared into the brush on the other side of the wall.

The silent vigil continued with only the sounds of nocturnal insect song in the grass around them and the hum from the houses down the hill where the occupants were kept warm inside, until the remaining lights and that electronic hum were cut off all at once.

Stefan's cold blue eyes shone in the starlight. Caterina's blade slid silently from its sheath as she pulled it free to raise aloft, glistening silver. *"Fear and...twice?...sacrifice,"* she ordered loudly enough to be heard along the wall, raising five pairs of blue eyes from their dark cowls.

For Ethan, it was fear that sharpened his vision and brought every stone and blade of grass between him and the nearest whitewashed house into focus as he followed with quiet footfalls toward the town. Caterina stopped and brought her hand up in front of him while the others disappeared into shadows surrounding the town.

His heart pounded traitorously slowly in his ears as a scream sounded in a house down the lane, voices started yelling in a house across the field, and somewhere a bell tolled.

Once the cries had spread to the whole town, Caterina moved again, making sure Ethan followed closely. Earnestly willing the ground to swallow him up, Ethan stopped at her gesture at the edge of a fence surrounding a house and some outbuildings.

"Go," her porcelain hand pointed to the barn. *"Retrieve a goat."*

Ethans eyes flicked between the old wooden structure and her face. *"A goat?"*

"One goat. Alive. Bring it here." She spoke clearly.

Stealing seemed a small sin to escape the night with, so, with no more hesitation, he stepped over the fence, feeling her melt away into the night which was only getting louder with the fear they had promised.

One goat... He eyed the tall wooden barn and managed to focus on the sounds within—sounds of milling animals only just catching the unease that permeated the night air. Ethan pressed against the wide double door at one end. It gave very little under his hands. Unsure if he could break through that with the force he alone could generate, and even less sure he wanted to, he took a step back and looked around the corner and then upward.

A darker opening yawned right above him next to a winch with a rope dangling from it. It wasn't as high above him as the staircase he traversed multiple times a day, and yet it seemed more unnatural that he should be able to reach it.

All the same, his leap reached it easily, and he ducked to avoid running into the top of the window frame while his feet slid slightly on the hay covered floor. There was movement, behind that wall of stacked hay bales, and a sudden gasp of breath. He snapped toward it, ready with an instinct beaten into him, but nothing leaped out, leaving him to take a breath of sweet hay dust and listen.

Moving animals beneath the floor he stood on. A scream outside muffled by the stacked hay.

A racing heartbeat and quick breaths.

Ethan crept around the wall of bales.

Pressed against the wall of hay as though to disappear into it, huddled a woman. Blond hair spilled over a face dominated by wide blue eyes. *"Please..."* Her soft plea was in modern Romanian.

Taken aback by the fear he incited simply by standing there, Ethan stared at her, too long probably, before turning away. "I'm not here for you."

"What-what are you here for?"

He snapped back to her, "You speak English?"

"Y-yes," she trembled. "Why do you?"

Because I don't belong here. Yet there he was, causing fear and taking a sacrifice. "I'm sorry for scaring you. I just need a goat."

Some of the fear in her face gave way to confusion. "A goat?"

"Yes. I'm supposed to return with one goat. Is there one you don't, uh, like as much?"

"The one with brown ears stopped producing milk..." she said in a daze.

"Right. Brown ears...Uh, how, exactly, should I get it to come with me?" He looked vaguely around for a rope.

She gaped at him, apparently baffled by his ineptitude or something. "Where are you from?"

"New York," the answer seemed ridiculous.

"But you are one of them?" She risked a peek around her hay bale wall toward the window where cries were still rising.

He looked down at his dark cloak, "Yeah."

"How?"

"They took me…" A sudden wonder hit him, "What is the date?"

"March tenth."

The world seemed fuzzy. "Seven months…I've been here seven months…"

The sound of her heart racing interrupted his thoughts, and her eyes widened again. "The stories–they're true. They take people–not just to kill but to become like them? *Strigoi?*"

He flinched at the name.

"How? Will you kill me? Or take me?" She huddled back against the hay again.

"No," he answered quickly. "I'm not–You're safe. I'm just here for a goat."

"They will kill someone?" she pointed out the window.

"Probably," he whispered. "Yes."

"Why?" her eyes searched his face.

Why…

"Why can they not leave us alone? They say you are stories, but I remember the last time–I was not a child. My grandpapa said we should go, visit another town on that night. But now they don't count the months but say you are only thieves, not demons…"

Ethan blinked, trying to make sense of her frightened words.

"Why are *you* here?"

Why? "They took me…"

"Why do you not leave them?"

Her question froze him. "I…don't know how…" He glanced vaguely upward.

"You cannot walk in the day? That is true?"

"Yes. And I don't know where I am." The simple truth that had started it all.

A motor started somewhere close by but was nearly drowned out by a desperate scream.

His reality came crashing back down, and hers. "Stay here. Hide. I just need a goat. Show me which one, and I'll leave."

She moved out of her hiding place and rustled through the stray hay to the top of a ladder that rose above the loft floor. "You can make them all leave?"

"No, but at least I won't be the reason they're still here." He watched her blond head disappear down the ladder before stepping off to land on the top of a stall rail below.

She gasped and jumped backwards.

"Sorry, sorry," he held up an open hand.

Eyeing him warily, she sidestepped to a shelf and retrieved a rope. "Here. A goat."

"Show me."

As she pushed through a gate into a pen on the other side of a low wall, the sound of a bleat rose to join the noise from outside. Ethan stepped down to walk to the gate and found her crouched next to a goat with its legs tied together.

His, "Thank you," startled her again, and she dropped the rope to retreat against the barn wall. When he moved to pick up the goat by the rope tied between its legs, he realized he had not been so close to another person from outside the cave since…since he'd been taken into it. The sound of her heartbeat pounded louder than the grunts of the goat, and he could feel her breath on his hand, almost smell the blood coursing through her. Human blood.

Ethan turned away, lifted the goat by the rope, and moved, almost fleeing, to the barn door. As soon as he lifted the broad wooden latch, the door blew in with a bang. The wind blew his hair over his eyes and brought screaming and smoke in with it. A woman's wail cut through the chaos outside. Amid it all, he knew only one thing: that he couldn't let them find and take that girl. He had told her that she was safe.

He dropped the goat, grasped the large door, pushed it back against the wind, and levered the board back into place. The girl cowered, staring at his eyes, and he realized they must have turned blue again with his own fear at what was happening outside.

Stepping toward her only heightened her alarm, so he stopped and held out a hand. "You need to hide again. They are everywhere." When she didn't move, he asked, "What is your name?"

"Iulia," she whispered.

"Iulia. I'm Ethan. I need you to come back up and hide in the hay. I'm going to scare the rest of the goats a little, so they'll make some noise so you'll be harder to hear, ok?"

Still watching him warily, she climbed into the hayloft as he ran along the front of the goat pen, rattled a gate, slapped a couple goats he could reach, and bared his teeth in a hiss at them. They responded with an appropriate amount of bleating and running into each other and bumping the pen walls with a general ruckus, so, remembering to grab the bound goat at the last moment, he jumped to the hay loft where Iulia was back behind her hay wall.

"Why would you help me?" she asked, still watching, as though trying to figure him out.

"The truth is, I don't have much power to keep my word that you won't be taken. All I can do is make you harder for them to find and follow my instructions." He held up the brown-eared goat and stepped toward the hay mow opening.

"Commandau." Her voice turned him back. "This village isn't on maps, but the nearest real town is Commandau." Stooping to brush the hay away from a section of the floor, she started tracing lines in the dust. "We are here. This is the mountains," she drew a wavy line. "Here is Commandau. To leave, you would have to get to Brasov," her finger drew a line along the edge of the mountains. "You can cross down to Bucharest from there. I don't know how you could get there fast, through the night…but many farmers leave keys in their trucks out here."

Realizing what she was offering, Ethan bent to study the lines in the dirt and memorized the names, the shape of the mountains, and the location of the cities. She made it almost seem possible to steal a truck and simply drive to the capital. What if it could be done? Could he still go back home?

A vampire shriek cut through the night just outside. He released the goat to bleat on the hay, and, with a hand against her chest, pushed Iulia between the bales. Finding himself tucked into the narrow place with her, his face above hers, her clear blue eyes searching his face in curiosity rather than fear, he wished, for a slow beat of his heart, that he could stay and hide with her.

"Ethan…" despite her slight accent, the name was his. Really his.

"Stay hidden. Live," he breathed.

She nodded. "Escape," she whispered back.

Looking into her innocent face, it seemed possible. Touching a blond curl under his finger on the hay beside her, he nodded, then leaned closer to her upturned face. Without even the time to fully form the thought of doing so, he touched his lips to hers, in a promise and goodbye, and left her, still and quiet, behind the hay.

After hurling a bale down below into the goats to stir them up again, he snatched up the rope securing the hooves of the goat and leaped out the window to land on the dirt between the barn and the fence—in front of another vampire who had been approaching the barn from the fence line where Caterina loitered.

Forgetting hope, repressing the thoughts of everything that had happened in the last minutes, and reminding his tongue of its permitted language, Ethan managed to look at the vampire with a flat expression and raised the goat, hanging upside down by its hooves bound in the rope, as an explanation. Choosing to dismiss the importance of that barn the best he could, Ethan hoisted the rope over his shoulder and pushed past him on his way back to the fencepost.

He was grateful for the chaos around him to distract from any sign of his relief when the vampire turned to follow.

At least one car was on fire down the road. Screams of fear still echoed, but there was also yelling, and a single shot rang out, the pop echoing down the street. Stefan and another vampire appeared out of a smoky shadow leading two bound young women. The one with long brown hair was shrieking endlessly, eyes mad with fear as Stefan dragged her by a rope that bound her hands. The other was blond and looked enough like the girl in the barn for Ethan to take a second look at her silent tearstained face.

Horror wasn't a strong enough thing to feel at the evil happening here. *Surely I have to do something—*

Caterina appeared to put a hand on his shoulder to remind him of his impotence before he could so much as finish the thought.

"Good," she nodded at the goat slung by the rope over his shoulder and gave him a push that steered him up the hill they had descended.

On their way up the hill, more shades coalesced into cloaked vampires. Two others carried goats, and one held a small squealing pig. Ethan's goat bounced upside down against his cloak at his leg, long brown ears flopping, an incongruous calmness to its fate.

Ethan was stepping over the low stone wall when something pinged off the rock next to him and then again a little further down. The cracks that followed were ear splittingly loud and disorienting enough that he would have frozen if Caterina hadn't knocked him down into a crouch on the ground on the other side of the wall.

Her eyes lit blue as she scanned him and raised a silver knife. With an order to, *"Stay,"* she leaped up to sprint along the wall toward the sound. The gunshots cracked again and again, causing Ethan to involuntarily wince, but he leaned forward enough to identify the gunman between an outbuilding and the wall. He was slowly aiming the rifle at the figure running toward him.

Caterina was an impossible target, one with the shadows as she skirted the edge of the trees and leaped the wall to him. She pinned his hand, which dropped the gun, against the side of the wooden building with her knife, grasped his throat with her other hand, and leaned in close to the man.

Stefan and several others shrieked victorious piercing notes as she stared at the once emboldened man, now shaking and crying under her gaze only an inch from his face. She held him off the ground by his throat, his struggles puny against her easy grip.

"He will serve as a warning," she proclaimed to them as they all moved closer to her.

"Fear!" several of them chanted in response.

Misinterpreting her words or resigning himself to his fate, the man calmed as she held him there a moment longer, smiling in his face. The tips of her sharp fangs glistened in the starlight as she bared them in a wide, almost ceremonious way before biting deeply into his neck.

Only a few twitches gave evidence of his dying as she held him fast with her hands and teeth.

And swallowed.

When she finally released the limp body, the smell of the blood that dripped from her mouth was enough to interrupt the calmness of the group. The bound girls screamed in the terror that is to know one's impending doom, while more than one vampire reached for one of them, causing Stefan to draw his blade as he ordered them to back off.

Not immune, Ethan couldn't tear his eyes from the blood on Caterina's chin. As appalling as her savagery was, it was the raw power over the man that shocked him. Surely a few vampires against a village could have butchered them all.

Caterina's clear order stopped everything, *"Enough. Return to the entrance. There will be feasting tonight."*

When others stepped around him to continue up the hill, Ethan placed a hand on the still-quiet goat's warm stomach and watched the two girls being dragged into hell and looked back at the dead man against the wall. *"Fear and* double *sacrifice,"* he whispered, wishing he didn't understand.

But he also understood that if he didn't move, someone would return to drag him back there too, so he lifted his goat and started walking.

18

The tree branches didn't sing and the stars didn't sparkle walking toward the mountain, but the cool mouth of the cave was still there to greet Ethan.

He was able to trail far enough back that he didn't see the girls when they were dragged away to those stalls, but not far enough to muffle the screams. When he reached the intersection where they still echoed, there was an impatient vampire who worked in the animal pens to take his goat. The goat might have a longer life than the girls, if it was to be put with the other animals and periodically bled.

The festive greeting of the returned party had crescendoed before Ethan walked into the main cavern, which allowed him to slink along the edge and leap up to his staircase relatively unimpeded. The moment he entered his room his legs gave in to trembling that dropped him to his knees.

What have we done?

He only crouched for minutes before Caterina's call, *"Dress for dinner!"* echoed through the halls. The long time of traveling and what had happened in the village must not have left much time to butcher the sacrifice.

I need to wash first. He wouldn't be able to scrub the guilt off, but he feared some scent or clue of Iulia might remain on him somehow, but surely she was safe now that they were gone. He yanked off his shirt and used the basin in his room rather than going for clean water.

The embroidered cuffs of his dress shirt dropped over still shaking wrists as he pulled it on. When Caterina appeared in his doorway, arrayed in sparkling finery, he barely kept his eyes from showing his swirling emotions.

"You did well tonight, Etan."

Simultaneously grateful for and disgusted by her praise, he waited for the "but" that hadn't yet come. As she reached to his neck, he stiffened, wary of her intentions, but when she floated away, he raised a hand to find a fine silver chain around his neck.

"I will see you at the feast." She left him alone.

⟩

The deep gong rang.

Expansive cave draperies and the crystal in the walls glistened in the flickering candle and lantern light, as did the throats and wrists and fingers of the milling black-draped guests. Caterina swept into her place beside the chair Ethan trudged up to, the embroidery in her gown playing its own dance with the flames. His focus dropped to the empty silver goblet in front of him, toying with him with its promises and shame as Lord Vasile proclaimed his standard monologue about victory and sacrifice.

After the first courses, when the blood glistened ready in its serving vessels, Caterina whispered over to him, *"Serve us."*

Ethan felt his legs obey her command, standing, while his eyes saw only the crimson surface of the liquid.

Which girl's was it? Who had they slaughtered and drained like an animal for the feast? Had it been only one, saving the other like leftovers, or had they taken some from both? Without drawing breath his chest heaved as though to sob, and, even without tears, the table blurred in his vision.

Stefan made an impatient gesture. Others were moving and pouring around the table while Ethan stood still. Caterina stopped Stefan with a flick of her finger and looked at Ethan, who found himself meeting her gaze.

What of it? her eyes asked. *Will you obey now, or later?*

What if he stood and protested the unjust butchery in front of those at the table? Did human life mean nothing?

But they all knew. They all drank. Craved. Reveled. It would serve nothing.

Absolutely nothing.

Looking at it paralyzed him with the sound of their screams and cries, so he didn't look. His hand shook, a last protest of his own body, when he grasped the silver pitcher and brought it to the edge of her cup, but she guided it with her own hand. He couldn't look at her face, at the proud expression that was likely pasted there. Stefan nearly poured his own, so Ethan was left to unsteadily spill the liquid that had only an hour before kept another person alive into his own chalice.

The others raised their cups while he fell into his chair off shaking knees.

Life.

That was the meaning of the word they chanted a moment before consuming it: *"From life to life."*

One of those girls had given her life so he could drink…this. He thought he would gag rather than swallow, but that changed as soon as the blood was in his mouth, and he drank like all the others, except for the grimace at the end when he dropped the cup to the table.

He sat back in his chair as his horror and dread swirled hard enough to produce a numbness that spread from the center of his chest. The resulting fuzzy lack of feeling let him sit listlessly until the candles burned low and others started dispersing merrily to other areas of the cave, and he climbed back to his room.

When he stood alone in his sparsely furnished room, the numbness threatened to crack, but then a single heartbeat from behind him offered a different option. Unsure what it meant, that she had come to him instead of Stefan on the night of a Great Feast, he turned.

"Cate," he whispered.

Her eyes lit blue.

And he reached for her first, pulling her close enough to feel something that wasn't numbness or pain or fear.

19

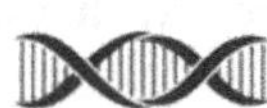

The morning after the feast, Ethan's feet wandered undirected along the cliff edge in an empty cavern. He'd started wandering when his mind wouldn't stop replaying the day before—or night, since it was clearly night outside the cave when they were awake.

When his next step hovered over emptiness rather than finding firm rock, he was forced to look up and realize he had strayed into unfamiliar territory. A look in either direction, and also up, showed gray rock and shadow with no recognizable features. He didn't have a good enough sense of direction to wander in such unfamiliar territory.

Of course, I probably wouldn't even be here to begin with if I had a better sense of direction. The thought smacked him in the gut while he was skirting around a deep shaft, knocking off his balance.

He fell.

Darkness rushed up, past him, swallowing him.

His feet punched through water to find the hard bottom only a foot below the surface, and his body absorbed the force by sending him into a deep bouncing lunge.

The pain of stung ankles and shock of the frigid water barely broke through the fog in his mind. He dropped to his knees and sunk down into the water.

What if he and Jack had only taken one different turn?

Despair threatened, beckoned him from the blackest edges of the darkness. *What point is there to living like this?*

He despised who he had become. What he continued to do. The morality he used to live by was twisted until he doubted it meant anything.

That shaft hadn't been deep enough, but perhaps there was another…

The babbling of the water pulled him out, tugging gently at his attention as it trickled away into the darkness somewhere ahead.

What if Iulia's right? What if I could still escape?

They had done their best to convince him that he could not survive anywhere else, that he needed them to live.

What if they are wrong?

Then he needed to get up. Get up and make some sound so he could tell where the open passage was and avoid smacking his head against an overhang. He needed to finish learning how to walk in complete darkness. He needed to be able to navigate the back passages. He needed to learn to fight the way they did in case he needed to fight his way out.

If they weren't wrong, then maybe life wasn't worth living. Then one day despair might win. But it would not be today. Today he would take one step to try to prove them wrong.

20

The Great Feast days kept recurring no matter what Ethan did or thought or focused on. Today he followed the back of Stefan's thick black cloak, wondering what new horrors the night might hold. The tension roiled in his gut, clamped tight around something in his chest, but a body could only take so much constant stress.

Somewhere in the curves of the underground canyon he stopped feeling it.

The numbness was so complete and sudden that he reached to touch the striations of the wall beside him to see that it still felt like coarse sand under his fingertips. It was like he was watching himself from outside his body, watching himself leap to the high ledge and keep his steps light over the uneven rocks of the old cave-in, seeing it happen without feeling anything about it. Immune even to the dark blue sky still blushed with pink at the west edge, he stopped by rote when the back of the vampire in front of him stopped after a few steps out into the world.

Luca had come from further ahead and was reporting something to Caterina, something that changed her demeanor.

That should have deepened the pit of dread in his stomach, but he couldn't feel his stomach.

They walked single file back the way Luca had come. The line stopped only a few minutes later, fanning out until everyone could see what was in the small clearing at the crest of the hill.

There were sheep tied to a tree. Next to them was a flat rock upon which sat several earthenware jars. The clear scent of human blood seeped from the jars, and held most of their attention, but next to them stood a man. Dressed in simple clothing and sporting short gray hair, he stood with shaking hands held palms out.

"Repeat it," Luca told the man in a version of Romanian that sounded more like modern Romanian than the language Ethan could now communicate in.

"I…offer sacrifice for…village…if not enough…sacrifice myself." Ethan made out from his short speech.

Some of the numbness started wearing off as he started piecing together what was going on. Every month they went to a surrounding village to obtain the sacrifice required, but there were cave openings miles and miles apart and seemingly a lot of small villages. They never went to the same village two months in a row. Rather, there seemed to be a standard rotation.

In the months following the fiery attack on the village from which he had taken the goat, tonight's village must have heard about it and was taking extreme measures to avoid a massacre by offering blood and animals and, just in case it wasn't enough, a volunteer willing to give his life for the village.

Ethan's breath caught in his throat as he wished for the vanishing numbness to return.

Caterina was a pragmatist, but also a master of creating suspense. After making a show of checking the contents of each jar and slowly counting, she stared down the trembling man, who somehow resolutely stared right back.

"Let him go. Your sacrifice is accepted."

After Luca made sure he understood and waved him away, Stefan started giving assignments. Feeling at once like all the air had been let out of a balloon, Ethan accepted the two sheep he was motioned to by the ropes around their necks and muddled back through the trees. The bleating animals broke the night quiet, but it was infinitely better than the human cries he'd been expecting.

The vampiress at the stables berated him for his poor handling of his sheep, naturally, but he shrugged her off and caught a glimpse of a brown eared goat in the stalls behind her. It was only a goat, but there was relief in knowing that one thing he'd done hadn't resulted in death. Not yet anyway. He almost smiled.

As he walked out, ignoring the side tunnel at the junction to the main passage, it seemed as though Caterina materialized in front of him.

"Come."

"Where?"

She swept away without answering.

No questions. He shut his mouth and followed.

The answer was the very place he was trying not to think about: the tunnel that led to the other holding stalls, where he had seen the boy hung upside down and drained. It was the place where he imagined the others were taken, although he'd never returned to find out.

As they descended, the sound of a quick heartbeat made his start pounding harder. By the time the tunnel opened into the wider subdivided space, the sound of the beating could be heard over the sound of whimpers, shifting on straw, and the rustle of clothing. The tension that he had naively let go of at the sight of jars and sheep came coiling back all at once, and he balked at entering.

"Come," Caterina repeated, having slowed but not stopped. Her tone was cool, but he knew that could change, and that she could make him obey.

What if it's not as bad as you think? Maybe you're just here for some standard chores or something? He made himself trudge after her, unable to keep from looking for the source of the sounds.

Although the artificial divisions along the wall looked like stalls, on the front of them hung black iron gates. In the first cowered a woman, recognizable as one of the two who had been taken from the village on his first trip out. She was dressed in clean clothes, but her hair was matted and her eyes glazed over, staring at nothing. They'd kept her alive down here.

The gate also made him realize that he had been there before, and not just the once to observe from above. He'd been only semiconscious when he'd been carried in, but he'd spent time in one of these cells. One further down the line, in the darkness…

"There will be no need for that," Caterina followed his gaze. *"If you obey."*

He was a fool for thinking hope existed in this place.

"It is your turn. You will kill today."

His vision sharpened as he jerked to look her in the eyes, begging for misunderstanding. *"Why?"*

"It is time."

"I am not injured," his mind spun out appropriate objections as he shook his head. *"The feast is tonight—I will drink then. This is not needed."*

Her leap forward put her face inches from his, even as he stepped back. *"I declare what is needed. You will kill now, so you are one of us."* He could taste her breath. *"You will kill now, so I know you will later, when necessary."*

"No."

"You will."

"I won't." His back hit the cool rock of the wall, stopping him from further retreat. He stared back into her dark eyes, seeing his own death in them, for killing, surely, was the thing they could not make him do.

Her eyes held only certainty.

He decided too late to fight back. Despite his attempt to spin away, she had him slammed face first against the rock wall in an instant, with his wrists in her hands and her foot in his back. When she brought his hands together to pull him away from the wall, he hopped up and rolled forward, wrenching his shoulder but yanking one hand out of her grip. Deciding the silver knife would have one use at least, he pulled it from the sheath with his free arm and slashed at her.

His blade was met with hers.

"It is necessary," she was still calm.

It wasn't—couldn't be. How could causing so much death be necessary?

She let go of his wrist and rained repeated rapid strikes at him with the glistening point of her knife, one edge then the other from a myriad of directions. He danced back, parrying but mostly dodging, twisting just out of its reach, or just within.

Blood seeped from a dozen shallow cuts by the time he realized he was being purposefully directed. She cut off his attempted leap upwards with a deep gash in his thigh and kicked him through a gate.

His feet found the floor before his body did, but they slid on the hay.

Metal clanged.

He was in a long shallow cleft in the rock wall, encompassed above and on three sides by natural cave walls with the open side lined entirely by iron bars. Caterina stepped a single pace away from the secured gate in the center.

She raised her chin, staring at him.

"No," he repeated.

When she turned away, long cloak sweeping behind her, and left him alone, he wasn't sure what to think. Too ragged to figure it out, he pressed his hand against the still oozing gash in his thigh, dropped to the ground, and leaned back against the rough back wall. With his legs extended in front of him, he could just touch the bars with his foot.

He couldn't see the other cells from his position, but he could still hear the one other occupant. He let fear bloom into anger at being left to once again wait and wonder at what new horror he would be forced to face and hit his head back into the rock wall.

Without the leverage or willpower to slam his head hard enough to take himself out of the equation, he did wait, for a while. Caterina returned, dressed for the feast in her glittering gown and delicate silver jewelry, but it was Lord Vasile, arrayed in his own finery topped by a rich fur coat, who drew his attention. He had not been a part of any of his training or punishments before, so why was the lord present for this?

Maybe he was needed for meting out death penalties.

Caterina walked up to the bars, within his reach. *"Will you kill?"*

It felt like a last chance. Still. *"No."*

Vasile nodded at Caterina.

She accepted his approval and turned toward something out of Ethan's line of sight.

"You have it?" she asked as Stefan strode in, still wearing his battle clothes.

"Yes." He nodded to two vampires who held a cloaked figure struggling vainly against their tight hold.

When Stefan reached for the cell's gate, holding a long naked blade in his other hand, Ethan instinctively scooted away from it. Stefan didn't enter, but held the gate open for the two vampires to shove their prisoner through the gate before slamming it closed again.

It was a human. He could hear it. Smell it.

She landed with a gasp and a cry at the other end of the narrow cell.

A siren started in Ethan's mind, and he stopped breathing.

They couldn't have. There was no way.

Blond hair fell from the hood, and blue eyes looked out at him as she pushed it off her head.

"Iulia."

<h1 style="text-align:center">21</h1>

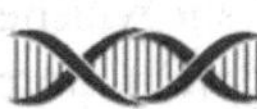

Iulia.

The lack of air in the room dulled every other sound.

"Ethan?" The terror in her eyes softened momentarily at the sight of him, but their cage and the others outside it threatened to reignite it. "What is going on?"

"As I said," Stefan nodded haughtily from the other side of the bars.

What was she doing here? How had they found out he'd talked to her? What— *"What are you doing with her?"* He slammed his hands against the bars hard enough to make them buzz, *"It's not her village's night! You can't take her!"*

Vasile turned his head and approached him slowly, meeting him at the bars. *"The rules are mine, boy. Your only choice is how to kill her."*

"I'm not killing her!"

"You will," he said casually, almost over his shoulder, as he turned in his flowing robe to leave.

Tears blurred Ethan's vision as he dropped to his knees. He couldn't make himself look back at Iulia. The cold hard truth was even if he didn't do it, she was dead. They would do it if he didn't. He had killed her already by talking to her in that barn. He was a fool.

Stefan agreed. *"Idiot. Take her. You are fighting what others would kill for."*

Ethan could only shake his head and slump against the bars. He couldn't kill her. However stupid and futile, he'd tried to protect her.

At Caterina's nod, Stefan thrust his long blade through the bars at Iulia. Ethan sprung forward, trying to hit the blade sideways to pin it between his forearm and the bar. Stefan pulled it free, the edge ripping Ethan's shirtsleeve, and held the bloody tip up to consider it with eyes

109

that had turned blue. Grinning, he gave the blade a slow sultry lick. *"She's a sweet one. Lucky dog."*

All at once the scent of her blood hit him, and he clamped his eyes shut against his own traitorous physical response to it. Stefan's laugh echoed in his ears as Ethan backed away from Iulia until his head hit the sloped ceiling.

When Ethan dared to open his eyes, Iulia was looking back at him with a tear on her cheek, holding her right hand tight to her left shoulder. Blood oozed from between her fingers, not fast enough to risk her bleeding out, but plenty to fill the space with the smell of it.

His head scraped against the rock as he shook his head again. *I won't.*

Iulia must have worked out by now how their imprisonment was supposed to end. "I'm sorry," she whispered.

She was sorry? *"Why?"* But what more could be risked by speaking his own language? "Why?"

"I couldn't stay safe. I didn't know they would return."

"It's my fault." Ethan's breath hitched. "It's all my fault...I couldn't...escape..."

Consumed with the sight of the one human he'd talked to in almost a year, the smell of her blood, and the taste of his failure, he paid no attention to whoever was responsible for the movement out on the other side of the bars until a shaft of pain pierced his thigh. His shriek echoed out into the larger chamber and skyrocketed Iulia's heart rate.

Caterina stood on the other side of the bars, holding a crossbow.

There was no sense in feeling the stab of betrayal. She had done it before. His hand quivered where it grasped the end of the crossbow bolt in his leg, but he didn't move to pull it out. *"Why don't you just kill me and finish it?"*

"I'm not killing you. I'm bringing you to life." She was so assured. So confident. How close would she bring him to death this time before snatching him from its jaws?

⟩

For a while, a long while, no one moved, other than Iulia's slight shifting on the hard ground at the other end of the cell. Caterina had settled onto a rock shelf outside, crossbow leaned casually against her knee, watching in a posture that said she was in no hurry. As the ache in Ethan's leg grew, stabbing him if he so much as tensed a muscle in his leg, so did his hunger, and the feeling that he had done it all before. Caterina thought all she had to do was wait for the hunger to

110

overpower his will, and he would kill the girl in front of him.

Was she right?

Caterina rose again, cradling the bow, to stand in front of him at the bars. *"Take her."*

It may have been weaker, but he still shook his head.

Pain stabbed again, in his side, knocking him to his hands on the floor.

Iulia gasped and covered a cry as he bared his fangs in a grimace, eyes undoubtedly blue.

When he grasped the wooden shaft, it stuck on a rib, sending sudden spasms across his whole torso and stealing any breath left in his lungs. Inhaling had the same effect, so he stopped breathing for a moment and lay as still as possible, still supported by one hand. *Maybe I should just push it further in.*

As though she'd read his thoughts, Caterina's hand folded over his, reaching through the bars to grasp the bolt tight before yanking it from his side.

It hurt so much he barely even felt her take the one from his thigh. By the time he could lift his head again, she was gone, leaving him in a shallow puddle of his blood next to Iulia and hers.

PART II
THE CITY

22

The barrage of sound was overwhelming. The clack of the subway wheels against the track below. The roar of the train engine. The echo of it against the tunnel walls.

There were also innumerable details Ethan could hear if he worked to divide the small sounds underneath the roar. The teenage girl chatting with her friend halfway down the car. The beep of the game in the hands of the man across from her. The clinking change in the pocket of the man at the other end.

And, barely audible under it all, quick steady heartbeats.

Ethan leaned against the back door of the last car on the A train with his hands in his pockets, nearly certain the familiar scene was a dream or hallucination. But the noise and blinding brightness of every light wouldn't have been present in his memory.

Nor would the date he'd seen on the metro card kiosk.

September 4th, over two years since he had boarded the plane for Romania.

What are you thinking? That you can re-enter your old life after two years? After everything that has happened? As what you are now?

He repeated an old mantra to himself: *One thing at a time.*

He could make it work. He'd done too much, become something else entirely before obtaining the perfect opportunity to flee. It had to work. After twenty-five months and three days, Ethan was back in New York City.

It had taken nearly two days to get to Bucharest and find a plane

115

headed to New York at a time he could risk sneaking into the cargo compartment from his hiding place at the airport. The plane had landed in JFK International Airport just after nightfall. The lights at the airport had made it impossible to simply slip out of the cargo compartment and down the runway unseen, but the orange reflective vest he'd taken from the empty cart had rendered him just as invisible until he'd followed someone into the terminal. Then he only had to join the masses headed to the Airtrain and subway.

Most of his dreams had stopped short at getting out of the cave, or maybe extended to making it to New York. He wasn't sure what all to do now that he was here, or even where the night would end, but he had worked out a first step.

While two days was a trivial time to go without food, finding a main source of his diet staple needed to be his first priority. Racking his brain for a possible source of blood in New York City, he'd come up with one answer: Chinatown.

So that would be the first stop.

He fingered the bills in his pocket. The clothes, shoes, and sunglasses he wore had come from a checked bag in the cargo hold of the plane. The money was from a wallet that had been too easy to take from a man in the airport. Those thefts had been necessary, but now it was time for a different set of rules. The old ones he'd used to follow.

Ethan exited the train into Atlantic Avenue station in Brooklyn, another place he knew like the back of his hand. However, tonight the bright lights made every dirty tile stand out, every beat of the subway bucket-drum performer reverberated in his ears, and every member of the steady 9:30 p.m. foot traffic pressed much too close to him.

At the top of one of the many sets of stairs on the way to the D train track, a small, "Woah!" stopped him. He quickly flattened himself against the sooty tile wall and watched the kid who had noticed him leap the whole set of stairs in one stride get pulled along by his mom's hand into the crowd.

Old rules.

Could he even remember what those had been?

If he was going to live in New York again, to get back to who he'd been, he needed to be like everyone else again, as much as possible. Everyone else was taking the stairs one at a time, or perhaps two at a time. He could do that. He would do that.

He swallowed and stepped back into the walkway to catch the D train to Chinatown in Manhattan.

み

The subway stop opened upward next to a park and a row of produce shops. The night sky glowed orange high above the tops of the rows of buildings reaching for it. Even under their shadows everything was overwhelmingly open. Ethan hunched his shoulders and focused on locating an open shop.

He stopped at the edge of an outdoor stall smelling of fish and slightly spoiled produce and took off his sunglasses.

"What you want?" A woman's voice demanded in a Chinese accent.

Ethan startled, "Um…I'm looking for blood. For cooking." The English words felt strange in his mouth.

She frowned and called over to her neighbor's stall in Mandarin, to a man who led him to a packaged dark red coagulated lump that read "pig's blood."

Trying not to grimace, Ethan considered it. Unpalatableness aside, could he even eat that?

"No, no, no," an ancient Chinese woman entered the store waving at him. "Not that. I have better. Come."

With a quick glance at the man, who shrugged him off, Ethan followed her across the street and down an alley to a small shop. A bell tinkled as they entered. She bustled into a walk-in refrigerator at the back leaving Ethan eyeing a row of white waving cat figurines on the counter until she came back out holding a round translucent plastic container. Red liquid swirled inside.

When she offered it to him with a pleased look on her face, he took it and cracked the lid, smelling it.

That's better. Maybe I can survive here.

"Pig?"

She nodded.

"Treated with vinegar?"

She nodded again.

He closed the lid. "How much?"

She told him.

He reached for the cash in his pocket, and she reached for a plastic bag.

"I will have the best when you need again. Come here."

"Thank you," he answered quietly.

Head down, fingers around the bag loops, Ethan headed back to the subway. *If only the next steps could go so easily.*

23

The thick stone steps and brown facade of the row house on Clinton Avenue in Brooklyn sat just beyond the glow of a bright streetlight. Various sounds of living—a jingle on a TV, the high bark of a dog, voices—trickled out from it and the row of similar buildings along the street, audible over the roar of the passing cars and the blaring ambulance siren three streets over.

Ethan had lived here.

Twenty-five months ago, he'd started every day in the basement apartment of this brownstone. Obviously, someone else would live in his apartment by now, but a friend owned the building. As a man without much family or other options, it had seemed to Ethan the best place to start.

He took a slow breath. If he was going to knock on doors, he might as well do it now, before it got even later. He had the best excuse for knocking on his own old door, so, before he lost his nerve, he walked down the few steps to the basement door half-under the wide front stairs and knocked.

A voice started answering before the door opened, "I called the plumber again. He said he'd be here tomo—" The tall thin man at the door stopped mid-sentence and gaped at Ethan. He had large ears and a long nose that stuck out improbably far from his face, giving him the self-acknowledged look of a mouse. His mouth dropped further open the longer he stood rooted in the doorway.

That had worked better than anticipated. "Hello, Garth."

Garth's mouth started moving without anything coming out. "Ethan!?" finally exited in a squeak.

"Yeah."

"What? You? How? You're dead!" tumbled out of Garth's mouth.

"I'm…not. I can explain." *Can I?*

"Where have you been?" his breaking voice squeaked louder.

"Um, can I come in?" Ethan shifted his feet.

"Yes!" Garth backed up a step but then reversed and threw his arms around Ethan.

Ethan forced himself to not react. To let him do it. To stand stiffly frozen until Garth released him and dragged him inside by the arm, stumbling over the threshold in spite of himself.

"I–wow I have so many questions," Garth let go and continued to stare. "Man, it's good to see you."

Suddenly overwhelmed, Ethan could only nod.

"Whatcha got there?" Garth motioned at the plastic bag in Ethan's hand.

"Um," Ethan took a couple steps to the kitchen side of the room and set it on the counter. "Can we just ignore that for now? It's hard to explain."

"Ok." Garth seemed oddly happy to do just as he requested and sat down on the couch. "Come on, sit down! I–what–I don't even know how to start! Where have you been?"

Blinking against the yellow overhead light, Ethan followed and lowered himself uncertainly onto the edge of the upholstered chair across from him. "Romania."

"All this time? What–wait, is Jack…?"

"Jack is dead."

"Oh man. Did you–I mean–are you sure?"

"Yes."

"Man! I'm sorry."

Ethan's gaze flitted around the small room, to anything except Garth's face. He was not at all sure how to have this conversation. Or any conversation for that matter. "What…what did you hear happened?"

"After you disappeared, Romanian authorities found the car you guys had rented somewhere out in the middle of nowhere at the bottom of a cliff." Garth made an explosion sound with his mouth and pulled his hands apart. "No one could explain anything else, but they said there were body parts…"

"Jack," Ethan whispered. "It makes sense. The car was there…"

"The car?" Garth dropped his voice too.

"I wasn't in it. Jack was already dead. Someone must have pushed it over to cover it up."

When he didn't go on, Garth asked, "What did happen?"

Ethan rubbed his eyes. There was so much he'd promised himself would remain a secret, so much no one could know about what he'd become. On the plane he'd considered what he would say if he got this far, but it was different, actually sitting there with a real person in front of him. His explanations sounded ridiculous now, and it was difficult to find the words.

"Hold up, what am I doing, demanding answers the second you walk in? What do you need?" Garth bounced up and started for the kitchen. "I have leftover takeout or we can call for something or–"

"No, I'm not–just water is fine, for now, if that's ok." Ethan's chest tightened.

"Ok, I have that." Garth let go of the refrigerator door and picked up a glass from the dish drainer on the counter to fill at the tap. "What else? Anything else right now?"

"No." Ethan stood without going anywhere. He took the offered glass from Garth and sipped carefully. It reminded him that he was hungry, but that would have to wait, so he sat back onto the narrow arm of the chair, mindlessly perching with a foot on the seat. "I was taken…" he tried to piece together some explanation. "And held underground by a…group. They killed Jack when they took me."

"Taken? By terrorists? They kept you hostage until now? Sorry–" he added when Ethan rubbed his eyes again, "You don't have to answer any of that. It's just, we really did think you were dead!" He dropped back onto the couch and stared at Ethan with wide eyes.

"It's fine. It's just hard to explain. Yeah, they made me work for them until…I found a way to get out. Two days ago."

"And you show up at my door! No, your door! This was your place. Oh man. I'm sorry–I took this apartment since it usually goes for the least, as a basement and all–shoot, I got rid of all your stuff, well except this couch was yours, wasn't it! That's terrible–"

"It's ok." Ethan interrupted without raising his voice, "I was…gone. What else would you…" He shrugged.

Garth leaned back again with a sigh and mirrored Ethan's rubbing of his own face. "Wow."

That was one word for it.

"What are you going to do now? I mean, do you know what you want to do?"

He wanted to get back here. And find real answers. *But…* "No, not exactly."

Garth slapped his legs. "Ok, then, you'll stay here tonight. And for as long as you need. 2B is supposed to be moving out next month, so we can even get you back your own apartment, if you want, by then. You want a shower?"

That was something he hadn't had in…two years. "Yeah, that sounds kind of good."

"Good! It's—well you know where it is. Go, help yourself," Garth stood only to sit down again and waved Ethan toward the bedroom door.

The short walk through the bedroom to the bathroom was like walking through a dream, and he was scared he would wake up at any second. He left the lights off without thinking and left the water cold when he found anything warmer to be uncomfortable. The water swirled at his feet, taking with it, he imagined, traces of coal, dust, and blood.

What are you going to do next?

He knew what he wanted, but how to do it, while avoiding the sun, without normal food, without someone finding out what he was…that was another matter.

Once done with the shower, a habit from another time had him opening the cabinet below the sink to pull out a towel. He paused, staring at it.

This had been his towel.

It spun his world back to a simpler time, before so much had happened. When he was another man. Was it even possible to live in that world again?

One thing at a time. Right now he could only crouch down in the small dark bathroom and breathe slowly until he could stand again and methodically put a stranger's clothes back on.

Garth's voice shouted from the other room, "You don't have a bag! You—well, I was about to offer you clean clothes, but there's no way you're fitting into my clothes, even if you have lost some weight."

"It's fine, these clothes are clean. I've only been wearing them for a couple hours."

"What?" Garth yelled back.

Oh. You can't hear as well. Like I could before…so many differences.

Ethan raised his voice and repeated his answer.

"Ok! We'll find you some more tomorrow."

An unpleasant smell wafted into the dark bedroom as he stepped silently through it. Garth had reheated the Chinese takeout after all. Ethan stopped in the bedroom doorway, which opened to the kitchen side of the main room.

If you're going to stay here, how are you going to hide? Doubts kept taunting him. *He's not going to stop trying to feed you. And he has eyes. Eventually he'll get curious and look in that bag by the microwave.*

So should he leave? Find another place, another way to live? But how? He wanted back in the lab that Garth worked in. He'd used to live here, in this apartment Garth lived in. Figuring everything out on his own, starting as a technically dead man, sounded impossible.

But to stay he would have to tell Garth *something.*

Maybe you could tell one person. As least part of it. Maybe he could help you figure this out.

The idea was horrifying and tempting at the same time. But how to tell him? The explanations sounded insane, even to him, and he knew they were true.

Garth seemed not to see him standing in the doorway until he turned and ran into him—or would have, if Ethan hadn't blocked him with an arm.

"Oh!" Garth leaped backwards, sloshing red sauce onto the floor, "Good heavens, I didn't see you there, in my…dark bedroom. Sorry!" When he kept apologizing, Ethan realized his posture was defensive, so he dropped his hand and slid sideways to avoid the red sauce.

"I know you said you weren't hungry, but I figured I'd warm it up and give you the easy option. Here's some egg rolls and sauce—woops watch that on the floor—and…"

Well, what are you going to do? his apprehension demanded over Garth's monologue about food that no longer held any allure. *Find a way to explain or leave?*

Ethan took another step back and pushed his damp hair off his forehead.

How do you tell someone you're a vampire?

"…and here's some fried rice and—hey, you ok? I mean, that may be a stupid question. We don't have to eat—I might have more, but…"

No use dragging your feet. "Do you remember Professor Burgess's class in undergrad? That thing he used to say, about being a scientist, how it meant you observed the evidence in front of you and followed it, even if it contradicted what you thought you knew?"

Garth set the food back onto the counter and turned to look at him. "Huh, that's been a while. Yeah, I remember it. Why?"

The words were stuck in his throat somewhere.

When he didn't answer, Garth took a step forward and really looked at him. "What…?"

"It's just, there's more, and, before I try to explain, I just need you to remember that. Ok?"

"Ok," Garth answered gently. "You know it's safe here, right?"

Not for you. Ethan shook that away and rubbed his eyes. "Before…before Jack died–We…were exploring this cave…" That part was hard to get out. After failing to swallow the lump in his throat, he plunged ahead. "We were attacked while we were in there. Then we got sick. I think Jack would have died, even if she hadn't killed him. He was vomiting, bleeding. I–it was different with me. They took me, and instead of killing me, whatever was passed to us in the bite changed me, my body."

Garth's eyes narrowed as he watched Ethan closely. "A bite from what? An animal?"

"No." *You sound insane.*

"I don't understand, Ethan. And changed you how?"

This is the most ridiculous…And since when did I stop thinking completely in English? Finding words shouldn't be this hard. Ethan ran his hand through his hair again. "The people who took me. One of them bit us." He winced his eyes shut so he didn't have to finish watching Garth's face twist in confusion. "I was sick and out of it for days, maybe weeks, I don't know. I was out of it for a while. When I was coherent again and could evaluate my condition, I noted several physical differences."

To his credit, Garth was still watching him, although with one side of his face scrunched together. "I'm trying," he lifted a hand. "I'm not totally following, but I'm trying. What differences?"

The fear and uncertainty roiling in his gut made it easy to let one show.

Garth jerked back against the counter, knocking the plate of egg rolls into the sink with a crash. "Holy bananas–your eyes, they weren't…?"

"Yeah," Ethan turned around, away from him to the other side of the room. *No going back now.* Stuffing the feeling down far enough to turn his eyes back wasn't as easy, but once he'd managed it, he shuffled around to face Garth again.

Garth watched more intently now. "What…"

"I think I have a lower metabolic rate, although I haven't been able to measure that definitively. My heart rate is lower, hair growth is slower, I eat less, sleep less, pee less."

After a moment, Garth stepped toward him. Ethan pulled back before realizing that he was reaching for his wrist, his pulse.

"Sorry," Garth stopped, hand in mid-air. "I was just–"

"Yeah." He turned his wrist over and extended it.

As soon as his fingers rested on Ethan's wrist, Garth paused and grasped his arm with both hands. "You're cold. I mean, you feel cooler, like I have a fever or something."

Garth's hands were warm, the same as every human he had felt in two years. "That fits."

"I think I forgot how to take a pulse." Garth kept moving his fingers around on his wrist.

"Just wait."

"I don't…is that it? That is…slow." He held tight for four slow beats of Ethan's heart before Ethan pulled his wrist back.

"Yeah."

"So…" Ethan let Garth think, almost able to hear his mind whirring behind his eyes. "I mean, do you think some of this could have been you adjusting to your environment? I don't know what it was like wherever they had you, but you were there a long time–"

"I'm sure there's stuff from that, but not what I'm showing you, Garth. This was all different as soon as I regained consciousness, all at once."

"I don't–"

"There's another thing that's easy to see." He bunched his lips together, hesitating uselessly. "My teeth."

"What? Wait, wait, wait–"

"I know how it sounds," Ethan's words ran over each other, "I'm not insane, at least, I'm not only insane. Remember–"

"Yeah, I remember, science class, I'm trying," Garth's voice had risen an octave. "Ok, teeth, so, show me?"

You're too far in now. Just do it. Ethan opened his mouth slightly and slowly pulled his lips back.

"What in the world…" Garth's exclamation was a whisper rather than a shout. He stumbled across the room to drop onto the couch.

Shutting his mouth again, Ethan backed up to the opposite wall and waited to see what would happen next.

It was a simple follow up question: "How do teeth change?"

"I haven't figured it out yet."

"What else?" Garth's eyes had a glazed appearance, as though he had given up trying to make sense of it all.

"Eyesight, I can see with less light, see further. This amount of light is bright. I can hear more, including the very irritating dog upstairs–you had a no pet policy when I was here."

"The tenant is a friend, she begged, I caved. But, drat, if he's at it now, that means 2A is going to complain at me again tomorrow—you can hear the dog from here?"

"That and everything else," he rubbed his eyes again. "I had no idea how loud this city is."

"*This* light is hurting your eyes?" Garth pointed to the flush mount light in the middle of the ceiling.

"I...yeah."

Garth only had to stand to reach the switch to turn it off, leaving the bulb over the stove as the sole light source.

The relief was palpable, allowing Ethan to blow out a slow breath as he sat in the chair across from Garth.

"You could have said something about it earlier."

"I couldn't figure out how."

Silence stretched, leaving them both with whirling thoughts.

"How–" Garth eventually started.

"I don't know. I've thought about it for two years, apparently, and it still sounds impossible. The best thing I've come up with is that the bite transmits a virus that can produce changes at a cellular level."

"That's not how viruses work."

"Of course it is, or it can be. We've found evidence of retroviral DNA in the current human genome and even figured out how to engineer viruses ourselves to make genetic changes as immunotherapy. I realize this isn't the standard viral pathogenesis, but it's not so far-fetched. The scale would be unprecedented, but this has to be something different than what we know. If I can get back into the lab, I'll–"

"You want to come back? I mean, of course you do, if you're you, but...I mean..."

Are you, you? That was the crux of the matter, really. "It's a fair question."

"No, not really. Sorry. Of course you're you. We're talking about changes to your body, not *you*."

Is that true?

"Going back to the lab may not be quite that straightforward, though," Garth stood and started pacing in a small circle. "They replaced you, because, well, you're supposed to be dead."

"Yeah, of course. I...I didn't think it would be easy. I didn't...really think that far..." Because he hadn't ever *really* thought he'd make it, not after all the time that had passed.

Garth paced back to the kitchen. "Is that thing about eating less why you're not..." he picked up the fried rice container.

This just isn't going to get any easier, is it? How much exactly are you going to share?

Ethan stood. "No. I don't know what exactly about my digestion changed, but I can only eat some basic stuff. Fruit, leafy vegetables, wine somehow. I thought what they were giving me was just restrictive, but when I tried something else, it didn't go well."

Garth's eyes darted to the undisturbed plastic bag on the counter. He wasn't dense–they didn't hand out PhD's to just anyone. It sounded all too cliche, but he had figured it out.

"I can't tolerate most protein sources–I don't know why–but it doesn't take much of…that to be enough for a day."

"Where did it come from?"

"A pig–but most recently from Chinatown."

Seemingly for something to occupy his hands, Garth picked up some chopsticks and took a bite of rice, chewing slowly. "So you brought Chinese takeout too, then."

Ethan sagged in a relief he hadn't known he'd been seeking and shook his head in incredulous disbelief that Garth was accepting what he was telling him.

Garth took another bite. "What? It's not like you drink human blood, right?"

Ethan stopped breathing.

But Garth didn't notice because he'd turned toward the high-topped table in the corner and plopped onto a stool. "Now. Go get your takeout and come sit down."

⟩

Caterina stood at the mouth of the cave at the edge of the fir forest watching the first rays of the sun brush the sky beyond the tops of the trees.

Etan had left.

He had been stubborn, rebellious, untrusting, yet he had been resilient and hard working when pressed to the correct task. He was well on his way to becoming the vampire she had envisioned on that first encounter, in the same place she stood.

Despite the early rebellions and resistance, he had recently been learning quickly and contributing well to their clan. Seeking to continue his advancements, she had pressed in and sought new challenges and rewards for him.

It was why she had sent him as the scout to the village three nights ago, before the Grand Feast.

When he had not returned, they had searched, but she had tarried too long before pursuing him. Had been too trusting. His trail had led only to the village, and not out of it. There were modes of transportation out of the village that would not leave footprints, but they had no time to follow all possible tracks before the sun would catch them all without shelter.

He was gone.

Like Dorin.

Bitterness rose into the back of her throat.

No, not like Dorin. Dorin had died, in her arms, by her knife so that his death was not the agony it would have been.

Lifetimes of men had passed before she found someone who might have come close to filling his void. Stefan had been there, yes, but Stefan had always been driven by simple means: power, popularity, diversion. Etan thought too much, felt too much, and had conflicting convictions. More like Dorin.

No, Etan had left her realm, but not the earth.

He was not utterly out of her reach.

She had ventured from their realm before, although it had been ages since the last time. Certainly there would be new challenges. Every time she entered the human world, new horrors were ready to be discovered, and yet she felt ready to meet them, eager even. If not for him, then for what reason would she leave? It was time to see what the world had become.

And find her vampire.

For even if she set aside her own feelings—she would not solely be driven by whim—there was convincing reason to pursue him: for his sake.

Etan would be a great vampire, or could be. As his flight showed clearly, his convictions were too conflicting. He did not understand who he was, what he was. He was her vampire, hers to mold since she had given him new birth, and yet he was not complete.

She would find him again, and she would make him great.

24

Ethan heard Garth stirring out in the main room. He'd insisted that Ethan take the bed in the relatively darker bedroom, even changing the sheets when Ethan continued to hesitate. Given the sunlight trickling in under the bedroom door, it was a good thing he hadn't argued harder against Garth taking the couch across from the high-set window next to the front door.

When Ethan eased the bedroom door open, standing obliquely next to it, Garth looked up with a startle before sighing back against the arm of the couch. "Whew. For a second I thought I had dreamed up last night."

"I understand the sentiment."

"Did you sleep?" A yawn cut off the question.

In truth Ethan had been certain that if he closed his eyes they would open back in the cave. "Some," he lied, "It's still loud and…weird, here. I'll get used to it." *Hopefully.*

Garth nodded toward the kitchen with another yawn. "You want coffee?"

Ethan glanced at the bright window, eyes narrowing against the glow of the sunbeam it cast over half of the apartment.

Garth followed his gaze with eyes still half-closed, but then jerked wide-eyed back to Ethan, mouth falling open, possibly further than it had yet. "You've got to be kidding me."

Wishing with everything that he was, and feeling shame well up at even this innocuous piece of the truth, Ethan dropped his tired eyes to the floor. "I—no. I think the issue may be UV radiation. I'm not sure."

Garth's flabbergasted expression didn't waver, "You turn to stone in the sun."

"No. It just burns, after significant exposure. Here," eyes down, he stepped into the sun beam and waved his arm around before stepping back. It was indirect, and, if he didn't look at it, there was no discomfort from a limited amount of time in it. "See, no stone. Right now, it mostly just hurts to look at."

Garth was still staring at him. Maybe everything he'd said last night had finally come crashing down in his mind.

"Do you mind if we cover it? For now?" As the basement window, it wasn't big.

"Yeah," as if waking, Garth jolted to action, standing and walking to Ethan. "I've got, um…" he paused in the middle of the bedroom as if losing his train of thought. "Here," he moved again. "A blanket and…there's duct tape in the bathroom. Under the sink."

Once Ethan retrieved it, Garth took the items into the other room and climbed up onto the chair to apply a liberal amount of gray duct tape to the doubled-over navy blanket and the plaster wall.

When the light had dimmed considerably, Ethan walked into the front room with a subdued, "Thank you."

"Don't mention it," Garth jumped down with a grunt and dropped the duct tape on the counter on the way to the coffee maker. "Oh," he stopped with the coffee bean bag in his hand, "Can you still drink coffee?"

"I…don't know."

"Want to try?" He clinked beans into the grinder on the counter.

Ethan decided abruptly and moved to join him, "Yes."

Garth jumped at his answer from right behind him. "You're quieter. Did you learn that, or was that an instant thing?"

"Sorry. Both maybe." *Has the coffee grinder always made that shrill squeal?*

"What do you want to do today?" Garth asked as he continued prepping the coffee.

"I'm not sure."

"Fair enough. It occurred to me that I may have shoved a box of your stuff in the back of this closet and never dealt with it. Want to help me pull it out?"

When Ethan nodded, Garth left the brewing coffee and jogged the four steps to the closet in the bedroom. After digging around on the floor under some hanging clothes, he switched to feeling around above his head on the top shelf. "Ok, here's something." After a tug, the cardboard box tipped, knocking a hat, a book, and a shoe from the top of it.

Ethan pulled the book from the air in front of Garth's face without him noticing, rested the black fedora on his own head, dodged the shoe, and caught the far side of the box.

"That's not as heavy as I—oh thanks. Let's just put it on the table, huh?"

Awkwardly letting Garth hold onto the other side, Ethan shuffled backward into the kitchen to the table and set it down.

"Where'd the hat come from?"

"Top of the box. There's someone approaching your door."

Garth turned to look at the closed door. "Really?"

Ethan deciphered some of the man's mutterings as boots clomped down the stairs to the basement door. "I think it's about the dog."

"I told you we'd hear from him this morning." Garth opened the door in the middle of the man's first knock, but the man recovered quickly and launched into his complaint about the yapping dog.

The room had brightened considerably with the door open, but the door was too sheltered under the front stoop to allow in any direct sunlight, so turning his back to the light and leaving Garth to it, Ethan opened the flaps of the cardboard box. It was mostly papers and folders. He shuffled through one of the folders to find records: copies of his degrees, a work contract, a lease agreement, a social security card. It was his previous life in a box. He stopped with an old New York ID in his hand, staring at his own picture.

Garth closed the door with a sigh. "Days like today, I'm thinking about moving to Jersey and hiring a super. So, did I keep anything good? Oh, hey, that might be useful. A picture ID has to be helpful when proving you're not dead, right?"

"Why did you keep all this?"

"Mostly because I couldn't figure out what to do with it. It felt wrong to just throw it out."

"Thanks for that."

"Remember it next time you notice you're living with a packrat. 'You never know when you might need it' has a whole new meaning now." Garth picked up two mismatched coffee cups from the counter and sink and reached for the coffee carafe. "You ready to try this?"

Ethan dropped the documents back into the box and stepped over to accept the mug.

When he studied it rather than taking a sip, Garth prodded, "Are we waiting for a reason?"

"It's hot," Ethan blurted one of the things in his mind.

"It's coffee. It usually is. You want an ice cube? C'mon, I don't know why, but I'm personally invested in this experiment." He slurped his own coffee loudly without taking his eyes off Ethan.

Ethan slowly raised the mug and took a small sip. As soon as the rich bitter liquid filled his mouth, memories of life before the cave flooded his mind. He grasped the counter, swallowing then sucking in a breath to steady himself.

"Hey, what's going on? We ok? Talk to me, man."

"It tastes like coffee," Ethan breathed.

"What?"

Ethan straightened. "It tastes right. Nothing tastes right, but that tastes like coffee."

"So that's good?"

He took another sip and closed his eyes. "I can't believe…"

"You kind of look like you're going to cry."

"This is going to sound weird, but I thought about coffee on quite a few mornings while underground."

"That's like the least weird thing you've told me yet."

That was probably true.

"And that's the first hint of a smile I've seen—more coffee for us."

Ethan held up a hand while continuing to cradle his mug with the other. "I'm going to take it slow."

"Yeah, ok." Garth didn't let it stop him from topping off his own cup. "I'm going to shower. Enjoy while I'm gone."

Ethan took another sip, unable to believe that one thing was the same as he remembered. His gaze wandered to the refrigerator where he'd stashed the container of blood and considered how his morning coffee routine had been replaced by a different liquid.

Although mornings had been evenings, outside. So, he'd technically already had blood 'today.'

But there was no one else to mete out his portion any longer. Ethan retrieved the container from the refrigerator and paused with it in his hand. Garth had watched him drink it last night, but it still felt like a shameful hint of truth, and he flicked a glance to the empty bedroom doorway before pouring some of the crimson liquid into his coffee. After washing the spoon and stashing the blood in the fridge, he took a sip.

Wow. There was only one thing that tasted better than that, but he banished that thought.

After a few more sips, he followed memories stirred by the coffee to the bookcase between the couch and the chair, still holding his mug in one hand. With one finger, he traced the narrow spines in the misshapen pile of science journals crammed onto a shelf.

"You have a little catching up to do, don't you? Two years in genetics research is a long time."

Ethan must have heard Garth enter the room, but his brain may have momentarily overloaded at the idea of reading again, so his voice startled him.

"Were you able to keep up with any reading?"

"No."

"Wow. You couldn't get science stuff, or like, *any?*"

Ethan shook his head.

Garth looked him up and down. "How did you, Dr. Ethan Dalton, survive *any* amount of time, much less two years, without *reading?*"

Ethan couldn't find an answer. He wasn't sure whether Ethan Dalton had, indeed, survived.

Garth took his silence in stride and moved the conversation along. "I have some stuff to finish at work–today's a deadline. Why don't you put a dent in that stack of journals while I do that and also tell everyone that you are alive and in my living room right now. Holy moly, this is going to be a crazy day!"

The offer of reading all day was an impossible and tantalizing offer.

"That is the second happiest look you've had all day, so I'm thinking you're on board. Maybe when I get back we can go expand your wardrobe. And replace anything else I got rid of. Oops."

Ethan's eyes shifted toward the window.

"Crud, sun! Ok, we'll figure it out. What pants size are you?"

Ethan had to twist and look at the waistband of the pants he was wearing to find the answer to his question, adding an inch to the length.

"Are you good? I just set the coffee maker again. Do you need anything?"

"No. Uh, Garth, don't tell anyone else."

"Tell them what? That you're here?"

"No, of course not. That…what I am. The physical changes." One person knowing might have been unavoidable, but others knowing was unacceptable. Dangerous even.

"Oh. Yeah, ok. I won't." After another hesitation, Garth walked for the door but stopped with it half open and looked back. "You will be here when I get back, right?"

"Yes," Ethan promised.

25

The flaking gray door squeaked when Garth gave it the required shove to open it into the basement apartment. Inside, Ethan sat at the high table, brow creased, with the end of a pen in his mouth, surrounded by open journal magazines on the table, counter, and floor, engrossed in what he was reading.

There you are.

The last 24 hours had been an impossible whirlwind. It wasn't every day you had a friend you'd thought long dead show up at your door. Despite instantly recognizing Ethan, and not at all noticing the physical changes he had since pointed out, Garth thought he seemed different. Instead of the self-assured nerdy genius, he seemed skittish and unsure of nearly everything. Of course, it was ridiculous to think that he could have gone through some of the stuff he'd said without changing. And that wasn't even addressing the physical stuff.

But here, at least, was the nerd he'd been missing. "Hey!"

"Hey," Ethan dropped the pen and looked up.

"You didn't have to try to get caught up all in one day."

Ethan looked down at the journals strewn across the kitchen as if seeing them for the first time. "I guess I did get carried away…"

"Have fun?"

"I…yeah."

Garth grinned. "Me too. I have never before been the instigator of such hub bub," he shifted the plastic bags he held, dropped one, and kicked the door closed. "I talked to the chairman. I talked to Carol," he referred to the department administrator, "I talked to Lee—oh, gee, I forgot to mention, uh, she's engaged now," Garth winced

135

sympathetically. It had been so long that he'd almost forgotten they'd been dating when Ethan had disappeared.

Ethan blinked a few times, but like he was trying to remember. "I…that's good. We, uh, went out for less than 2 months, right? I didn't expect…"

Relieved, Garth nodded, "Right. Yeah. And I talked to Steve–who didn't believe me by the way, but never mind Steve. They all want to see you. Carol is already trying to figure out how to get you back to work up there. Oh, and she recommended a lawyer friend, because coming back from the dead is probably going to be a lot of paperwork. I called him and set up a meeting tomorrow evening–just after sunset–but we'll have to go to midtown because I don't think he makes house calls."

"Wow." Ethan looked stunned.

Well, that was quite a lot, wasn't it? "Good wow? Because we could take this slower, you know–"

"Yes, good. Thank you. This is…great."

"Ok good." He walked by the table to drop the bags onto the counter. "Sorry, you may not be interested in much of that, but the fridge was empty, so…" With little idea what his friend ate now, he'd simply restocked as he normally would. Some of the contents spilled out when he dropped the handles, and Ethan caught an orange that rolled off the counter while Garth picked up the nearly-empty bag of coffee next to the coffee maker. "I should have gotten more coffee. How much did you drink today?"

Ethan's lips parted for a beat before he answered, "I didn't seem to get a buzz from the caffeine, and it didn't make me sick, so…I don't remember."

Garth was happy there was something normal he could offer. "Good then. We'll get more tomorrow. Talk to me about the sun thing. The chairman was asking about a meeting Friday morning. How does this work? Do you think we can get there without burning to death or anything?"

The orange bounced back and forth between Ethan's hands as he seemed to consider the question. "There's the tunnel from the subway stop to the hospital, right? I used to walk outside, but there's a way to get through the hospital to Hammer building, isn't there?"

Garth closed his eyes and traced a mental map of the campus, from the hospital to the research building and across the street. "Yes! I think there is. Oh, but it involves an overpass which is basically made of glass. And I don't think it's particularly shaded. Does glass help?"

Learning the new Ethan was going to be interesting.

"I don't know," he continued juggling the orange. "But it's not that far. The subway entrance to the C is just around the corner from here. If we leave before the sun comes up over the houses across the street, then the overpass is my only exposure. Should be inconsequential."

Was that excitement Garth saw in his friend? He knew he was in there somewhere. "Sweet. I'll text Carol and let her know that the 8:30 option should be good."

Ethan bit into the orange.

The image jarred Garth for a second. With his lips pulled away from his teeth for a large bite, his elongated canines looked so much more like fangs piercing into the orange skin. *This is real, isn't it?* "Huh."

Ethan abruptly pulled the orange from his mouth while simultaneously trying to slurp the dripping orange juice from his lips, "Sorry."

You gotta keep your thoughts in your head, Qualls. "No, no need. You're fine. I'm just still processing the stuff you told me, and it's kind of hitting home at odd times. The way you bit the orange, it just looked a little…" Garth waved his hand, trying to say the right thing and quit saying the wrong thing.

"Like a vampire."

Garth sucked in a breath. It had seemed less real when that word had just been in his head.

And now he could actually see Ethan drawing back into himself. "But it doesn't matter how it looks, huh? Eat that however you want." He was still saying the wrong thing. Time for another subject change. He walked back to the bag he'd dropped by the door. "I got you some stuff." He pulled a collared shirt, a couple T-shirts, and a pair of pants out of a bag. "Figured you might want to change at some point. I draw the line at buying another man underwear or shoes, but at least you can change for tomorrow, and maybe we can stop at a store tomorrow night or order some things. Also, earplugs and a sleep mask. Maybe that'll help sleeping."

Ethan had gone quiet again. He'd never been a terribly gregarious person, but now everything else in the room seemed louder than Ethan's soft, "Thank you."

"I'm just helping out my friend, man. Happy to do it."

26

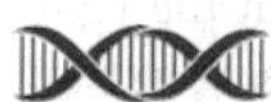

Ethan washed his spoon before sitting down with his cup of coffee. Garth's morning preparations bustled along in the background as he pondered the day before him. He had actually slept a couple hours the previous night, and his dreams had been mercifully vague. Even so, waking had left a remnant of a dream-like quality over the morning. After all the times he had thought of coming back, of what he wanted to do in the lab if he ever got back, it didn't seem possible that it was real.

"You ready?" Garth cheerily entered from the bedroom.

Ethan swallowed bubbles of unease and more coffee.

"Yeah, ok, me too. Coffee first."

The trip into midtown the previous day to meet the lawyer had been almost too easy. With all the city lights it felt more like traveling during the day, but without the threat of burning. They'd given the lawyer all the information and proof Ethan possessed that he was still him, and he'd promised to start working on the interesting problem right away.

Today was the next test, or so it felt. Today he would go back to the Genetics Department at Columbia University. While the sun was up.

Once his coffee was gone, Ethan started, "Garth. Do I look like Ethan Dalton?"

"What do you mean? Of course you look like you."

"I'm serious. Look at me. What are people going to see today?"

Grateful for Garth's serious expression as he leaned forward to study him, Ethan sat still under his gaze. Garth had seemed to take Ethan's story so easily that Ethan was concerned he didn't completely grasp his new reality. But then Garth didn't, and wouldn't ever, know everything.

After a moment Garth said, "You're a tad thinner. Harder maybe, but you look like the same person, Ethan."

It sounded honest. "You can't tell? By looking. That I'm a vampire?"

Garth swallowed. He had trouble with that word, regardless of how he wanted to seem to brush it off. "No. I can't. Maybe avoid biting into any oranges," he gave a nervous laugh, "but I can't notice anything about your teeth when you're just talking, and you're not exactly prone to super wide smiles." He raised a finger, thinking of something, "If there's anything, it's going to be how you react to something. Like the way you were all cringy about the lights was a tad odd. Or like now when you are obviously listening to something somewhere else."

"2A is confronting the dog owner right now."

"Fiddlesticks!"

The side of Ethan's mouth tugged nearly into a half-smile. "Thank you for the feedback. Could you…tell me if I'm acting strangely? I'm concerned I may not notice that I'm doing something wrong."

"Yes. That I can do. Today I am your guide back into the world." Garth regained his former exuberance and checked his phone. "Sunrise is now. You probably have half an hour before it is actually visible in the street."

Ethan picked up the black fedora from the top of a stack of journals and put it on.

Garth did a double take over his coffee cup. "Not that there's anything wrong with it, exactly, but is that the style we're going with?"

It didn't clash with the gray shirt and black slacks Garth had bought him. "Isn't it your hat?"

"Actually, I'm not sure."

"Is it better than a hooded cloak?"

Garth lifted his index finger, "Yes. Yes, it is. Do you have one of those?"

It was in the cargo compartment of that airplane. "Not anymore."

"Ok. Because that's probably something to avoid if we're not going for the…vampire look."

"You think?"

Garth's chuckle seemed relieved. "I don't think there's a hood, but the coat we ordered arrived." He picked up an orange, reconsidered it, and set it back down. "It's still in the box on the chair."

Ethan washed out his mug before he stepped to the other side of the room to retrieve the long black trench-style coat from the box. "I owe you."

"It's not like I'm strapped for cash, while you literally have nothing. Hey, what even happened to your bank account?"

Ethan shrugged. "I guess we'll find out." He put the coat on, appreciated the way the collar would turn up to cover his neck, and looked back at Garth for approval.

Garth cocked his head. "The hat and the coat kind of give you a private eye vibe, but I think you somehow pull that off. Go with it."

Ethan accepted the approval and found his sunglasses on another pile of journals. They went into his shirt pocket.

Garth's coffee mug clanked into the sink. "Let me grab my bag."

When they descended the stairs into the underground subway station, something in the back of Ethan's head relaxed. As he had every morning twenty-five and a half months ago, they took the C train one stop to transfer to the express A train which they rode underground through Manhattan.

The Washington Heights 168th street subway stop was more brightly lit than its Brooklyn counterparts. Large fluorescent lights illuminated the arched ceiling, and doorways were paved with tan tile bordered with more intricate mosaics. Ethan slipped his sunglasses on with a quick dip of his head while Garth followed the signs for the hospital to a wide underpass that led under the street. In the middle of reaching to move his ID badge to a more visible location, Garth paused with a look at Ethan.

"Sunglasses," Ethan guessed.

"Well, yeah, they're a bit conspicuous. I don't know how much pain it's going to be with all the fluorescent lights and white walls in here, but if you could bear it…"

He'd endured pain for worse reasons. "Yeah, I've got it." He pocketed the sunglasses and forced himself to keep his head up and eyes open but was not completely able to keep from blinking more rapidly. "Let's go," he prodded as Garth continued to watch him.

The crowd of people in scrubs and business clothes thinned out as they walked down a back hallway. "This might take a little trial and error," Garth said. "I can't remember which elevators back here actually go to the third floor."

The scent of human blood tainted the air. Somewhere down that intersecting hall.

"That's not it. The emergency room is down there and should definitely be avoided."

Definitely. Ethan picked up the pace he hadn't meant to slow and snapped his attention forward again. *No more. Not here.*

Garth's educated guess of which bank of elevators to try proved correct, and they made it to the overpass with only one wrong turn. When sunlight faded in under the fluorescents, Ethan put the sunglasses back on and turned his collar up.

"Here we are," Garth announced belatedly. "How do we do this?"

"Just go." Ethan put his hands into the coat pockets and tilted his head so his face remained in the shadow of his hat as they walked along the glass-lined bridge over the street below. It took an annoying amount of effort to fight the instinct to cringe back from the sunlight, but he did it. If he was going to re-enter his old life, he would learn to bear the light and the noise and the openness the same as he had learned to embrace the darkness and quiet of the cave.

"Shoot, we have to walk along the windows for a second here," Garth whispered loudly after they'd crossed the bridge.

"It's fine."

Once they turned onto an internal hall out of the sunlight, Garth let him walk about ten steps before stopping to scrutinize him.

Sunglasses already off, Ethan looked back with an intentionally casual look and adjusted his coat collar down. "See. No spontaneous combustion."

"I'm starting to wonder if you were yanking my chain."

"I wish," Ethan rubbed his eyes before stopping himself. "We have to go down again, right?"

"Yeah, let's try that stairwell. So did the glass help?"

"Not really in the overpass. The windows on the building may be tinted, but it only helped a little."

"What does it feel like?" Garth's voice echoed in the stairwell.

"Ever been irradiated?"

"Can't say as I have."

"I admittedly don't have a control exposure to compare either, but I think it would be similar," Ethan dropped down a whole flight of stairs at once.

Garth startled. "That's new."

Old rules. "Yeah, I'll watch that."

"I mean, I'm the only one in here, so you can do whatever."

But he wouldn't always be. Ethan started taking the stairs one at a time. One more underpass later, they were there—greeted by the lobby of the research building. It was like a familiar grandparent's hug, but after he'd grown up and wasn't sure he fit anymore. Everything was the same. Except him.

Stepping into the elevator next to Garth still felt right, though.

The elevator doors opened to a hall lined with mostly offices. The yellowed linoleum floor was the same, but the walls had been painted, a shade of beige that was neutral and yet clashed slightly with the floor. Ethan could feel his heart thud in his throat as he stepped out and followed the repeating line of orange-brown wooden doors away from Garth into the maze of halls.

There it was. His door, still with the scuff on the bottom left. Someone else's name was on it. And directly across the hall…Jack's door. It had someone else's name on it too, but he couldn't see what it said because Jack's face floated into his gaze, blood staining his mouth.

Ethan blinked hard, but it didn't clear his vision, and he backed into the wall, watching the flash of her knife and the blood pouring from Jack's throat.

"Ethan?"

Garth's voice, not Jack's.

"I'm sorry…" Garth whispered and stopped next to him.

At least he didn't go through the hell I did.

Garth's concerned face jerked back slightly. "Uh—eyes—"

"I know." It hurt more than he'd thought it would after everything, but Ethan managed to focus on the door and took a shaky breath. *Good bye, friend.*

A subtle vision change let him know his eyes returned to dark gray, but he turned his gaze to Garth to confirm.

Garth's expression relaxed, and he nodded.

Ethan blinked again at the glare of the lights but raised his head and squared his shoulders. "Is Carol still in the same office?"

"Yeah. You sure you're ready?"

Ethan nodded stoically.

Garth turned and retraced their steps past the elevators to the empty front room of an office suite. The printer on the left wall was complaining loudly. A set of bulky leather chairs flanked a coffee table in the center of the room, and a bank of metal filing cabinets on the right wall evened out the furnishings. A head of cropped gray hair styled into carefully messy spikes was just visible through the glass window of a door on the back wall. There was a gasp, a burst of a squeal, and the petite woman in purple glasses and a skirt suit shot into the room. "Professor Dalton!"

Her excitement was infectious, and Ethan found himself almost smiling. "Hello, Carol."

"Ooh, I can't believe you're here!" She bobbed back and forth. "Come in, come in!" She waved them over to the leather furniture, grasping his arm when he stepped forward. At least she hadn't gone for a hug. "I am so glad you're here, son."

She'd called him that since he'd shown up in her office as a grad student, but he'd never been able to outgrow it. The sincerity in her eyes made him relax a measure. "Me too."

"Let me take your coats! And coffee? Do you still take one sugar?"

"Just black, thank you." She'd always somehow been able to remember every single person's coffee or tea preference.

"Dr. Qualls?" she asked from the breakroom through the other doorway in the back wall.

"Yes, ma'am," Garth answered.

She bustled back out holding two white coffee cups. "Did he just ma'am me?" She addressed Ethan.

"I was never quite able to break him of the habit." He took the offered cup.

"You'd think he would have learned by now." Carol retook her seat after handing Garth, a Texas native who had been in New York City since starting college, his cup, then fixed her attention back on Ethan. "I like the hat."

Ethan shot Garth a look. If Carol liked it, that was that.

"Oh Ethan," she gave a big sigh, "We thought you were dead, son."

"That's what Garth said. I'm sorry."

"To think the whole time…Mmm." She shook her gray-spiked head.

Ethan adjusted his hold on the hot cup and took a sip of coffee.

"And the first thing you do is come back here? Dr. Qualls said the main thing you want to do is come back to work."

"This place was home for fifteen years. Where else would I go?"

"You spent more time here than anywhere, didn't you? Always working, this one. I suppose I couldn't expect anything else. You can be sure we'll take you back. Dr. Qualls thinks the doctor he works with is looking for a PI, for one idea, but I'll let the chairman discuss that with you. Can't steal all his thunder, now can I?"

"I appreciate your efforts. I don't expect anything."

She started to wave him off, but then, "Ooh! The other matter! After Dr. Qualls came in the day before last announcing you like a herald, I looked into some things. When everyone thought you were dead, well, did you know you had this department listed as the beneficiary on your accounts?"

Ethan mentally pried into dusty memories, "I did…"

Her mouth was open in disbelief. "That sum, young man. Do you not have any family or anything?"

"You're right here," Ethan replied matter-of-factly.

There was no stopping the hug after that. Gripping the chair arms kept him from warding her off, but he couldn't keep the tension from his body. Friendly contact seemed unnatural now, especially warm contact with the pulsing of human blood underneath. He was getting more used to hearing Garth's heartbeat and having him around, but he hadn't tried to embrace him since the first night.

She gave him a tight squeeze before releasing him and making a furtive swipe at her eyes. Ethan looked down for a quick moment to reset his expression to something somewhat neutral.

Garth seemed to be trying to decide whether to be concerned or amused.

"Well," she steadied her voice, "Rest assured we will figure out how to get it back to you."

"What was it spent on?" Ethan asked her after remembering they were discussing his life's savings.

"Spent on? I'm not completely sure. But there was a grant to a lab. And some equipment purchases."

"The new sequencer," Garth blurted, making a connection.

Ethan looked between them. "I don't need back what has been spent."

"But certainly–"

"If I get a job again to pay expenses, I don't need it."

"But, son–"

"I don't need it, Carol," he insisted.

She closed her mouth in acquiescence. "I'll talk to the chairman," she nodded. "Meanwhile, I think there are some others around this place who would like to see you."

"Thank you." He considered his empty coffee cup for a moment, then stood, took Garth's cup, and strode to the break room before she could stop him.

The expected, "I've got that–" followed him, but he had one sudsy and washed in the small sink before she got to the door.

"I know you do, but it's no problem," he placated her and finished the other quickly. "It really is good to see you."

Her stern posture wilted, and she let him follow Garth out into the hall.

"What was that about?" Garth asked in a low voice.

"Until I know how…" he looked vaguely down at himself, "I'm going to be extra careful with any potential exposure. Including saliva. You should be too," he added when Garth frowned.

The sound of conversation burst out of a room down the hall, and a couple students he didn't recognize walked past, one with a, "Hi, Dr. Qualls."

The person behind them froze in the middle of the hall. Her dark almond eyes widened as her full lips formed Ethan's name.

Now the memories flowed, but too much had happened since then for more than a memory of a feeling to remain. "Hi, Lee."

A voice from behind him interrupted with a curse and, "Dalton! There's no way Garth was telling the truth. How–"

Word was spreading around the floor. Realizing the crowd was only going to grow and could trap them in the hall, Ethan turned and put his back against the wall to at least avoid being surrounded. He took a slow breath and reminded himself that he was not in actual danger. There was no reason for the unease in his gut, no reason for his eyes to turn. No reason for any expression other than a slight smile.

Thankfully, Garth stepped in to intercept Steve so Ethan could address Lee.

"Congratulations," Ethan motioned to her left hand which bore a glittering ring.

"Ethan, I'm sorry–"

He shook his head to interrupt her. "For what?"

Her eyes searched his face. "I didn't know."

"How could you? No one did. I'm glad you're happy. You are happy?"

"Yes," she answered. "I am. But I don't regret our two months."

"Neither do I." It was the last thing he remembered not regretting. He swallowed. "Who's the lucky guy?"

"He's a banker. Crazy, I know."

"You deserve a good kind of crazy."

She smiled softly, but the growing crowd vied for his attention, and he found himself fielding greetings from old colleagues, some students and fellows he wasn't sure if he was supposed to know, and one he did.

"Dr. Amin." She had been doing her post doc in his lab when he'd left and had practically been his right hand. She was wrapped in a long white lab coat and looked awestruck.

"I couldn't believe it when Lee told me the news. It's so amazing to have you back, Dr. Dalton," her voice bubbled.

He realized he'd seen her name in another place. "You took my office."

"Oh, yes, I–"

"I'm sorry, that came out wrong. Of course you have my job–the job. You were the most creative mind in my lab. I couldn't have handpicked anyone better for it." Ethan continued to stumble through what he was trying to convey and realized she was starting to tear up.

"You have no idea what it means to hear you say that. I wondered what you would think of my heading your lab, if you would think it was a good choice or bad. We don't usually get the honor of hearing what our heroes would think of us."

Hero? Her words made him sick. The hall seemed to tip sideways, causing Ethan to actually steady himself against the wall.

"Hello Dr. Dalton, it's good to see you," a dark-skinned woman with a wide smile interrupted. "The chairman is hoping you'll join him in his office. He considered coming out here, but I decided perhaps a rescue would be in order."

"Thank you, Doris. It's good to see you too," he thanked the chairman's administrative assistant, glad he and Garth had reviewed names.

Doris led him and Garth through the crowd that parted before her through a double-wide wooden door into the corner office.

"Fiddlesticks," Garth muttered.

Ethan might have chuckled if he hadn't been biting back his own curse.

The corner office, obviously, was lined with windows.

A quick jerk of his head dropped the rim of his hat a fraction which allowed him to hide from the glare just enough to look into the room toward the department chairman, who stood in front of the 16th floor north-facing window. Perpendicular to him, the east-facing windows let in floods of sunbeams.

"Dr. Ethan Dalton," the deep voice boomed from a tall man with thinning hair. "It's not every day I get to welcome a dead man into my office. This is truly a first." He stood behind his huge cherry desk and extended his hand to Ethan.

Maybe I should have hung on to that hot coffee cup. Abruptly aware that his hand would feel cooler to the chairman's warm skin, Ethan rubbed his hand in a few quick strokes along his pants at his thigh before shaking his hand. "Dr. Grant. It's good to see you as well."

"What a tale. You really must tell us what happened over there."

The awkward silence stretched as Ethan couldn't come up with an appropriate response.

Dr. Grant finally glossed over it with an invitation to sit, and Ethan and Garth nearly ran into each other as they both headed for the same chair. Apparently realizing it was the chair the furthest from the window, Garth gave the right of way to Ethan, but not before making the moment even more awkward with his abrupt direction change.

This isn't going as well as it started.

"I hear you'd like to come back to work." Dr. Grant continued. "I'd like to offer you a position. In fact, I think I may be out a department administrator if I don't, judging from my conversation with Carol just now," he gestured to his phone. "It's not quite as simple as offering you your old lab back, though."

"I know. I just met–saw–Dr. Amin. I wouldn't want you to." Mentally vowing to never leave the hat at home, he tilted his head just enough to keep his face in its shadow and tried to ignore the feeling of heat on his jaw and neck.

"Dr. Qualls and I had a chat yesterday, and the PI of his lab is looking for an academic PI. I haven't had time to talk with her, as she's on the medical side, but if you are interested, it may be something you could start soon. And then I could have you do guest lectures, mentoring and the like, other things we can add to your plate, until things shake out further. It may not be ideal, but it would be the quickest way to get you back in a lab if that's what you're after."

Principle investigators, PI's, typically headed their own labs, leading a group of students and new PhD's who were doing post docs, like Garth. Sharing a lab with a medical doctor would be new, but he couldn't just expect them to manufacture funds for a new lab for him to head just because he'd appeared again. "That has potential. What's the lab's focus of study?"

"Blood production. Hematopoietic stem cell regulation. Blood cancers."

Garth had failed to mention that. "Of course it is."

"Is that a problem?" Dr. Grant asked.

"No, no. It's an area of interest actually."

"Great. Like I said, the PI is an MD, but don't hold it against her, she's actually great to work with. I'll call her and get you together. Maybe drop a note that she'd be lucky to have someone of your track record. If Qualls didn't put that bug in her ear already."

"I appreciate it. It doesn't sound like a bad way to get back into things."

Dr. Grant nodded. "Carol also just told me about your offer regarding the funds that were donated on your behalf. It's incredibly generous. Please let me know if there's anything else we can do for you."

Ethan shook his head, "I couldn't take anything back from the department. I…may like to take advantage of some of the new equipment on occasion. I have a couple new questions I've thought of recently."

Dr. Grant gestured with a welcoming hand. "By all means. Give it some time and research and I may be able to get you a team to chase it if it pans out."

"I'm happy to start slow. I appreciate everything."

The chairman went on about some details. Ethan nodded and agreed until he couldn't pretend to ignore the sunlight on his neck any longer and decided that cutting the meeting short would be less disruptive than any alternatives. "Thanks. Again." He stood, keeping his hat brim angled at the window as he rose. "I don't have a new number yet, but I'll be in touch."

"I'll get it to you," Garth offered as he abruptly stood to follow Ethan's lead to the door away from the windows.

"Great, sounds good," the chairman agreed, rising as Ethan left without further ado.

As soon as they were in the hall, Garth pestered, "You ok?"

"I need a second," Ethan answered tersely and pushed into the nearby restroom. He stopped Garth from reaching for the light switch with a stern, "Don't."

"Right. Yeah. Not touching it." Garth stood just inside the closing door.

Ethan knocked the hat off his head to the floor, yanked his shirt cuffs upward on his forearms, turned the sink on, and reached under the cool running water. It was enough relief that he couldn't resist splashing it onto his face and head before shaking drops out of his hair and staring up at the shadowed ceiling tiles. His eyeballs felt as though they were full of sand. Maybe it wouldn't always be quite so hard. He should be able to adjust some to the lights, surely. The sun was a different matter entirely, but there wasn't much danger of him earning a corner office anytime soon.

Garth started feeling his way along the wall toward Ethan.

"Watch out for the trash can."

His knee collided into it with a metal clang anyway. "Oh, you mean *that* trash can. How well can you see in here?"

"There's plenty of light coming in under the door."

"Plenty, huh?" He didn't seem to agree.

"Sorry."

"Nah, it's fine. It's not like it's hurting me to stand in the dark for a minute. Are you ok? You were making me forget that it probably wasn't easy out there."

Ethan stepped up onto the counter and sat down with his back against the cool glass. "I'll get better at it."

"I'm saying you're doing great."

You can't see me shaking in a dark corner. Ethan leaned his head back and let everything slow back down.

"On the upside," Garth broke the quiet he'd let stretch out for several minutes, "Our lab is in the hospital tower, so no sun bridge. Assuming that all works out."

Ethan nodded and, when Garth remained silent, added, "That's helpful."

A few minutes later, Garth checked his phone, which lit the room, and noticed where Ethan was. Ethan deflected his reignited concern but ultimately agreed it would be a good move to head back to the apartment.

Since Carol was multitasking fighting with the copier and trying to explain something to a grad student, she let them retrieve their coats from her office with only an exuberant wave and an oath that he'd return again soon.

Ethan led the way back through the maze of halls and stairs, cursing the direct sun as he picked up his pace in the overpass. He held the elevator to let Garth catch it before the doors slid closed leaving them alone.

"I think you paid better attention than I did on the way in this morning," Garth commented over the sound of his elevated heartbeat during their descent to the basement.

Ethan let his statement echo unanswered in the metal box.

He breathed again once they entered the underground walkway to the subway station and forced himself to shorten his gait to match Garth's on the stairs down to the tracks. The weight of Garth's watchful eyes hounded him to the end of the platform where he leaned against the tile wall. Garth waited for the roar of the departing C train to fade before asking in a casual tone, "What language was that?"

The question didn't make sense.

"Back before the overpass. Was it Romanian? Sounded like a curse maybe."

Oh. So much for thinking in English. "An old version of Romanian, I think."

"You must have learned it pretty well…"

"No one spoke English."

"Hm," Garth grunted. "Sounds about right. Put me with a bunch of people who don't speak English? I'm screwed. You? Meh, just learn the language, no biggie. You always were the biggest brain around."

Afraid he might not be anything any of these people thought anymore, Ethan looked away.

27

"Dr. Dalton." The slim woman in the white coat radiated professionalism and approached from the hall rather than the closed office in front of Ethan. "I'm sorry if I made you wait."

"You didn't. Thank you for setting this up so quickly," Ethan answered. It had only been five days since their meeting with the chairman, which was record timing for any job interview to be set up, much less in such an odd case.

Dr. Miller, Moraine—as the badge clipped to her white coat read—unlocked and opened her office door. "Come in."

He did and took the seat she motioned to.

"I had barely mentioned the idea of bringing on another PI, sometime in the future mind you, and now all at once have pressure from the administration, not to mention Dr. Qualls, to take you on immediately. So tell me, Dr. Dalton, why do I spend my precarious budget on you instead of new equipment and possibly another post doc?"

Ethan had to give her credit for being forthright and to the point. The straight-backed Dr. Miller had finished her question before even getting to her desk.

"I'll have to ask Garth to ease up. He's just trying to help, but may be a tad overzealous."

She gave a tight-lipped smile. "I've worked with him long enough to roll with the punches."

"To answer your question, I honestly don't care much about my paycheck. Give me what you would give the post doc to start with, if you need to. I know I have a couple years' worth of research to get

153

caught back up on. But I can promise you dedication, and I have no desire to wrestle for control or anything. I will follow your lead in your lab."

Her dark blue eyes gave him a second look. "Devaluing yourself instead of talking yourself up. That's a new one for an academic."

"You know who I am. You have access to my research. I don't think there's much point in repeating any of that."

"Former primary investigator of your own lab and senior author on a paper published in Science," she cited his previous accomplishments including publication in the prominent journal. "My question remains. Why do you want this job? To just jump back in at the first thing they offer?" Her eyes were intense, but her face was honest and open. Yes, she was direct, but her questions were valid. Why sugarcoat it?

She was someone he could work for, he decided at once. "I spent the last two years a hostage of an old underground terror organization without access to the outside world. When I dreamed of making it home, I didn't picture family or my apartment or food or any of those things, I only saw this. This lab, these walls, these people. I want to be here, doing this. What you pay me doesn't matter anymore. My position is irrelevant. Getting back here, doing this work, that's all I care about."

She was watching him carefully. "What if I don't want the hassle of a celebrity returning from the grave to deal with?"

Ethan acknowledged that concern with a nod and countered, "What if a little notoriety could be used to leverage a few more resources? Maybe even a new grant at some point."

"Are you better at writing grant proposals than Dr. Qualls?"

It's not as though Garth doesn't know it. "Yes, I think that's still the case."

She leaned back a degree and considered him. "The lab can't afford your old salary, but I can rustle up something halfway respectable. We have more grad students than I have time to adequately counsel, so if you're willing, I'll pass you one, or two if we get another. I have one project I can think of to hand you, and your chairman was talking about adding lectures and a genomic project."

"That sounds perfect," he broke in honestly. Everything he'd said in her office was true, even if he'd left parts out. She was his way back in, and he would take anything she offered.

She inclined her head in acquiescence and considered him again. "Students, and others, will ask about your time away." There was a question in her statement.

"You can repeat what I told you."

She accepted the answer but added a friendly warning. "There will be conjecture added to it by some."

"That's fine." It would be better than the truth.

"All right, then. You will let me know when you're employable again?"

That was one way of putting it. "I will. My lawyer has promised to make quick work of annulling the death certificate, but apparently it isn't a common problem." He leaned forward to take one of her cards from her desk.

"I'm sure it isn't."

She stood, so he followed suit, replacing his hat on his head as he did. "Thank you. For taking a chance with me. I owe you."

"We'll see if I can collect on that." Her extended arm invited him to exit in front of her.

"I'll let you know when I'm legal again," he gestured with her card.

"Good. Feel free to let Garth give you some orientation before you leave today."

"Thank you."

She strode away with the quick purpose of a busy doctor, leaving him to retrace his way down the hall to Garth's office.

It took a minute for Garth to notice him standing in his doorway. "Oh! Hey. That was quick."

"She's no-nonsense, isn't she?" Ethan observed.

"True enough. Soooo…"

"I don't think I'm quite what she wanted, but I start as soon as I'm officially alive again."

"Yes!" Garth spun his chair in a seated victory dance. "Ok, so what's next for today?"

"She said you can 'orient' me."

"Sweet. So. This is a computer."

"I do remember that," he replied dryly but with a hint of a smirk.

"Yes, and the most important thing is–"

"The location of the brightness control." Ethan scooted a second chair closer to the edge of Garth's desk.

"Huh, good question." Garth peered closely at the screen and clicked around for a moment. "Wait, here we go. There. Any better?"

It was almost tolerable, so he gave a shallow nod before asking, "Did you have time to find some of the things I asked you about?"

"Yes!" Garth yanked his deep desk drawer open to show a stack of various medical equipment. "There are advantages to working in the hospital."

"Thanks." He stared down at the pile with growing apprehension. It was so much different than that first time he'd tried to take his pulse without even a clock.

"Do you want to document this in any certain way to start with?" Garth had a spreadsheet pulled up on his screen.

Ethan shook his head.

"Cool. By the way, you look the same as I remember, but I pulled up an old picture," he angled his phone toward Ethan, "and it pretty much confirms that. Your hair's a little longer, you maybe put on a little muscle, but it's not really like you could even get much paler," he snickered.

Garth was right…wasn't he? Yet, staring at the picture seemed like staring at another man completely. He did look similar, certainly, but he couldn't help but envy that man's innocence.

"Teeth…" Garth continued typing. "Is it just the upper canine teeth that are longer?"

"The bottom one's are too, slightly," Ethan bared his teeth for Garth for just a moment.

"Interesting. And the rest seem the same?"

"Yeah."

More typing. "Hey, can you do the eye thing on demand?"

Ethan let his anxiety flare before answering, "Yes." It took a beat of silence for Garth to look back at Ethan.

"Woah," his startled jerk knocked his chair into the wall.

"Sorry." Ethan pulled back.

"I did ask, didn't I? You're good. So, how do you turn them back?"

"Calm down."

"You look calm already."

Ethan focused on a random spot on the wall and took a deep breath, allowing Garth to watch his irises return to dark gray nearly instantaneously.

"Huh," Garth pondered. "Does that come with any, like, benefit? Why do they change?"

"Vision gets a degree sharper. It's related to any strong emotion, as far as I can tell."

Nod, and more keystrokes. "All right, measurement time." Garth pulled out a thermometer. "Here, start with this."

Ethan took the probe and put it in his mouth while Garth fished out a small pulse oximeter from the pile and held it out for Ethan's finger. When the thermometer beeped, they both angled to look.

"Ninety-five point nine. A tad low, right? Which makes sense given how you feel to me. Woah-kay, but more normal than your heart rate of 30." Garth pointed to the pulse ox read out.

Ethan kept to himself that it might be elevated above his baseline due to the anxiety that wouldn't calm as easily as his eyes. "Clean the thermometer," Ethan stopped Garth before he set it down.

"Right, yep, I have bleach wipes somewhere…"

Leaving Garth to rummage in a bag behind him, Ethan reached to type the numbers into the document on the computer. Garth tossed the container of wipes to him, and Ethan caught it with his typing hand without looking.

Garth leaned over to the computer. "Okay, temperature, oh you got that. Heart rate…and your oxygen level is 100%, so that must be working for you ok. Blood pressure?"

When the automatic blood pressure cuff produced the numbers 70/35, a far cry from the normal standard of 120/80, Garth asked, "Do you think that's right?" He typed them into the document. "Maybe it is right. Everything else is low, right?" He turned to the drawer again, "Now for the fun stuff. Audiometer."

"Got an instruction manual?"

"You think we can't figure it out?" He handed Ethan the headphones and fiddled with the buttons and dials. "I think this is frequency, and then volume…put the headphones on."

Ethan did, but then yanked them off with a curse as soon as Garth pushed a button.

"Right. Too loud. That was in English, by the way."

"I…" Ethan tried to figure out why it had been more natural. "We're in the lab. I only think in English in a lab."

"That kind of makes sense. Here, try again."

"I can hear it from here," Ethan said, still holding the headphones in his lap.

"Fine, fine, lower… now?"

"I can still hear it."

Garth stared at him flatly and toggled it down lower, again.

Ethan put the headphones back on. "Just drop it all the way down."

"Confident, aren't we?"

But when they were finished, he'd been able to hear the entire frequency range of tones.

"I got that from the audiology lab too, so it's not even the most basic." Garth picked up his phone and tapped as he talked, "What is the normal hearing range…wow. So, you can hear at least way better than a normal human. Maybe into dog range here."

Or bat.

"The next one is not so high tech," Garth continued as he held up a sign topped by a big letter "E" and tossed a tape measure at Ethan.

"Now I know you're doing that on purpose," Ethan accused when he snatched it from the air next to his face.

"If I am, it's for science. Your reflexes are crazy. Now measure out 20 feet."

When he did and looked back at Garth's goofy grin and the vision card, it was clearly not far enough, so he handed Garth one end of the tape, opened the door, and walked backward until it was difficult to focus on the bottom line of the card. The tape measure read 100 feet.

"A O H G E R," he read the bottom line.

"Did you memorize it?" Garth called.

"R E G H O A."

"Like you wouldn't be able to say it backwards if you had it memorized?"

"I can see it, Garth. And stop yelling. We did just establish that I can hear everything, didn't we?"

"Oh yeah. Come back then, and turn off the light on your way in." He stepped off the end of the tape leaving Ethan to handle its recoil back into the roll. It was easy retribution to turn off the light without warning when Garth was still in the middle of walking back to his computer. "Why do I think that is not the last time you're going to do that to me? Fine then. Can you see this?" He held the card up in a random direction.

"There's still too much light."

"Say what?"

Ethan grabbed his coat from the back of a chair to drop at the base of the door.

"Is that pitch black enough yet?" Garth's eyes moved blindly around.

"It's closer."

"Can you still read?" the card waved in his hand.

"Y T A N D L."

"So, no?"

"It's the second to bottom line. I do have the bottom one memorized now. I'm not sure how measurable this is though."

"How about I'm the control? I attest that, right now, I can't even see the card. And I am holding it. Hit the lights."

After a beat of hesitation, Ethan flipped them on and sat down slowly.

"What's with the return of serious face?" Garth asked.

For a moment it had felt normal to banter with Garth, but reality pulled at Ethan. He'd wanted solid confirmation for so long, but every measurement they took was illustrating to himself, and to Garth, how different he now was. "It's all so abnormal."

"That is the point of this exercise, right? To get facts. Real comparisons."

"Yeah." It also made it harder to hope he could simply fit back into his old life.

"Do you want to go to the next thing?"

Ethan sat up straight. "What is it?"

"This one I nabbed from physical therapy, but not before I asked him how to use it. It's a dynamometer to measure strength." Garth demonstrated its use and recorded his own measurement, acknowledging, at Ethan's sideways look, that he wasn't the most fabulous example of strength.

Ethan squeezed it without fanfare and handed it back. Garth's muffled squeak of surprise was telling. "Well…you are stronger than me. Did you work out at all?"

"Yes."

"In what way?"

He didn't answer.

"It doesn't matter. We knew that environmental factors would come into play. Observations only right now. Let's try a couple other muscle groups, as the PT was explaining."

There was a temptation to hold back and not try as hard.

Come on, if you're going to let him participate in this part, why not go all the way so his assistance is relevant? Ethan questioned his own thoughts while going through the exercises Garth demonstrated. Several exercises and absurd numbers later, Garth abandoned it and led him on a "field trip" that ended in the stairwell.

"Ok."

Ethan just waited for more.

"Can you hear anyone else in here?"

After a door slammed somewhere above, Ethan answered, "No."

"You said something about being faster and jumping further. So. How far can you jump, exactly?"

The staircases extended both up and down, with a narrow gap between the rails just wide enough for something to fall the entire height. "This isn't exactly a standardized question. Are you making this up as you go?" Ethan stalled as he visually traced the metal rails through the five stories above.

"Maybe I am just curious, but does that make it a less valid question? 'When we don't know what's important, you just record everything,' right?"

He couldn't exactly reprimand Garth for quoting their favorite undergrad professor when he'd started it, could he? Still, he hesitated. It felt like going naked to show Garth so much.

"I mean, I guess it's not necessary. If you don't want to," Garth started to backpedal.

"It's not enough of a straight shot to show you a maximum."

"The ten-story stairwell isn't high enough?" Garth's voice cracked.

"No, it would be, but there's not quite enough room to jump straight up."

Garth's eyes narrowed.

"Fine. I'll show you," Ethan muttered. "What's the point otherwise." He took half a flight of stairs up in one stride. From there, he used a step onto the rail to vault up a full flight onto the rail above and across from him. He continued up, stepping back and forth on the edges of the treads and the rails from his position in the center vertical gap until he reached the top floor.

The view back down showed just enough space, so he stepped off and fell straight down until he reached the fifth floor. A kick off the opposite rail landed him squarely on the landing in front of Garth. He had to duck to avoid knocking his head on the stairs above, so he landed in a crouch and stood up to meet Garth's bug-eyed gaze.

"That…was the most amazing thing I've ever seen."

Ethan wasn't sure what to do with that.

"Seriously!" Garth gaped upward again. "Did you just wake up one day able to do that?" He pointed upwards.

Ethan shook his head. "I woke up one day able to jump to a two-story cliff but fell over when I did it. I could land a drop like that without getting hurt, and usually hit my feet."

"Something is definitely different about your bones, muscles…"

"And nerves."

"How did you learn to do all that, then?" Garth motioned vaguely upward again.

A pause. "Traversing a cave. It was big. A lot of cliffs and ravines."

"Huh," Garth thought about that. "When you said underground, you meant cave not bunker. No stairs, huh?"

"There were a few stairs." He looked back at the stairs in front of him. "But I realize now they were significantly steeper." And that was enough storytelling. He tensely turned back to the stairwell door.

"So," Garth followed, "I'm just thinking how much more we could figure out with some access to MRI, bone density, other tests. And someone actually on the medical side. Dr. Miller is a hematologist, and I know others. I know you said not to tell anyone, but…"

Ethan stopped and made himself think analytically before answering. Or tried. "No, I…forget what I want for a second. What do you think? About sharing this. With how many? And where does it stop?"

Garth's posture became serious. "It feels like you may be right. We don't really know what we're dealing with yet, and what happens to you if a whole team knows…or more. Ok, fine. Me and you, until we know more. We may be limited, but we'll make fine work of this little mystery, won't we? We got it."

That almost felt like hope.

"Do you want to hang out until dark or head home now?" Garth opened the door to the hall.

"Waiting sounds easier."

"Sure thing. I was going to go straight from here to church, usually do on Wednesday evenings. Want to come? We meet in Bay Ridge, a couple blocks from the subway, so it didn't sound like such a good idea Sunday morning, but it'll be dark tonight."

Garth's religious kick had started sometime during grad school, but Ethan didn't think he'd tried to get him to join before. Regardless, Ethan wasn't interested. He'd been to hell, and no one else had rescued him. He'd had to get out by himself. "Not really my thing," he replied.

"Ok," Garth answered easily.

"I…would like to detour to Chinatown on the way back."

"Oh, now you're getting demanding, asking that we stop for food," Garth turned playfully sarcastic.

"I could just ask for lunch money and go alone."

Garth laughed. "I still don't know how you survived on that one container of…for a week."

"It's a big container."

"One of these days we will have to figure out the secret of your metabolism. You could be the cure for world hunger."

"It's not a good cure." Mirth evaporated from Ethan's voice.

"Ok, ok, sorry, bad joke. We'll do it your way. One step at a time."

28

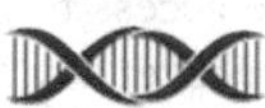

"Good morning," Dr. Miller effectively called the room of people to order. Standing straight in her white lab coat with her blond hair twisted up in a clip, she bore the air of authority gracefully.

"It's 7 a.m. on a Monday," someone groaned.

"Then we really do need to get a move on, don't we?" The bright-eyed doctor was undeterred.

Ethan sat quietly in the back of the room, overwhelmed by his new reality. The underground passages and crisscrossing subways in Manhattan had proven their worth, giving him a way to attend quite the series of meetings. In only five weeks, Carol and others from banks and the university had helped make him legal again, given him back a bank account, and gotten him started in his job.

Dr. Miller continued, "Our first order of business is to welcome the newest member of our team, Dr. Ethan Dalton. Most of you will recognize his name and know he has extensive experience heading his own research project a couple years ago, so I don't need to carry on about that. He will be contributing his experience to our lab, mentoring a couple of you—no need to look so happy to escape me, Rav—taking on as many lectures as he can be persuaded into, I think, and also lending his lab skills to the genomics lab downstairs. Considering our frequent utilization of the sequencer down there, perhaps we can take advantage and push our own samples just a little further in line?" She smiled in gest, but a meaningful look suggested there was some earnestness to that hope. "I need to round on a few patients this morning, and Dr. Dalton has some orientation things to attend to, so we'll keep this morning brief.

"Some quick introductions," she addressed Ethan directly. "Our post-doc Dr. Garth Qualls needs no introduction, as you've worked with him before, and, I recently learned, went to undergrad with him. You'll know more about him than I do, I'm sure. These are our PhD students, Rav, whose last name we try not to pronounce horribly, and Abby Douglas. Dr. Alena Bianchi is an MD completing a research year during residency. If you have time before your next orientation duty, take some time to get to know everyone, and, everyone, show Dr. Dalton around. My request for additional office space was not granted, unfortunately, so the rather inglorious temporary solution I have come up with is to move the ancient records out of the closet that adjoins this room. The desk just fits in there." She spread her hands apologetically, "It is all I have access to at the moment, but at least it will offer some privacy. I believe Dr. Qualls has offered to trade, however."

"Yes, I did," Garth interjected.

"There's no need. It'll be just fine, thank you," Ethan replied.

"Now that I know the history between you two, I may let you sort that out yourselves." She gave a nod and clapped her hands together once. "All right. Let's get through some things, and then Dr. Bianchi and I will go round on some patients."

She concluded a few minutes later and left with her resident.

As soon as the door closed behind her, heads and chairs swiveled toward Ethan. He pushed down bubbles of unease and quickly decided to take the offensive rather than get stuck answering questions. He pointed to the dark-skinned woman nearest him, "PhD student. Abby Douglas, right? Yes, thank you. Have you started your dissertation research?"

"Yeah, I started last semester. I'm looking at stem cell regulators causing aplastic anemia."

"She has sixty little helpers, but they have to live in the research building," Rav added.

"Using mice models? Oh, interesting." He couldn't resist giving a side eye to Garth, "Are you her adviser?"

He was rewarded with snickers from the students and a contrived glare from Garth as Abby nodded.

"Ok, Rav, what is your whole name?" Ethan turned to the Indian student.

"Ravinandan Suryavanshi," his tongue bounced over the syllables.

Ethan pondered the sounds, silently testing the rhythm out with his tongue. "Ok, once more?"

After hearing it again, he repeated it back to Rav, "Ravinandan Suryavanshi?"

Rav looked stunned, "Yes! I think you're the first white person to get it on the first try. No offense!"

"I'll take it as praise." He repeated it a couple more times to get it in his head. "We'll see if I can remember it. What is your dissertation focus?"

"Uuuhhhh," he shrunk dubiously into his chair.

"Right, so we have some work to do on that."

Now comfortably on to the topics of their studies, he let them lead the conversation a bit more and also show him around.

He'd already been to Dr. Miller's office, and Garth's, both down the hall. And, of course, the 16th floor of Hammer building across the street held Carol's office, auxiliary offices, lecture halls, and some lab rooms—one of which apparently held sixty mice. The big equipment, such as the DNA sequencer, would be housed in their own special labs. In the sequencer's case, it was the genomics lab downstairs. There it could be accessed by those with permission and the techs who knew how to use them.

This lab room, dubbed the Miller Lab, had white walls, a white linoleum floor, and was lit with enough fluorescent lights that it practically glowed. The walls were completely lined with tables and counters except for a tall refrigerator, the main door, and a closet. The tables held computers and various lab equipment including microscopes, a couple microwave sized appliances with blinking lights, and some stations set up with test tube racks and pipettes.

Rav led the way to the closet door. It opened into a narrow space lit by a single bulb on the ceiling. A desk was wedged across the middle of the room with only a foot to spare on one side, and one filing cabinet sat behind it.

"Wow," Garth grunted.

"I found a mini fridge to go under your desk, Dr. Dalton," Rav offered. "Because if you ever get caught with something in the lab fridge, Dr. Miller will burn you at the stake."

"Good to know, Rav. Thanks." Ethan tempered the relief he felt at entering the small dark room. "This will work fine. I know I didn't exactly give Dr. Miller much notice."

Since only one to two people would actually fit in the room at one time, though, he followed them back out into the main lab.

"When is your next thing?" Garth asked him during a lull in the conversation.

"Uh…" He really was going to have to get better at keeping track of time again.

"Phone calendar, maybe?" Garth prodded.

Ethan frowned at him.

"Seriously?"

"The thing still hurts to look at," Ethan deflected in a low voice.

"You turned down the bright–"

"Yes."

"Hold on, there has to be an app or something, give it here."

Ethan handed him the phone from his pocket.

"Isn't there an app or something to reduce light on the phone screen?" Garth raised his voice and polled the room. "For when staring at it gives you a headache or whatever…"

Rav raised a hand. "I know of a good blue light filter. And it lets you get a lower light setting too, I think."

Garth slid Ethan's phone down the table to him.

Only a minute later, Rav rolled his chair over and held the phone screen toward Ethan. "Here, look. I just downloaded this and gave it permission to do stuff. If I turn on the filter…"

"Oh. That's actually better."

"And you can change light levels there."

Ethan swiped it down to the lowest. *Now this I can actually work with.* He looked over at Rav. "I don't suppose you can work similar magic on a computer?"

He shrugged. "I can at least look. Maybe there's an add on or something in the settings."

Ethan reached under the table for the canvas messenger bag he'd found in the back of Garth's closet, pulled out his new laptop, and handed it over.

Within minutes Rav had the computer screen at a much more usable light level.

After he and Abby excused themselves to go to a lecture, Garth grinned over at him.

"What?" The screen brightness hadn't seemed too much of a stretch to be a normal question, had it? And Garth had started it.

"You seemed like *you* just now."

"Oh." Maybe there was still some of Dr. Dalton in him. "It felt…good." He scanned the room of familiar equipment. "It was the mouse comment, wasn't it?"

Garth grinned wider.

"I can't quite believe you got me back so fast."

"It was Carol's doing, wasn't it? You had her on your side in less than two sentences, and she was all in."

"You helped," he looked back to his now usable phone. "A lot."

"If you write that grant proposal that Dr. Miller has been bugging me about for weeks, it'll all be worth it." Garth languished sarcastically. "Wait, why am *I* wincing at the lights now?"

"Power of suggestion. Send me the grant info. I'll see if I remember how to write in full sentences." There was his calendar app. "Ah, I am supposed to be somewhere."

29

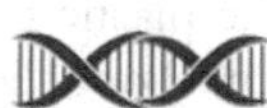

"Hey."

"Hey!" Garth gratefully looked up from his computer screen and returned Ethan's greeting. "Find where you were supposed to be?"

"Yes. Got an orientation to the next gen processor downstairs. That thing is amazing." Ethan was actually wearing his whole, naturally crooked smile–the left side of his mouth pulled back more than the right revealing just the front of his crowded teeth.

"Right!?" Garth was quick to agree enthusiastically. "I mean, I'm sorry we spent your life savings, but that thing is worth it."

"It's at least five times as fast."

"I *know.*"

"And you don't have to…" Ethan pantomimed a small repetitive action.

"Yes! It just does the whole thing!" Garth hadn't been sure if pushing to get Ethan working in the lab again so fast had been the best idea, but his excitement confirmed that it had been after all. "I just realized how jealous I am that you actually get to work down there with it and not just send them stuff."

"I am not sorry about it. The tech…Jessica, was running me through the set up. Man, I'm going to forget someone's name at some point."

Garth laughed. "I think that's allowed. It'll be ok. I still forget all the time."

"You never forget anything." Ethan dropped into a chair and pulled his hat down lower. "You think anyone would notice if just a couple bulbs went missing in here?"

Garth leaned back and considered the lab ceiling and its six industrial fluorescent lights. "I mean, if we were really gradual about it, and maybe even took out a couple in the hall so the difference wasn't stark."

Apparently that was enough permission. Ethan stood and stepped up onto the back of his chair in a smooth motion to reach for the light above.

The back of his spinning, rolling office chair, with the toes of one foot counterbalanced on the arm.

"Oh—ok. We're going for it now. Sure. That doesn't seem like the safest place to stand, though."

But Ethan's balance was incredible. The chair didn't move under his feet at all as he pushed the plastic pane up to reveal three white fluorescent light tubes. He popped one slightly out of place, rather than remove it completely, replaced the cover quickly, and stepped off the back of the chair to land seated with a poof of air.

The lab door opened a second later.

How did the man concentrate on any one thing while still able to hear what was going on outside the room?

Garth shut his gaping mouth as Ethan rose again and made for Carol, who was holding at least one too many things so that only her purple glasses and gray spiked hair were visible above the pile.

"Thank you, son," she relinquished a cardboard jug of coffee to him and proceeded to a mostly empty table. After dropping disposable coffee cups, sugar, creamer, napkins, and a large tray onto the table, she held out an ID badge already connected to a retractable lanyard clip with a DNA double helix on it. "I brought you this. HR finished printing it, and I stopped by security to get you the appropriate access. If you find you need to get somewhere that it doesn't let you, just call them and ask for Gary."

"Thank you, Carol." Ethan accepted it with an air of reverence.

She pulled the lid off the large round tray. "I also brought you something as a welcome home."

The tray on the table held cannolis from Tony's—those were Ethan's favorite.

Or had been.

"Carol, you're incredible."

"Psh." But she smiled and handed him one on a napkin.

Garth hadn't seen Ethan eat anything remotely close to a cannoli since being back. But Carol hadn't taken her eyes off him.

Ethan's hesitation was subtle—maybe Garth imagined it—before he took a bite.

Chewed.

Swallowed.

Only when Carol turned back to the table to pour some coffee did Ethan press a knuckle to his lips to stifle a gag.

Well. It must really stink to come back and find that your favorite food in the world tasted bad enough to gag you.

Carol stuck close to Ethan, only half-turning to hand Garth a cannoli, and Garth could find nothing to do to help. Ethan managed to finish it, probably with a straighter face than Garth, considering Ethan shot him a warning look over her shoulder. He wished he could just stop the "power of suggestion" thing, because the best cannoli in the city was tasting a little flat right now.

"How is being back?" Carol asked.

"He was just singing the praises of the new sequencer," Garth offered, giving Ethan a chance to wash down the last bite with some coffee.

"Good. I did think that was the most appropriate thing bought with your funds."

Ethan almost succeeded in suppressing a cough before agreeing, "I would have bought one myself if I knew what it was capable of."

Carol nodded again. "Yes, with that and the grant to your old lab, I guess I can understand why you made the decision you did, not taking it back. We really don't deserve you, though."

Ethan shook his head modestly. "I'm glad they got something too."

"You know they haven't changed the name. It's still the Dalton Lab."

There was some blinking to absorb that, and something of the haunted look stole back into his eyes. "I…They should take Dr. Amin's name. I'm here…now."

"Perhaps you're right. It's less a tribute to your life's work when your work isn't finished, now isn't it?" Carol could be profound.

With the sixth sense of an unpaid grad student, Rav walked in just then and went for the food. Ethan must have used his arrival as a distraction to escape, because when Garth looked around, he wasn't in the room anymore. Not sure if there was cause for his concern, Garth excused himself and opted to check the restroom down the hall first.

The sound of retching and splashing from a stall answered his questions.

Ethan's black tennis shoes visible under the partition confirmed it was him, so Garth said, "It's me," just so Ethan wouldn't think someone else had walked in.

At the sound of Garth's voice, Ethan dropped back to his hands and knees on the floor and promptly vomited again.

Garth waited for him to finish and flush before walking over and leaning against the sink. Ethan slumped to his seat against the stall wall, still clutching his abdomen with a pained expression.

"Is this what happens when you eat something off your diet?"

"It's what happened the other times I tried," he caught his breath with a grimace that revealed his teeth. "This was faster though." When he launched back toward the toilet, Garth found himself studying the water stain on the dropped ceiling square above until Ethan once again sagged to the tile floor.

There was blood on his lip. That couldn't be a good sign. "Uh…"

Ethan wiped his mouth with the back of his hand. "It is what I put in my stomach this morning."

"Oh, right. That makes sense then." *Duh.*

He still looked miserable. "It kind of looked like it didn't taste that great. Is that usually the case? Can you tell if something is going to make you sick?"

Ethan glared at him before leaning back to the toilet again.

"Sorry, bad timing.…"

Garth tried again to look away but found Ethan's white knuckles grip on the base of the stall partition as he endured some longer lasting heaves. Finally, Ethan slid back to the floor again and dropped his head back against the partition, answering between heavy breaths, "I've only tried a couple things, but no, they didn't taste right either."

"I'm starting to understand why trying coffee was such a big deal," Garth replied. "I can actually see you breathing hard–are you ok?"

"It's quite the workout, trying to turn your insides out–ah–through your mouth–" The grunt and grimace belayed his attempt to lighten the situation. At least he was distracted enough to miss Garth's momentary stare at the blood drop that dripped from his elongated canine while his lips were pulled back.

Reading Ethan's abrupt glance at the door, Garth started in that direction in time to catch the man in blue scrubs and warn him away. He took his time walking back to his spot at the sink to let Ethan retch again in peace.

When Ethan again wilted back to the door of the stall, Garth quipped, "It turns out you can look paler. Who knew?"

Ethan only managed a grunt in response.

"Surely there's nothing left in your stomach."

"Someone needs to convince it of that." But he managed to breathe through another cramp without vomiting.

"Sorry you hate cannolis now," Garth offered after a few silent minutes.

"Yeah…thanks."

"If Carol had any idea what you went through to save face in front of her–"

"You're not going to tell her," Ethan retorted.

Garth held up his hands in surrender.

A phone beeped.

"Shoot."

"What is it?" Garth asked.

"I'm supposed to meet with Dr. Miller to go through some stuff with the students."

"Oh, you mean you're actually using calendar reminders already? Goodness, Rav did in half a day what I couldn't in a month."

His glare held little fire.

"You want me to find them and make an excuse?"

Ethan shook his head. "Just give me a minute. I'll make it."

Garth shifted against the sink but gave him about ten quiet minutes before Ethan moved again. He went forward to his knees, used a grip on the stall wall to push to his feet, and made it a step before swaying.

"Take it easy," Garth stepped in to support him. "I'm getting a flashback from undergrad."

Ethan pulled away and made it to the sink to brace himself against it with his hands. "I think I only went to the one party," he grunted.

"So, you remember it too. Or…at least the aftermath."

It got a half-smirk from Ethan.

"Are you sure you're ok to meet them?"

He turned the water on. "Yeah. I'm now hungry and nauseated, so I think it's going in the right direction."

"I could grab some fruit from the cafeteria–"

"I'll be fine until tonight." He splashed some water onto his face and into his mouth to rinse it out.

"You sure?"

"Yeah." There was determination in his face as he stood up straighter and checked his clothes for evidence of the misadventure.

Garth could still see him breathing, though, and faster than the four times a minute they'd counted before. "Ok.…"

After drying off with some paper towels, Ethan cast Garth a look for a final check.

"You're good. Definitely not puking your guts out a few minutes ago."

"Very reassuring."

ק

The smell of cannoli and cake still permeated the lab when Ethan walked back in to find Dr. Miller, Rav, and Abby gathered at one of the tables. Trying not to look like it was a relief, he sank into a chair and rolled over to them. "Sorry I'm late."

"You're fine. We were just reviewing some lab protocols," Dr. Miller said.

"Did you get a cannoli?" Rav waved the one in his hand in front of Ethan's face.

His, "I did," came out a little pinched.

"Rav, this part of the lab is still functioning as a lab, not a break room. No food, please," Dr. Miller intervened.

Rav shoved the whole thing into his mouth and dropped the paper plate into a trash can, redirecting his attention to her looking somewhat like a chipmunk.

"Now. What's the next step in DNA extraction?"

The process should have been something Ethan could do in his sleep, so he mostly worked to sit calmly and pretend that his insides weren't still at war. And that he wasn't hungry. And to not flinch at the whir of the centrifuge.

Maybe he should reconsider bringing "lunch" with him to work. When he'd made the argument to Garth that he didn't need to eat that many times a day, he hadn't considered a scenario that involved him regurgitating everything he'd eaten in the last 24 hours.

Dr. Miller transitioned, "Application time," and retrieved some new test tubes from the refrigerator. Each contained swirling crimson liquid. "What do we want to know from these samples?"

"From the mice?" Rav asked.

They weren't. It was obvious to Ethan the instant Dr. Miller uncapped one.

"These are blood samples from some current patients of ours. We also have samples from healthy volunteers for controls, including a lot of people who work here and are invested in our results." Dr. Miller's voice droned in the background.

Ethan carefully kept his gaze down and stopped breathing.

It was one thing to get used to and dismiss the smell of humans constantly around him. It was another to have blood waved under his nose. When he knew it would soothe everything going on in his stomach.

Dr. Miller was looking at him, waiting for an answer to something that had stumped the grad students.

Unfortunately, he hadn't heard the question.

She answered it herself and moved on smoothly, covering his blank stare, but he kicked himself mentally. There was nothing to make her question that equivocal decision to let him join the team like not knowing the basics.

To top it off, Garth walked in and plopped down next to him. Knowing Garth would undoubtedly still have an annoyingly close eye on him, Ethan started breathing again. The scent of the blood was slightly contaminated by the chemical used to preserve and process it. He focused on that smell, the wrong part, and tried to listen more closely.

Until Garth extended a sample toward him. "Want to get back in the saddle?"

Ethan sat perfectly still. "I'll take a back seat today. You can show us how it's done."

He would manage to handle and process human blood samples—it was a necessary part of the job. He'd known that when he chose to pursue the fastest option back into the lab.

Just not today.

30

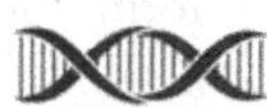

The door opening startled Ethan, a sure way to prove how immersed he'd been in thought, but when it was Garth who nosed his way into the genomics lab room, the coil in his chest relaxed.

"Hey, there you are," Garth sounded relieved. "It's after six. Did you get my texts?"

Right. They'd been finding each other and leaving the lab closer to 5:00 p.m. all week. It took a pat of his pockets and paper print outs on the desk to locate his phone, which showed several texts from Garth. "Sorry, didn't hear it."

"Is that what we're going with?"

All right, "I wasn't paying attention."

"Clearly. What are you working on?"

When Garth leaned over to read one of the reports, Ethan reactively tensed before forcing himself to relax. He'd already decided to let Garth help with the physical stuff. Which would include that.

The genotype report simply read, "Error: invalid specimen."

"How did you prep the sample?" Garth asked, ready to solve a technical issue.

"I processed specimens all morning with Jessica. I remember how to do it."

"What sample did you use?"

"Mine."

"Huh?"

"Cheek swab. Retook it twice."

Papers shuffled. "You're running a genotype on yourself? Why?"

"It's the fastest way I could think of to check a theory." It hadn't

177

been hard to prep his own sample and send it through one of the more basic genotype assays. The genotype was a common test to run that identified a few thousand single nucleotide polymorphisms (SNPs), specific genetic areas known to differ among people. They were used in studies and sometimes clinically–for example, to identify particular cancer risks. Measuring SNPs with genotyping was faster than whole genome sequencing, but it used predetermined assays and computer software, which is where the problem had come in.

"What are you looking–?"

That pause would mean Garth had reached the bottom sheet, the one that suggested helpfully: "Error, analyze human specimen only."

Ethan waited for him to process it and look up, which he finally did tentatively, still only able to form the beginning of a question, "What…?"

It means I'm no longer human.

He couldn't speak the words aloud. He'd lost track of how many times he'd thought it, but seeing it in black and white in front of him had rooted him to his seat.

"You think…."

"My DNA has been altered," Ethan managed to summarize. "It always made the most sense, as a theory." He looked at the paper still in Garth's hand and swallowed hard. "I don't know how, but something transmitted in the bite…changed my DNA."

"This isn't conclusive–"

"It would have spit out a normal genotype report otherwise, Garth. I've run one of these on myself before, years ago. I don't have it now, but I know it was a typical report. And I know the machine is working– I ran 20 of these today. It can't process my genotype because the markers aren't…typical. It's different. Wrong."

Garth's gaze flicked back and forth between the paper and Ethan, his expression worried.

Conversely, Ethan was feeling more and more settled, the longer he sat there. An answer was better than questions, even if it confirmed a fear. Able to move again, he started clearing the computer's history before reaching for the print outs.

"What's next?" Garth asked, following his lead and handing him back the papers.

That thought required a slow deep breath. "I can run a genome-wide sequence. Analyzing it might be troublesome. I don't have my original genome to use as a comparator." Instead of looking at specific sections of DNA, a sequence would give a picture of the entire genome. But if the software had trouble analyzing it, Ethan would have to manually make sense of the extensive list of data.

"If you started with a standardized human genomic map as a template…or we could try RNA sequencing." Rather than mapping all the DNA in a cell, sequencing RNA transcripts would essentially tell what genes were turned on and turned off.

"That will take forever."

"Not with the next gen processor," Garth pointed across the room. "And it's not species specific. It can detect RNA sequences without having predetermined genomic sequences…" he trailed off, apparently realizing what he'd implied with the use of the word "species," and comparing Ethan with "human."

But Ethan had already been to that thought and back.

"Ok, those are good thoughts," Garth recovered. "But maybe I can also tweak the genotyping software. I can talk computer. Let me try a few things. And I know a couple people in the data wrangling world who might be able to help."

"Don't–"

"No, I won't give specifics. Never will, unless you tell me to."

Still not sure how it had become Garth's project too, but sure it would be nearly an impossible project alone, Ethan nodded gratefully.

"Do you have more samples already processed that I can work with?"

Ethan handed him two tiny plastic-capped test tubes. "Let me get this cell culture set up to incubate. I'm going to run a karyotype. See how crazy this is." The karyotype would let him look at the DNA visually, as it was naturally packaged for cell replication into chromosomes. It wouldn't give the detail he was looking for, but it would let him know if there was a drastic change and tell if Garth's venture into tweaking the genotyping software was worth pursuing.

Garth nodded without saying anything, which could only mean his brain was whirring too quickly to put into words.

After stashing some test tubes in the back of the incubator, stuffing the reports into his own bag, putting the machine to sleep, and turning off the only remaining light that was on, Ethan led the way out. "We can walk outside," he offered after a quick check of the weather app on his phone.

When Garth still only nodded, Ethan started bracing himself for the barrage of questions that would follow so much silent thinking.

It started as they descended the subway steps. "How long did it take? For the changes to manifest? You said it happened mostly all at once, but for DNA changes…"

Ethan had used the silence to decide he would give Garth a bit more than the little he had divulged so far, at least sticking to scientific topics, so he answered after swiping his metrocard and walking through the turnstile, "I don't know, exactly. Besides having no way to keep track at the time, I wasn't completely conscious for part of it. Maybe a few weeks, but I don't know for sure."

"What…what was it like?"

Ethan flinched involuntarily. "It hurt. Everything hurt. Until finally it was like something short circuited in my brain and reality kind of went wonky for a while."

"I guess that makes sense if even your nerves were changed somehow." Garth was still thinking. "What about the others…there? What did they look like?"

"There were common characteristics. Everyone had dark hair, dark eyes. Everyone is this shade of Caucasian, although that may be environmental. Height varied, both genders, but no one was heavy."

"They were all…?"

Vampires. Ethan nodded once.

"How many are we talking about?"

"Twenty-eight." He'd included himself. "Twenty-seven…"

Getting answers had Garth on a roll. "And they all had the same physical changes?"

"*Yes.*" The Romanian word came out without thought. Under Garth's look, he shifted his feet uneasily on the dirty concrete platform and tried to pull his sense of reality back. "Yes," he corrected. "Teeth are the same, strength, balance, diet, aversion to sun, eyes that change…" His gaze drifted down the dark tunnel. Still the words he sought were harder to find in the right language.

"The first description you gave, hair color, eye color, and such, you had before the hypothesized genetic changes. Any idea if it was the same for the others?" Garth continued.

"I don't know. They were all there years before I was taken. I was a…rarity."

"Just wondering if you all had a similar phenotype before the changes."

Ethan had thought the same thing, but his mouth was muddled about which word to form, so he just nodded.

Face still scrunched, Garth tried something else. "If they could change others with just a bite, why weren't there more?"

"Jack reacted differently. I think it was killing him. Maybe it takes a compatible genome…" His analytical brain kicked back on, processing in light of his new information. "The gene pool around the mountain isn't diverse. They only killed locals, never bit them and waited to see if one would change. They must have stopped trying. Until new blood wandered in…"

"Wandered in?" Garth's prodding was gentler now.

The subway platform faded out of focus. "Jack was obsessed with hiking and stuff, you know. When we ended up in the middle of nowhere, he still managed to find an opportunity, even a cave. She found us, even though we were at the edge of the cave. We got away after she bit us, but it was too late…"

"She?"

"That's enough." Too much, really.

Despite the language change, Garth got the message. "Ok," he took a step away, giving him space. "Thank you for answering."

Speaking about it made it real again, while he'd rather it remain a nightmare. No one needed to know what he'd been. He'd much rather be Ethan Dalton.

31

The razor pricked his neck with a sharp pinch. Garth gave an unmanly yelp and reached for the toilet paper.

"You ok?" Ethan called from the kitchen.

"Yeah, yeah, fine! Stinking too-dull razor is also too sharp. Trying to stab myself in the neck, but no worries," Garth yelled back, before he remembered not to yell, and turned on the sink to rinse his razor.

What time is it? The question drove him through the bedroom, still holding the toilet paper against his neck. "Do we have a lab meeting at eight or nine?"

Ethan sat at the tall table in the corner with a coffee cup in front of him. When Garth walked into the room, he looked up at Garth only to jerk his gaze back down to his coffee.

Almost as if…

But no, that wasn't possible.

And he said he didn't drink human blood, only the pig stuff.

Or had Garth been the one to say that?

What if…

Surely not. They worked with blood samples all the time at work. Had he been weird about it at the lab? *Hold on, what about the first day?*

And Garth knew that look.

"Huh." His neck was still bleeding. "Hold on–" he spun back into the bedroom. Stop bleeding first, in case he was right, then talk.

⸻

Ethan shoved his nose back into his coffee cup to try to override the scent of Garth's blood. *Stop it,* he ordered himself. *You don't need it.* It didn't matter that it would fill that remaining void that was never quite sated despite eating better than he had in the cave. He needed to forget it was an option all together.

Garth had just surprised him.

The pig blood sweetened coffee was plenty.

When Garth walked back in, his heartbeat was much too fast. What had happened? Had he done something or was it something else? Ethan looked up, seeing the band-aid on Garth's neck despite focusing very hard on only his eyes. "You ok?"

Garth hesitated.

Tension coiled in Ethan's chest.

Garth walked in and leaned against the counter. "I…have a question. But before I ask, I'm going to tell you something to explain why, ok?"

Ethan waited.

Garth shifted. "After undergrad–well, do you know why it took me four extra years to get my PhD? Why I had just started my post- doc when you left?"

That required a change in direction of thought. "You mean because of the accident?"

"Not just the accident. What happened afterwards."

That felt like another lifetime. "I…I lost touch for a little while, while I was buried in my dissertation. I'm sorry–"

"You didn't lose touch. I pulled away. From everyone. A few months of oxy had me all in, and when the doctors stopped giving it to me, I found another way to get high. I was addicted–I am an addict. It took almost dying to get me out. And Jesus, but that's another story. So, I know that look."

Ethan absorbed that fast ball of information. "What look?"

"*That* look. The one where you want so much to look, that you look everywhere else instead, or else you might do more than just look."

Ethan's gaze was frozen on Garth's eyes.

"Did you drink human blood?"

Regret and shame, heavier than an ax blow, smacked Ethan in the chest, knocking a gasp from him. It took everything he had to push down the feeling to keep it from his eyes.

But it was still way too much reaction to hide from Garth.

He had his answer.

"Ok…" Garth took a deep breath as his heart rate sped up even faster.

He wasn't running yet.

Rationalizations poured out before Ethan could stop them, "I didn't know what it was when they first gave it to me. Then I tried to refuse but wasn't given a choice. It really was mostly animal…"

Garth was nodding. Not running.

"I won't drink it here."

Nodding. "It's ok. That's what I get for assuming. I didn't really think…well that sums up the problem, doesn't it? Do you want to tell me about it?"

With everything in him, he didn't.

Garth got it. "Ok, that's fine. Just tell me about the addiction part."

The what? Ethan stood and shook his head. "There's no…you don't know what you're talking about."

"Ok, I might not. Just answer this one question, if you don't mind. What did it feel like when you drank it?"

The rush of feeling, the memory of it, made it to his eyes and sharpened his vision.

Garth jumped. Took a stumbling step back.

There it was.

Fear in his eyes.

No.

Ethan grabbed his hat and coat and yanked the door open, leaving behind another friend.

32

Ethan couldn't stand still on the subway platform.

You told him part of it. Tried to explain rather than leave. But he saw more. Too much.

When the eyes of the others waiting were all turned away, he grasped the edge of the gate separating the platform from the tunnel and swung around it, landing softly on the maintenance walkway on the other side.

A few steps into the subway tunnel, he was hidden from any eyes. Any judgment. He was alone where no one could see him run. Leap. Stare blue eyed into the dark. Shriek at the lights and roar of the trains.

Darkness and silence were so elusive in the city.

Wind stirred up by the subway train tugged at his coat and hat.

Emptiness gnawed at him.

Memory of that wholeness, feeling sated and calm, taunted him, making his hands shake.

Was Garth right? Was he nothing but a tweaking junkie?

He was a fool to think he could change by simply escaping the cave. What they had done had changed him, even more than his DNA.

Now he was having trouble remembering why he'd made the decision not to drink again. Did he even know for sure that it wasn't physically necessary for his inhuman body?

The agony drinking it had caused, that he had helped cause, the death toll…he'd told himself he didn't have a choice. Was it true?

Did he have a choice now?

He wouldn't kill again to get it, but…

But…

As long as that word was allowed to hang in his mind, he was a danger. Garth was right to be afraid of him.

If he determined that he couldn't live without it, what was there to keep him from repeating previous actions and becoming the evil he sought to escape?

Time to leave.

＞

Ethan ultimately swung back onto the next subway platform and rode the A train uptown, trying not to think. The noise and press of people around him helped. And didn't.

In his dim cramped office off of the Miller lab, he pushed all his focus into the problem of the grad student who sat in the spinning office chair across the desk from him.

"Rav, this is too broad for a thesis," he gestured to the document on the desk. "It needs to be a question with a measurable answer."

Rav dropped his head back against the chair, still spinning, "I don't know how to narrow it down."

"What you have written here is an overview of the subject. You need a single question."

"Like what?"

"This is your thesis, not mine. I'm not going to give it to you."

Rav sighed and let the chair slow to a stop.

"You said you have an exam today, right? Go. Worry about that today, then come back to me next week."

"Yeah…" He got up in a dragging way and opened the door. Since the door opened out, it didn't hit the chair, which actually belonged in the larger lab room. But Rav must have forgotten that he'd rolled it in to begin with, because he left in a slump without a look back.

Garth was out there. He'd arrived only a few minutes after Rav had come in for his meeting.

Rather than make him come into the confined space, Ethan figured he should go out there and get out what he needed to say while the presence of others tempered his threat.

He stood. It was tempting to simply step over the desk, but he didn't want to risk getting into the habit and then doing it in front of someone without thinking, so he walked sideways in the foot of space between his desk and the wall and pushed the chair through the door into the lab to roll to an empty spot in front of a table.

Garth looked up. "Ethan—"

Ethan avoided looking at him but stepped close enough for him to hear easily. "I'll move out tonight."

Garth's whisper grew in volume, "Move out? No, no, don't you go anywhere—"

"You're right to be afraid. I'm sorry I let it go so far."

"I was just startled. You laid a lot on a guy. I just needed a minute! But I'm getting a handle on it. You are not allowed to leave. This isn't something to try alone, ok? I may not know everything, but I know that."

It didn't make sense.

Ethan risked a look at his eyes.

There was no fear there now.

Why?

Garth's voice dropped back down, "Maybe I can help, somehow. What's the longest you've gone without it?"

Unintentionally, Ethan's gaze flicked to the calendar on the wall.

"*This* is the longest? Right now?"

"Stop."

"It's unfortunate it's so ubiquitous. Do you have a long-term strategy?"

Ethan turned to leave.

"Wait, wait, ok, sorry. You're right—wrong time. Ethan?"

He stopped, his back still to Garth. "You don't know what you're talking about," his voice was flat.

"Maybe not. Just come back home tonight. Don't leave over this, right now. Ok?"

⟨

He hadn't answered.

Garth watched Ethan walk out of the lab, shoulders slightly hunched over, without another word.

"Fiddlesticks." Garth clamped a hand over his mouth and leaned his elbows onto the table. Everything had sounded a little insane before, but it had just taken a sharp curve to Crazy Town. Had he really just been prodding a vampire into admitting he was addicted to drinking human blood? Maybe that's why he hadn't seen the signs before—it had seemed impossible. It was real life, not silly stories. Ethan was still flesh and blood, not dead, not supernatural.

And yet, this part was true.

Now what? God help me, what do I do now?

189

Ethan avoided Garth by working in the genomics lab for the rest of the day but had to return upstairs later to get his bag. Before he got to the lab, Dr. Miller's voice caught him in the hall. "Ethan."

He pivoted back to the slightly ajar door of her office. "Yes?"

She waved him in and pointed at her computer screen. "This grant proposal you just sent me is the one I gave Garth two months ago."

Grant proposal. He'd sent that to her last night when he had not been sleeping. If he'd thought the dreams had been bad before, today definitely wasn't going to improve them. "Yeah, I owed him one. Well, a few."

"Did he give you something to work with?"

"He—a little. Not much. But it's due in a couple weeks, and there's some clinical information that you'll need to add, so I wanted to give you time to do that."

"You haven't even been here for three weeks, and this is thorough." Her brows arched in a doubtful yet awed look.

He shrugged. Truth be told, he'd gotten bored with the longer than necessary nights and so had started working from the apartment bedroom while Garth slept. The proposal, only requiring research into the files and typing, had filled the time. "I had time. But feel free to send it back for edits if something doesn't look right, or…"

A flame caught his eye.

It burned on the wick of a small candle in a glass at the edge of her desk and gave off a soft clean scent, but it was the yellow flickering light that transfixed him. A light he had lived in for so long and yet not seen in two months.

Dr. Miller was saying something about knowing she shouldn't have the candle in the office but secretly using it because it helped her relax, but Ethan was seeing a coal lantern and a rock forge.

"I'm sorry." She reached to extinguish it.

"Don't." He jerked back to the present. "I mean, it's fine."

"I didn't mean to stir up memories." She relaxed the hand that had reached for the candle, letting it burn.

How long had he stared at it? For her to notice? But maybe it was ok. Maybe it didn't give away anything, really.

His gaze drifted back to the flame. "Not every memory is bad," he whispered.

Without moving to interrupt him, she observed, "I imagine that doesn't make it less confusing."

He blinked because she was correct and stepped back to interrupt the thoughts anyway.

"The proposal looks great, but I will let you know if it needs anything." She said it slowly, allowing him to transfer back to work mode and remember what they'd been discussing before transitioning with, "Rav is trying to get everyone together for drinks to celebrate finishing his exam."

That wasn't a good idea. "I'm going to have to decline." He backed toward the door. "I'll see you tomorrow."

33

Two months back in the city. Three weeks back in the lab. Every time Ethan thought a part of him fit, something happened to remind him how he didn't.

He'd gone back to Garth's apartment, as asked. Since Garth had gone out with Rav after work, Ethan had avoided him by pretending to be asleep when he got back to the apartment. He'd been staring at the stained plaster ceiling in the light of the microwave light glowing 3:56 a.m., wondering how it was possible to miss parts of something he hated, when he'd abruptly decided there was nothing keeping him from going back to the lab, where he had projects that he'd started days ago but hadn't had uninterrupted time to complete.

Since no one who arrived after Ethan knew how long he'd been in the lab, no one questioned finding him there when they came in. He sat at a table in front of a microscope fitted with a camera, looking at slides and clicking at the computer next to him. He ended up with the task of training resident Dr. Bianchi with the process, but as she had the uncommon skill of following the written directions from a lab protocol correctly, it hadn't been a difficult task so far.

She sat before a similar microscope focused on tiny snippets of gray-banded lines. The chromosomes he was visualizing weren't the same as hers, but she didn't know it, and they looked quite similar at the moment.

"Yes, that looks right. Chromosome nine," he answered her question and ignored Garth who walked in and sighed. Considering all that Dr. Bianchi had already accurately accomplished in her first attempt at the procedure, he should have been more encouraging, but when he opened his mouth, "Keep going," was all that came out.

"Thank you. I do need to meet Dr. Miller in a few minutes," she replied.

"That's fine. You've got everything documented so you can pick it up later if you want."

She nodded and started filing her slides.

Garth waited for her to leave before plopping into her vacated seat. "Morning. How—"

"Fine," Ethan interrupted without looking up from the microscope.

"Ok." His terseness only put Garth off for a moment. "I'm glad you came back last night."

It seemed he might be about to keep pushing, but Dr. Miller walked back in with Dr. Bianchi to retrieve something. Instead of continuing the conversation, Garth sat fiddling with the microscope.

"Don't you have something else you're supposed to be doing?" Ethan asked.

"This is what I think I should be doing right now. Hand me a slide."

On the other side of the room one of the women opened a specimen tube. Ethan didn't know which because his attention flicked straight to the open container of blood on the counter before jerking back to his computer screen.

Garth sucked in a breath.

Ethan remained motionless until the women walked out. Then he stood, sending his stool rolling backwards, and fled toward his office.

"Hold on, you're just leaving a research task half done? And leaving it out? Especially what I think this is?" Garth called across the empty room at his back.

It stopped him. Disgust and anger curled his lip but stopped just short of his eyes.

Garth opened his mouth, paused, then, "We don't have to talk or anything, ok? Let's just work on this."

The lab had gone from feeling like freedom to feeling like a trap. But what else was he supposed to do? For the first time he was close to actually getting answers.

He sat, picked up two slides, and handed one to Garth.

They worked side by side for half an hour, alone in the room, and mostly quiet except that Garth was humming. Ethan wanted to be irritated at the constant noise emanating from him, but it was occupying the part of his brain that wanted to wander down dark paths, letting him focus on his monotonous task.

Ethan sat up from the microscope and rubbed his eyes.

"Want a break? Or," Garth scanned the empty room, "Less light? Also, I just sent you another one."

Despite seriously considering taking out another light bulb, Ethan turned to the screen which showed the digitally combined chromosomes they had pieced together.

"This is yours that we're working on, right?" Garth asked.

"Yeah." There were 22 squiggly X's displayed on the screen.

"Ok, because that looks pretty typical so far, yeah?"

"Yeah," he repeated.

"Not that I would have expected it to be wildly different. Considering you still pretty much look like you..."

But he couldn't see what Ethan thought he saw. It wasn't visible on the screen either, making him question his eyes and squint into the microscope again.

"What did you just figure out?" Garth asked when Ethan leaned back and brought a knuckle to his lips.

"I'm not sure," Ethan muttered as he pulled up a 23rd blurry X and a Y on the computer. "Here's the last one." He told the computer to analyze them into artificially stratified columns and print them, then laid the printouts on the tabletop next to a standardized human example.

Garth leaned forward next to him, peering down his long nose in study mode. After a few minutes, Garth broke the silence. "Ok, I see an atypical variance in this band here," he pointed.

Ethan nodded.

"Yeah..." Garth scanned for another moment before adding, "But that's it. Nothing crazy, no 24th chromosome or anything."

But there was still the other thing. Ethan stood, stuffed the folded report into his lab coat pocket, checked the clock, and retrieved his hat from his office.

"What are you thinking?"

"I need a better microscope."

"Why?"

"I can't explain it. Just come on if you're going to."

The sun was annoyingly bright in the overpass as Ethan jogged through it and strode for a lab deep in the research building. Garth's breath wheezed through his nose by the time Ethan badged into the dimly lit room with specialized equipment and an especially expensive microscope. He retrieved a slide from the cabinet that he had started preparing a couple days ago when he had first noticed the abnormality that only he seemed to be able to see on his new karyotype.

"Florescence microscopy?" Garth asked. "What are we looking for?"

Ethan set up the slide and bent to visualize it. "Telomeres."

"Telomeres?" Garth parroted.

Ethan panned across the slide. *I was right.* "They're too long." He clicked to send an image to the computer screen, which Garth promptly bounced over to.

After a moment, Garth leaned against the table and peered closer. "These are yours? How old are you again? Thirty-eight? Why are your telomeres this long? And why are you even looking at them?"

There were so many details Garth didn't know. "The others..."

"In the–" Garth dropped his voice even though the room was empty, "In the cave?"

"I told you everyone looked similar. Including in apparent age. But everyone else was actually much older."

"What do you mean? How much older? How do you know?"

"I don't know exactly."

"But?"

"The last one to join before me arrived just after the war."

"What war?"

"World War II."

"That was...so you're saying there were 90 year-olds who looked like they were in their 30s?"

"They were the youngest."

Garth's elbow fell off the table. "And you think this is an explanation?" His whisper was a hiss now. "Something repaired the telomeres on your chromosomes?"

"Maybe keeps repairing," Ethan muttered as he printed a report so he wouldn't have to stare at the brightly lit screen. After spreading it out next to the reports from his pockets, he studied the first verifiable evidence behind a two-year theory. One blurry gray line that should have been a different shade and some fluorescent chromosome ends that were too long.

"It's a variance not before identified in human karyotypes and the undamaged telomeres of a child," Garth summarized.

"There are probably other smaller changes, but that's going to take a different view," Ethan added.

"Speaking of which," Garth pulled a packet of swabs from his pocket. "I think I may have the genotype software tweaked, but I need another sample."

"Really?"

"I mean, you woke me up leaving before five this morning, which is the worst time to go back to sleep. So. I had to do something."

Unable to argue that, Ethan took the swab and paused with it part way to his mouth. "Careful with this. I still don't understand how it was originally transmitted."

When Garth nodded, he ran the swab along the inside of his cheek and recapped it himself. "And don't leave it out where it can get mixed up with the others."

"Yeah, that might be hard to explain. Although if it comes back with an error message, it'll just be assumed it's degraded or user error or something."

Ethan reached back to the computer to copy the results from the florescent microscope to his own archives and delete it from the common drive.

While he worked, Garth's heartbeat accelerated, and he opened and closed his mouth without saying anything.

"You might as well say whatever it is you're not saying." Waiting for him to say it was worse.

"How do you do that?" Garth's stool squeaked.

"Your heart rate keeps jumping."

"You can hear my heartbeat?"

He kept his eyes on the screen, "Anytime there's not so much other noise to drown it out." He was pretty sure he'd admitted as much before, but it held extra weight after yesterday.

"I just…want to help. Handling addiction alone isn't a good thing to try."

Ethan shook his head.

"See, I was gonna wait, but you asked first."

Ethan fought down anger at Garth, at himself, at the whole situation. "There's nothing to help with. You can't–I can't–fix it."

"I know. But you're not denying it anymore, and they say that's the first step."

The glare Ethan shot him was flat and cool.

"I know it isn't the same, ok? I don't know your experience, any more than you know mine, really. But you can't do it alone, I do know that, and this isn't exactly a story you're going to share with anyone else right now, am I right? So, we start here. You can talk to me, maybe I just listen or maybe I can help with the temptation."

"Which can include *you*." It just slipped out. Or maybe he wanted to see if it was possible to bring the fear back.

"I get it," Garth answered with barely a missed beat, "But I'm not scared of you, ok?"

"Maybe you should be."

"Maybe…but I'm going with this for now. What makes it harder?"

Ethan turned away, rubbing his eyes. "I don't know, Garth."

Garth's wait for more was unsettling in its patience.

"It wasn't exactly an issue before. We drank it once a month, a single cup. In between there was no access to…humans. The only time I ever drank it outside of that was when I was significantly injured."

"Oh. Ok. Injured?"

Ethan only nodded.

"How? Why then?"

"I heal more quickly than before, but I think my metabolism must go up when healing a wound, because I'm…hungrier."

"And *that* blood is better for…?"

"It's more…yes." He stood up, knocking his stool into the wall.

"Yeah, ok," Garth leaned back. "Thank you for sharing."

I didn't sign up for an AA session.

Garth continued to summarize, "So ample supply is a new problem. But avoiding hunger is helpful?"

Even when Ethan avoided answering, Garth caught some hint of an affirmative.

"Then yay Chinatown. Ok…Oh." He looked at his phone and squeaked. "I'm late for a lecture–Good thing we're in this building or I'd lose them to the 15 minute rule!" He jumped up with a hurried promise to return to the topic later.

Ethan returned to the empty Miller lab and worked until the never-ending light and noise overwhelmed his attempts at concentration. He left the lab but paused in the stairwell. The idea of entering the crowded subway didn't seem a much better option for decompressing.

Instead, he dropped down five flights of stairs, grasped the handrail, and swung around the last half-flight to land on the thin rubber soles of his shoes on the bottom stair. The door to the basement was locked, but not well, and opened under his shove.

Flickering lights lit the abandoned dank hall, but he found a panel of switches that shut them all off. The residual light from the stairwell was adequate to weave around the collection of old wheelchairs and assorted broken medical equipment. When he made a right turn and closed a fire door, it gradually, wonderfully, faded to utter darkness.

Relieved of the burden of constant sight, he felt lighter. Sounds were muted and there was even a damp coolness. There were no expectations, no one to hide from. Just darkness.

The darkness beckoned him to explore its depths, so he answered with a click from his throat and listened to the echoes off the harsh floor and walls.

LIFEBLOOD

34

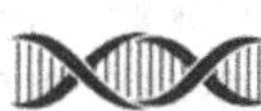

David Seeley hummed the opening lines to "Look Down" from *Lés Mis* as he moseyed into the basement of the medical towers.

The lights were out.

He stopped short of bursting into song at the chorus to listen instead. This wasn't his usual post, but he was pretty sure it was right for the basement to be empty and unusual for it to be completely dark.

Since he was alone, there was no need to pretend he couldn't see with the light from the stairwell glowing under the door, but the Maglite was a good tool to surprise someone up to no good. It was also the heaviest thing in his belt and thus the best weapon he was allowed, so he pulled it from his belt and held it, off, in his hand as he edged into the darkness.

After a couple turns and long stretches of hall, the darkness did become absolute, but all was still quiet.

Or…Wait. Was that clicking? It almost sounded like…But he hadn't heard anyone use that particular sound in ages. He stopped and leaned an ear slightly forward, listening.

The sound stopped. Was that a breath?

Time to stop playing around.

He clicked on his flashlight. "Campus security. Who's down here?"

Twin points just below his eye level reflected the light.

He froze and watched his vision sharpen. "What are you–"

The shadow was moving at him before he could finish his sentence.

Seeley dropped the flashlight to keep it from swinging around and messing up his own vision, set his feet, and extended his fists while the other vampire took two quick steps up the wall to spin a kick aimed at his head from above. A quick duck saved Seeley's face, but the foot still connected with one of his broad shoulders and knocked his punch wide.

Seeley cursed and spun to face the vampire whose momentum had taken him over his head to land lightly on the floor. Fangs bared in a hiss, he launched back at Seeley, spinning in close and leading with those fangs.

"Woah, take it easy!" Seeley managed to connect a punch to his jaw but cut his hand on the bared teeth. Without taking time to reset, Seeley kicked out. It made the other leap back to avoid his kick and put him partially in the beam of light.

A Columbia ID hung from his shirt pocket.

"You work here? Wait!" Seeley extended both hands in front of him and took a step back, trying to avert another charge. "I'm a security guard. I work here too! You're a professor?" He tilted his head to read the ID card on the still crouching vampire. "How have I never seen you before? Never mind, it doesn't matter." He slid back further, hands still up. "Just hold on half a second! Dr...Dalton?"

His blue eyes bore into Seeley. "You work here?" It was a hiss.

"Yes!" Seeley gestured to his own uniform and ID badge. "For six years now."

"What?" Dalton's expression twisted.

"I know it's not that long, in the grand scheme, but it's worked out pretty well. Nothing compared to what you've managed, apparently. You hang out with all the other doctors and professors? How does that work? Hold on—"

Dalton bolted down the hall, and Seeley started to follow but then rolled his sore shoulder and thought better of it. If all he'd seen was the guy's behavior and confusion, Seeley would have sworn he was a young one. But young ones didn't fight like that.

The army had taught Seeley to fight, in his first life. That Dalton guy fought like a vampire—like an *old* vampire, with all the flipping, leaping, and leading with his teeth.

Seeley stooped to pick up his flashlight and examined his bleeding knuckles. At least he couldn't complain about being bored tonight.

⸙

Ethan's chest was in a vice. Surely his ribs would crack from the pressure. Or maybe he'd break in half.

It was quiet in his dark corner, since the tapping steps of the security guard's boots had retreated. No one else had entered his hiding place. Nothing lingered out in the black void. Still he couldn't breathe. The world became a nebulous vapor as reality morphed around him.

How is there one here?

There was no denying what the guard was. It hadn't even taken his eyes changing to see it. He was quiet, quick, comfortable with the dark. And he looked like one. A vampire.

No!

Ethan had rushed him without thinking, as if to beat a ghost out of his world. He didn't belong. This wasn't supposed to be that world.

But there was more.

Six years.

Ethan didn't want to believe him, but he'd said it like it was common knowledge. Implied that it could have been longer.

There had been a vampire in New York years before Ethan had even left for Romania.

How is that possible?

How is any of it possible?

It changed everything.

There was no true escape.

What now?

With enormous effort, he inhaled and forced his brain to re-engage. Everything had changed, and yet nothing had.

He had to keep searching for the source of his transformation. If vampires had spread throughout the world, if they lived around him, in this city, that only highlighted the importance of understanding what created them.

It also meant one other thing. Someone else was living the same way he was trying to—had for at least six years. So maybe it was possible. Maybe he, a vampire, could still live as Ethan Dalton had.

35

Something was buzzing. His phone. *Where on earth is that thing?*

Ethan found the right desk by feeling for vibration but then had to shuffle through papers and pick up a couple open books to find it on the flaking desktop at the bottom of a stack. It stopped buzzing as soon as it was in his hand.

Four missed calls from Garth. *Shoot.* Garth. What was he going to tell Garth?

Answerless, he hit the button to redial, tucked the phone between his ear and shoulder, and turned back to the microscope.

"Oh, good, you are alive," Garth's tinny voice blared through the phone.

Right, no need to hold it. Ethan dropped his shoulder and let the phone fall to land face up on the desk beside the microscope. The clock on the screen showed 9:23 a.m.

Oh. "Yeah…"

"Sorry. Not that you need to check in…or that I really need to know where you are…but, did you decide not to come back, or…"

"No. Just got caught up. I'm in Hammer building, third floor, 309, virology lab," Ethan reported, eyes still shifting between the microscope and his laptop screen.

Nothing. He would tell Garth nothing about the other vampire. Not yet.

"Virology? Sure, why not? Um…Can I come over?"

"Yes. Please."

"Ok…I'll see you in like, an hour…"

"Ok." Ethan hit the red button with his thumb and paused.

205

9:24 a.m.

Is someone else going to come in here? No—the phone also said it was Saturday. *Good.* He picked up another slide and paused.

Garth already knew more than he'd intended. He would wait until he had more answers to say anything else. Until then, he'd keep him away from any other vampires. Too many humans he valued had died at their hands already.

ꓘ

Ethan heard Garth's footsteps enter just over an hour later. "Huh," Garth took in the state of the room. "I guess that answers the question of where you were last night."

"Sorry. Lost track of time." After the world had ended in the basement, Ethan had come to the virology lab to find more answers.

"Clearly. Did you find anything interesting?"

"Maybe." Ethan looked up for the first time and took a breath to try to organize his thoughts. Garth was holding out a thermos and an orange. "Thank you," he accepted them.

The thermos smelled like pig blood, not coffee.

He looked back at Garth.

"What? I can pour," Garth defended. "But I don't know the rules of how to warm it up, so it's cold."

"That's fine—thank you," Ethan repeated. He'd found that he could mitigate some of the refrigerated staleness from the blood by warming it slightly, but he wasn't going to be picky today.

"Do you want to show me what is going on in here that's kept you busy all night?" Garth asked.

"Yeah." Ethan set the thermos down on top of a book and pointed to some petri dishes lined with pink agar balanced on the edge of the desk. "Bacterial cultures. Blood and oral."

"Yours?" Garth verified as he bent to examine them.

"Yes."

"There's nothing growing."

"Right."

"When did you start them?"

"At the beginning of the week."

"Blood should be sterile, but why is there nothing on the oral ones?"

"Not sure, but I moved to viral cultures."

"That explains why we're in *here*."

"I needed a cell line for the culture," Ethan agreed with a glance across the room at the biological safety cabinet covered with a filter-containing hood. That was where he'd avoided contamination while carefully inoculated several cultures. "I started them…13 hours ago." He gestured to the slide on the microscope, "and I'm already getting cytopathic effects."

Garth bent over to peer into the microscope eyepieces and reached to dial the light up brighter. "The cells are broken–lysed. That's a sign of viral infection."

"Yes. I'm also running plaque assays." Ethan pointed to a pile of petri dishes lined with a purple substance. Some were full of holes like Swiss cheese.

"These show the same thing as the lysed cells, right? Evidence of a virus?"

Ethan had done more work with viruses in the past and had also taken advantage of a couple textbooks overnight. "Evidence of viral infection. Each clear bubble is an area where the virus killed the cells and spread further."

"There are quite a few holes here."

"It's fast. But it takes a decent dose to cause an infection at least. I did a gradual dilution." He pointed to a pile of plates at one side that had no holes as evidence.

"This virus is from your mouth?"

"Blood. Those are saliva," he pointed to another stack. "The results are more mixed–not every one shows virus. I don't know why."

"Somehow you have no bacteria in your body, but there's a virus in your blood. What is it?"

Another point of his finger at several sets of plastic dishes. Each contained multiple wells with a clear fluid in them. "I ran ELISAs. All negative."

"Testing for specific viruses with known antibodies? Yes, ok, which one's did you check for?"

"Everything I could find a reagent for in all the rooms I have access to. And one I didn't."

Garth paused. "All negative."

"Yes."

Tracking with him now, Garth summarized, "So there's a virus, but you can't identify it with the tests we have for known viruses. You think this is it, don't you? You were thinking virus from the beginning."

"There aren't many natural processes that can introduce new nucleotides into a cell. And it's the only thing that I've found so far. It could be inconsequential, but why is there one virus, and nothing else?" He leaned back in his chair. "The process that changed my DNA was triggered by something transmitted by a bite. Symptoms started less than 24 hours later. I have no way to be sure, but I think Jack would have died within another day or two, unless there was something that could have been done to counter it. This virus would be transmissible, and," Ethan gestured to the slide on the microscope again, "fast acting. What is harder to understand is how a virus would have changed the DNA in my cells rather than just use them for replication that would kill them, like a virus normally would. Like it did in Jack. Maybe it's something specific to my genome, some marker or compatibility…"

Garth nodded slowly. "What's next?"

"I took a tissue sample to see if there is still virus in the cells, spun it down," he pointed to a couple test tubes sitting upright in a tray. "I need the electron microscope to visualize the virus."

"You know Steve works over there some. You could ask him. Wait, tissue sample from where?"

"I just cut a little wedge of skin and muscle." His shirtsleeves were rolled up, so he rotated his left forearm to show a large band-aid.

"Ow."

"It's fine. It won't take long to heal. I want to sequence the viral DNA, or RNA, but I'm going to have trouble separating the viral genetic information from mine since the software won't identify mine as human." Ethan picked up the orange and tossed it between his hands. "Since it seems to take a decent dose of the virus to be infective, small exposures shouldn't be worrisome, which means you're safe to wash my dishes…" His train of thought was abruptly arrested by another idea that made the orange a focus of study.

"What?" Garth prodded when he didn't continue. "What's with the orange?"

"Just a theory," he said faintly.

"About?"

"Why there's only virus in some saliva samples." He stopped short of bringing the whole orange to his mouth with a glance at Garth.

"I don't care, bite it. So why?"

Opening his mouth nearly as wide as the orange, Ethan sank his elongated canines into the orange skin and held it there, noting the squeezing sensation along the sides of his upper jaw where he thought saliva glands would be. He pulled the orange from his mouth without sucking up much juice, and pondered it again. "What if the saliva released with a bite is what contains the virus?"

"You mean like when you bite down?"

"It would ensure a concentrated dose when someone is bitten. And explain why a bite turns someone and a kiss doesn't."

"We know that?"

Still staring at the orange with his bite impression in its thick skin, Ethan started to reach into the cabinet above his head but then remembered what had happened the last time he'd done that.

"Could you get another plate from in there?" he asked Garth.

Garth eyed the cabinet directly above Ethan's chair. "From there?"

"Yes, please. I'm going to compare this to a sample from my regular saliva."

Garth figured it out as he disengaged the cabinet's safety mechanism to open it. "Ooh, this is a UV sterilized cabinet. But the light goes off as soon as you open it."

"It actually takes a second."

Garth squinted one eye in thought. "Was that a problem?"

Ethan held out his right forearm, which bore a raw linear red line.

"Oh man! That looks like it hurts." Garth angled his head sideways to study Ethan's arm closer.

"Yes, it does."

"It is UV that you react to."

"I think that's confirmed, yeah."

"Well, now I know you're not joking about sun exposure. Did it get your cheek too?" Garth reached toward his face.

Ethan flinched and snatched Garth's hand before it reached him.

"Sorry, sorry! My bad! Ouch, that's a grip."

Ethan released his hand as abruptly as he'd grabbed it. "Sorry."

"No, my fault for reaching into your space. I know it's a thing, it's fine."

Ethan shook that off. "My face was behind my arm, so yes, it's slightly burned. The light is pretty bright." It had taken an hour for the dark blob to fade from his vision after the flash of light, but he could see fine now. "Can you tell?"

"Uh…" Garth studied it from a cautious distance. "Not unless you know to look, I think."

"Ok, thanks." He set his arm back down on the table at an angle that avoided the burn.

"Are you ok?"

"Yeah, it's just pain. It'll heal, if a little slower than other stuff."

"Oh, what about the transilluminator in the lab?" Used in their lab to prep samples for DNA analysis, it also emitted UV light.

"The safety mechanism actually works on that, apparently."

"Huh," Garth grunted in a way that indicated he'd figured something out and handed down the specimen plate Ethan had asked for. "You can actually see the ultraviolet light. I can't see anything but a faint blue glow on the bulb. Hey, does the sun look different than it used to? Bluer?"

Had the sun looked more yellow before? The air seemed to thicken as he realized he couldn't quite remember what it had looked like before. He knew daylight hadn't always appeared as harshly bright, but suddenly he couldn't quite picture how it had been.

Apparently spotting some change in his expression, Garth attempted to buoy his tone. "It just makes the brightness level make more sense, if you can see a whole other light spectrum, you know, not earth shattering." He paused. "I wonder if you can see infrared…Anyway. Saliva swabs. Here we go."

After they had the new sets of purple lined plates inoculated with saliva from the orange and from his mouth, Ethan started straightening things up.

Until Garth's heart rate sped up for no apparent reason.

Ethan glanced at his chest. "What?"

Garth hesitated.

Not a good sign.

"This isn't about yesterday—or the day before—but my tenant in 2B is supposed to have finally moved out. The plan was always to get you your apartment back, and I think we can do that now. I could probably move up today even."

Related or not, a little more space would help him keep his new secret. "Good."

36

"What's the verdict?" Ethan asked once Garth had barged back into the basement apartment, momentarily flaring light in the dim room.

"Tenant–and dog–gone! It's all mine now. After I clean it." He made a face. "It's slightly unfortunate that I know her, because she shouldn't really get her whole deposit back."

The sun had been shining its possibly bluer rays across the street when they had jogged the short distance from the subway. Now Ethan felt caged in the basement, unable to escape circling thoughts about the other basement last night, and regretted leaving the lab. It was easier to pretend the world hadn't exploded when there was something to keep him busy. "Want help?"

"Uh, sun?"

"It doesn't take very long to walk up the front steps."

"The apartment has two windows."

Right. He dropped his chin back onto his fist.

Garth held up a finger. "But one has blinds still on it. And the other is on the alley side with only indirect sun, and we could cover with something like that," he pointed at the blanket that was still taped to the window, "If you're ok with the ambient light." He was starting to look hopeful at the idea of help.

The light level was still occasionally overwhelming, but the constant exposure to lights at the lab had built up his tolerance, and Garth wouldn't care if he wore his sunglasses. "It'll be fine."

"Sweet! Let me just…" He darted off.

A few minutes and two door slams later, he was back. "Ready!"

After retrieving his coat, hat, and sunglasses, Ethan followed Garth

211

out the door, up the few steps to the sidewalk, turned to bound up the Brownstone's broad front steps, and ducked through the main door into the narrow entrance beyond.

Garth slammed the mercifully windowless door behind him and turned to scrutinize Ethan. "Ok?"

"Still not fun, still not spontaneously bursting into flames," Ethan returned blandly.

"Just checking. Now that I know the UV thing is legit."

"If we lose the ozone layer I'm especially screwed," he retorted.

"Ha. No moving to Australia for you." Garth led the way up the creaking staircase to the empty second floor apartment.

One step over the threshold into the bright front room, the odor of wet dog smacked him in the face.

Garth mirrored his grimace. "I'm going back to my no pet policy."

"I'm good with that."

"So, I'm thinking since the bathroom is the windowless room, it may make sense for you to start in there."

"That's the most disgusting room, isn't it?" Ethan read right through that.

Garth's innocent look wasn't very innocent.

Unfortunately, given that he was wincing against the rays filtering through the blinds, the logic still held, so he shed his coat and hat onto the floor by the door, took the bathroom cleaner and brush, and retreated into the cramped dirty room.

As if scrubbing the grime off the bathtub could really distract him from last night's revelation and the questions that wouldn't stop invading his thoughts.

He crouched into the bathtub and sloshed a generous amount of bleach into the scummy tub. The fumes stung his nose, and the splash of bleach stabbed fire in his burned arm.

Dang that hurts. He leaned forward, braced himself against the tub, and shook out his arm. It wasn't a bad injury, barely enough to increase his appetite, but its naggingly persistent sting wasn't helping his state of mind.

As he recovered and started scrubbing, Garth continued muttering from the other room as if narrating, "Did you ever clean your kitchen? I'm a bachelor, and my counters are not this sticky. Why didn't I just get a cleaning service? Qualls, you are too cheap for your own good. Please, please, tell me you didn't leave crap in your fridge, ehhhh—whew empty, but then why does it still smell, gah! I need more bleach. And a mop. What is that? Is that blood? Tell me you didn't murder someone up here."

Ethan leaned out of the bleach fume filled bathroom and inhaled for the first time in two minutes. "Not blood."

A quiet pause. "Well, that is incredibly good to know. Thanks for that. But I still need to figure out how to get the stain of whatever isn't blood up. Can I have the bleach?"

A push sent the bottle sliding across the wood floor into the front room. Even with the bleach, scrubbing at the stained grout wasn't working, though. "I think the shower grout might be beyond saving!" Ethan remembered to raise his voice.

"Yeah, I thought that might be the case. As long as it's surface-layer clean, I can move in and then get someone to come fix it. I'm not stupid enough to do my own tile. Hey, I'm going to move your stuff!" Garth had been doing well speaking at a normal volume despite being in the other room, until that last statement. Then his voice moved to the bathroom doorway. "These yours? Wow, how much bleach did you use? How are you breathing?"

"I'm mostly not. I can hold my breath for a helpful amount of time. Yes, those are mine."

Garth shook the carton of cigarettes. "When did you start smoking?"

"The other day," he answered vaguely and kept scrubbing.

"It doesn't really work to try replacing one addiction with another." Garth's tone changed.

Ethan straightened and leaned back onto his heels. "It's not—I don't think I get anything from the nicotine. It was just a spur of the moment thing, something different…to taste."

Garth didn't look convinced. "So…just, as your landlord—"

"I'm not smoking in the apartment."

"It's just it would really affect—"

"Garth, I won't. I get it. Ok? It was just something else to do. Outside."

"Pretty sure 'something to do' is how addictions start."

Ethan shook his head and leaned back over to keep scrubbing. "It's not hurting anything."

"Except your lungs."

"I breathed coal smoke for two years with no apparent effect. I don't think the occasional cigarette is going to do it."

"Huh. Really?"

Ethan chucked the scrub brush into the bottom of the tub. "Yes."

But Garth was full into thinking-mode now. "Do you think the changes in your telomeres could affect the rates of cell mutation and cancer?"

"I don't know. Maybe. No one there seemed to have any issues."

"Apparently not, if they were…however old. Or maybe just better cell regeneration–how's your arm?"

Ethan was flinging his arm again, as if to shake off the sting. "Fine, I just splashed bleach everywhere." His T-shirt left both forearms bare for examination, and his left forearm bore only a small scab while the right still had the angry red line.

Garth pointed at the scab. "Is that the spot you cut this morning? You did say it would heal faster than the burn. Why is that?"

"I can only guess that something about the radiation damage takes longer to repair."

When Garth slid down to sit on the floor with his fingertips propped together, Ethan decided the bleach fume-filled bathroom wasn't where he wanted to have the impromptu brainstorming session and scooted out into the hall to join him.

"Or what if it's your immune system that is primarily different? Have you been sick, at all, since…"

"No. But I wasn't exposed to much–"

"You drink raw blood every day."

That was a valid point.

"You said all the cultures were completely sterile, but the human body isn't sterile. There are all kinds of bacteria that should be in places like your mouth, at least. How is it possible for an immune system to be that efficient? Can you imagine…"

Don't even go there. "We don't know enough yet, it could be a direct effect of the virus for all we know."

"Assuming that the virus is even what you think it is."

"Right. There's a long way to go."

Garth's head dropped back against the wall. "Still, it's quite something to be immune to illness, cancer, and aging…"

And they live everywhere. For lifetimes. Knowing how long they lived, why had he assumed no one had ever left? Or that his cave was the origin point? Why wouldn't they be all over?

But then how does no one know?

Ethan eyed Garth, who was still staring into space, and crawled back into the bathroom. "Just stop bugging me about the cigarettes."

"Oh yeah…fine. But it's not like you have to be a case study with them."

"Why do I have to explain myself to you?" Ethan shot back.

"Ok, ok," Garth eased back. "I'll leave you alone. I gotta find the mop."

า

After Garth declared the apartment clean enough, they started moving some of his stuff. At first, Garth piled some things into a box and moved it up to the narrow portico on the first floor where Ethan retrieved it and moved it the rest of the way up. When enough sunlight faded to leave Ethan more comfortable, he went down to the basement himself and started with a couple boxes of books.

After carrying one up, he came back to find Garth staring down at the second. "You know that's too heavy to actually move, right?"

Except it wasn't. "I'll hold the bottom." Ethan unceremoniously picked it up and moved to the door to the sound of Garth's sputtering. "You were there when we measured strength on the thing from PT," he called back.

"Yeah well…it's different in context."

That was true for a lot of things.

Garth wanted to leave most of the furniture, but Ethan made him take the bed. He promised to order his own because there was no way he was going with Garth to Ikea as he suggested. Until it was delivered, he'd use the couch. Or the floor. Or whatever.

Due to the narrow staircase, the mattress proved more difficult to get upstairs, but he managed to wrestle it through the door and into the single bedroom. As he stood there considering that they should have brought the bed frame up first, the scent of blood wafted into the room. The same exact scent as when Garth had cut himself with the razor.

Ethan dropped the mattress to the floor with a thud. "Garth! You ok?"

Only a scraping sound answered his call. He started for the open apartment door. "Garth?"

Garth's nose pushed around the edge of an upright boxspring as he hauled it into the room with a squeaky gasp. "Yeah?"

"You ok?"

"Yeah. Almost got stuck on the landing there, but made it. Couldn't let you entirely show me up."

Ethan scanned him, but he looked fine, so he eased back a step.

"Why?" Garth asked.

"Because…you're bleeding."

"I am? Are you sure? Are you sure it's me?" Garth let the boxspring lean against the doorframe and looked down at himself.

"...Yeah."

"I don't—oh, here," he held up his left thumb which bore a cut down the back. "There must be something sharp on the bottom of that or something. Didn't even notice. It's fine."

"Ok." Ethan made himself start toward the bedroom, but Garth's next question pulled him back.

"Are you saying that you not only can smell this amount of blood from the other room, over that bleach, but you can recognize it as mine?"

"Yes," Ethan answered stiffly. "Apparently. It's...familiar, from before."

"Huh, mental note, if I ever get kidnapped, definitely leaving you a blood trail. Hey—"

Ethan started mentally cursing Garth's persistence.

"You said something about this being a bigger issue when you're hurt. Does your arm count?"

"I'm fine. Here, give me that."

Garth started to reach back to the boxspring but stopped to suck the beads of blood off his knuckle.

Cursing his own brain, Ethan shook his head as though to physically banish that image and spun back to the bedroom.

"Oh, shoot, that was—stupid. Sorry! I'll be back..." Garth stammered from behind him until footfalls sounding down the steps announced his retreat.

Letting himself groan aloud, Ethan kept moving, dragging the boxspring into the bedroom and returning downstairs.

When he met Garth outside again, he sported a new band-aid on his hand. "I'm sorry about that, it was really inconsiderate."

"It's fine," Ethan kept walking down the basement stairs.

"I mean if someone taunted me like that..."

That made him pause mid-step. It didn't seem possible that Garth could understand at all, not with what all Ethan hadn't told him, but then he said something relevant and made Ethan second guess his assumption. Maybe it wasn't so bad that he knew what he did. "It's fine." He stepped down the last stair. "It's your thumb. How many times have you done that without thinking? Let's just move on."

37

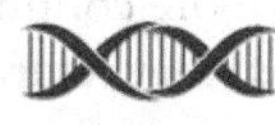

The windows of the old church were narrow but reached as tall as the arched roof and were many in number. Thus, Caterina only emerged from her hiding place in the ancient stone walls once the sun had set and no longer cast its glare through the glass onto the whitewashed dome above the hall. At the late hour, she could perch on the balcony next to a hanging tapestry, behind one of the pillars standing sentry along the hall, and watch the few humans who lingered below on the wooden floor among the pews.

As she had not been in Brasov, now a large city within sight of the ancient mountains, when the church had been built, she did not know whether she or it were older.

Lifetimes of men before, her people's reign had extended further from the cave into the world. The vampires were known to men, welcomed in strongholds of dark stone during the day, and paid much tribute by some to protect their lands.

In many of the towns at the base of their mountains there were similar simpler buildings–churches, built for worship and also for safety. There people often fled for refuge from the raids from other men. In such a time, in such a stronghold, her lord had given her life.

As time marched on over these lands, some men who dared to stop their tribute would take sanctuary in these churches from the retribution of the *strigoi*. Only once in living memory was such a retreat successful.

Ranks of vampires had surrounded one secluded village that lay in the shadow of the ridge of mountains to the north. They had advanced to find each house empty. At the center of the village there was a whitewashed stone building bearing a cross on the domed roof and another on the barred door. It was there that the whole of the town had gathered together and whispered their prayers and songs as their attackers silently advanced to raze it to the ground.

Though the doors had been mere wood, they had not given way under the charge of the vampire warriors. The iron lock would not break under any blow. The wood shingle roof would not light from the fire of their torches. When her lord had reached his own hand to the door, the cross carved upon it had burned his hand as if alight from the sun. Those who tried after him were burned the same way, until the sun itself was just below the horizon.

They had abandoned the small town to its church. Through the ages, before they had become more confined to their stronghold, there had been those who argued that they return. Those who had been there never agreed.

Somehow the legend had persistently followed the tales of the *strigoi*, but those muttering their soft prayers below were not safe from her.

She had no reason to harm them this night. It had come time to abandon her role as ghost in the cathedral towers. For two cycles of the moon she had lingered, listening, learning, remembering. There was no need to hurry. The observations had taught her tongue the nuances of the Romanian language that was now spoken and reminded her of what she knew of several other languages as well. She observed the humans' movements and interactions, their use of known and new machines.

As a whole, these humans were not so different from those with whom she had interacted so long ago; although certainly the way they functioned was not the same. The knowledge she gained in Brasov would allow her to move about and effectively follow Etan in the new vast and noisy world.

She could not know for certain where he had fled, but she knew where she would begin her search. Caterina ran her finger along the small stiff card she held in her hand. Reading was another skill she labored to recover. The symbols she had once read had changed in form more drastically than the spoken languages, yet she had worked these words, in Etan's first tongue, to their meaning.

"Department of Genetics and Development. Columbia University Medical Center. New York, New York."

PART III
A NEW WORLD

38

"Send Jon in there."

Feeling a stab of betrayal, Jon looked at his upper-level resident across the nursing desk. "Why have I got to stab the old gal?"

Taylor pointed at him. "*That's* why. Right there. Your accent will charm her and get her to give up some blood."

The nurse standing next to him started to nod.

"And we're running short…" Taylor trailed off, clearly wanting to avoid the topic they were all trying to avoid.

Jon felt fear try to creep up the back of his neck.

"Here," Taylor handed him a stack of blood collection tubes, needles, and tourniquets. "Just go lay on the British all thick and get back here before the trauma gets here." Taylor gave him a pat on the arm as he left.

It sent sharp pains into the ache in Jon's shoulder.

"You ok?" the nurse asked. He didn't remember her name but knew she'd worked in the emergency department long enough that she knew what she was doing better than he did.

"Fine." He started for the curtain-enclosed area where the elderly lady in question was. As a first-year resident in a New York City hospital, grunt work like drawing blood was practically his job description, so being assigned to it was no surprise. The troublesome part of the job was the patient. Violet Mince had been in the ER at least once a month since Jon had started rotating there, and she was well known to refuse most recommended medical treatments and complain about the rest.

Taking a deep breath hurt in his chest a bit. Everything was sore, but his persistent pounding headache and the chest pain had him thinking that, to top off the week, he was probably coming down with something as well.

Nothing for it. Go on.

Jon brushed past the curtain and leaned into his London accent as instructed, "Afternoon, Violet. I'm Dr. Holloway. I need to get a bit of blood from ya so we can get you feeling better again."

She turned her watery eyes up at him. "Ooh, you're a new one here, aren't you?"

"Yes'm. Started a few months ago." He sat on the squeaky rolling stool next to her narrow cot, set the supplies down on the blanket that covered her legs, and put on some nitrile gloves. "May I see your arm?"

She actually gave it to him without argument. Now, if he could just find a vein somewhere under that papery skin that would bleed enough to fill his four tubes.

"Where are you from?" she predictably asked.

"I grew up in London. Came to New York for medical school." Every vein that looked like a candidate was already covered with a purple bruise.

"I look like a pincushion, don't I? That one is still tender."

"I'm sorry," he laid her arm gently back down and leaned over to look at her other hand.

She heaved a sigh. "I know I'm a bother. I just don't want to die alone like Janice…"

Jon stopped and took her hand, to hold it rather than examine it. "You're not alone, Violet."

Not like Pete. And Jake.

Jon's other hand gripped the cot's side rail.

A tear dripped from Violet's eye. "Can you stay with me?"

He blinked hard. "As long as it takes me to get blood. But I'll come back to check on you. And at this rate, it'll be some time before I can find a good vein, so no worries."

⇗

The slate-colored sky still glowed enough to make Ethan blink and wish for sunglasses as he followed Garth out of the hospital building onto the sidewalk. Dread consolidated in his stomach with every step toward the bar around the block.

"Why are you so tense about this?" Garth crossed the street next to him with a throng of other pedestrians.

Ethan had been informed that the lab-wide outing for Abby's birthday was not optional. He probably should have been grateful to Garth for getting it changed from lunch to drinks after work, but at the moment he just wished he could have gotten out of the whole thing. "I don't know how to be...social."

"Now that doesn't make sense. You talk to these people all day long. How is it different in a bar?"

"Different rules..."

"Rules?"

Yes, rules. He'd maybe regained a grip on the old rules associated with the lab, but going out with people constituted totally different rules–any guy who'd ever gone out on a date with a coworker should know as much.

The bar door jingled as they entered. Although the bar wasn't brightly lit, it buzzed with conversations, clinking glasses, TV screens showing news or sports or financials–too much to take in at once, and too much to tune out. Overwhelmed by it, Ethan followed Garth to the raised bar where he'd spotted the rest of their team.

Being forced to take a seat on a stool with his back to the constantly changing environment of strange noises didn't make him less jumpy. After he'd glanced over his shoulder for the fourth time, Garth leaned over and asked, "Ok?"

"Yeah. A lot of noises," he replied and tried again to focus on Garth to his left, and Dr. Miller and the rest of their team seated on stools to his right, while the back of his mind insisted that there were too many potential threats in the room. Acknowledging the existence of vampires in New York had put him on constant alert.

The bartender asked him for an order.

When Ethan hesitated, Garth jumped in, "He's got some wine selections back there."

"If you describe what you like, I can pick something, sir," the barkeeper added.

That was achievable, wasn't it? "Uh, thanks. How about a red with some bite, not too sweet."

"Very good, sir, and for you?" He turned to Garth.

"Sweet tea, Wes. Thanks!"

Oh. Garth had gotten their outing changed to drinks, but didn't drink now...Because of the drug history?

"No, I don't drink, but he'll actually brew the tea sweet," Garth answered his unspoken question and flashed him a look that said it didn't matter because the tea was a big deal. "Also, can't beat bar snacks." He added a mumbled, "sorry," and subtly pointed at the hat Ethan still wore.

"It blocks that screen," Ethan whispered with a tilt of his head at the flashing TV above them.

"Fine."

Barkeeper Wes returned with a small amount of red liquid in a stemmed glass and offered it to Ethan to taste. Ethan inhaled at the rim of the glass without drinking and answered, "That'll be fine, thank you."

"Abby, you mentioned wanting to try wine," Dr. Miller added, "Why don't we follow the connoisseur's pick?"

"You may not like–" Ethan started.

She brushed that off, "I should try something new now and then."

He could at least remember how to buy women a drink. "Bring the bottle then, Wes?"

The bartender nodded and retrieved a maroon bottle to set in front of Ethan and two more glasses for the ladies.

Ethan picked up the open bottle and leaned across Dr. Miller to serve Abby first. "I'm afraid I'm not a bartender with portions memorized," he confessed but nevertheless smoothly poured the wine into her glass with a twist at the end to stop the flow and moved to serve Dr. Miller without a spilled drop. Once he'd served himself, they all toasted to Abby's birthday.

Settled onto his stool, canted back slightly to let Garth talk past him to the girls and Rav, he listened to their chitchat, pretended this was his world again, and tried not to let it startle him every time the door opened or the waitress clinked glasses behind him. They were still talking about research stuff, but what else did they ever really talk about? Even Dr. Miller had relaxed her demeanor and laughed at something Garth said.

There was still had half a bottle of wine in front of him, so when the ladies' glasses were empty, he leaned forward to refill them.

"Half portion this time, please," Dr. Miller requested.

Ethan nodded as he served her. *"My Lady."*

No, that's not right.

Her kind, intelligent eyes raised in question of the Romanian title. *Not at all.*

He wasn't there, and it was as blasphemy to use that title, the title he wanted to strike from his mind, on Dr. Miller.

I shouldn't be here.

Without another word, he set the bottle down on the bar, slid from his stool, picked up the coat draped across the back of it, and exited out the door into the chill air outside.

That's why, Garth, he ranted in his mind. *Because I wasn't good at social things before, and now all the rules are mixed up in my crazy brain.*

Snowflakes danced in the headlights and the streetlight above him. Higher in the sky, no stars shone brightly enough to overcome the city lights, but a nearly full moon managed to break through. He held onto the sight for a moment. The moon had always been new, or nearly so, when they ventured from the cave, so it was the first full one he had seen in some time.

Realizing that everyone else standing on the sidewalk was smoking or talking on the phone, he pulled a cigarette from the pack in his coat pocket and lit it with a single flick of his lighter. The taste of smoke mixed with wine. It wasn't the same, but why did he crave the things he'd sought for so long to escape?

Because he'd been striving to ignore background noise like the jingle of the bell on the door, it failed to warn him of Dr. Miller's arrival. She spotted him with a wave.

Ethan dropped the cigarette and stamped on the butt.

"No need to stop on my account." She stopped next to him and looked out into the street. "I may spend half my day educating patients on avoiding risky habits, but I'm not hypocritical enough to lecture my colleagues on their coping mechanisms."

Unsure if he had exhaled the last breath of smoke, he turned his head away to avoid blowing any in her face. "I'm sorry," he said stiffly.

"For what? It sounded nice."

"It wasn't meant..." *for you.*

"It's ok. There's no need to explain. I convinced Garth to let me come out instead of him, because I know he would try to get you to go back in there, but I'm not. Not that you need my permission to leave, of course."

"Why?" He leaned back against the brick wall behind him and whispered it to the snowflakes.

"None of us knows what you've been through." She mimicked his posture. "So who are we to tell you how to deal with it? How to get back to 'normal'?"

She stayed that way for a while, watching the snow rather than him without prodding him to break the silence. Her shiver broke the spell, but as he turned to address her, she stopped him. "It's ok. I should go back in for Abby, and I'll see you back in there, or I'll see you tomorrow, either way, ok?"

Somehow her permission did affect how he felt about remaining outside. Relieved of the burden of immediately returning, he lit another cigarette and let his swirling thoughts follow the snow as it burned down. When the thoughts kept coming back to Dr. Miller, he made the decision to go back inside and focus on the people in front of him rather than the ghosts in his head.

The inside of the bar wasn't any easier to relax in, but Garth had scooted over a stool, so he took up the one on the outside of the group, gave contributory nods once in a while, and finished his wine. Mercifully, since the next day was also a work day, no one was set on the gathering being an all-night thing. Less than half an hour later, Ethan followed Garth back out into the night.

The snow had stopped. Shadows clung here and there to the buildings wherever the lights failed to completely shine around a corner or under an overhang.

The alley across the street had a deep hole darker than the surrounding shadow.

"...subway right there?" Garth's voice vied for his attention.

"Go ahead. I just thought of something I want to check at the lab."

"I can come—"

"I'll meet you at home." Ethan didn't look back until he'd crossed the street, and then just to make sure Garth hadn't followed.

The hole in the shadow consolidated into a figure blacker than the darkness. It stepped forward out of the alley, shadows clinging to the billowing coat and hood, and stopped on the sidewalk out of the direct streetlight. The black coat, shined dress shoes, and manicured hands became instantly more distinct as Ethan's vision sharpened.

Vampires lived in New York City.

And apparently not all of them wore innocuous security guard uniforms.

Ethan stopped in the middle of the sidewalk and brought his weight forward onto the balls of his feet. He drew his knife into the palm of his hand and held it hidden with the blade up against the back of his arm.

The specter dropped his hood back to reveal neatly styled black hair and a deliberate shadow of a beard. Jet black eyes lingered at Ethan's knife hand. "This isn't the way first meetings usually go." His smooth voice emanated from lips that appeared to naturally sneer up at the edges, showing the tips of his elongated canines when he spoke.

And how is that?

"Interesting," the vampire continued when Ethan didn't answer or so much as twitch in response. "You're not at all what I expected to find in a new vampire who just appeared in my city. Who are you?"

"I don't answer to you," Ethan hissed softly.

"In that case, it may be time to introduce myself." His manner was relaxed but superior, and his speech was that of a practiced politician. "I am Caspian. You are in my city. All vampires here do, as you say, 'answer' to me, in some way."

Vampires. Real in New York City as well as Romania. The world was upside down.

"Who turned you?"

Turned. Not the English interpretation he'd been imagining. Too trite. He remained silent. Strangers didn't get to just claim authority.

"Not feeling conversational? Well then, I'll go. What do I know about you, Dr. Ethan Dalton?"

Ethan blinked.

"I know what the news said. You disappeared, presumed dead for over two years, and now, poof! You're back. Ever the smart doctor of–genetics, wasn't it? And, clearly, a vampire. It leaves quite a bit to the imagination. I'm sure there's a fascinating story there."

Not one I'm interested in sharing.

Caspian's black eyes ventured to a point behind him. "And you told a human."

The knife hilt swiveled in his hand to drop the point down as Ethan darted a look back to an empty subway entrance and took a step to square himself between Caspian and the stairs Garth had descended.

"That's your pressure point, then. Interesting again. Calm, I'm not going after him for it, but we will need to discuss the rules."

"What do you want? I'm not going with you." It took strange deliberation to speak the words in English.

"You mean besides answers? But never mind, I'll have them eventually," Caspian sighed dramatically and spread his hands. "You don't have to come, I suppose–although the subway is about to empty, and you are presenting an interesting spectacle at the moment. If you cannot calm your eyes, at least sheath the sword."

The concrete under his feet hummed at the arrival of the train beneath. Not eager to draw attention either, Ethan moved his knife into the folds of his coat and, to spite Caspian, pushed down emotion far enough to change his eyes.

"There is more to you than meets the eye." Caspian's mouth

sneered into a smile. "As I said, you don't have to come anywhere, but be aware you're shunning a good time. No? Then for now the only thing you *must* do is abide by the code."

Ethan gave a silent snarl.

The smile disappeared. "Calm. I won't have to be the one to kill you if you don't follow it. It's simple: No one is to know what you are. It seems you may have broken it already, but assuming that mousy fellow who follows you everywhere is the only exception, it can be permitted."

Rules.

"Is he the only one?" Caspian pressed.

"Yes," Ethan answered primarily to protect Garth.

"Good." Caspian relaxed his posture again. "Just think of the alternative, if the general public knew. Good, I can see you have. At least I'm not dealing with an imbecile. If you continue this charade, make it a good one. When you can't any longer, you can still come to me. If you kill anyone, don't let it reach the point of alerting the authorities—otherwise I will get involved. If you are injured, do not, under any circumstance, seek traditional medical care. I don't know what you study with your fellow doctors of philosophy in there, but it cannot be anything related to your new self. Consider what history the scientific community has with that which is not understood or expected."

Ethan swallowed.

"Discovery cannot be allowed, and especially not in this avenue. Understood?"

Ethan gave a single nod before trying a wary step away.

"Yes, fine, I won't stop you leaving. Just know, now that you've brought him into it," he nodded toward the subway entrance, "The same rules apply."

Only the pedestrian walking behind him kept Ethan from baring his teeth.

"I do wish you'd reconsider your standoffishness." Caspian shrugged. "Oh well, for when you do need help," he extended a business card toward Ethan and, when Ethan didn't move, flicked it to lodge against his shoe on the sidewalk.

Without retrieving it, Ethan stepped further away and left the card to skitter away in the breeze. "Don't follow me."

"I don't have to," Caspian stepped back to rejoin the shadows.

<h1 style="text-align:center">39</h1>

Smoke wafted up from the snuffed cigarette butt and mixed in a swirl with the condensation from Ethan's breath, dancing with the invisible questions.

Caspian. With his billowing hooded coat and cold superior tone, he seemed to represent everything Ethan had fled to return to New York, where he wanted nothing to do with the world he'd left. He wanted only to live here, to be what he'd been.

But, like him, the world wasn't all it appeared.

Ethan had stalled by the side door to the research building, perfectly still, contemplating what answers were worth. He wouldn't go with Caspian, but he needed to know something.

So, in an instant, he leaped forward, slowing only for as long as it took the electronic lock to read his key card.

The object of his current question was not difficult to find. When Ethan spotted him sitting casually at the security desk just around the corner from the door, he retreated into the stairwell and left only the sound of the door latch closing behind him.

It was enough to draw his quarry's attention, and soon there was the tap of boots in the hall outside, disembodied footsteps without any other sound accompanying them. The stairwell door opened inwards, admitting the broad-shouldered guard. When his glance up found Ethan balanced in a squat on the stairwell railing one landing up from the door, he stopped short and deliberately dropped his hands into an open posture. "I wondered if you'd be back."

"As you said, I work here."

"Ah, I get some conversation this time. Neat."

"Who are you?" Ethan wanted answers, not conversation.

"David Seeley, campus security guard," his hand gestured as if presenting. "And you?"

"How long have you been here?"

"One sided conversation, huh? Well, I've been in the city for about twenty years. It's a little easier to get around here than most places, you may have noticed."

"Where did you come from?"

Seeley sighed and crossed his arms. "I was turned in Spain, on the way back from 'Nam, technically. Made it back to Pennsylvania before I was all in. You know normally, in conversations, there's a little back and forth."

Ethan snarled a soft hiss. "Who did you tell about me?"

"No one–"

"Then why did he show up right after I ran into you?" Ethan dropped to the landing and stepped down one stair.

Seeley loosened his arms and straightened. "I don't know what you're talking about."

"You're going to tell me you don't know Caspian?"

The recognition in Seeley's eyes was answer enough. Anger turned Ethan's eyes blue.

"Ok, take it easy, just–" Seeley backed into the stairwell door. "If he found you, he did it on his own."

"You expect me to believe–"

"Everyone knows Caspian. He knows everyone. He rules this town, at least the–our part." Seeley leaned forward again, standing his ground. "That doesn't mean that I talk to him."

Ethan let a sharp hiss express his opinion about that statement.

Seeley's hand twitched. "You think I would be here if I worked for him? I am here, working a job, because I live on my own. Alone. I'm here in the city because it's practical, and because people barely look at you twice. I can blend in. Disappear. But I don't want anything to do with him and his company."

"Then how did he find me?"

"The question is, how did he not find you earlier? He knows everything that happens in this city, or at least that's the shtick. You must really be out of his usual circle."

That sounded like a line. Ethan scoffed.

"Seriously. I haven't even seen him in months."

"How many others are here?"

"In Manhattan?" Seeley restated as if the answer were obvious.

"More than any other city, at least in this country. It's been that way for decades. We just agreed the subway system is a tad conducive to a sunless lifestyle."

Ethan swallowed and made himself take a breath. There was never to be any true escape. That world had been here all along.

"It's actually really interesting that you just now ran into Caspian. I bet that threw him off."

For a split second, Ethan wondered if David Seeley would be different from those he'd escaped, and another question slipped past his lips. "Do you kill people?"

Seeley's face hardened as he answered slowly, "No—not now, or here, since I've worked this job." His bottom jaw jutted out as he worked it, showing his bottom canines, before he continued, "But…I have…haven't you?"

That was enough.

Ethan fled the rock that slammed into his gut with a leap up the stairwell.

No, nothing was different. Ethan wanted nothing to do with others and their rules and their manipulations. Answers were only worth so much. He wouldn't trust his own judgment of another vampire.

Better to stay alone.

40

Garth turned to look for Ethan, saw nothing on the empty subway platform, and turned back—only to find him right in front of him.

"Good grief," Garth muttered. It wasn't that he couldn't see Ethan move—it wasn't like some vampire movie with his movements all fast and blurry and accompanied by a whooshing noise—he just seemed to move when you weren't looking at him. Glance down, glance back, there he is. And he didn't make any sound whatsoever.

It made for getting startled a lot.

Without a word, Ethan led the way to the underpass.

Garth sighed as he followed. Since he'd moved out of the basement last week, he'd felt Ethan close off. It was harder to get a conversation going, and he hadn't shared any research updates recently. At least Ethan had answered his basement door at 5:59 a.m. coffee cup in hand.

And now Ethan wasn't in front of him anymore.

Where...?

Behind him. He'd lost him at an intersecting hall.

"What's up?" he backtracked to ask.

Ethan bore an unsettled expression. "You don't hear the screaming?"

He totally did, but, "Well, yeah, but I was trying not to. That's the way to the emergency room. I don't really want to know what's going on down there..." It was a man's screams, and they just kept going on and on with barely time for a breath.

When Ethan still didn't move, Garth prodded, "We should probably keep going, or...?"

"Yeah." He resumed walking but was still distracted when they boarded the elevator.

"Were you able to get to the electron microscope yet?" Garth tried again when they walked into the empty lab room.

"Not yet, but I've got to get downstairs. See you later." More deflection.

"Ok. Later."

⌐

The figures on the bright screen blurred, and Ethan winced into the palm of his hand. Those screams from the hall haunted the brief darkness of his closed eyes. The agony in them had felt…familiar.

The screen still made his eyes burn after another look, so he momentarily gave up on it, clicked to logout, and walked out of the genomics lab with a quick, "Back in a bit," aimed at the tech. Without consciously deciding to, he found himself heading in the direction of the emergency room.

He didn't have to go very far down a back hall littered with stretchers before he identified the cries of the same man, coming in gasps and moans. He was trying to speak to someone, perhaps a doctor, or maybe a friend. Camouflaged in the white lab coat he hadn't removed, Ethan edged down the hall, focused on the voice speaking to the yelling man.

"Try to take a breath and tell me what's going on. The pain meds should be kicking in, but I need you to talk to me, Jon."

"I d'nno—everything hurts!" The words forced through clenched teeth were in a British accent, glossing over the "r".

"I get that, but work with me, man. When did this start? When you were attacked?"

What?

"No. After. A day or so ago—but only getting worse!"

"You went to the hospital up there, right? After the bite. Did they give you anything? Tetanus vaccine, antibiotics?"

One word struck Ethan like an electric current and rooted him to the spot against the wall.

"I don't think this is tetanus, Taylor," the British man panted.

"Ok, I know. Let me get the nurse to give you more pain meds and start fluids and more antibiotics. I'll find Dr. Jones."

The man in scrubs and a long white coat swept out of the room. Ethan turned away until he passed.

The more he heard, the more familiar it was getting.

Too familiar.

Ethan took three steps away down the hall before getting stuck again.

You can't just leave.

He's not my responsibility.

What is going to happen to him here? That doctor doesn't seem to have a clue what he's dealing with. You need to do something.

Do I? What would happen if I hadn't heard? He would still be here. I just wouldn't be involved.

But you did hear.

Ethan rubbed his eyes. He didn't want to get involved, yet it was curiosity that finally won out. *I'll just see if this is even what I think. Probably I'm just seeing things where they aren't, because of what I am.*

That conviction wavered as he entered the room and saw the man curled into a fetal position against the side of the stretcher, moaning and panting. His hands gripped his dark tangled hair as he looked up at the sound of Ethan's footsteps, a plea for him to be the source of relief.

"You're not the nurse," he croaked.

"No. I'm Dr. Ethan Dalton." His brain started analyzing. Could that man become a vampire? His skin was more tanned than Ethan's, with a slight olive tint, but he had the dark hair and eyes they all seemed to share, and if his skin tone faded from lack of sunlight…

"You're not an ER doc," he grimaced.

"I know. But I'm not sure they can help you. I know the pain is overwhelming, but I need you to focus on me for two minutes. Your life may depend on it. What is your name?"

"Jon. Holloway. Doctor–a resident."

A doctor here? He was wearing sweat-stained blue scrubs. "You were bitten by something?"

"Yea," his accent and a wince bit off the end of the word.

"Where? How long ago?"

"We were camping, upstate, three days ago…"

Upstate. That was unexpected. Or was it? "We? What happened to the others?"

His face crumpled in more than physical pain. "They're dead."

Ethan blinked. *So familiar…* He followed the scent of blood to a bandage on Jon's left shoulder. "Here?"

His head dropped to the stretcher mattress as he nodded.

Ethan unceremoniously pulled the tape away from the wound,

evoking a gasp from Jon and another blink from himself.

Wounds crisscrossed over each other so that the whole area resembled something that had been assaulted with a butcher shop cleaver. Maybe he'd been wrong—the wound looked more like a mauling than the clean bite he'd borne on his back two years ago. *Still, it's not as though your teeth couldn't do this damage to skin, is it?*

He dropped the bandage and stepped back to ask, "Did an animal do this?"

Jon's heavy breathing hitched. "I d'nno."

"A person?"

Jon's dark eyes darted to his in shock. And haunting.

Ok then, Ethan swallowed. Three days. "A couple" days since the pain started. He'd postulated that Jack would have died in three days max, and he didn't see any bloody vomit in the hospital room. If Jon was beginning the process Ethan had gone through, the agony wouldn't end soon.

Ethan started backing away. That was his curiosity satisfied, and not in the way he'd been expecting, so now what? Ethan had nothing to do with the man or the vampire who bit him, so why should he get involved now?

Haunted eyes bored into him, begging him to be the one with answers.

But the answers he had weren't good. Better to…just leave him?

The warnings from the other night, from Capsian, rang in his mind. *Under no circumstances seek traditional medical care. I won't have to be the one to kill you if you do.*

Could he just leave him to probably be killed?

Well, that wasn't really the question, was it? The question was, *would* he?

Would he leave one more ghost to haunt him?

Maybe you can do something about this one.

"Look at me." Ethan got Jon to open his clenched eyes again. "Listen closely. I know what did this to you."

"How could you—"

"Something did the same thing to me. The doctors don't know. They can't help. What's happening to you isn't normal."

He had Jon's attention now, but he was still shaking his head.

"You can stay here if you want, but what they do won't help, and may kill you."

"Can you make this stop?"

If only. "No. And I can't take away the pain. Nothing can, I think."

His whole body shook as he groaned, "I think I'm dying."

"No, I don't think you are." Ethan stepped to the side as a nurse walked in with a syringe.

"Jon, I've got some more pain meds, ok?" she said. "Let me see your IV, ok, there. Try to relax, that's got to start working soon."

Ethan didn't really know if it would work or not, not having had access to modern medicine during his turn, but the pain of having every cell in your body rewritten, reconfigured, didn't seem like something that could be relieved.

Once the nurse left, Ethan waited, letting Jon have a few minutes to process and see if the medicine helped, but his moans only grew in volume.

"What can you do?" he finally gasped.

"The virus transmitted in that bite will change you, your body. I don't know how to stop it. But I can keep you safe and be there when it's done."

Can you keep anyone safe?

Jon rocked back and forth. "I don't—you're mad."

"I know. But it's still true." Ethan motioned to Jon's shoulder again, "What did that?" It was the one point that couldn't be denied.

Jon just groaned.

Having had about enough of standing in the ER trying to convince the guy of something he didn't want to know himself, Ethan started to turn away.

"I don't believe in monsters…" Jon spit out, as if arguing with himself. He glared up at Ethan from under his contorted brow. "What happens next?"

"If you want me to take you with me, you need to tell them you're leaving. I don't want them to keep looking for you."

His shaking hands gripped the stretcher rail. "I don't think I could walk."

"I'll come back and get you, but I'm not sneaking you out if someone is going to search for you. Do it now, if you're going to." Ethan edged out the door and down the hall, questioning his actions with every step.

Jon yelled out, louder than even before. After someone else in blue scrubs darted in, Ethan could hear Jon yell that he was leaving, that nothing was working, and that he was going to get out of there.

Once the nurse had scurried back out, Ethan strode in and reached over the stretcher rail for a grip around Jon's shoulder. "Time to go." The scent of his blood caught him in the face.

It wasn't right.

That's as sure a sign as any, he thought as he pulled Jon to his feet only to catch him under the arms when his knees buckled.

"Try not to scream," was Ethan's only advice as he pulled Jon's arm over his shoulders and grasped him around his waist. Leverage was the issue, rather than strength, when it came to carrying him, and his grip slid when he reached to open the stairwell door at the end of the hall.

After getting half-shoved into the stairwell, Jon dropped to the hard floor, shaking with the effort of not crying out.

"You're already doing better than I did. I am sorry for this. But it seems it really is the best way." Ethan took hold of one arm and one leg and hoisted the man onto his shoulders to carry him down the stairs. The light faded as he found his way into the abandoned sector of the basement.

There was a room with thick walls, possibly originally shielded to protect some radiation-producing exam equipment that had long since been relocated. It seemed as good a place as he could currently think of to hide a screaming person he didn't want to be found. He dropped Jon onto a rickety stretcher from the hall and pushed it into the room.

Jon grabbed for his spasming leg and moaned.

"It's ok. This is as far as we're going right now." Ethan didn't know what else to do, but getting him away while he was capable of speaking had seemed paramount.

"What is happening?" Jon gasped again, "What are you doing—"

"You're changing," Ethan repeated.

"Why?"

"The thing that bit you transmitted a virus that is rewriting your DNA."

"That's not—"

"It's possible. I have evidence," Ethan replied softly, stoically.

"Into what? A monster?"

"Not if you don't want to be. We don't have to be…"

Surely we don't have to be…

41

Can anyone else hear the screams?

Ethan could only hear them when he stood in the hall outside the shielded room where Jon lay in torment., so maybe they weren't audible to anyone else.

It sounded like Jon was dying, or begging to. The basement Ethan took refuge in had become just another hell.

He opened the heavy door and closed it quickly behind him. Jon lay on the stretcher where he'd been for the last day. The sheet and blanket Ethan had retrieved had only become twisted up as he writhed and screamed. He was conscious, maybe, but less coherent. His eyes stared through Ethan, not focusing.

Feeling utterly unsure about what to do, he'd almost gone back to find the security guard for help, but still one fact stopped him: he didn't want to do things their way. Unfortunately, that left him figuring out what to do based on his own experience, which wasn't only lacking, it had to be the most terrible example to work from that he could imagine.

As he watched, Jon's hyperventilating breaths suddenly caught in a choking gasp, and his eyes rolled back into his head as his body arched and started jerking. Ethan jolted back in alarm. Maybe he'd had everything wrong. Maybe Jon was dying—but this was nearly familiar too. Ethan could remember exploding sensations, even visions, once he'd lost sense of time. Could that be what a seizure was like from the other side? There would have to be a reaction to having nerves reconfigured.

After a minute or so, Jon's body relaxed, and he became relatively calm. He stirred, moaning, but did not resume screaming, nor open his eyes.

Now what…?

He might remain this way until it was over. Ethan just had no idea how long that would be. The only thing he could firmly recall after seeming to explode with pain was…blood. The blood and her.

Jon would need blood when he awoke, wouldn't he?

It wasn't as though Ethan hadn't considered how to get some. The blood bank was three floors up. It contained human plasma, platelets, and scores of bags of packed red blood cells. In possibly the stupidest security oversight in hospital history, Ethan's badge gave him access to the lab's back door.

There was still a question: what in blood was of the most nutritional importance to his new body? Would the packed red blood cells, having most of the plasma and white blood cells and platelets removed, still provide what was necessary, or would he need plasma, or have to find pre-processed whole blood?

There was one way to find out.

There was really no other way to do it. He didn't know what made human blood different for him, not specifically. And if he was going to be ready when Jon needed it, it would be best to get started now. It was late at night. There might only be one tech on duty.

Before he had finished thinking it over, he was in the hall behind the blood lab. He checked for cameras, tugged the brim of his hat down, and slid along one wall to avoid getting recorded, just in case. If no one had any reason to look, maybe they wouldn't search the door logs.

It only took a swipe of his badge for him to slide inside and let the door close quietly behind him.

He listened.

The tech was up front by the window to the hall on the other side. She was opening a refrigerator door and talking to a nurse about a patient in an ICU. With silent steps, without even the sound of rustling of clothes or footfalls, Ethan walked between rows of refrigerated cases and noted what was in each. He stopped at one with a glass door that held dark red bags labeled with bold blood type letters and expiration dates. If he took a common type that was about ready to expire, or even found some already expired bags, no harm would be done.

The conversation from the front fell silent, and footsteps warned him to slip into a shadow next to an upright refrigerator. After the tech bustled past and settled in front of a computer with her back to him, he eased out and into the front of the lab that she had just vacated.

The line of refrigerated cabinets continued into the front. He scanned the rows of packed red blood cells, skipped the ones with labels noting they had been allocated for a patient already, and found a row of A+ with a listed expiration date of tomorrow.

There. The only thing between him and it was the electronically locked door. He closed his eyes and recalled the tones that had beeped when the tech had opened the door to retrieve the blood moments ago. With one ear toward the back to ensure she kept humming and typing, he pressed each numeral once to hear the tone they made. After only two tries for the correct sequence, he held the open door in his hand.

Thirty seconds somehow passed in a flash as he stared at the bag. A beep warned that the door was ajar, loud enough to rouse the tech in the back.

Time to go.

He grabbed two bags, tucked them into his shirt through the buttoned front, and closed the door. The window to the hall was sliding glass and just large enough for him to fit through. He dove through the narrow opening at an angle, landed smoothly into a roll on the floor, and reached up from his crouch to push the window closed again.

He retreated quickly to the room across from Jon's in the basement and removed the bags. His body heat had warmed the one closest to his skin the slightest amount, but it was still cool.

He'd never tasted it cool.

But temperature shouldn't make a difference.

Time to test the theory.

The port on the bag was sealed, designed to be pierced by the spike of IV tubing, but he had something sharp of just the right length to open it the same way.

The scent punched into the gloomy room.

"From life to life," he whispered to the darkness. And drank.

He knew at once it was right. Wrong—too cold, stale, concentrated, and lacking some subtle note—but also right. The sweetest, most wonderful thing he'd ever tasted.

Drinking as if from a straw, he downed half the bag before pausing with his shaking knuckles against his lips.

You're a fool. A demon—strigoi—

Stop!

Will this work or not? He yanked himself back to the question that had started him down this path: was this adequate?

He hadn't eaten in two days. Consumed by what was happening with Jon and trying to appear upstairs in the lab as expected, he hadn't been home. He would finish it and see if he felt sated.

As if he couldn't already tell that it would leave him immensely satisfied and simultaneously craving more.

42

It was a roar. Made up of footsteps, train clacks, automobile growls, voices, and an electronic hum.

It was trumpets sounding. All varieties from the crammed roads to the ringing in human hands to the blaring of the trains.

It was a flood of lights. Red, green, blue, yellow. All bright, from all sources. The towering structures. The streets. The never-ending line of vehicles, blinding with their glowing eyes. The hovering flameless torches suspended above.

It was a leap into a pool of scents. Smoke, foul in its aroma. Simmering oils and nuts and strange meats. Rotting refuse. Humans.

Piles and parades and cartfulls of humans. Pressed in and pouring out from everywhere.

Caterina hovered at the edge of a tower of brick in the night that was brighter than day. The throng would not even notice if she entered it, but rather than attempt such mingling, she leaped to an iron platform suspended on the wall next to her. It ascended upward, and she followed it to the top. From there the sounds softened to a background cacophony. The lights spread out in all directions, giving sparkling definition to the land that was cut off by shadows of water on all sides.

This was New York City? A glowing, vibrating island containing more humans than imaginable.

It was most overwhelming. Shocking. Deplorable.

And pregnant with promise.

To find a single person in this boiling stew of humanity would be nearly impossible.

She could hope finding a single vampire would not be.

43

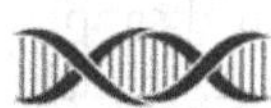

How long could a human go without food and water? But then was Jon still human?

For a few days after his first seizure, he'd seemed to take sips of water all right. Then he'd gone still. For a week and a half, he'd been seemingly comatose without so much as a twitch in response to Ethan.

If Ethan hadn't known that there had definitely been no modern medical intervention in the cave where he had turned, he may have given up and sought an expert by now. Instead, he sat on the counter across the room from Jon and continued the hazardous task of struggling to catch onto memories he'd rather leave buried six feet down.

The only slippery images he could hook from the time between first losing consciousness on that fur covered ground and waking to Caterina were nonsensical dreams. If they had done anything to help him through the turn other than leave him completely alone, he didn't remember.

What if I have this all wrong?

A choking sound broke him out of the memories, and he leaped over to the stretcher. Jon's unconscious form twitched, but rather than arching as if starting another seizure, he gagged and started coughing. Ethan gripped him by the jaw to open his lips, spilling blood-tinged saliva containing several hunks of something from his mouth.

Ethan released him and reluctantly leaned forward to examine what he had spit up.

Teeth.

Had he cracked them during a seizure? But they looked like several full teeth. Ethan reached for Jon's face again, but Jon clenched his jaw with a harsh, grating moan.

Ethan studied him, tried to see him turning into a vampire. *If I can't watch DNA change, who can?*

He pulled a couple swabs from his lab coat pocket and uncapped them to swab the bloody saliva he'd just been offered. Bloody—but the human scent had faded completely. It had lost the sweetness, leaving a metallic tang and nothing more.

Maybe I don't have everything completely wrong.

Ethan retrieved the teeth and left Jon where he lay, still again.

Once back to his office, he dropped the teeth to the top of his desk. Was that the answer to how teeth changed? They fell out and were replaced by new ones? It seemed simple, looking at them. There were more than four teeth in the pile, though. There were canines and also molars. Ethan ran his tongue along his teeth. He hadn't thought anything other than his canine teeth were different.

Something about the whole thing wasn't right.

Time to look closer. He retrieved the capped swabs from his lab coat pocket.

His office door was being pushed open, and Garth's voice rose above the background sounds of conversation out in the lab, "Hey, you do still work here. How's—"

Ethan swept the teeth off the desktop into a drawer.

" —it going?"

"Fine."

Garth eyed the swabs still in Ethan's hand. "Have you made any more progress?"

"I…got a visual of the virus." Ethan switched gears, opened the laptop on the desk, and clicked it to an image as Garth closed his office door behind him. "This is the virus present in my tissue, blood, and saliva from a bite," he turned the laptop around.

The grayscale image from the electronic microscope showed a cluster of viruses, each with a circular band surrounding a darker inner core of squiggles.

Garth leaned forward. "You still think this is it? The source of—" he dropped the last word to a bare whisper, "vampires?"

"Until I'm willing to inject a live person with it to see what happens, it's still a theory. But yes. The structure is consistent with a retrovirus, but I still can't find an exact match in any databases, nor can I find anything else in my blood or tissue samples." Ethan reached under his desk to stow the swabs in the refrigerator.

"Huh–Is that a bag of blood?"

Can't you just–Ethan flicked the refrigerator door closed and spit out, "Yes."

"Uh, why–?"

"Testing theories."

"What theories? Where did you get it?"

It doesn't matter. "The blood bank."

"Have you gotten blood from there before?"

Ethan's lip curled, "No."

"Ok, sorry, it's just–that's blood just sitting right there, right, which seems like kind of a temptation, and you've been a bit off recently–"

"Get. Out."

Garth took a step back. "I'm just–"

"Now." He let all of the day's frustration loose to affect his eyes, suddenly not caring about hiding it from Garth if it would make him leave him alone.

Garth understood the message. He backed into the door and fumbled the knob open. "Ok. Ok."

The door closed after him.

Only minutes later, Dr. Miller entered the lab outside and asked, "Ethan in?"

"Uh, I think he could use a moment–" Garth stammered.

"Stop with the excuses!" Ethan yelled through the door while shoving his emotions into a box where they couldn't show in his eyes and jumping his desk to yank the door open. "I don't need to be minded!"

Garth backpedaled further into the room before stopping to take in his dark-eyed glare. "Fine. If that's what you want."

Ignoring the hurt on Garth's face, Ethan swung back toward his office.

Dr. Miller's tense voice followed him. "Ethan, actually I have an emergency I was hoping you could help me with."

That didn't seem right. He stopped. "What do you mean?"

She was flushed and breathing quickly. "Do you speak Romanian?"

That was even more unexpected. "Some, but–"

"I'm in the middle of a procedure with a patient," she broke in to explain. "I thought she'd had everything explained, but she's upset, and it's difficult to stop now. She doesn't speak English, there's no family, and I can't get the interpreter up here now. I know it's not fair to ask, but could you try, please?"

"What I know isn't…yeah, fine."

"Thank you." She spun back to the hall and rushed at a pace near a run to a procedure room. He hurried to follow, sure he had just made a mistake but unable to think clearly enough to see a better course of action.

They pushed into a sterile room full of voices. A woman lay on an exam table in the middle of the room, clearly in distress, crying out and speaking rapidly in modern Romanian. The male nurse in scrubs next to her held her still by her shoulder and was trying to explain, but she didn't understand his loud English any better than she understood the white-coated resident who was trying to steady a large needle embedded halfway into her hip.

"Quiet, everyone!" Dr. Miller ordered. "Ethan." She motioned him to the patient.

The nurse and resident stopped, but the woman continued to cry as Ethan hesitantly approached the side of the table opposite the resident with the needle. He focused on the woman and tried to decipher her words. "She's saying something about you killing her."

"What?"

"He can speak–?"

"She doesn't understand what's going on," Dr. Miller confirmed.

Ethan crouched to her eye level and spoke in the version of Romanian he knew, *"No, no. They're not killing you. They're trying to help."*

Her eyes darted to him but still creased in confusion.

"Not killing. Not hurting. Helping." He tried to simplify his words to make it more likely she could interpret his ancient dialect into something she could understand. "What are you doing?" Ethan directed the question in Dr. Miller's direction.

"A bone marrow biopsy. We gave her local anesthetic, but it isn't always completely effective, and she started screaming hysterically as soon as the needle touched her iliac crest. It's already in her bone—we need to finish. We were planning to take another sample from the other hip if she calms, but we can skip it if she can't."

Ethan blinked rapidly. He didn't know the words for any of that in the archaic Romanian much less in terms she might understand. He tried, *"You're safe. They need to finish the…test."*

"It will kill me?"

"No! They're taking small…tiny…," he tried different words, *"bone only."*

Although still breathing fast, she stopped struggling. Tears streamed into her hair and she sobbed another question.

Ethan didn't understand. *"What?"* He bent to try to keep eye contact as she turned her head.

"...break bone?"

"No. Not break bone. Tiny piece. To help know how to make you better."

"Make better?" She stilled.

Ethan nodded quickly, and she gave a slow nod back. Ethan met the resident's gaze over her. "I think she gets that you're not trying to hurt her."

"Well, that's good."

Dr. Miller blew out a breath. "We never would have started if I'd known how little she understood."

"I'm going to advance this just a little more," the resident said.

The woman cried out again, *"It hurts!"*

"I know. It's all right. Almost done."

Another woman's cries mingled with hers. Another face.

Ethan sucked in a breath.

"It hurts! make it stop!" He couldn't tell if the cries were coming from the girl in front of him or the one in his memories.

Clamping his eyes closed made the other girl's face clearer, but when he opened them back and tried to focus on the woman in front of him, her face still seemed to morph in front of him. He grimaced before remembering to pull his lips closed with another sharp inhale.

"It's almost over," he whispered to both girls.

The scent of blood floated through the air.

Ethan gripped the edge of the table, unable to keep the images from stuttering in front of him like damaged film.

Was the taste a memory?

"Ethan?" Dr. Miller's voice called from far away. Her hand, though, he could feel before it touched his arm, and it was in his grip in an instant.

She froze then relaxed her hand. "Ethan," she spoke calmly, quietly. "We're done. She's ok. It's over. I'm going to back up, if you let go. Ok?"

"It's over," he repeated, interpreted.

"Ethan?"

He heard her voice, but as though from outside himself, and couldn't stop the images from playing out.

"Don't," Dr. Miller stopped someone who moved toward her. "Ethan. Can you open your eyes? You're here. In the lab. With me."

Ethan shook with the effort of prying his eyes open. He stared down at the table in front of him, struggling to see it.

When Dr. Miller gently flexed the hand in his grip, he let go at once.

She took a slow step back.

"Do you want to do the other biopsy?" the resident asked.

"No, we need to stop." she answered quickly.

Ethan focused on the Romanian woman's face again, smelled her blood.

"*All done?*" she asked.

"*Yes. Done.*"

He left quickly.

The bathroom down the hall was a refuge of habit. The lights came on due to a motion sensor and made him flinch. The reflection of evil stared back unbidden from the mirror in front of him, blue eyes peering back as if to reveal his true nature. They taunted him, *You may fool them, but I know what you've done.*

Regret hung on to his windpipe and twisted.

There was more than one face permanently imprinted on his mind's eye, with tears, fear, and pain etched on their features. He grasped for the smooth hard edge of the counter with bloodstained hands.

The breath he finally forced out became a high shriek as it caught on tightened vocal cords.

The bathroom door opened.

He ducked his head down and away from the door and mirror.

You may fool them…

"Ethan?" Dr. Miller's voice bounced off the hard walls and fixtures. "Are you…? I'm sorry. I'm sorry I asked you to do that."

Ethan couldn't look up.

"I needed help, but I didn't consider…I don't know what that brought up for you, but thank you for helping me."

His throat tightened further.

"Ethan? Is there anything I can do?"

"I'm fine," he forced out and turned half toward her without raising his eyes, to try to prove it, to her at least.

"Thank you for helping her when I couldn't."

Fool…

He nodded once.

It got her to leave, slowly with a final glance back.

Then he struck the light sensor with the edge of his hand, cracking it and disabling the light, and slid down the cool tile wall to the floor. Darkness didn't hide the ghosts. They lingered, haunting him despite his hissed threats and tears.

44

Leaned back in an actually ergonomic office chair with his feet on the desk, David Seeley lazily eyed the old monitors on the other side of the cramped office. They displayed stuttering footage from a few security cameras, but it was one of the older buildings on campus, one of the most understaffed, and thus the quietest.

It was his favorite post.

The lights were dim, especially if he turned off the one at the end of the hall that flickered psychedelically, and the empty halls and rooms were still and cavernous enough that he didn't really need the monitors to tell him if someone stepped an echoing footstep into his domain.

He had made a couple rounds through the building to check doors and show off the security uniform to anyone who might think the building was abandoned at night and could now settle into the most relaxing moment of his week.

Until a door two floors up clicked shut.

He sat up with a frown and scanned the monitors again. There were only two that might have shown anything from that direction, and both were clear—or was that movement?

Forget the ancient cameras, time to go look. He stood and strode to the stairs that he took on his toes to keep his boots from broadcasting his location. Since the building was too old to have the motion activated overhead lights, the hall was dark, but the offices behind these doors had windows that let in enough street light for him to see. He walked the length of the hall, listening.

Nothing.

Blaring notes pierced the quiet, momentarily disorienting him.

What in the blazes—

That was the security alarm for the locked lab one floor up.

Seeley bolted forward and bounded up the stairs to the floor above. The door responsible for the alarm would be only a few feet to the right of the stairwell door—

The hall was empty.

His radio was starting to get busy with staticky voices demanding answers about the alarm that was too overbearing for him to hear much else. Seely pushed through the door that should have been locked. The locking mechanism that bolted the door to the ceiling was bent inward. Someone had forced it.

How…?

First things first. He needed to answer the radio—he was pretty sure someone had just called the police—but to do that he needed to silence the outrageously shrieking alarm. He found the control and switched it to off, breathing relief as he keyed the radio. He identified himself and gave the door's location. "It's been forced open. No sign of an intruder yet."

Pounding footfalls in the stairwell announced his supervisor's approach as clearly as his answer on the radio, but Seeley didn't wait for him to search through the offices and lab rooms on the other side of the door.

There were still no sounds of rummaging around, no footfalls, no breathing, not even a heartbeat within his range of hearing.

By the time his supervisor got to him, he had laid eyes or ears on the entire space without a single thing to show for it. He'd also pulled out his Maglite and clicked it on, because it wouldn't make sense to be found searching in the dark, but his supervisor turned the overhead lights on as he approached.

"It's all clear. There's no one here," Seeley reported.

"Then where'd they go? Someone forced that door."

"I know. I'll check down the other way. Did I hear PD get called?"

"Yes, although I'm not sure why. Someone will need to go down and meet them."

"Will do." Seeley started down the hall. He usually preferred it when he could get through a shift with basically no interaction with anyone else, but that also meant a lot of boredom. Sometimes it was difficult to choose between quiet and interesting.

Tonight was definitely erring on the interesting side.

He searched the length of the hall. As far as he could tell, the rest of the floor was also entirely quiet, so he opened the door to the stairwell on the opposite end of the floor and almost stepped on a small rectangle of something.

He retrieved it and looked it over as he descended the stairs. It was a University ID. Someone must have dropped it. But—he gave it a second look as he pushed out of the stairwell into the main floor—it belonged to Dr. Ethan Dalton.

He could certainly be Seeley's ghost, but why would he be breaking into a place he probably had access to? It might make more sense that he had simply dropped it or something and it had no connection.

Hold on.

Boot clomps on the hard floor.

Someone was walking around on the ground level.

A figure rounded the corner and started toward him. Something was off. Something subtle about his movement wasn't right.

Seeley brought up the Maglite that was still in his hand and clicked it on.

The dark-clad man instantly dropped his gaze to the floor, but not quickly enough for Seeley to miss the subtle light reflection in his eyes.

Within a second he'd studied him again, taking in the lanky limbs, young face, reddish brown closely-trimmed hair, the easy gait, the steady heart rhythm, and the subtle movement of an ear listening for his.

Lycan.

That would explain the bent door locks.

Selley's upper lip pulled back from his teeth in a sharp hiss as his vision sharpened.

The reaction from the lycan was immediate: mid-step he dropped his weight to a slight crouch, set his left hand at his belt, and held his right open and ready at his side.

His pupils dilated to fill his irises with darkness.

But his next response was surprisingly calm. "Easy. Security called for police. I'm just responding."

The silver shield on the left side of his uniformed chest registered. "You're a cop?" Seeley asked incredulously.

"And if I'm not mistaken, you're a security guard."

"Yeah, but—"

"What, just because I can go outside during the day?"

Seeley's snarl returned.

The officer tilted his head subtly. "Look, my partner is walking in behind me. Is he going to find a cop and a security guard or something else?" His eyes resumed a normal appearance as he straightened slightly, offering his own answer. Aside from some working of his jaw, he seemed completely calm. He had to be the weirdest lycan Seeley had ever met.

If we're not fighting, then, Seeley blinked his eyes back to brown.

The officer took that reply, released his grip on his flashlight, and went completely back into cop mode. "Found the security guard, Smitty," he called behind him.

"Finally." The lycan's older, grumpy looking partner ambled up behind him. "So what's the deal?"

Seeley answered, "An alarmed door was tripped upstairs. It leads to a research lab. The locks were forced, but there's no one up there."

"Anything stolen? Other property damage?" Smitty pulled a notebook from his pocket with a huff.

"I don't know for sure, but I was at the door within seconds of the alarm going off. I searched the area but didn't see, or hear, anything." Even with the blaring alarm to disable, Seeley should have been able to detect someone running away, and the office and lab area had no other entrance. He would have found anyone hiding in there. Their intruder was a literal ghost.

Or else a vampire.

The lycan cop's eyes narrowed briefly.

"You want to show us or what?" Smitty asked.

But Seeley didn't have to walk them up or make any more decisions, because his supervisor arrived and took over the conversation.

With another glance at the lycan in an NYPD uniform who was clearly trying to appear as though he weren't paying as intense attention to the surrounding dim halls as he was, Seeley eased back out of the fray to take up position against a wall.

The whole thing ended up becoming a lot more work and mess than it was worth.

He gave his same brief report of what had happened four times. The cops and Seeley's security supervisor, and *his* supervisor, must have tromped up the stairs to the third floor a dozen times. Seeley participated in the building wide sweep that, of course, turned up nothing. Whoever had opened that door hadn't been there three seconds after doing it; they certainly weren't there later. The security cameras were absolutely no help, despite a review of all the footage for hours before the alarm went off.

He thought the whole event was coming to a close when his supervisor appeared again, more disgruntled and disheveled than he had been an hour earlier. "Seeley, make another round, outside. We checked the doors, but search the surroundings."

Seeley quickly checked the clock on the wall. 6:05 a.m. Avoiding people was one reason he preferred the night shift, but the other reason was close to presenting itself. Good thing it was December, but the sun would still rise–

"Could I actually use him to get a copy of the security footage?" the lycan officer asked. "I know it didn't show much, but we should check again."

"Yeah, fine. Seeley, get that for him. Louis! I need you to make another round!" His supervisor barked to another security guard.

Seeley froze for a moment, processing the fact that the lycan had just rescued him, before he moved again to the main office where he could get a copy of the footage. The lycan followed, quietly, and waited in the doorway for Seeley to download the footage.

The name placard under his badge labeled him Officer Sanderson. The strangest lycan he had ever met. Seeley couldn't make himself thank him, but he gave a nod as he handed over the flash drive.

Sanderson nodded back, took the drive, and walked out.

Forget interesting. The night was officially weird.

45

Garth plodded into the lab, plopped into a chair, and tapped the spacebar to wake up the computer.

His eyes wandered to Ethan's dark office door.

He hadn't talked to him in over a week, and the only time he'd seen him was in the meeting two days ago. Ethan wanted space, to not be hovered over, so Garth was giving it to him. It had nothing to do with getting told off in front of Dr. Miller despite only ever trying to help him in the impossible situation.

Garth looked back at the computer screen but didn't see the email he clicked on aimlessly.

Dr. Miller strode in holding a piece of paper. "Garth. Good morning! How are you? Is Ethan around yet?"

Garth shrugged.

She tapped gingerly on Ethan's office door, and it opened only seconds afterward.

"Hi. Good morning." She hesitated.

Ethan looked a tad subdued, not that Garth was looking.

Dr. Miller took a breath, "I'm sorry for that request last week. I didn't think it through, obviously–"

"It was valid," Ethan interrupted, hunching his shoulders further. "I'm sorry I couldn't be better help."

I missed something.

"It's not your fault."

Ethan didn't look convinced. Garth focused on his email.

"That aside," she continued. "This seems to have been a difficult week. We missed you this morning."

Ethan didn't answer.

Should Garth tell him? Or let him struggle, alone, like he'd asked.

C'mon, Qualls, get over yourself.

"Abstract writing workshop," Garth whispered. It had been on the calendar for weeks, and Ethan had been notably absent.

Ethan's lips moved in a silent curse. "I'm sorry. I've–it's been–"

"Everyone is allowed an off week," Dr. Miller interrupted. "And if you need me to take Rav back, I can, and you could drop the–"

"No, that's not necessary." Ethan started searching his pockets, presumably for his phone.

"Check your desk," Garth suggested, but Ethan shot him a glare, so he shut up.

Nevertheless, Ethan came walking back out of his office with his phone. "I'm sorry. I'll refocus. What else, besides finding Rav to reschedule our meeting, is a priority by tomorrow?"

"We're reconvening in a few minutes in here. And you might want to check your calendar invites." Her posture had softened.

"Right."

"That aside also, I have some exciting news. Want to hear it?"

When Ethan just looked at her, Garth interjected, "Yes. Please."

"We got the grant."

It took a moment for Garth to absorb the impact of her calmly delivered words. "We–seriously?"

Ethan managed to look less worried.

Garth whooped.

Dr. Miller smiled with the relief of a known financial future, at least for the short term. "So, really I'm thanking you for writing the proposal," she told Ethan.

"Part of it," Ethan still played himself down. "But that's great. Amazing. Did you tell everyone else?"

Her smile softened her usual clinical demeanor. "I'm doing it now. The students will be here in a few minutes."

Ethan turned away and muttered something about reviewing the workspace documents.

When he returned a few minutes later with a stack of papers, Dr. Miller nodded at him. "I think I'd prefer to look at it on paper too, but I'm always stopped by the printer's sign, 'do you really need to print that and kill a tree?'" She paraphrased the actual sticker on the printer.

"It's printed double-sided if that helps…" Ethan flipped through the pages.

"I'm not saying it should stop you. And I'm all in on that

justification. Seriously, though. Thank you for your help on the proposal. We may actually be able to get somewhere on this study."

Garth was starting to feel like an awkward fly on the wall.

"Of course," was all Ethan muttered, still focused on the papers in his hand.

Once she had walked to the front of the room, Garth sighed, "Definitely the right decision to pass that on to you. You're making me look bad."

Ethan grunted and addressed him for the first time, kind of, "Not even sure why she's putting up with me at the moment."

The room started getting more crowded as the students arrived, and Rav began his gossip topic for the week. "They still haven't figured out who broke into the research building over the weekend. Did you hear about that, Dr. Dalton?"

Ethan gave a noncommittal head motion.

"Someone broke a whole door in but didn't take anything. Steve says that his security guard friend said it was like a ghost."

Garth frowned and glanced at Ethan again. *What are the odds?* It was harder to guess when he didn't know what Ethan was up to anymore.

Once Dr. Miller shared her news about the grant, bedlam erupted for several minutes. Keeping an eye on Ethan, and trying not to look like he was, Garth was relieved to see him relax a little and get lost in the research schematics in front of him as Dr. Miller managed to redirect the meeting back to the task at hand.

Twenty minutes into debating the wording of a small section of the abstract, Garth watched Ethan lean closer to the paper in his hand with a look he recognized from the old days.

What did you just figure out? he mentally questioned as Ethan dropped the paper, pulled something up on his laptop, scrolled, clicked, and picked up the page again, looking back and forth with his knuckles at his lips.

Dr. Miller must have noticed too. "Dr. Dalton?"

"Hold…" Ethan raised a finger and kept scanning the screen in front of him.

Garth leaned over to see what he was so engrossed in. "Huh." It was a paper that had been published last year, but it wasn't directly linked to the stem cell line production they were looking at now.

"Did you test for interleukins in this study?" Ethan looked up.

Dr. Miller looked between him and her screen, "Why?"

"Go back a page–there." With a blink at her bright screen, Ethan leaned forward and started pointing out some correlating research.

"Look at the percentage of the variants–there. It's not what you meant to find, but here," he motioned at his own screen, "the findings looking at IL-2, they have an even larger percentage of that variant."

"That study's from over a year ago," Rav said.

"I wasn't here then," Ethan replied. "But I'm looking at it now."

Dr. Miller stepped to his side to look at the computer screen he was clicking on. "We weren't looking at that…"

"No, but what if it does have a cross interaction with this stem cell line production, because here–"

"I see it. Garth!"

He grabbed for his computer. "I'm pulling up everything from that study."

"Just print it off," Dr. Miller ordered. "How did I miss that?"

"You weren't looking for it," Ethan answered and dropped to the floor with his papers and pen to spread out.

"It's a good thing you just got us a grant, Ethan, because I think you just found us another rabbit to chase." She dropped down next to him.

And you wonder why she puts up with you. Garth shook his head as he jogged to the printer. *You crazy genius.*

꘏

Ethan rubbed his eyes and set the page down. He'd chased their new rabbit all afternoon until he was left on the floor of the lab alone. Except for Garth at the table at the other side of the room.

They'd been able to work together, for a while, until everyone else was pulled away by other commitments. Then they'd drifted apart, but Ethan knew he was still keeping an eye on him. Relentless in his watching.

It was tiring.

Before he could shuffle all the papers together and retreat into his office, Dr. Miller walked in. "Any last thoughts?" she asked Ethan.

He retrieved a page of scribbled notes. "This, but I can type it up on the workspace."

"May I see it first?" She took the page from him. "Garth, did you get those numbers sent?"

"Yes, I did. But it may be a while before we get it back. My go-to statistician Ms. Becker had the gall to take the whole week of Thanksgiving off, but I'll get with her in a couple weeks at least."

"All right, thanks. Sounds good. Ethan, this is your cue to go home, unless you're up for a drink or bite with me on the way out?"

"Not tonight, thanks."

When she'd walked out, Garth sighed loudly from his table. "You know she was just inviting you, right? I wasn't included."

Ethan paused. That didn't make sense. She'd just seen him have a full-on meltdown and then had to reprimand him for ignoring his job.

And that was just the stuff she knew about.

He shook his head to banish the thought of a one-on-one date. It wasn't a good idea. "All the better then."

"You know, you don't have to talk to me. I get it. It's ok. But you should talk to someone," Garth persisted.

"Just leave it alone, Garth. Go home."

46

The grayscale circles were broken. Every one, every cell visible through the microscope eyepiece on the slide below the lens, was broken.

Ethan had taken a break from trying to look at his own DNA to look closer at the virus. He'd attempted to isolate the viral genetic information from a sample he'd taken from Jon early on, but the sample was contaminated by other common viruses and bacteria, so his search was inconclusive. And what he'd found had inconsistencies.

But there were plenty of questions to address.

If the virus is what had changed him, why had it killed Jack but not him? What made him, and maybe Jon, different? Why did the vampires in the cave not even bother to try to turn the locals around their mountain?

How was it possible that it had infected people around the world without the world at large knowing?

That question made the others sound less intimidating but also made them more relevant.

So, he was trying something new.

There were things he couldn't risk taking a lot of from the university labs, like the immortalized cell line used to incubate virus in the lab. But what he had ample access to was his virus and a lot of randomized samples of blood and cells that made their way through their lab for testing.

Regular cells didn't live long on a slide, but the virus was fast. Fast enough, he thought, to kill cells before they would naturally expire.

In his first experiment, he had exposed cells on two different slides to his virus.

A sample of his own cells hadn't been destroyed yet.

These cells, from a randomized study sample taken from the lab, had.

So, he was testing more.

It was impossible to know how many he would have to try to find another one that didn't lyse, like his. Or maybe it wouldn't work at all. There was nothing to do but keep trying.

He'd set up more samples yesterday in the virology lab to avoid contamination, but then, after checking on Jon who hadn't seemed to have changed at all, Ethan took the slides to evaluate the results in the empty Miller lab which was all quiet after 10:00 p.m.

He'd been at it for a while when steps tapped in the hall outside. Despite the late hour, the lab door opened, illuminating the room that had previously only been lit by his dim computer screen. He spoke to keep from frightening the person who entered, "Moraine."

It didn't work. Dr. Moraine Miller gave a short, startled cry, and a tube from the tray she held dropped to the floor with the tinkle of broken glass. "Oh my word," she gasped. "What are you doing in here in the dark?"

Realizing that she wouldn't be able to see as soon as the door clicked closed, Ethan stood quickly and hit the light switch. "Sorry, I didn't think anyone else was still here." Blinking against the sudden fluorescent light, he cautioned, "Hold on—the glass."

Her heeled dress boots stepped to the side, and Ethan reached for the tilting tray of capped test tubes in her hand. "I'm sorry, I was trying to avoid scaring you."

She let him have it. "It's fine, not your fault. I didn't expect anyone else to be here either, although perhaps I should know better by now." She shook her head at him before stooping to the floor.

"I'll get it." Ethan crouched more quickly and carefully brushed the small pile of glass together.

"I'm going to be checking all the dark silent rooms for you now."

He accepted the piece of paper she offered to act as a dustpan and lifted the gathered glass into the nearby trash can. "I had a computer on."

She looked doubtful.

"But Garth did threaten to put a bell on me once."

Her alto laugh lightened the room. "I would like to see that."

"He clearly hasn't succeeded yet." Ethan brushed the rest of the glass into the trash. "I didn't see a label on that tube. Do you need to know what just broke?"

"It would seem I managed to drop one of the empty ones, so no harm done. I got caught in some long meetings today and was just trying to get some work finished so I'm ready for tomorrow. Are you working on the secret project that's going to get you your own lab back someday soon?"

"I—no. I'm just…"

She dismissed his attempts to find an acceptable explanation. "Don't worry. I know I won't get to keep you forever. And I don't need to know what you're doing in your off time at," she glanced at the clock on the wall, "1:15. Wow, time got away from me further than I thought. I'll see you in the morning—later in the morning."

She was wearing her long gray coat rather than her lab coat and had a scarf draped around her neck. "Are you walking to the subway?" he asked. It was getting on the late side, even for New York City, and the trains would be less frequent now.

"No, I live just a few blocks north. Quick cold walk, but a faster commute than yours and Garth's."

For as many people as traveled through Manhattan on a given day, there weren't huge odds of being touched by crime in their area. But even the city that never slept got considerably less busy in the early morning hours, leaving more room for activities hidden from the eyes of authorities. And that didn't take into account what he now knew lurked in the city's shadows.

She must have read his concern on his face. "Yes, it's late, but campus security is still around for half the blocks. I'll be fine. Unless you just feel like a brisk early morning walk."

Maybe he recognized what she was doing, but her comment about security had not increased his comfort level. "I would. If you don't mind waiting just a moment for me to close this up and get my coat."

"Of course." Her deep blue eyes smiled at him.

By the time he returned with his hat, coat, and messenger bag, she had pulled a gray knit hat over her golden hair and wrapped her scarf tighter around her neck.

He gestured for her to lead the way and followed her into the elevator and out a side entrance. At the first step outside the building and the familiar constraints of their established relationship, a coil of discomfort took up residence in Ethan's chest, stopping any chance of starting a conversation. Whether or not Moraine noticed was unclear, but she didn't try to break the silence and seemed content to simply walk next to him across a crosswalk and along the nearly empty sidewalk for two long blocks.

As they approached another crosswalk, she gestured to a bar across the street that was still lit with people visible inside the front window. "I just realized I never ate dinner, and I have nothing at home, and I happen to know that they have good pub food and a wine list."

It sounded suspiciously like a well-executed trap. "Moraine…"

"They're quick. It won't take long. Join me?"

You already decided this would be a bad idea.

When he continued hesitating, she added, "If you'd prefer not to, I assure you that I can make it home the rest of the way just fine. But I would appreciate your company."

I don't want to leave her alone. It's just a quick detour. He nodded with a slow sigh.

Her eyes lit up victoriously. "We can cross now if we hurry."

He stepped faster to join her jog across the road and took hold of the cool metal door handle to let her into the warmly lit bar, asking himself the whole time what he thought he was doing.

The current occupants were an interesting mix of other workaholics eating or enjoying a late happy hour, a smattering of college students, and a collection in the corner wearing the blue scrubs he often saw in the hospital halls. Only a couple of men in the corner appeared to have been there long enough that they risked falling asleep in their booth.

Moraine slid up onto a brass stool at the bar with an open one next to it and handed Ethan a menu. "There is food on the back there."

"I ate earlier," he grasped at an empty excuse while opening to the wine selections. "I'll get a drink…"

Her nod accepted his statement naturally. "Considering my fried food choices, I'm going for a beer tonight. I haven't stopped here quite often enough to know the other good options."

"That's all right. One of these will be fine."

She ordered chicken tenders and an ale. Having the practice of the last time he'd ordered wine with her, Ethan selected quickly and added their menus to a stack to his left.

Too bad he wasn't any better at social conversations. Yet, somehow, she made the silence almost comfortable with her casual lean against the bar and contented watch of the people around them.

After they had been served their drinks and he'd taken a sip of the maroon liquid in his glass, she asked simply, "Any good?"

He gave her a nod. "Better than I expected."

"You have to love New York for that. The best food and drink can be found in the most obscure places." She took her hat off and pulled out what she'd used to pin her hair up, running her hand through it so the blond waves settled onto her shoulders.

Ethan redirected his study to the glinting bottles behind the bar.

"Have you found anything especially good recently?" Her gesture at his glass clarified the subject of her question.

"I got a couple bottles from a place in Brooklyn. One was pretty good."

She accepted her food from the bartender. "I'm getting better at choosing wines. The first charity event I hosted I think I just guessed and pointed."

"Do you still host events?" He wasn't sure how she would have fit more activities into her schedule, but somehow it didn't surprise him.

"I do, actually. It may not seem so, as bad as I am at social things in the lab, but," she shrugged, "I actually enjoy putting together the details of these parties. More than actually going to them—that's probably my problem."

That he could understand. He relaxed a little and offered a thin half-smile

"At least with the charity dinners, there's a purpose. Then if I have to hobnob, I know I'm doing it to earn money for the cause."

"Are they pretty big events?"

"Mmhm," she covered her mouth politely while finishing a large bite. "There's one at the end of the month to raise money for the Leukemia Research Foundation. I have a friend in the foundation who knows how to get the right people invited, so I can focus on planning the party. I actually got a room in the Met for it, so that's always a draw."

"Nice," Ethan acknowledged. He was cultured enough to recognize that hosting a party at one of the most famous art museums was pretty fancy.

"It's the 29th—no chance of getting New Year's Eve, of course, but it will still be festive. Would you eat a fry or a few? These are good, but I don't need them all at two in the morning."

"No, thanks. I'm good." He took a sip of wine and let her eat some more while debating with himself whether to acknowledge that he remembered what he'd promised her in that interview three months ago. Finally deciding it would be petty to avoid it, he haltingly started, "I…do remember that I promised you use of my notoriety in some capacity. If it hasn't already waned enough to not be useful."

Her look was gentle. "I was willing to let you off the hook, considering how much you love social events."

"Ah, you noticed that…" He took another sip with an

acknowledging shift of his eyes.

"It's ok. You're allowed. But, if you're actually offering now, I will happily take you up on your offer. Dropping your name may get me some people I wouldn't normally draw. And you're welcome to bring Garth as a wingman. Although, please don't think I'm ever asking for monetary contribution. You've given more than enough on that front. Or had it stolen from you, as the case may be."

"It went to a better use," he replied quietly. "Although that's not supposed to be public knowledge."

She just smiled coyly.

"I can come on the 29th. You should probably send me a calendar request though."

"I can do that. And thank you." She took a long swallow of her beer. "I have preyed upon your goodwill for long enough, but I have never been good at chugging beer, so bear with me another minute, and I'll be ready to go."

She carried too much of an elegant air for him to imagine her ever chugging anything. "Take your time."

Nevertheless, she was done quickly, prompting him to finish off the last of his wine and motion to the bartender for the check.

"Mm, I've got it," she reached for the slip of paper he brought. "This was my suggestion."

"You pay me enough to buy a drink," Ethan replied with a shake of his head.

She paused with a press of her lips. "Then buy your own if you must, and I'll get mine." She deliberately laid a bill large enough to cover hers and an ample tip on the bar.

Ethan acquiesced, added his own payment to the stack, and picked up his hat.

"Ready?" she donned her own warm accessories quickly.

Nodding affirmatively, he motioned for her to again take the lead and followed her out onto the street. Snow had started to fall again, but lightly, the flakes seeming to hover endlessly in the air until they were mixed together by a gust of air from a passing bus.

The quiet between them felt more friendly as they walked around the block and down the length of another. Their interactions hadn't been that awkward, and she seemed strangely content to pretend with him that his flashbacks and freakout episode hadn't happened.

"My apartment is just on the other side of this block," she pointed. "I might have gone around if I were alone, but we can cut through the alley half way down if you want to take the more straightforward route."

"I'm good with either." But she was huddled into her coat against the bite of the wind. "We can cut through."

They briskly crossed the street and entered an alley between brick buildings. As they were crossing an access lane to the rear of a produce market, quick footsteps slapped concrete from the shadows. Ethan turned to see a bulky figure pull a black ski mask down on his face and barrel toward them. A smaller man stepped alongside from out of his shadow and yelled, "You two! Stop there! Drop the bags!"

"Empty your pockets! Give me your phone!" The other man demanded at the same time and thrust forward a knife clenched in his bare fist.

Moraine gasped. Ethan's step back brought him against the brick wall. The two men spread apart in front of them to block an easy escape forward or back the way they had come. Both held blades that caught a glint from the streetlight back at the alley entrance. Heartbeats thudded over each other. The taller man in front of him yelled again, "Now! Wallet out of your pocket. Drop the bag!" His jacket rustled as he extended the switchblade in his hand.

No.

Ethan had no desire to cower. Nor was it necessary. He stepped forward, caught the large man by the wrist and the shoulder, and pushed.

The man plowed face-first into the brick wall on the other side of the alley.

Ethan spun and grabbed the other man's forearm just as Moraine yelled and raised a small black cylinder at his face. Only Ethan's quick duck avoided the pepper spray that caught the masked man squarely in the eyes. With a howl of pain, the thwarted mugger stumbled back, nearly onto his accomplice.

Satisfied that they were going to be slow to get up, Ethan followed Moraine forward to the edge of the alley where she stopped against the wall of an apartment building. Her breathing and heart rate were still escalating despite the quick conclusion to the ordeal, and she stared ahead without focusing on Ethan.

"Moraine." She'd reacted quickly in the face of the threat, but now fear had frozen her. He'd seen enough of fear to know she would need some help moving on, so he gently took her upper arm and guided her toward the street. "You're ok now. Let's get you home."

Once they reached the street, she started moving under her own direction again, and her steps became more urgent as she rushed into the portico of a building entrance lined with small gargoyles. He let go of her but kept following through the entrance and up a flight of stairs to a door in the first-floor hall. When her hands were still shaking enough to lose grip on the keys she pulled from her purse, he plucked them from the air before they dropped to the floor and caught her wrist to ease it back so he could unlock the door.

Her blood pulsed under her warm skin.

He let go and allowed Moraine to stumble slightly over the threshold. Salt marks glistened on the wood floor behind her boots. She dropped into a chair next to a glass dining table while he stood just inside the door, the doorknob still in his hand.

"You're safe now."

She covered her face with her hands.

Except that I'm here. He turned to leave.

"Wait. You can't just go back out."

He could. He should.

But instead he eased the door shut behind him and waited.

"I'm sorry–" she started.

"Why?" he asked. "You were attacked. It's ok to be shaken up. Also, you waited until after chasing them off very effectively."

She looked so vulnerable sitting there, peering over her finger tips at him. "You seem fine."

"That's not fair..." He looked away. *Don't use my reactions as a standard.* And anyway, she had seen him broken recently too.

The kitchen was on the other side of the table. "Can I get you some water?" He started for it. It was just one of those things that people did when they had no idea what to do for someone who was hurting, but it was all that would come to mind. Taking her silence as assent, he found a glass on the counter and filled it at the sink.

"We should have called the police," she muttered as he set the glass in front of her.

"Don't worry about it. They're gone now." He sat on the edge of the chair around the corner of the table from her.

"No, it's not..." She ran her hands over her head to push her hat off and her hair away from her face. When she started speaking again, her eyes stared at something unseen on the opposite wall. "When I was in college, I was attacked." The spike in her heart rate attested to the intensity that memory still held. "I was ashamed–" her voice quivered, and she swallowed. "And blamed myself, so I didn't say anything to anyone afterward. Two weeks later, another girl was attacked, in the same place I had been. She was killed."

Ethan couldn't watch the pain in her eyes.

"I can't help but think that if I had gone to the police, maybe they would have caught him before…Maybe she would be alive."

The haunted expression echoed something in the back of his mind. "You couldn't have–"

Her voice became firm, "I won't make the same mistake again."

Ethan nodded slowly. "I'll do it. I'll make a report. Tonight. You don't have to be there."

Relief brought tears to her eyes, but she blinked them away. "Thank you." Then she reached for his hand.

He dropped his hands into his lap. After a beat of silence, he added, "They didn't have a chance against your pepper spray skills."

She blew out a nervous chuckle. "Can you stay? Just thinking about going back out there–"

He stood. "That's not a good idea."

"I mean on the couch, Ethan. I'm not trying to insinuate anything."

"I'll be fine. And you're ok now. You're…" *Safe.* He couldn't get the word out.

She picked up the glass in front of her. "Then could you at least get your own water and give me just another minute?"

"Yeah." Giving in and grateful for the excuse to walk away, he retreated to the kitchen nook and found a glass in the second cabinet he opened. *If she knew who she was really asking to stay…* It was only a lie that he should make her feel safe. If she'd known the truth, the fear in her eyes would have a different cause. Wouldn't it?

He returned to sit, pushing his chair back slightly to avoid brushing against her, and they sat in a different kind of silence holding water glasses.

"Ethan…"

He waited for her to continue.

"I'm sorry for being insensitive. You just jumped back into work so fast, I gave no regard for the trauma you must be working through. I should know better."

Ethan blinked. Again. "You weren't…you've been the most sensitive…"

"Do I remind you of something, or someone, who hurt you?" she whispered quickly and didn't look at him until she'd finished asking.

He froze. "No," he breathed. "No, not at all."

Her hand reached for his again.

He stood and eased back a step.

"Then why," she asked softly, "Do you try so hard to avoid

touching me?"

You don't understand. You don't know what happened to the last woman I…touched.

He took another unsteady step back, toward the door. "It's not her that you remind me of." Another step back. "I'm not…" *who you think I am.*

Her eyes searched him.

"You remind me of the one *I* hurt."

Without waiting to see the confusion settle fully onto her face, his hand found the doorknob behind him and pulled the door open, and he turned to hurry through it.

I shouldn't have done that.

But what if he hadn't?

Stop it.

Too much feeling. Too much in his head.

Just do the next thing.

Which right now was filing a police report while it was still the dark hours of the morning.

47

Garth walked into his office but didn't sit down. He'd argued with himself, or maybe God, the whole subway ride uptown. It didn't seem worth fighting to get his friend to talk to him when that's not what he wanted. If Ethan just wanted to be left alone, why couldn't he just do that?

But then Garth was reminded of his own story, and where he might be if no one had come after him.

Ethan wasn't so different. It took dogged persistence to befriend an addict. He should have more resilience.

So back out of his office he went, into the lab to stop in front of Ethan's closed closet-office door. Ethan hadn't been home, or he hadn't answered his door, so he must be in the lab. Or at least if he wasn't, Garth had no idea where else to look.

There was no response to his tap on the door.

Despite knowing that there was no way he wouldn't have been heard, Garth pushed the office door open to check anyway. "Ethan?"

But there he was, head and shoulders resting on his desk, motionless. Garth had never gotten close to Ethan when he was sleeping without him waking instantly. At least he twitched in apparent sleep so Garth could breathe away the fear that he was dead in his office.

"Hey," Garth reached for one of his splayed arms, "You ok?"

Garth's world spun.

Pain rang deep in his head—something smashed into the back of it.

The wall.

He was pinned.

He couldn't inhale.

All he could see were cold blue eyes.

Primal panic froze him in place. An impossibly strong hand held him by the throat. He couldn't even raise his arms or turn his head as bared clenched teeth hissed closer to his face.

The world spun again.

Suddenly Garth wasn't against the wall anymore but instead falling head over heels through the door of the narrow office.

"Go!" Ethan's voice, but raw and hoarse.

As soon as up was up again instead of down, Garth pushed with his heels and elbows to scoot himself across the hard floor of the lab. His gasp caught in his sore throat and started a cough.

When he could breathe again and hear over the pounding in his head, he looked back into Ethan's office. He couldn't make out details of the figure leaned over the desk, but could hear it moan.

"Ethan?" His voice shook. He couldn't stop it.

"Just get out." The still-blue eyes focused on him were enough to make him obey, quickly, but he stopped on the other side of the main lab door and leaned against it.

⇗

Images crashed through Ethan's mind: rock, darkness, blood—remnants of a dream that clouded reality. A pulse under his fingers, fear in the eyes—Garth's eyes—here, now.

The effort of pulling back from what he'd started felt like physical pain. He groaned and planted his shaking hands on his desk. As his surroundings coalesced back into reality, the agony of what he'd almost done shot through him. Another moan escaped. Trying to get a grip on the world around him felt like slogging through quicksand half blind.

He took hold of the sound of Garth taking a deep breath from behind the lab door and followed it. Then the next.

Heart beats slowed. Hands steadied.

He dropped into the chair behind him and stared into his hands. *What just happened? How did I let it?* He'd been tired, exhausted really, but that was barely an excuse to not hear Garth's approach. With everything that had been going on, his head wasn't in a good place. And he'd drunk human blood. More than once. The desire for more was something he couldn't dismiss as lightly as he'd tried to.

"Hey, can you hear me?" Garth's voice came through the door, remarkably steady considering he should have been far away by now. "It's almost seven. Others will be showing up soon. I'm going to wait as long as I think I can, but then I'm going to come back in, ok?"

Why?

"I can't just leave…and let someone else…"

Ethan pushed his hair out of his face, trying to push everything back—hunger, confusion—it was all tightening into shame deep in his gut.

It would be better for Garth to leave. How was he supposed to face him after that? His tentative grip on humanity slipped through his clammy palms. In seconds his actions had betrayed more of his secrets than he'd shared with Garth in months.

The clock said it had been twenty minutes when Garth spoke again. "I just saw Dr. Miller's office light come on, so I need to come back in now, ok?" A minute later, the door eased open and admitted Garth with his heartbeat sounding like a jackhammer and hiccupping when he caught sight of Ethan sitting in his office. "Hi?"

Ethan knew he needed to say something to show Garth that he wasn't still out of control, but it was hard to get the words out. "I'm sorry," he finally rasped.

Garth relaxed his shoulders a measure. "We're going to have to do that later, ok? People coming. Am I right that it might be better to get out before you get kind of trapped in here?"

How are you still here? On my side?

But he was right.

Slowly, so slowly, Ethan stood and padded to the doorway of his office.

Garth's eyes checked his, now dark, and he nodded with a look on his face that said he had firmly made up his mind about something. "You don't have to come, but my office has an easier escape route."

Ethan took a step into the lab, paused to let Garth open the main door, then followed at a distance down the hall and around a single corner to Garth's office. He only wanted to flee, to hide, but couldn't quite push down the burning feeling that he owed Garth more. An apology, or explanation, something. Anything.

So, he hovered in the open office doorway.

"Are you ok?" Garth ventured from inside.

"Am *I* ok–"

"Well, are you? You wouldn't have done that if you were. You aren't–"

"You have no idea what I'm capable of," Ethan's voice chilled. He hadn't known himself, before. Maybe he still didn't.

Garth paused, just for half a second. "Maybe not, but I know you're dealing with something. In any case, I should probably have known better than to wake you up."

"Garth–"

"Maybe a lock on your door if you plan on sleeping in there–"

"You need to understand–"

"Maybe if I had some idea of what has been going on–"

"Garth, I could have killed you!"

Whether because of the words or because his eyes flickered blue, Garth went silent and took a step back. "I get it." His hand went to his throat. "I do understand."

Ethan shut his eyes, backed into the doorframe, and worked to calm his breathing that felt faster than it was. Feeling strangely unsteady, he slid down to the floor.

Garth sat down against the same wall, next to his desk. "Could you tell me what happened?" he asked quietly.

More answers were the least he was owed, but that didn't make it easy. Eyes still closed, Ethan answered, "You woke me out of a dream…I couldn't figure out–I didn't know what was real until…"

Garth sighed, "Ok, that makes sense. And makes it at least partially my fault."

Ethan shook his head. *Only if you don't know how much I wanted to do it. How easy it would have been.*

"It's ok–it *is*, now. Maybe you're right, maybe I needed to understand a little better, ok? You can bet I won't make the same mistake again…" He fell quiet, but Ethan heard the remaining unasked questions, saw them when he finally opened his eyes to see Garth massage the front of his neck.

"Is your throat ok?" he asked instead of answering.

"Yeah, I think so. Getting strangled is just a new experience, you know, and the movies never show that it's sore afterwards. But everything still seems to work fine, so pretty sure I'll live."

He'd nearly forgotten how humans reacted to injury, that there was still danger of it worsening after the initial impact, and worry refilled his stomach like gnawing acid.

"Really, I'm fine."

"I'm sorry…"

"I think you've officially said that enough times–"

"For…" *the other stuff.*

"Oh." Garth somehow seemed to get it. "In that case, me too. I haven't exactly been a great friend recently either."

Quiet stretched. Garth stood first. Would he leave now?

"Wait, I…"

"You gonna actually tell me the rest?" Garth paced a small circle in front of his desk. "Sorry, I didn't mean to be demanding. You don't have to tell me anything. I just know something has been going on with you and wish you'd just say what. That's all."

Again, he was right. Trying to work alone was proving disastrous, but telling Garth more seemed impossible, as bad as the day he'd arrived on his doorstep. How to even start?

Garth knew enough to start getting nervous the longer he stared up silently. He caught Ethan's glance at his chest. "Well, yeah, the longer it takes you to say it, the more the suspense builds. Just spit it out already."

"I'm not the only one," Ethan forced out.

"The only what? Wait, the only…" Garth cast a glance to the hall and skipped the obviously implied word. "What do you…You mean here? There's someone else *here*?"

Ethan scooted into the office and closed the door. "There has been, apparently, since way before I even went to Romania."

"Huh?" Garth's face scrunched.

"That cave isn't the only place they…we, live. There are some here, too."

"What–how is that–how do you know?" Garth's constrained pacing sped up.

"I met one. A few weeks ago. He was *working*, blending in…but it was easy to tell, now. He said he's lived here for years."

"What?"

"And another found me when I was outside the bar. Said he was in charge of us here," he sneered the words.

Garth's hands clamped against his cheeks, making it look like he was squeezing his round eyes out. "Oh, man. How is this even possible–" He dropped his voice to a harsh whisper, "How does no one know!"

Ethan's head shake came in stutters.

"I'm starting to get why you've been a tad tense." Garth dropped his head back to stare upward. "Why didn't you say anything?"

"There's more." If he was going to spill it, he might as well include the other part.

"How is there more?" Garth's voice squeaked.

"Remember the screaming we heard from the emergency room last month? I could hear more than just the screams. He said something about having been bitten."

Garth's eyes bugged further.

"I went back to check on him. It wasn't right. It felt…familiar. I moved him. He's in the basement. He's…changing…" Or the cliche word Caspian had used, "Turning."

"All this time? Is that why you've been spending the night here?"

"Mostly."

"Where–" Garth's voice broke, making him clear his throat, "did you say you have him?"

"Downstairs. I need to check on him this morning." He stood and reached for the door but hesitated at Garth's step forward.

"You're not keeping me out of it now!"

That hadn't been working that well anyway, had it? "Fine. But you have to be careful. Caspian–the one 'in charge'–knows about you, that you know."

"How–?"

"There are rules," he spat the word, "Chief among them that we're not supposed to tell anyone what we are. That includes you, now, since you know. I don't know what happens if we break the rules, but don't you risk it, not right now. I told him to leave us alone, but I don't know if he will."

Wordlessly alternating between nodding and shaking his head, Garth followed him to the stairwell. Ethan dropped down three flights without thinking and had to wait for Garth's quick stuttering steps to catch up before he pushed into the still-dark basement corridor.

Garth promptly tripped into a wheelchair.

"The light's at the other end of the hall."

"It's–ow–ok. Hold on for a sec and let me just get my phone out. Watch your eyes." Light flared into his darkness. "Ok, I'm coming, keep going."

The thick-walled room didn't let the sounds of Jon's incomprehensible moans reach even Ethan's ears until he made the next turn, and Garth was oblivious to it until Ethan jimmied his self-fashioned locking mechanism from the top of the door and shoved it open.

Odors of sweat and urine and something sick filled the dim room lit only by the emergency light near the floor. Garth stopped short of fully entering the room while Ethan moved forward to check on the writhing figure on the stretcher. "Jon?"

Jon's bare chest rose and fell in fast panting breaths. He'd stirred from his silent, still coma to start twitching and moaning again. Dark hair lay plastered against his sweaty face, and although his eyelids flickered, he made no reply or sign that he perceived his surroundings.

Garth clamped both hands over his mouth. "Ethan, he looks like he's dying."

"I know."

"How do you know he's not?"

"I don't. Not for sure. But it doesn't feel like that's what is happening."

"'Feel like'? This man needs to be cared for by doctors—"

"They can't help him now. His blood, it's not…he's not human anymore, not completely. It's changing him."

Garth's lips had gone pale, and he sat down where he stood, perhaps rather than pass out. "This is like what you went through?"

"Yeah…it seems right."

"How long does it last?"

"He said he was bitten…maybe 24 days ago now, and he was conscious only a few days after that. His body seemed to shut down for two weeks, and he's just started moving around again, but not conscious. I don't know exactly how long this part lasts."

"But…How often does this happen? How does it not get noticed? What if you hadn't heard…?"

"I don't know. Maybe someone usually finds them. I have no idea."

"Can't you ask one of the others you were talking about?"

"No."

"But maybe they would have a better idea what's going on with him?"

"I don't care," Ethan replied flatly. "I'm done being told what to do by vampires."

Garth didn't have a reply to that, but Jon shifted in his stupor, baring his new sharper teeth in an unconscious moan that ended with a grating rumble.

Garth gasped.

"There's something else…" Ethan started.

"Did he just…" Garth pointed vaguely at Jon. "Growl?"

Yes, I think he did.

"Can you…make that sound?"

"No," Ethan answered. "I can't." He'd even tried, after the first time he'd heard Jon do it. He started to leave again. "Come on, if you want the rest."

<h1 style="text-align:center">48</h1>

On the way back to Ethan's office they ran into Dr. Miller in the lab.

Garth saw Ethan noticeably tense.

No minding. No excuses. Just be quiet, Garth chanted to himself.

Ethan seemed about to brush past, but then he stopped and addressed her, "I took care of that report I said I would file Friday."

"Thank you." Her voice had a different quality than it did when Garth told her he'd finished something. "Do you need anything from me for it?"

"No." Ethan seemed about to say more but then continued on to his office.

What was that about—never mind, just stay with him. He'd just been invited in again. No wasting it. Especially not when what was going on was so much more than he'd dare suspect when he'd pushed Ethan to tell him.

Ethan perched on his office chair and opened his computer while Garth closed the door behind him, turned on the light, and started pacing in a very small circle. "You ran some tests on him?"

Ethan clicked while speaking, "The first saliva samples were still contaminated with common bacteria and viruses, but this week they aren't, and I isolated this from his blood." He spun the screen to show two grayscale images, each of a dark inner blob surrounded by a circular envelope. Viruses.

"Right, you showed me yours—this is it?" He pointed to the one on the right, and Ethan nodded. "Did you confirm it's a retrovirus?" Garth remembered what he'd told him back before they'd gotten sidetracked by blood and egos. He also remembered reading about the

281

use of retroviruses in immunotherapy–how they were used to insert new genetic information into cells to correct defects. Retroviruses had taught scientists a lot about genetics and were known to be able to insert sections of DNA into the human genome that persisted for life and were even passed on from generation to generation. What had been described was nothing of the scale of Ethan's virus, of course, but still, it almost made sense.

"Yes," Ethan confirmed.

"And you were right about him, weren't you? These look the same–no they're not, quite. That capsid structure is different from your virus."

"It does look slightly different," Ethan agreed. "But it's still not consistent with any known viruses."

"Do you think it's mutated? Like you encountered an old strain, and this is what's around on this side of the ocean?" Garth leaned forward until his nose almost touched the dim screen.

Ethan threw up his hands. "Enough to change the whole envelope structure? I don't know. I think I've isolated the viral RNA from Jon. But I still can't isolate it from me, so I can't compare it. His virus has the same components as known complex retroviruses, but it's also bloated with extra-long RNA strands, a lot more than any of the ones we know about. Maybe that's because the entirety of the changes made to our genomes are much more extensive than the ones we know about. I'm still trying to untangle it to make any sense."

Garth considered Ethan. These were great findings, but there was still something else.

"I just keep thinking, what if I'm completely wrong." Ethan rubbed his eyes.

Garth paced to turn off the overhead light. "You're not completely wrong. I'm seeing what you're describing. And he's clearly changing. I saw the teeth, heard…." What had he heard exactly? He leaned his elbows on Ethan's desk next to the computer.

"But I'm not right, either." Ethan searched the darkened room before looking back at Garth. "There's this story I can't get out of my head. It was told like entertainment, almost acted out." His eyes closed again.

Oh, we're talking about vampires from the cave.

"I thought they were just stories. Fairy tales. But why would they be, if I exist…"

Garth bit his lip.

"There used to be an enemy–of the…clan, the vampire, uh, group that lives in that mountain." He shook his head as he started tripping over his words.

I wish I knew another language so well as to think in it. Probably not one I learned stuck in a cave against my will, though.

"The enemy was strong, like us, not like humans. There was a war, or something, that went on for a long time, before we–they–the vampires–destroyed them, killed them all. They were described as mindless beasts, but also sometimes as cunning, and they roared and tore things apart with their teeth and claws."

Garth closed one eye as he mentally searched for the connection.

"They were portrayed as our equals. Not beasts, not human, but some abomination that had to be destroyed for the good of the land. What if…what if they were real? What if Romania isn't the only place they existed, either?"

"I'm not sure I'm following. You think the creatures in the story were actually similar to the vampires? Like, humans infected by a virus? What does–"

"They called them *Pricolijk* or something like that. I don't know if there's an exact translation or…but I think part of the word might mean 'wolf.'"

Just like that Garth's stomach felt like he was in free fall. Again. "You're not saying…"

"If I exist, why not them?"

"Uh…" *Because this stuff isn't supposed to be real.*

"You're right. He," Ethan's point downward was just visible in the light from the screen, "*is* changing, but it's not right, not like a vampire. But the *Pricolijk* were always described as growling." He rummaged in a desk drawer and handed Garth a paper.

Garth had to flash his phone light at it to read it.

It was a genotype result with an error message.

"I've seen this," Garth noted.

"It's Jon's."

"Oh." He looked at it again as though it said something completely different now. "His genotype is unreadable too–so you're right. Do we know what it changed from?"

Ethan handed him a completed genotype result. "This is his from the first day he was here. Reportedly day four after he was exposed. I got the error message from the check swab sample from day 18."

"Amazing. You've been documenting the whole thing. If I can get the genotype to read, we can compare them and see what changed."

Ethan clicked to something else on his computer. "I found my original genotype from some old archives. There's one change I can see so far from the partial genotype you got to work."

Garth did a double take. "All right! We should have looked for that before. Isn't it nice we use ourselves as standardized patients so often." He leaned his chin onto his hands and grunted thoughtfully. "So, this is a lot more information than you had a couple weeks ago."

Ethan stopped to consider it. "I suppose it is."

"How are you keeping this all straight and finding breakthroughs in the lab?"

"Not very well. Clearly."

Garth let that one go. "What can I do? Besides get you a new shirt. You've been wearing that for a while, and if I noticed, then one of those girls on our team is bound to notice."

Garth snickered at Ethan's look down at himself and vowed not to let himself get shoved away again. It had never been about him. It had been about way too much more. His friend needed help. He would have to get used to a little persistence.

49

Something was different about Jon tonight.

He was calm.

Most of the tension had left his body, and instead of writhing and grimacing, he lay as if asleep with an occasional twitch. But he wasn't as out of it as before either. When he stirred, he seemed to come so close to opening his eyes that Ethan thought he might wake.

Four weeks since the bite and he might actually be on the other side.

So now what?

Deciding to ease him into the crazy new world, Ethan left to retrieve a couple bags of blood and a thermos and returned to find Jon stirring just enough to offer him his first sustenance besides some trickles of water in over three weeks.

The flicker of doubt that it was the right thing to do was snuffed when Jon swallowed twice and relaxed back with an expression of relief, eyes closed, a single drop of blood dripping from the corner of his closed mouth into his beard.

ר

In the morning, Ethan left Jon sleeping to attend to some lab business and ended up caught by Garth hovering at his office door. When Garth insisted on following Ethan downstairs, he didn't bother to argue but made him promise to stay behind him at all times.

Glad he had already refilled the thermos, Ethan grabbed it from the cart in the basement hall and eased into Jon's room. The only lights were the two emergency lights near the floor. The stretcher sat against the wall above one of them.

When he entered, Jon's head turned toward him. His black curls and beard were tangled and matted, his cheeks were hollowed under his cheekbones, but he was finally alert.

"Hi, Jon."

"Where am I?" he rasped in a British accent as his brown eyes darted between them and the door. "What's happened?"

"I'm Ethan. This is Garth. I met you upstairs in the emergency room. Do you remember?"

He scooted away from them closer to the wall, wincing at something. "What've you done with me?"

Ethan stopped in the middle of the room and spoke calmly. "We're still in the hospital. This is the basement. I brought you down here to get you away from the people who didn't understand what was going on." *Never mind that I didn't either.*

Jon stared out at them with a frightened glare. "You said you were a doctor."

"Dr. Ethan Dalton. I have a PhD in genetics."

"Knew I didn't know you," he coughed. "You said…what's happened to me?" He looked down at his bare chest and the sour-smelling sheets tangled under him.

Ethan risked a step forward and extended the thermos. "Let's start slowly, ok? Here."

Jon looked skeptically at the thermos, as if it could be a trap, but once he'd taken it and risked a sip, he started gulping.

"Take a breath." Ethan reached for him only to have his hand forced back. He snapped his attention down to Jon's hand and swallowed his surprise that he'd been so easily overpowered.

Once Jon had emptied the thermos, he relaxed. An enviable peace settled into his eyes as he sat against the wall and looked down at the thermos. "What is this?"

"The answers aren't going to be as fast as you want, Jon. I promise I will do my best to answer everything I can, but I need you to–"

Jon lunged forward and swung the thermos at him. "What happened to me?"

Newly convicted that he didn't want to arm wrestle him, Ethan ducked and slipped to the side. He knocked the thermos to the ground with a quick flick of his wrist, then came up short at the look in Jon's eyes. It wasn't just the anger and fear in his face–his pupils had expanded to cover the entirety of his brown irises with blackness.

Letting his own eyes turn blue was only partly a conscious decision. Jon jerked back.

With a quick glance to check on Garth and his pounding heart, Ethan eased back a step and held his hands out, palms up.

Jon's breaths were coming in quick gasps now. "What…"

"What is the last thing you remember?"

"I–" Jon winced and reached a hand up into his tangled hair. "The ER. Everything hurt…you said you could help."

"I said they couldn't help. I was right. You said you were bitten, and not by an animal. The bite transmitted a virus that has changed your DNA and so your body. I have run some tests and have evidence."

He was shaking his head. "That's not possible."

"It is, apparently. I will show you if you give me time. But I need you to calm down and take a breath, and please don't try to hit me again."

His glower barely wavered, but his pupils constricted back to their normal size, and his breathing started to slow. "What do you mean, 'changed'?"

Ethan nodded. "I'm also a bit new to this, ok? Some of it we're going to have to find out together." He turned slowly to the sink across the room and reached for the mirror above it. It popped off the wall with his yank but cracked up one side.

His image in its cracked surface threw him into the past like a jump into frigid water. The memories and reality swirled around him.

"Ethan?" Garth's voice.

Ethan grabbed the counter and inhaled, a gasp above the swirling water. *I can't do what was done to me.*

"Hey," Garth's voice softened as he leaned toward Ethan, keeping a pace away. "It's ok. We're here together, ok?"

Blink. He focused on Garth's face, managed to push Caterina's blue eyes from his mind's eye. "I've got it." Ethan shook the memories from his head and turned back to Jon with the reflective side of the glass toward him.

Tentatively, with wary glances thrown at them both, Jon leaned forward to look. After a moment, he asked, "What's the catch?"

"Open your mouth," Ethan said, feeling the uncertainty in Jon's face in his own gut.

Jon did, and jerked back.

"And your eyes," Ethan whispered.

Ethan was the one holding the mirror, so it didn't fall to the floor as Jon gaped. "How…" He started hyperventilating.

"Your old teeth fell out a couple weeks ago, and you grew those in their place." A small answer.

"What else?" Jon gasped.

Setting aside the mirror, Ethan leaned forward. "I don't know entirely. You saw my eyes—I have also had my DNA rewritten by a virus, but it's not the same one. I don't know what all has been altered for you, but with your permission, I'd like to find out."

50

Jon suspiciously allowed Ethan to take his blood pressure and pulse with the machine that Garth retrieved. Ethan took his own for comparison and to show they were telling him the truth. Jon's vitals were slightly low but much closer to a normal human's than Ethan's were. Jon's temperature was 99 degrees Fahrenheit, slightly warmer than the human normal rather than the cooler 36 degrees of Ethan's.

Jon couldn't see as well in the darkness as Ethan could, but he could still see better than Garth, and apparently better than he had before when he'd needed glasses. Unlike Ethan's lack of beard growth, Jon's had grown thick, and his nails were long and hard, almost claw-like—although Ethan cut Garth off before he could observe that aloud.

It was the beard that had Jon asking how long he'd been in the basement.

"You've been here over three weeks since I found you in the emergency room. It's December 7th."

He gaped and cursed, "How? What did you tell..." He scanned the room for the invisible ramifications.

Ethan continued, "You had nothing on you when I brought you here, and almost immediately you weren't able to communicate. I had no one to tell anything. We can help you get in contact with whoever you need as soon as you are strong enough and after you understand more about what has happened."

"It's not so simple. I'm a doctor, in residency. Missing that much time...I need to call my program director. If they think...what will..." He tangled his fingers into his hair as panic stole back into his eyes.

"I get that it's a lot, but let's take it one thing at a time. Tonight I

289

can—"

"You going to stop me leaving?"

"No, but I can't help you if you leave."

"Why should I believe any of this?"

"How do teeth change, Dr. Holloway?" Ethan challenged. If he had a scientific background, all the better. He could work with that. "Why do my eyes turn blue and yours black? Why can you hear my slow heartbeat?"

Jon's eyes bore into him as he quieted, listening. "It's not possible," he whispered.

"And yet here we are."

After another tense moment, Jon dropped back onto the stretcher. "How did this happen?"

"You remember," Ethan replied, quietly.

The fear on his face said he did. "The virus came from…that thing? Was he that way, because—Am I that now? How is that—It growled, like an animal…"

"You've made the same sound. I heard it."

Panic laced his voice and sped up his breathing. "I'm a monster?"

Garth answered, "No. You still choose who you are. But your body has changed."

I was made into the image of my attacker, but maybe you don't have to be. "Look at me, Jon," Ethan leaned forward. "It's too much to get it all right now. Focus on right now. One thing at a time."

He wasn't sure he was going to do it, but then Jon dropped his shaking hands from his face and looked at Ethan.

"How do you feel right now?"

An unsteady breath. "Knackered. Beaten up. Hungry."

The last one was less expected, but if he had longer hair and higher vital signs, maybe his metabolic rate was also higher, meaning he'd need more to eat. "Ok, the first two make sense, and I can fix the last one."

As he left to refill the thermos from the bag still lying on the rolling cabinet across the hall, Ethan came to the quiet understanding that the next few days were going to be far from easy, and also that he had gone too long without eating. Without an immediate way to remedy either, he returned to the room to hand the thermos to Jon, who looked it over suspiciously.

"What am I drinking?" There was the question again, asked with a glare that said he knew.

"It's blood." Ethan told the truth and ignored Garth's glance. *I'll tell him the rest. Just not yet.*

"*Why* is it blood?" Jon's animated enunciation left his subtly elongated canines just visible.

"Because, in my experience, it is the most nutritionally dense food that I can digest. Your…response to it so far suggests you may have similar…nutritional needs."

"Because it tastes good instead of terrible and I want more?" Jon's voice shook.

He'd never said as much in front of Garth, but, "More or less, yes."

Jon turned his glare onto the thermos. "This should be revolting."

"I know."

"Why isn't it?"

"Different…taste buds. Digestive tract. Nutritional needs. I don't know entirely."

"Why can't I eat something else?"

"There are probably things you can eat. I can't digest a lot of food—it just makes me sick—but there are some things that I tolerate, and are good. I don't know for sure if the same foods are what you need or not. I was going to wait until you're a little stronger before trying. Eating the wrong thing could make you violently ill."

Jon cursed.

"Yes," Ethan agreed, "but you get kind of used to it."

It was enough at least that Jon willingly lifted the thermos to his lips and swallowed quickly.

Watching someone else drink the blood in a room saturated with the smell of it jerked at Ethan's desire for it. He turned away, thinking he'd covered his response decently only to hear Garth's heart rate speed up. Shaking his head to ward him off, Ethan addressed Jon again, "I can take you home tonight, but I need to go upstairs for a couple hours to wrap something up."

"Home?

"My home. I don't know where yours is, but better my place than here. Then we'll figure out the next step. Ok?"

Jon dropped the empty thermos and leaned back, apparently exhausted.

"I know it feels like you want to do everything right this minute, but I need you to try to take one thing at a time. Drink that and rest for a couple hours, and I'll be back. We'll get out of here and keep figuring out…how things work now."

⅄

Garth watched Ethan sink into a chair in the empty lab room with the posture of someone who had just been beaten up. He knew that Ethan hadn't told him everything that had happened to him, and that some of it must have been quite traumatic. It was why he tried not to pry too hard. Ethan must have re-lived some of it while they were talking with Jon. He didn't usually speak in Romanian for no reason anymore.

And then there was the other thing. Garth might have zero experience being a vampire, and he might not know how it made Ethan feel to drink human blood, but he saw things. He saw the way Ethan looked or didn't look at the blood. He saw the defensiveness when he started keeping it in the office. He knew how to tell when someone was taking something that altered how they felt. He knew how to spot twitchiness and craving.

Absently rubbing his throat, Garth left Ethan there, grabbed a thermos of pig blood from his own minifridge, and returned to find him in the same position. "Here."

Ethan's forehead creased. "Why…?"

Garth shrugged. "Hungry's bad. So, just in case."

Holding it without moving for a moment, Ethan added, "I need to get out of whatever we have going on tomorrow."

Garth nodded and reached for his phone, "I'll send Dr. Miller an email, let her know we're helping out a friend with an emergency."

Caterina had taken a human. One from the teeming thousands.

No, she was not injured or threatened and had no need to walk in the sun, but starvation was its own torment. The only animals she had been able to find in the foreign city were the rats, whose blood tasted as foul as the refuse they ate. The city bursting with humans would be unlikely to feel the loss of one. It would discover no reason to fear or hate a lone *strigoi*.

She retreated with the drained body deep into the underground tunnels and disposed of it in a shadowed crevice. Even there, the light was never ending, seeping from dirty yellow lights spaced much more closely than necessary for sight. The roar of the trains and the traffic above was similarly ubiquitous. There was no true darkness or silence to be found.

As she stepped over a pile of decaying material and chirped at the rats to prod them from her path, she felt eyes watching her movements.

She was not the only *strigoi* in the underworld of the city. The humans had taken no notice of her, yet she had not gone utterly unnoticed.

She stepped to more secure footing on the artificial ledge at the tunnel edge, swept her cloak aside to leave clear reach for her weapons, and clicked in her throat. The lights left no question as to what was in front of her, but hearing was better for searching the obscured side tunnels and shadows. The sacrifice of the human proved well-timed. Caterina could face the approaching vampire well strengthened.

Vampires. Another lingered behind in a shadow.

One landed from his well-executed leap more loudly than necessary in front of her. His appearance had been curated to mimic the humans closely, with cropped hair and a collared shirt and tie. Without greeting or introduction, his first words to her seemed to be a challenge. The words were not all clear to her, but she took the meaning to be a citation for her killing openly and without permission. His leer suggested he had some authority, or represented it, and took too much pride in his position.

Caterina remained still, poised to move but with no need to initiate it. *"Who are you to challenge my purposes?"* she asked in her own tongue to see if he would understand.

He did not. And he made the mistake of drawing a blade.

Without warning, Caterina leaped to the side, braced a footstep against the tunnel wall, and swiped the overconfident vampire's weapon arm with her knife. She spun to avoid the crimson spray and placed a single kick into his back to throw him off the ledge onto the tunnel floor among the liquified refuse and rats.

"Well done." The smooth voice emanated from the shadow further down the tunnel.

Caterina regained a motionless position, ready but silent. Curious.

The vampire moved more quietly, gliding from the shadow as though a part of it, and examined her with a faint smile. "Who might you be?"

A strange greeting. At least he didn't start with a challenge. "Caterina," she granted him.

"Caterina," he repeated it as though tasting the name. His quick words left some without meaning. "How many strangers…enter my realm…?"

"Who are you?" she asked.

He stepped closer. "I am Caspian. This city is mine."

How interesting. She smiled. Now she was getting somewhere.

51

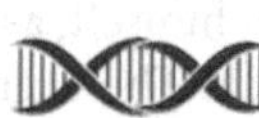

"Nice place."

Ethan gave the basement apartment door its required extra nudge open and tipped his head toward Garth. "He owns the building."

"Ah," Jon nodded, "That's…great." He had spent most of the taxi ride silently staring out the window, looking twice at sights he'd probably seen dozens of times. Although he'd jumped at the car horns, he hadn't seemed to mind the myriads of lights that glared along the way. Ethan found himself curious about how Jon was seeing the world and realized that must be Garth's viewpoint with all his tests.

"It's a one bedroom, but Garth swears the couch is as good a bed as his." *And smells a tad like him, and I have exactly one set of bed linens.* "You have an extra clean sheet or blanket?" he asked Garth who had followed them in.

"Yeah. I'll bring it down and anything else you can think of."

Jon had nothing but the blue scrubs they'd snagged from the emergency room for him to wear, but he was more likely to fit into something of Ethan's than Garth's. "Thanks," Ethan opened the refrigerator to find a fresh container from Chinatown. "And for stocking up."

"No problem."

He felt Jon's eyes as he poured himself a mug. "You want some?"

"Yea." His tone was sheepish.

I guess we're doing this now. Ethan inhaled slowly and handed it to him. Dread turned his stomach, so he put the container back without pouring his own.

John took a swallow. Looked down at it. "What is this?"

295

"Pig's blood." Ethan answered steadily. In the background, Garth's sudden heart rate spike indicated he'd just caught on.

"It doesn't taste like before." Jon's upper lip curled in a touch of disgust.

"It wasn't pig's blood, at the hospital."

"What was it then?"

I can't do this with you here, for more than one reason. Ethan looked Garth in the eyes. "I need you to leave."

To his credit he moved nearly instantly. "Ok. I'll bring you a sheet and blanket in—when you text me."

The door closing behind him sounded like a sentencing. Ethan met Jon's dark eyes firmly. "It was human."

He felt the punch to the gut himself, as horror dropped Jon's mouth open and turned his irises black. The wait to explain until Jon got past the initial blow felt interminable.

Jon glared savagely. "What did—how could you! Why?"

Ethan had to blink away the image of a mute young man, strung upside down. "After…turning, you needed a lot of nutrition quickly. Human," he nearly stuttered the word, "blood works better for that. But now, you're past the hard part. This," he pointed at Jon's mug, "should be enough. I'm sorry. I had to give it to you, as far as I know." The thick red liquid sloshed in the mug. "Try to forget it, if you can. This is it now. And we'll try some other things that you can probably eat…"

Jon backed away with what could only be described as a snarl and dropped his mug on the counter. "I don't want any of it."

"You do need this."

"No."

"If you don't—" Ethan leaned closer, "If you don't eat it, you will find what you crave elsewhere. You will hear, smell it in them," he ticked his chin at the blanket covered window, "and you will take it." Blue eyes now inches from Jon's black ones, he breathed, "Unless you want your friends, coworkers, your next patient, or the woman next to you on the subway to become as food to you, you will drink this. Because you need something. One or the other."

Jon lunged at him.

Ethan's backstep pivoted to avoid the chair behind him, but Jon wasn't as surefooted and plowed into it. His anger wasn't done with Ethan, and he swung back toward him with an uncanny growl.

Not surprised by the outburst, or blaming him for it, Ethan let him rage. An attempted hold of Jon's punching arm proved unsuccessful against his angry strength, so Ethan twisted away and blocked against blows by redirecting the force of his swing or simply ducking out of the way. It was not the first time he had faced an opponent stronger than he was, but the fight with Jon was made significantly easier by the fact that Ethan was still quicker.

Garth's apartment was not as good at getting out of his way. When Jon's fist punched through the drywall behind the place Ethan had just been standing, he darted into the center of the room. "As willing as I am to accept your blame for the way I handled this, I can't let you destroy this place." His attempt at diplomacy was met with another snarl, so with a kick off the counter to gain velocity, Ethan grasped Jon around the wrist and swung it into a position behind his back that he could hold steady by virtue of leverage, at least long enough to make him pause. "You have a right to be angry, but this needs to stop."

Jon moved to throw his back into the wall. Ethan released him, dropped to the ball of one foot in a squat, and spun out of the way. *Fine then, your way.* Using the opposite wall to launch off of, Ethan spun into a flying roundhouse kick that caught Jon in the temple and landed light on his feet.

Jon collapsed into a heap on the floor. It made him pause long enough to suck in a breath, and it seemed that the pause rather than the blow finally took the fight out of him, because he dropped his head into his hands with a sound that was more sob than growl.

Letting the blue fade from his eyes, Ethan perched on the arm of the upholstered chair that lay sideways in the center of the room and again waited.

"Why?" Jon gasped.

"I don't know. I don't have all the answers."

Dropping to his seat on the floor and leaning against the front of the couch, Jon heaved breaths through a gaping mouth and rubbed the side of his head.

"I'm sorry for that," Ethan said.

"Mum would have said I deserved it. Always cursing my thick Irish head."

"Irish?"

"Born there. Raised in London. Med school and residency here…at least I was…"

"Your skull is even thicker now, probably along with all your bones."

"How do you know that?"

"I would have cracked it otherwise," Ethan admitted. "And so are mine. They don't break as easily. And you're stronger. You're slightly stronger than me, but Garth or any other regular person isn't going to be able to stand up to you, now. You have the ability to easily overpower and hurt them, whether that's your initial goal or not. You need to understand that before you go back out there."

Jon dropped his head back against the couch cushion.

Ethan smoothly stood and retrieved his mug from the kitchen. "Finish that cup, and I'll brew some coffee. If it's the same for you, it'll be one of the few things with the same taste you're used to."

"This is mad."

As he picked up his phone to text Garth to leave the sheets at the front door, Ethan had to agree.

<h1 style="text-align:center">52</h1>

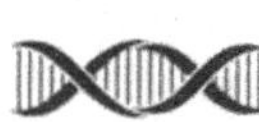

That was the sound of the front door squeaking open.

"Jon?" Ethan called, simultaneously shutting off the shower water and stepping out to drip onto the bathroom floor. When only the outside sounds of traffic answered him, he grabbed the towel off the rack in a rushed attempt to mitigate the dripping, snatched up his pants, and stuffed one leg in. Somehow balance kept him from tripping over his other pants leg as he yanked them on the rest of the way, buttoned his pants, and pulled on the shirt he'd left on the bed while walking into the disheveled—and empty—front room.

"Jon!" He yanked the front door open to stop at the threshold with a curse at the sunlight. *What are you doing? If you don't get yourself hurt, it's going to be someone else. Should I have said more last night?*

He had to go after him.

Hat, on. Sunglasses, in hand. Coat—no coat on the hook.

Forget the coat, just go find him. He leaped the steps to the sidewalk, turned one way then the other, and pulled the hat down further, wishing he could see past the glare better. "Jon!" He sprinted down one block of row houses. Stopped to listen with his eyes closed.

Traffic. People. A horn. A dog. Nothing abnormal.

Cursing again, he ran down the street, then turned to run completely around the block of row houses and shops.

He stopped back in front of the apartment with nothing to show for it except a startled older woman shouting after him. *This isn't going to work!* Ethan spun in another useless circle, scanned the street, and shoved his hands into his pockets in a futile attempt to slow the rising sting in them. He couldn't stay in the sun much longer if he wanted to

299

stay functional—*wait, there!*

Risking direct sunlight in the face by looking further up the street, he finally spotted Jon, ambling down the sidewalk, gaze flitting back and forth, chewing something, utterly unconcerned about the sunlight he was standing in.

Biting back some more creative curses, Ethan sprinted toward Jon, dodged a dog walker and three other pedestrians, and grabbed his arm with a hissed, "What are you doing?"

Jon jerked. "Ay! What are you—I was tired of being trapped, and hungry. I don't know what I was looking for, but then I walked by the butcher back there, and—ease up, what's the rush?"

"Just come on." Ethan continued to pull on his arm to speed up his walk.

"Why do we have to hide out—"

"You may be fine out here, surprise and congratulations, but I'm getting second degree radiation burns. Let's just finish the conversation inside—go please." Ethan nudged him toward the basement stairs, then, when he still wasn't moving fast enough, impatiently shoved him through the door.

Jon stumbled into the overturned chair in the middle of the apartment and turned back to Ethan, who leaned against the closed door and heaved a breath of relief.

"What—"

"And you took my coat," Ethan accused with a grimace.

"Borrowed—I don't have any of my own clothes." Jon indicated the scrub pants he was still wearing under Ethan's long coat.

"Are you eating raw meat?" Ethan pulled off his sunglasses and tried to blink away the pain the sun had seared into his eyes.

"Er, yeah, it was sitting there in the window, and I thought, there, I just need to actually *eat* something of substance. I was going to bring it back and cook it, but once I had it…it tastes good raw, which isn't right." He frowned at the paper bag in his hand.

"You feel ok? Not sick?"

"No?" There was uncertainty in his inflection.

"Maybe you can eat it then. It would have more calories than blood." Ethan grunted as he pushed away from the door and knocked his hat off on his way to the sink.

"What did you mean, about being burned?" Jon asked. Ethan put his hands into the running water. The sting took away his breath to answer, but there was apparently enough visible evidence on his face for Jon to turn the light on—making Ethan flinch—and walk over to look closer.

When he leaned in, Ethan gave a quick warning hiss.

After responding appropriately with a step back, Jon continued to study his face, then looked at the covered window, the door, and back to Ethan.

Ah. Ethan turned the tap off and spun to face him. "It's real."

"But, you're…" He retreated further.

"Yes."

Incredulousness filled his expression. "Then what am I?"

"Not the same, obviously," Ethan eyed the window, "And yet similar. After I was bitten, when I was taken to live with a group like the one who bit me, they told stories of a group called *Pricolijk*. I don't know for sure if they were referring to those changed by the same virus as you or not, but part of the word translates, I think, to 'wolf.'"

"You're saying I'm a werewolf." He backed into the couch and dropped down onto it, breaths coming in uneven gasps.

"It's not as if the terms are accurate anyway."

"You're completely mad."

There was that option.

A knock at the door interrupted, and Jon wasn't listening well anymore, staring at nothing with a horrified look in his eyes as his chest heaved, so Ethan stepped over to let Garth in.

He entered tentatively. "You ok? I thought I saw you outside a few min–" He cut off, making Ethan at least a little curious about what his face looked like.

"He went in search of food. I went in search of him." Ethan waved at Jon and walked back to the counter.

"Food?" Garth clarified, squeaking a little.

"At the butcher shop. It turns out he can eat meat. So, that's probably useful."

"Oh. Can you?"

"Eat meat? Raw, a bite or two. More than that," Ethan made a face. "But then I don't need as many calories, so," he shrugged.

"What happened?" Garth asked, looking at Jon.

"I'll pay for the drywall patch." Ethan referenced the hole in the wall above his head.

"Oh." Garth looked around at the toppled furniture as though noticing it for the first time before repeating, "What happened?"

"He had a right to be angry."

"Are *you* ok?"

"He's stronger, not faster," Ethan summarized.

"Stronger." The word was full of doubt.

"Yeah. Slower reaction speed though, I think."

"Oook." Garth wore a familiar, overwhelmed gape. "And now?" He pointed to Jon, who hadn't moved besides to hunch over further.

"He understands." Reaching to rub his eyes stretched the sore skin on his hand and face, so Ethan stopped with a wince. "He can call home, figure out life, now, whenever he's ready. I won't chase him if he leaves again."

"Understands?"

"What I am. What he is—as much as I know."

"All of it?"

"Enough." He pulled open the refrigerator and reactively shook out his hand at the sting the action added to his fingers.

"How long were you out there?"

"I don't know. Fifteen minutes?" Garth was making a sympathetic face when he turned around. "What does it look like?"

"Like a sunburn, I guess. I've just never seen you stay out that long."

Ethan drank straight from the container. "There's a reason I try not to make it a habit."

Without comment, he let Jon stand, sit, stand, start pacing a short section of floor, and drop back onto the couch with his hands in his hair.

There was no way he was doing anything right. Why hadn't he just left Jon in the emergency room? Jon wasn't a responsibility he was equipped for or wanted. It might not have been worse if someone else had found him. He might not have been killed. But was the alternative that he be made into the image of his attacker, as Ethan had been? What if there was another way?

Jon needed to know what Ethan did. At least most of it.

Shaking his head at the decision he made, Ethan took another swallow, set the container down with a grimace, and walked across the room. He righted the upholstered chair across from Jon and sat down. "Ok. Ask. I'll answer anything I know."

After staring at him blankly for a moment, Jon finally croaked, "How did it happen? What you are?"

Ethan took a breath. He could make Garth leave again, but he wouldn't stay gone. He was too doggedly persistent. It already had him in danger, from Ethan, now Jon, maybe from Caspian and the others. He might need the answers as badly. Even if it stung Ethan to give them.

Still opting to stay as vague as possible, he told Jon the short version of how he and Jack had ended up in the cave in Romania. "The next day, we both started getting sick, like you did, but he was worse off. I'm pretty sure it was killing him. Then she came back, killed him, and took me to their cave. I turned there, like you did in the basement."

"She?"

"They. There were over twenty."

"They fed you blood?"

"Yes, human at first, or when I was injured. Otherwise, we drank animal blood from the livestock they kept."

"Injured?"

"My metabolism seems to go up when healing. Something about…human blood seems to work better under those circumstances. Although that doesn't mean it's necessary."

"Where do you find humans in a cave in Romania?"

Refusing to break eye contact, Ethan shifted subtly, feeling the ache of his shoulders under his shirt. "You take a sacrifice from surrounding villages once a month."

"You…" Jon gaped. "Did you kill people?"

But there was the one question he wouldn't answer.

Ethan shoved every slippery emotion deeper down, further from his eyes. "People were killed. I was there. I escaped when I could figure out how."

"How did you escape?"

By becoming one of them. "I took advantage of the right moment."

Jon looked at Garth, who was leaning against the counter, heart pounding. "He's not the same."

"No. He's human." When that seemed harsh, he attempted to rephrase, but, "His DNA has not been altered," didn't seem much better.

"And he knows? What you are?"

"Yes."

"Then why is his heart rate so fast?"

"Oh great, two of you with super ears," Garth muttered.

"I generally avoid talking about my time in Romania. He doesn't know every detail. But I told you I'd answer your questions."

"I can seriously hear everything."

"So can I."

"And the smells?"

"You mean the blood?"

"No, I mean *everything*." He waved at the door. "Rubbish, sewage, those dogs, the bakery," he jabbed a thumb in the direction of a store two blocks over, "The butcher, the veg stand–and people smell–everything."

"Uh…" Garth and Jon were both looking at him for answers now. "No, that's different. I can smell and differentiate blood with odd accuracy, but not everything, I don't think."

"Right…" Jon fidgeted, pulled his feet up onto the couch, dropped them back down, and shook his head again.

"When I got back," Ethan pushed his autobiography forward to safer topics, "I found I'd been declared dead. Garth helped me fix that and get me back to work. Everything I told you about the virus, DNA changes, is what I've discovered in the last few months at our lab. And I found out Romania isn't the only place where we live–there are others who appear the same as me, here. When I saw you in the emergency room, I thought you were one of them, but it seems I don't fully know how this world works yet."

"There are other–others like me here?" Jon didn't say the word. To say it made it real.

"I haven't seen any, but I didn't know to look," Ethan answered.

"This is mad," Jon waved aimlessly.

Ethan didn't disagree.

"These things aren't real! How could it be that these things actually exist, and no one knows about it? Isn't it more likely that we're the ones who have lost reality?"

"I thought of that." Ethan started to rub his eyes again. "But I'm a scientist. There are measurable differences, observable changes–and a plausible explanation. And you and I are not the only ones who can see them." He glanced back at Garth.

"I think I'm maybe not crazy. At least completely," Garth offered.

"What happened to you? Do you mind telling us the whole story?" Ethan asked Jon.

Jon looked away, absently rubbing his shoulder. "I was camping, upstate, with four mates. I said I'd been camping, but they didn't think it was real, American roughing it. We were out in the middle of nowhere, with three tents and a fire." the faint smile at that memory dropped into an expression of disgust. "It was the middle of the night. Everyone was asleep, at least Pete was–he snored like an engine…Then something started growling. I–I thought it was maybe one of the others joking, but then they were yelling something about a bear. I'd never seen one. I looked out, there was something ripping into one of the others. There was screaming. I found Pete, but," his hand clenched into a fist, "There was blood everywhere. I tried to find where he was injured, but there was no pulse. Jake–he was dragged right out of the tent…" He clenched his fist at his mouth, as his pupils expanded to turn his irises to circles of black.

"It's ok–"

"I thought it had gone, but then it had me. There wasn't any fur," gasp, "but he growled, and bit, and…" He dropped his hand from his shoulder to look at his fingernails, hard and sharper than they should have been. "When it let go, I just ran. The keys were in the car. I didn't even try to find the others…" He inadvertently bared his teeth at the thought. "But there were no more screams…"

"I'm sorry."

Jon's black eyes met Ethan's again.

"There's nothing you could have done. I tried to save Jack, but I couldn't, either."

His pupils constricted, leaving his eyes brown and his head hanging.

"What did you do next?" Ethan asked.

"I drove to town. Ended up at the hospital, maybe from habit, I d'nno. They patched me up, took a statement. Supposedly someone went to investigate our campsite–I didn't go back. It was reported as a bear attack. I think I believed it because I wanted to…until I came back and instead of getting better, everything just kept hurting worse until I couldn't stand up, head exploding–and you show up in the ER and say you know what it is that attacked me."

"I…was not entirely accurate. But not entirely wrong."

"And now what?" Jon dug his hands into his matted hair. "I just go back to life like you did?"

Is that what I've done? Ethan wasn't sure anymore. "I'm not going to tell you that it's been easy, but it helps that I live where the subway is underground and work in a windowless office. And that I found an old friend who, for some reason, believed my crazy story and wanted to help."

Jon's amber eyes flicked back and forth between him and Garth. "I don't have the sun…issue."

"That has to be an advantage," Ethan agreed easily. "We–I can try to help, however I can."

"I'm in too," Garth threw in. "I don't know if I could actually do anything, but I'm in."

"How are you at making up cover stories? Because I just missed weeks of residency and have no idea how to explain it and get back in."

"Not that bad, actually," Garth replied.

Blowing a breath through his lips to keep from groaning as he stood, Ethan walked stiffly to the kitchen side of the room and braced himself against the counter where Garth leaned.

After taking a step to the side to give him some space, Garth asked cautiously, "You need me to leave?"

"No. I just don't feel great." Ethan ticked his head at the door.

"Oh, from the sun?"

"Yeah." He stared at the container of blood he'd left sitting on the counter and had to preach the message he'd given Jon yesterday to himself for a solid minute before he could make himself pick it up. The nausea was starting to become more than a background sensation.

"You think it's like radiation sickness? Affecting not just the skin?"

Ethan twitched his head in a possibly affirmative tilt.

"Can you think of anything that could help? I mean, like cool water or something?"

And darkness. "Maybe."

From the couch, Jon started, "Er, sorry I gave you second degree burns. I didn't…"

"Not your fault. I should have…I don't know. Done something differently. You didn't end up with a very competent guide to help you out with this."

Jon's lost expression drifted away to the door.

"I'm going to go finish the shower I was taking." Ethan set the container he couldn't drink any more from in the refrigerator and stepped toward the bedroom. "If you touch Garth, I'll kill you."

"Yea. Right. Wasn't…going to." Jon stammered after him.

The darkness in the bathroom relieved the pain in his eyes but raised the ghosts. He turned on the shower and leaned his forehead against the cool wall without bothering to remove his clothes as the water droplets whispered back the question in a hundred murmured voices: *Did you kill?*

53

It had been agony beyond reckoning, to lie in that narrow rock cell, sticky with dried blood from the wounds they kept inflicting, his stomach cramping so hard it might have cut him in half. The worst was knowing that the one thing that would stop it all was there within reach.

Tears stung the burned skin on his face, but Ethan couldn't let himself rinse them off with the cool water. He deserved so much more suffering.

"I'm sorry, Iulia."

In the end she had asked him to finish it, to do it cleanly and quickly, to prevent someone else from doing it differently.

"It's ok," she'd whispered.

That invitation, enticement, had been too much.

And so nothing would ever be ok again.

He'd ended their torment with his teeth in her neck.

When it was done, after he'd drank long enough that she was limp and her heart went silent, he'd laid her gently on the hay strewn ground and felt something click deep inside.

She hadn't been the only one to die that night.

Was he insane, as Jon accused, because he thought he was a vampire? Or was he insane because he thought he could be Ethan Dalton again when that man had surely died?

"Ethan?" Garth's voice came from outside the bathroom door. "You ok? Jon said he heard something weird."

"Stay out."

"Ok, I understand. I mean—not technically, but I'm not coming in, ok? I'll go keep an eye on Jon, so just, take your time. Holler if you need something."

✗

"Is he ok?"

Garth settled onto the stool across from Jon, where he sat with the laptop Garth had handed him a few minutes ago. *Depends on your definition of "ok,"* he thought. "Yeah. It just hasn't been the easiest morning ever."

Jon grunted with an expression that said, "No kidding."

"Did you get in?" Since Jon didn't have his phone, Garth had set him up with his computer to try to access his email account as a way to start contacting someone.

"Yea…I just don't know what to do now." His eyes glazed over. "I was in that basement for weeks, what do I tell…" He leaned back and searched the ceiling.

"Yeah. And the rules," Garth mused.

"What rules?"

"I don't know, exactly, but Ethan said that one of the vampires here told him the number one rule here is to not tell anyone else about them."

Jon stared at him.

"But you're right. The whole truth may not be the best thing to tell anyone, and I'm usually a fan of the truth. Ethan has a version that he tells others—well there's not much to it actually. He just says that he was taken hostage by an underground group in Romania and escaped two years later. It's true, it just…leaves out the really confusing parts. It sounds like the cops upstate already started a story for you and blamed the attack on a bear?"

"Yea." He looked lost.

"Ok, and then what happened when Ethan found you?"

"I was…falling ill. I tried to go to work in the ER and became a patient instead. He told me to tell them I was leaving because nothing was working. Then…I don't know. I was in the basement."

"Ok, so you were attacked, got sick, left the hospital where everyone knows you, and ended up in a different hospital for an illness for a while? Almost true."

Jon scratched his head. "It might be plausible that I was admitted a John Doe until I regained consciousness. But it'll have to be a hospital a good ways off, as I know someone at most of the ones around here."

"Just figure out which one, and you've got it. You woke up when the infection cleared or whatever. Sounds like you could possibly forge some records if you need them for work stuff, huh?"

"I d'nno, maybe." He stared into the vague distance, his foot bouncing faster and faster, until he jumped to his feet, then froze with a look at the bedroom door as if caught.

"What?"

"I d'nno, I need to go for a walk or something, but—"

"He said you were fine to go now. And I can tell him where you went."

After borrowing Garth's phone and an old hoodie so he wouldn't have to steal Ethan's coat again, Jon left.

Alone, Garth rubbed his face, looked around the room, and thought about the last three months that had just crescendoed in the last 24 hours.

Qualls, you are so far down the rabbit hole now.

It was something researchers aspired to, to find something that changed the rules of known reality. But this was something altogether reality shattering. He was also concerned about Ethan, who was injured and upset about something or other that had come up during that conversation with Jon.

You know which question, you just don't want to think about it.

To avoid thinking, he wandered about the room instead, righting a lamp and tidying some things that had apparently gotten knocked everywhere last night before ultimately retreating to his own apartment for some breakfast. Given the diets of his downstairs companions, he doubted either would appreciate his eggs and toast.

When he returned to the basement, Ethan's bedroom door was open to an empty room and Jon wasn't anywhere to be found either.

Well, now what?

It only took ten minutes of pacing before Jon returned, nearly falling through the door he threw open while looking at the phone in his hand.

"Hey, how was the walk?" Garth greeted.

"I called my Mum."

"Oh! That was probably a good place to start. Does she live here?"

"No, London."

"That might be good, considering it's kind of hard to hide big changes from moms. How was the call?"

"Er, she was glad to hear from me—started crying actually. I've been declared a missing person."

"Oh. Well, that's better than being dead. It sounds like the John

Doe story could fly ok."

"Yea, she believed me," he winced, probably at the idea of lying to her, "but it's easier to believe than…" He looked down at his nails, hard and long and definitely resembling claws. When he sat back down with the computer in front of him, he seemed frightened.

"You don't have to do everything at once. Like Ethan said, just do one thing at a time."

"It's been so long already–I don't know what happens to my place in the program if I'm missing."

"The residency?"

He nodded. "It's all I've been working towards for…years. If I don't finish, I don't work as a physician."

"Will one more day, or even a couple, make that big a difference? While you get a handle on things? After a month?"

"I d'nno." He leaned back and reached for his hair before stopping to look at his nails again.

"We could start by letting you feel more–uh, normal," Garth pivoted mid-sentence to avoid the word "human." "I have a razor, if you want it. I don't know if I have a file that's going to work on your nails, but I bet Amazon does, and we have same day delivery. We could order some clothes too, while we're at it."

Jon nodded. "Yea, all right. Wait, is he still here?" He jabbed a thumb at the bedroom.

"Apparently not. But I'm sure he'll be back." Actually, Garth was surprised he had gone back outside while the sun was up, but he opted to play it down a little.

After ordering things and letting Jon trim his beard and use his laptop to contact his landlord, Garth ended up slaughtering orcs and trolls online with the sound muted while Jon dozed on the couch for a few hours.

Garth woke him by screeching the front door open to retrieve the box from the doorstep, noting out of habit that the sun had just dropped behind the buildings across the street. When he turned back, Jon was sitting stark upright. In the current light level of the apartment and as dark as his eyes were naturally, it was difficult to see if they were the huge-pupil black.

"Hey," Garth started cautiously and held up the box. "Delivery. You ok?"

Jon slumped back, rubbing his hands over his recently shaved jaw, "Yea…just, forgot for a second."

"Understandable. This must be super weird."

He grunted, "Yea."

"I think I've got some of your stuff here."

"Thanks." Jon took the box from him and ripped open a flap with shocking ease that had him giving his own hand a second look.

"How are you feeling?"

"Er–" By the ashamed look that flashed over his face when he looked at Garth and then the fridge and then the floor, Garth had a guess.

"Hungry?" Garth started walking for the fridge where he'd stowed the bag of ground beef from the counter earlier.

When he pulled it out, Jon eyed it uneasily. "What if we cook it?"

"You want to try? Sure. Ethan doesn't like cooked meat, but then he doesn't really eat meat at all, so who's to say you can't? We'll have to do a little discovery here and there won't we?"

After retrieving a pan from the recesses of a cabinet, Garth formed a rough patty and started cooking. He didn't get very far before Jon gave him an uneasy look.

"What?"

"It's only…that smells rather terrible, actually."

"Ok," Garth answered easily. "Maybe that answers that question. You just grab a plate and the rest of that," he pointed to the bag, "And I'll just have this one, if you don't mind."

When he was done cooking it, Jon tried a single bite to confirm its unpalatableness, then Garth took the rest, jogged upstairs to retrieve some ketchup and pickles, and returned to finish it at the table.

Jon's sudden glance to the door was all too familiar for Garth not to recognize. The door opened before Garth could take a step, and Ethan ducked through and shut it quickly, although the sun was already down.

"Hey. Where have you been?"

"Lab." Ethan's voice was quiet and flat as he doffed his hat and jacket.

"I thought we were all squared away to have the day off."

"Needed some things." Ethan stepped toward Jon. "How are you?"

"Fine." He shrugged. "I don't really know." He told Ethan about calling his mom with the cover story they had come up with and checking his email but not really doing anything else about it yet.

After a quick, "Thanks," aimed at Garth, presumably for staying with him when he hadn't, Ethan pulled a stack of papers out of his bag. "I promised you evidence."

54

Garth watched Ethan set a few pages from the top of his stack onto the table in front of Jon. "This is the virus I isolated from your blood. There are details on the other pages, but I ran a lot of tests trying to identify it, and I cannot. It has not been described in any literature. There is another virus in my own blood, different, but also not identifiable.

"This," he added another two pages to Jon's stack, "Is your original genotype. And here is a partial I ran on your current genome. It isn't complete, because the computer software has trouble finding the correct markers on our new genomes, but the genotype whisperer has promised to keep working on it." He shot a glance at Garth. "In the meantime, this does show two SNPs that are different from your original genome. This one is in the same place that mine has a change. That one is different."

Garth pushed the empty plates aside and leaned around Jon to see what he was pointing to. "You did a karyotype too?"

"Yes." Ethan shuffled papers and dropped one with the pairs of banded pillars onto the table. "The only change big enough to see is at the same location as mine."

"Someone is going to have to refresh my old med school knowledge, mates," Jon interrupted.

"We're looking at the same DNA, just from 10,000 feet packaged into little x's," Garth offered before asking, "Did you do a FISH on his too?"

"Yes." Ethan retrieved a printed visualization of his telomeres obtained using the immunofluorescence technique.

They were long. "How old are you?" Garth asked.

"Twenty-eight, why?"

Oh boy, this is a fun one.

He actually heard Ethan take a deep breath.

"Telomeres are DNA end caps or something, yea?" Jon tried.

"Yes. Represented here." Ethan pointed to the page, at the fluoresced portion. "They act to protect the DNA when cells replicate. They typically get shorter as we age."

"Right. And?"

"The other vampires in the cave–most of them appeared to be as old as I am, but I realized they had been there for far longer. Some of them for over 100 years."

"Ay?" Jon's mouth dropped part-way open in a baffled expression.

"It seems that some of the DNA changes caused by the virus affect aging. Delay it, or prevent it."

Jon's curse called the validity of Ethan's claim into question.

"The telomeres on my chromosomes are the length that a small child should have. So are yours. And since I have your original results, from the first day I found you, to compare to, I can confirm they are longer than they were before you were infected. It would seem that you may, from now on, age very slowly."

"That's impossible."

"As is the rest of this. Yet, it seems to be fact. I will add my own observation that, personally, I have not gotten sick in the last two years, excepting reactions of my body to food it can't digest and the sun. I haven't identified the specifics, but I think there are differences in how the immune system works. It's an assumption that you will be similar. Additionally, most injuries heal more quickly–a small cut will heal in a day, a larger injury in a few days. I don't know what effect, if any, the differences in your metabolic rate will have on those time frames."

Having given up on words, Jon just gaped at him. Garth took advantage of the pause and reached for the paper in Ethan's hand to examine the results he hadn't seen before.

"They were over a hundred? You actually know that?" Jon finally spoke again.

"Some, much over," Ethan answered stoically.

"Wha…and no getting sick?"

"It seems so."

"I need a drink."

"In my experience, substances such as alcohol, nicotine, and caffeine don't have the same effect as before. I don't know if it's due to a nervous system change or if it will hold true for all drugs."

Jon glared at him.

There could be advantages to that. Along with the obvious disadvantages, of course, Garth mused.

"Anything else?" Jon challenged.

"Yes." Ethan dropped the rest of the papers onto the table and reached into his bag to retrieve a couple specimen containers and swabs. "There are a few other things I can tell you, and I'd like to test to confirm others."

Jon got up and paced the length of the apartment before coming back. "Let's have it, then."

"Safety first. For those around you. The virus you carry can infect others, obviously, and can change DNA as it did in your, or it can kill, which I think is actually the more likely result. The virus is present in your blood, as mine is in mine, but not in huge quantities. From the testing I've done, it doesn't appear that someone is going to get infected by a tiny bit of virus, and it dies quickly on surfaces, so unless you exchange a significant amount of your blood with someone, they're likely fine even with casual exposure."

"Right. That sounds…good."

"Saliva is more complicated. For me, regular saliva carries no virus, but saliva released when I bite into something contains a significant dose. So, passing saliva by having someone drink after me, or with a kiss, would have very low risk. But a bite is another matter. As we can both attest to."

Jon rubbed his shoulder.

"I would like to confirm that it is the same for you, by swabbing your mouth and then having you bite down." Ethan reached for an orange off the counter.

"Yea, fine."

After he'd swabbed his mouth, Ethan handed him an orange. "Now bite this."

"Why an orange?"

Ethan's head shake was irritated. "I don't—for consistency's sake, ok?"

Garth watched Jon bite it, admitting to himself that there was something instinctively fearsome about watching his subtly curved, pointed canines and abutting molars sink into the fruit's thick skin. It was so incongruous with the concerned and confused but regular-seeming man standing there holding the orange.

"Did you test other bodily fluids?" Jon asked.

Ethan swabbed and bagged the orange. "Urine is clear. Nothing obvious in stool. Semen contains no virus. At least for me."

I had no idea you tested all that.

"I can check yours if you want," Ethan added.

"Yea, er, maybe later, or, I'll let you know."

"Incidentally," Ethan continued while sealing the specimen bag, "You may also be sterile. Children of vampires were never mentioned, despite activity that should have led to the consideration. I theorized that something about the changes prevented procreation, and it turns out it is as simple as sterility—no sperm."

Jon's reaction was one of absorbing enough blows to finally be knocked down. "Oh," he grunted and dropped back onto the stool.

"Sorry." Ethan took in his reaction and paused. "I can't know for sure it's the same, unless you decide you want me to check."

Garth managed to keep his questions inside his head.

"What else?" Jon dropped his hands from his hair.

"We don't have to talk about everything all at once."

"What else do I need to know before I call my program director and try to get back? Can I even do this anymore?"

Ethan seemed less sure for a moment. "I think the main issue goes back to the blood."

Jon frowned and started to speak.

"You had the same reaction as I did, so I think I know what I'm talking about, all right?" When Jon slumped back, Ethan continued. "You're an emergency room doctor?"

"Trying to be," Jon mumbled.

"How many of your patients are bleeding when you take care of them?"

That seemed less a problem until you said it that way. Garth started holding his breath and waiting to be kicked out again.

"If you can't avoid it, then you need to be ready."

"To what?"

"To treat it like nothing special. Like everyone else does. To not taste."

Jon looked away. "That's disgusting."

"Is it?"

Ethan's question hung in the air for a minute before he spoke again. "Don't let yourself get hungry. It's good that you can eat meat, but drink some too, just in case. I'm still not sure what it is about blood that is special. Some things, like injury, increase your metabolism and hunger. Anticipate it. Keep blood and food on hand even if you think you don't need it in case you discover something we don't know. Don't let your guard down–around your patients but also friends, those you're close to." He shifted. "And you should probably be exposed to it in close quarters again before it's your patient in the hospital. So you can decide if you can do it."

"How?"

"We'll figure something out before you go back–No."

Garth hadn't even been able to open his mouth before Ethan spun back to him. "What?" he tried an innocent look.

"It's not a good idea. I won't have him looking at you that way–"

"What about yours?" Jon interrupted Ethan.

"It's not the same." Without fanfare, Ethan lifted his own wrist to his mouth, pierced the skin with a single nick of his tooth as though it was the most basic of actions, and held it toward Jon, who studied the drop of blood for a moment.

"Oh."

Ethan nodded, agreeing with an apparently obvious point that Garth completely missed.

"It smells more like blood should. Not like…"

Ethan nodded again. "Yours is similar, although I can tell the difference." After removing the drop of blood with his lip he dropped his arm but tensed when Jon's gaze moved back to Garth.

Managing to swallow his disturbance, Garth spewed his argument, "It's just, I'm sitting right here, plenty of blood, while you're looking for some, so he can know how to react? Seems like a pretty straightforward answer."

Ethan was getting shifty on him.

"Small quick cut, you chat, I leave to get cleaned up." He shrugged. "Easy peasy."

Ethan shook his head and stepped into enough light for Garth to notice the remnants of the sunburn on his face. Ethan had been acting better, so he'd forgotten for a moment, but maybe there was more to his current attitude. "Or we can do it another day or whatever."

"Could we not wait?" Jon cut in. "I need to figure out what I'm doing. If he's fine with it. I won't touch him, and you wouldn't let me anyway."

Deciding not to push Ethan, Garth just waited.

Ethan closed his eyes over the space of a slow breath. "There's a knife in the drawer behind you. Cut your arm, not your hand, and don't make it deep. Leave when I tell you and go upstairs."

"Yep." Garth pushed up his sleeve and turned around to open the drawer before he lost his nerve, because, the longer he thought about the idea, the worse it seemed. "Ready?"

Ethan turned to face Jon, putting his back to Garth and leaving him a clear path to the front door. "Yes."

Cutting himself on purpose required more than one try–he chickened out with the blade touching his skin the first time–but he did it, a short nick on his forearm, careful to avoid any large veins, eyes flicking up afterwards to watch the two others in the room.

It dropped a cold stone in his gut to watch Jon's eyes change, but that eased when Ethan moved to put himself squarely between them. Looking back down only to make sure the blood pooling on his forearm wasn't dripping to the floor, Garth kept his nerve and stood still, ready but waiting for Ethan, who would probably have told him the complete trust was foolish but didn't get to tell him who to trust.

Jon had dropped his gaze to the floor.

"You want it." Ethan wasn't asking.

Jon's brow drew tight, but he didn't move. His gaze remained locked on Garth's wrist as he started shaking his head and ultimately pulled his eyes back to Ethan. "That's…completely unnatural."

Quiet, tense minutes stretched on, while the only drama was Garth using his shirt sleeve to keep the blood from dripping off his arm, until Ethan told him to, "Go." The blue in his eyes just visible when he turned his head to the side made Garth hesitate. But then he opted to take it as a kick in the rear to get him through the stubborn door and out into the night.

Had Ethan been out of control or threatening Jon? Or did it really matter, considering that he was outside, and they were inside, and maybe he had been able to give Jon what he needed.

Never mind. Just go Google what gets blood out of shirts.

⌐

A tension eased in Ethan's chest with the banging of the door, and he watched his vision change as the blue vanished from his eyes. "You don't need it," he told Jon, who had dropped his head into his hands.

"Are you sure?"

"It has to be." It was just as well he couldn't see Ethan's face give a different answer.

"Yea." The other man's voice sounded steadier than Ethan's own. Perhaps he could hold on to that resolve. "Ok. Will it be easier next time?"

"No," Ethan answered. "How do you think that went?"

Jon plopped onto the couch with a shrug. "I d'nno. Fine. I just stood there."

"Your eyes changed."

He looked up. "Really? The pupils? Like when I had the mirror…?"

"Yes. Can you tell? My vision sharpens with the color change."

His gaze bounced around the room. "I'm not sure. Why do they…?"

"Mine change with a threat or anger or craving, or any especially strong emotion."

"How do I change them back?"

"Feel it. And then choose to feel something else."

Jon scoffed, stood, and paced two steps and closed his eyes trying to follow the ethereal instructions.

When his eyes were brown upon reopening, Ethan's faith in him was significantly bolstered. "Good."

"You sound surprised."

"It's not easy. You're doing well. However, to work with others, you will need to learn to not let them change at all."

"How?"

So much hope placed in his terrible explanations. "Learn not to feel."

"That doesn't sound possible."

"Practice. Until you can, learn to notice immediately when it happens and don't let them see. I don't yet understand all the repercussions of giving away the secret, but I know there are consequences."

"Is it the same for you? When you smell it?"

"How do you think I know?"

"Is that why your eyes…?" He motioned at them.

"There's more than one emotion that causes it, remember?" Ethan opted for ambiguity as he started for the bedroom.

"Wait—what else?"

"Jon," Ethan leaned against the doorframe, "I don't know. I'm still figuring it out myself, ok? And even if I knew it all, I couldn't give it all to you right this minute. I have told you all I can think of. And I'll continue to be around to help, to figure things out. But I've given you all I can today. One step at a time. Please."

55

It took one second for David Seeley to go from bored and relaxed to completely alert. He'd been leaning against the wall behind the churn of other gray security uniforms waiting for the bland shift change report when the supervisor walked in with two NYPD officers trailing him.

"We've got two off duties with us tonight." The bald Hispanic supervisor pointed lazily with his thumb to the two officers. The tall young one scanned the room until his gaze landed on Seeley. His supervisor continued, "Seeley, you are my senior down here tonight and were moaning about your assignment–take one and stick him where you don't want to be."

You've got to be kidding me.

"Since the break in, we're being asked for more coverage without more bodies, so give me some walking patrols, and if you're at monitors, watch them please. Good night."

Seeley waited for the small crowd to file out of the room before he approached the officer, whose casual posture was a contrast to the abrupt tension in Seeley's.

"So, I'm with you," Officer Sanderson intoned.

"What are you doing here?"

"Owens said his usual partner called out, said I should come over and take a shift." A tilt of his head indicated the other officer who was already down the hall with another security guard.

There had to be more to it, but the lycan officer stood relaxed as though it really were just another day at work.

"Seriously?"

"Why not?" the officer returned.

"All right, Officer Sanderson, guess you're with me then." As wrong as it felt to turn his back on a lycan, Seeley stepped past him to lead the way to his assigned post.

As they descended to the ground floor, Sanderson asked, "You ever find your intruder?"

Is that why you're here? "Nope. Still a ghost."

Sanderson's grunt could have meant any number of things.

Seeley stopped at the security desk at a side entrance of the research building that connected to the hospital a short way down the hall. He tried to go through the routines of his job despite Sanderson's eyes on him, exchanging brief pleasantries with the security guard who was going off shift and stepping behind the desk next to the bank of old video monitors.

"There's a small door in the hall down that way—you can see it from here." Seeley pointed it out to Sanderson. "They want that manned at least for the better part of the evening, so that's you. The door should be locked, but everyone who works in the building has access, and there's night classes, and some of the professors keep weird hours."

Sanderson nodded.

"They should all have ID's."

"Yep, got it." He started that way, alert and looking around every corner, but otherwise relaxed. Seeley couldn't help but picture a golden retriever at work and tried not to snicker as he walked the other way to a small, oddly-located waiting room. The green vinyl chairs were all empty, and the TV unattended. "Right on…" Locating the remote, he flipped it onto the Rangers game and left the door open. It wasn't the marathon of old musicals that ran on Wednesday nights which he would have usually turned on, but it wasn't like he was going to admit that particular preference with a lycan listening to everything he did. And anyway, he did like hockey.

Back at his desk, he updated the log and toggled through the camera feeds but couldn't escape the unease that the cop down the hall could hear everything he was doing as well as Seeley could hear him shift in his creaky chair and tap his heel repetitively.

Might as well take advantage of it. "So, you're really a cop."

A muscle behind Sanderson's jaw tugged his ear back a little, but he didn't respond.

"I know you can hear me. I can see your ear twitch." Seeley persisted.

With another glance around, as though to ensure himself he was alone, Sanderson answered, "Yep."

"As yourself. Not impersonating someone else?"

"It's not my first name, but yes, I, myself, am an officer. You work here alone?"

"Is that why you're here? To check *me* out? No, it's not a company job. I too am honestly, gainfully employed. It's not that weird."

"Not that common either. Did they want eyes up here for some reason?"

"Ease up, I'm not Caspian's bug. I don't work for anyone except the college, all right?"

"You're a loner."

"It's not that dangerous in the city. There's…potential backup. I'm just fine and not interested right now."

Sanderson looked around the corner at him. "Maybe we do have something in common."

"You got into the NYPD without someone greasing things?" Seeley shot back skeptically.

"You just told me you're in this job honestly." He returned to staring at the door.

"But all I needed was a good enough backstory for a basic background check and a reference. Then, interview a tall, broody, fit guy for a security night shift job, easy in. The NYPD has a whole academy, physical training tests, health checks?"

"It helps that I don't get sunburned in under two minutes."

"Oh lay off." Seeley rolled his eyes. "I get that you have a physical advantage already. I was trying to ask an honest question."

Sanderson answered after a moment, "I passed the academy. The PT was easy, just have to be consistent. Most of the health checks are cursory. I had a guy I used for blood work once."

"You must be watched like a hawk though."

"A lot of the time."

"Why risk it? Why put yourself through that?"

Sanderson paused again before answering, "To do something good. Thought there ought to be a way I could use my skills for the good of society instead of…" He shrugged.

Seeley pondered that. "But, New York City, really? A small town had to have been an easier option."

"That has occurred to me," Sanderson agreed flippantly.

The overhead speaker crackled out an announcement.

"Code purple?" Sanderson asked.

Seeley stood and started down the hall. "Let's go. Did they not give you any kind of orientation?"

"You were there for the whole thing." Sanderson jogged to follow.

"The five-minute roll call thing? Good grief, they must really be hurting for help. Code purple equals crazy patient going ballistic, and they need muscle to hold them down while they jab some happy drugs into them. I'm *campus* security, not hospital, but I hate this post because it is too close. We still have to respond to the crazy who somehow made it to this lobby–there."

A balding man too large to be completely covered by his blue patterned hospital gown which gaped open in the back turned in frantic circles in the small lobby that served as the hospital entrance on that side of the building. Catching sight of Seeley, he froze and turned his wide unfocused eyes in his direction. "They're coming! Get me out! The moon–it's full! It's rising! You have to get me out!"

Seeley couldn't help sliding a slow side eye to Sanderson.

After a quick press of his lips, Sanderson gave a single head shake.

"This is definitely the beginning of a bad joke," Seeley cracked dryly and looked back at the man who was waddling toward the sliding doors to the outside. "We need to stop him from leaving. You want to get him or should I?"

"He's big enough it should probably take two people," Sanderson replied.

Seeley groaned. "Fine, come on then. That's the cavalry with the happy drugs." He waved toward two people in scrubs jogging down the other hall.

"Sir," Sanderson stepped around to angle himself between the man and the door, "I need you to–"

"I need to leave! I have to–get off–get off!"

Seeley dodged the swing at his head and caught one arm, but he watched Peter take a flailing punch to the chest before grasping the man's other arm. It didn't take much of a combined push to get the man to his knees, and they held him, squealing, in place on the floor while the nurses injected him.

The scent of the blood drop from the injection site wafted through the stale air. *At least you're human.* Seeley looked vaguely away while they waited for the drugs to take effect. Feeling Sanderson's eyes check him, he realized he wasn't the only person who had just thought that. Camaraderie with a lycan…was officially the strangest feeling ever.

The man started to go limp in his grasp, and they completed the hand off of the man to the increasing number of nurses and other scrub-clad helpers.

As they walked away, Seeley brushed the front of his uniform, as though to get the crazy fat man scent off of him. "This is why I don't work in the hospital. Bleh. Why do they smell like that?"

Sanderson snorted.

"If you can smell so well, then how do you even live here?"

His companion just flicked his eyebrows in acknowledgement.

They strolled back down the hall. "Well, that was the most exciting thing to happen all week. Between the break in and our crazy guy, I'm starting to think you're bad luck. You really are all in on looking normal, huh?" Seeley tapped his own chest at the spot where Sanderson had taken the punch. Surely the lycan would have been able to grab the man or something to avoid the hit if he'd wanted to.

"You're the one who just observed that I'm in a highly scrutinized job."

"Yeah…" Seeley studied him again, "You're weird."

Sanderson shrugged, accepting it.

After settling back behind his desk, Seeley checked the clock. Sanderson had gone a whole five minutes before starting the foot tapping again.

And his luck didn't continue. By 11:07, Seeley had enough of his chair creaking and foot tapping. "You up for a patrol wander?"

His, "Yep," sounded relieved.

"Ok, traffic through that door should be about nil by this time of night, and I can see it, so just walk a big circle, starting that way. Yeah. Stay on this floor. Pretty sure a cop should be able to handle it. If you get lost or see something off, just howl or something and I'll come find you."

"I don't howl," he replied blandly and walked away.

"Yeah." Seeley snickered to himself. "I figured."

56

Jon was pacing. Back and forth across the apartment.

Back and forth.

Ethan felt like he was watching a tennis match. "You could go for a walk outside instead of wearing a groove into the floor in here." He was starting to wonder why he hadn't stayed at the lab over the weekend. It would have definitely been more peaceful.

Jon stopped long enough to glare at him and snapped, "Am I distracting from study time?"

Maybe I could still go back to the lab. "What's going on?" Ethan tried. He'd only had Jon as a roommate for a few days, and it was clear he was not the type of person to sit still for very long, but today something had him at a new level of restlessness.

Jon threw his phone into a couch cushion and kept pacing. "I don't know why this is so complicated."

It was a fair guess that his complaint had something to do with getting back into his rotations at the emergency medicine residency he had been working in before disappearing almost five weeks ago. Although Ethan had been making more of a point of being around on his off hours in case Jon needed help, he was feeling less useful as the days ticked by. Jon was currently less worried about what changes the mysterious virus had made to his body and more concerned with getting back where he had been before it had all happened.

Understandable. But Ethan knew little about how to navigate the medical education system. He sighed and engaged tentatively. "You seemed optimistic after the meeting Thursday."

"That was when I was told I could restart rotations and finish what

I missed at the end of the three-year residency. Now, there's apparently someone else on the rotation I would restart and the paperwork is hung up somewhere. My visa should not even be an issue if I am technically still in the program, but there's some dodgy paperwork somewhere with the missing person something–I d'nno, but January is not even three weeks away and apparently there's even some threat of deportation now if I don't restart work." He threw up his hands and groaned in frustration at the ceiling.

When the groan ended in what sounded much more like a growl, he swung in an angry circle.

Ethan couldn't blame him, but he was going to make them both crazy if he kept that up in the cramped room. "You're too worked up. Go for a walk and maybe we can talk it out again." *Or get Garth to come talk. He's better at this.*

"You go take a walk," Jon snarled.

"*I* can't right now, but you can. Please, get out of here. Go."

Jon growled at him again, a deep low sound from his chest, and Ethan hissed back without moving from his perch on his stool. Something in the exchange, perhaps its absurdity, stopped Jon's prowling. With a broody glare but without any more sounds, he grabbed up his jacket from the hook by the door and stomped out, yanking the door shut with a screech behind him. Ethan took a slow breath of relief at the quiet–or what would have been quiet if the upstairs neighbor hadn't had the TV blaring.

⟩

The cold air bit at Jon's face but did little to cool the heat dampening his hair and making it cling to his neck.

His feet pounded rhythmically on the cement path around the huge park ten blocks south of Ethan's apartment. Snow lined the iron fence and the branches of the bushes. A woman in perfectly styled workout gear glared at him from her position next to a bench. The irritation burning under his skin had started to fade to the background as he worked his muscles hard, but her passing glance flared it anew.

Jon pushed harder, pumping his arms and sprinting down the ice-lined path. He should have been more out of breath. Shouldn't he?

If only he knew how it was supposed to be. If only one thing would go as it should!

Some reasonable corner of his brain argued that if he couldn't handle a literal walk in the park, then handling residency was going to be impossible. Never mind that he may end up back in London in a few weeks instead, where not a single soul knew what had happened to him.

As if anyone here really does.

A dog yapped at his passing.

He almost growled back.

Stop!

He stumbled to halt at the edge of the huge stone pillars at the north side of the park. Pressed his palms against the cold smooth rock.

Since he'd woken up in that hospital basement, everything had been loud, smelly, and hard to ignore, but today everything seemed loud*er*, more distinct, and harder to ignore. Every small stimulus had become a barrage of thorns, tearing at his nonexistent patience. Car exhaust. Tapping footsteps. Roaring engines. The scurry of tiny squirrel feet in the tree above him. The piercing shriek of a passing ambulance siren.

Wait. There's something.

He started walking again, kept thinking, turning the sudden thought over. He still had an active EMT license.

Before starting medical school, he'd worked in the city for a full year as an EMT for a private EMS agency on a 911 response ambulance. During medical school, he'd even continued working enough shifts in a per diem capacity to keep his license. He'd only stopped once he'd started residency six months ago. The agency would still have his paperwork.

What if he could get his old EMT job back while the residency sorted its paperwork out? It might at least help him avoid deportation for lack of a job.

Jon lost track of how many loops he made around the huge park before panting his way down the steps into the apartment again.

Ethan sat, still as ever, at the table behind his computer, and Garth leaned against the counter.

"Any better?" Ethan asked dryly.

Jon's grunt came out oddly rough.

"You went for a run?" Garth asked.

Jon sat where he stood, realized the cool floor felt good, and lay all the way down. "Yea. Round Prospect Park."

"That's a good ways."

"Went around three times, I think."

"Wow. Can you run faster? Or have better endurance? Now?"

"I d'nno, Garth," he snapped, then ran his hands down his face. "Sorry." He glared at the ceiling which was doing little to muffle the artificial sounds of gunshots and yelled curses accompanied by a soundtrack. "Everything is more annoying today. D'nno why."

"Oh," Garth bounded forward and held out a pair of headphones, "That's why I brought these down. Noise cancelling."

Jon sat up to take them. "Thanks."

The relief they provided was like jumping into a pool. The sounds from outside the apartment become muffled and indistinct, like they should have been. He flopped back to the ground with a sigh. "That…is better. You have some of these?" he directed at Ethan.

"At work sometimes." Ethan's voice was softer but still plenty clear enough. "I use them sometimes, but they make this background hum."

"I don't hear one right now."

"Hey, you got your stuff?" Garth pointed to the stack of boxes in front of the bookcase.

"Yea." Jon had arrived at his old place to find his landlord had already sublet his room out from under him, but at least they hadn't had time to dump his stuff. "At least I've got clean clothes and my computer back."

Garth nodded. "I still think it's ridiculous they gave your room away so fast."

Jon agreed with some choice words.

"I might have an apartment you could rent if the tenant on the third floor follows through with breaking their lease next month. We'll see."

As if Jon could afford a flat in Clinton Hill. "When did you buy this place?"

"I didn't. Science nerds don't make that much money," Garth chuckled. "I inherited it from my great aunt. Apparently I was her favorite nephew or something."

"You're the one who moved here from Texas," Ethan supplied before eyeing the ceiling.

"Ok, you've both done that now. What are we listening to?" Garth asked.

"TV," Ethan answered.

"Sounds like a war movie or something," Jon added.

"Fiddlesticks! His neighbor is going to be complaining again."

"Does he ever *actually* curse?" Jon asked Ethan.

Ethan gave a terse shake of his head.

"I generally don't think it would be edifying and try to avoid it," Garth answered for himself.

"He's odd." Jon frowned up at Ethan as if he had something to do with it.

"I don't think he'd be standing here if he weren't," Ethan replied matter-of-factly, then returned to the previous topic. "Did you carry all the boxes on the subway?"

Jon eyed the stack of four boxes on the other side of the room. "Yea. It's easier to lift them, I think."

"You're going to want to watch stuff like that." Of course Ethan had brought it up to start a new lecture. "Anything that draws attention to your differences could mess up your ability to blend in. Also…"

Jon bounced to his feet and scowled at him.

"You keep asking, 'what else?'" Ethan retorted. "I don't know how you were at self-control before, but it's likely to be more difficult now."

Jon pulled the headphones off and paced the floor. "What?"

"Generally. Impulse control…can be harder. You may find yourself acting on an idea before you fully think it."

"How would you know?"

"I don't, for you. But that's how it is with me."

"You." Jon stopped pacing to gape at the man sitting completely motionless in the corner.

Even Garth looked confused.

"Not everyone exhibits it the same way. And I've had practice."

Jon threw his hands wide in exasperation. "Seems I've plenty of time to figure more stuff out."

"Did you hear more from your director?" Garth asked.

"Only more about the problems keeping me from starting back on rotations."

"Maybe it's not a terrible thing to take it slow betting back into it?"

Jon huffed a growl in Garth's direction.

Ethan was on his feet in an instant and in Jon's face before he could so much as flinch. "Not him. Back off."

Jon backpedaled into the chair. "All right, all right." He held his hands up in surrender, not eager to get another thrashing by the vampire—of all the maddest things to think—and sat down over the arm of the chair his knees buckled against. "Sorry."

"He's fine, Ethan," Garth coaxed from the kitchen.

Ethan returned to his table, eyes fixed on Jon.

Trying desperately not to growl back again, Jon plucked the headphones off the floor where they'd fallen and dug his phone out of his pocket. "I'm going to try something else," he muttered.

"What's that?" Garth sat on the couch.

"I'm going to try to work as an EMT again for a while." He found Tony in his contacts. Tony would remember him, and they always needed another EMT.

"EMT?"

"I still have my certification. It'll keep me from deportation, maybe, and at least keep me from being stuck in here all day."

Ethan seemed to appreciate his last reason, at least.

57

Wait, finally?

Ethan leaned in even closer to the microscope eyepiece and kept turning the knob to move the slide in a linear pattern. He'd brought the microscope into his office to avoid questions while he studied his latest group of slides.

Footsteps approaching his office door threatened to break his concentration. They were Garth's. He wouldn't be as fooled by his quiet dark office as the others.

"Yes."

Garth's knock stopped short at his answer. "Ok, then." The door opened to admit him.

"Just wait a second." Still scanning the slide, Ethan groped along the desktop with his left hand until he located a pen and started scribbling notes on the paper lying there. For the first time in 62 samples, the cells on the slide were intact, rather than in pieces.

After scrutinizing the last corner of the slide, he lifted his eyes from the microscope to see Garth standing dutifully in the middle of the floor, leaning in slightly to see what he was doing.

Noticing him disengage from his state of concentration, Garth blurted, "Since when are you left handed?"

"Huh?" Ethan looked down at his left hand, which still held the pen, then at his right, which had just let go of the microscope knob. "Since…the adjustment knob is on the right and the pen was on the left."

"You mean you can write with either?"

"Apparently." Had he done that before without noticing? He

usually picked up the pen, or pipette, or whatever he was using, with his right out of habit, but it hadn't felt odd to write with his left.

"Have you always been ambidextrous and I'm just now noticing?"

"No, not always." But he'd definitely sparred with a knife with either hand equally without questioning it.

"So it's new. Not only are you quicker and better at fine motor skills, you can do it with either hand. Can you do everything with the left as easily as the right?"

"I hadn't noticed until you said something, but possibly."

"Huh. Well, that's a new one for the list. What did you find?"

"Cells that didn't lyse." After looking back at the side to see what sample number it was, he finished his notation.

"Hold on, what are we talking about?"

"I've been exposing different samples to the virus. It infects within hours, so I have been watching for cell death on simple slides."

"Right," Garth followed. "You said you were going to try that."

"So far, every single sample, except mine to the V virus and Jon's to W virus, have lysed."

Garth's lips pinched at the labels he'd given the viruses, but he continued nodding.

"I'd started wondering if I had things wrong. If maybe the exposure to the virus made our cells react differently, or maybe this method of testing just isn't viable. But this sample didn't lyse."

"Whose is it?"

Ethan picked up the sheet of paper he'd been scribbling on. "I've been testing extra samples from Moraine's research, and a couple other sample pools I got access to, so most of the identifiers have been removed. All I know is adult Caucasian male, mid 30s."

"So, the theory is that if this person were infected with your virus, he would have become…" he waved at Ethan, "Instead of dying quickly?"

"Yes. But not mine. Jon's." He picked up another slide, "The same sample cells lysed with exposure to the V virus. I still haven't found one that hasn't."

"Interesting."

"Obviously I can't prove the theory, but this might mean it's at least viable."

"What are you hoping to do with the information, assuming it means what you think?"

"I'm not sure exactly. I'm just looking for anything that helps me understand why. How does it work that it kills some–possibly most, if this model is right–and changes others? I had thought to access genotypes of those with positive results and compare them to see if it might be some specific profile, but I'd need quite a bit more data at this rate. And that's supposing that other factors like age or something else don't come into it." It was a daunting undertaking to think about.

"What's the next step?" Garth asked.

"Rerun the sample. Then keep going."

"You have more of Jon's virus?"

"Yeah." He retrieved a purple-lined dish. "This will keep a sample alive for a little while, and since I live with the carrier, it's easier to get more."

Garth was giving the dish a worried look.

"I know it's a dangerous idea to have it sitting here, but I can't just swab my own mouth to get more of this one. I keep it locked up. And it doesn't last more than a couple days alive even in a culture."

"I mean, yeah, of course, it just seems…weird to think about. That's a pretty bad mortality rate."

"Fortunately, it is hard to keep alive outside a compatible person's body."

Garth tilted his head at that and fiddled with the bottle in his hand.

"Why do you have sunscreen?" But suddenly Ethan didn't want to know.

Garth held up a finger and rubbed his nose with a look that he usually wore before trying to talk Ethan into something. "Ok…"

Ethan started to object out of habit.

"Since you are sensitive to UV, have you ever considered trying sunscreen?" Garth set the orange and white tube onto Ethan's desk.

He hadn't, actually, having been too conditioned to avoid the sun altogether. "I'm not sure. Clothes delay the burning only slightly–"

"There's a thought. They do make UV shielding clothes, don't they? For beach stuff. But I didn't have time to find that today–wrong season and all. We'll have to make do with this for now."

"Why do I need–"

Garth held both hands out as though to placate. "I don't know if they meant to tell me, but I just got the scoop from Rav and Gabby. The grad students are about to kidnap you. To take you to a surprise celebration for getting the grant."

"That's–not a good idea."

"Which is why I'm standing here. I don't know where it is, or how they might try to take you to get there, but I do know it's before noon, so…" He gestured at the sunscreen.

Ethan started to stand. "I'll just leave for a bit—"

"No, you can't do that either. Carol planned it."

He didn't want that to matter as much as it did. Every graduate of the program and every professor owed Carol something, or a lot of somethings, and snubbing her just wasn't acceptable. He stopped where he stood with a sigh. "I'm not eating another cannoli."

"No, let's not repeat that one. I'll stick close enough to eat whatever gets put on your plate." A grin split his face.

Ethan grunted acceptance.

"She apparently tasked the grad students with getting everyone there, and they have taken that a little too seriously. You and Dr. Miller both have managed to garner a reputation of being too busy working to celebrate."

"She just doesn't like being the center of attention. She plans whole charity dinners."

Garth's eyes narrowed. "Ok, I think I knew that, but how do you know that? Have you been actually *talking* to her?"

Ignoring that question, Ethan asked, "So why do you get told about the surprise?"

"Maybe I don't have the same reputation. Maybe I'm more approachable." He raised his chin.

"Not enough to get told where it is." Ethan gave the sunscreen bottle a closer look. It was labeled spf 100.

"Yeah well. If the shirt only gives so much protection, do you want to try this on everywhere?"

Shaking his head, Ethan shed his lab coat and started unbuttoning his dress shirt. *This is a terrible idea.*

"I'm thinking the weather will hopefully keep us from hanging out outside for terribly long, but I don't know about windows and the like. Just put your lab coat back on for added protection maybe. Here, want me to get your back?"

Ethan looked up from his study of the glob of sunscreen in his palm to give Garth a warning glance.

"Ok, fine." Garth backed up and continued on while Ethan wiped the glob over his arm, sparing a stray thought that the cream wasn't as cool on his skin as he'd expected. "Put your sunglasses in your pocket, right? You could put your hat on already, but then there was talk of putting a hood over your head to, you know, complete the kidnapping scenario, so I'm not sure what would happen to it."

"Seriously?" *Of all the terribly bad ideas…* They would never get close to succeeding unless he deliberately let them.

"That's why I'm warning you," Garth reiterated.

As he pushed away thoughts of what he could have done to people trying to restrain him, a vision of someone else's possible reaction popped into his head. "Did you say they're going to kidnap Moraine too?"

"Yeah, I think so."

"You need to warn her."

"Why?"

It wouldn't end nearly so badly as trying to surprise him would, and she would undoubtedly cope fine in the end. Still, after learning about her history and seeing the fear in her face after the attempted mugging, he found himself wanting to spare her any even a moment of panic that could result from someone grabbing her or trying to force a hood over her head. It might also spare a grad student an eyeful of pepper spray. "Just tell her. Now. Please."

"Ok." Garth was taken aback but moved to comply, careful to pull the door closed behind him.

By the time Garth reentered with a knock, Ethan had covered as much of himself with the sunscreen as he could and set the half-empty tube back on his desk so he could put his shirt back on. "You told her?"

"Yes, I did. And I should probably get out of here so no one thinks I did just that. You have a little–hang on–" Garth reached for his phone and clicked on the camera. "Here, look for spots to rub in a little better."

Ethan stiffly scrutinized his face and reached to rub in a spot on his left ear. "This is ridiculous."

"Yeah, but it'll be pretty cool if it works, right? That's better. I can't tell now that you're wearing sunscreen in December. Ok, I'm gonna get out of here."

"Good, because someone's coming."

Less than a minute after Garth left, enough time to don his lab coat, make sure he had his sunglasses, and sit back in his chair, a ski-masked Rav noisily stole into his office and squeezed past his desk to grab his shoulders from behind.

Ethan picked up his hat from the desk while allowing Rav to put a black hood over his head, careful to stay still and calm. When Rav dramatically ordered him to come with him, he complied, standing and following the pressure on his arm, and resisted the sudden instinct to click his throat in order to navigate while blind. Instead, he let Rav lead him, still managed the stairs more fluidly than his kidnapper, and didn't even pause when he was led out the door into the sunlit sidewalk.

At least the hood lent a little protection for his face. He started counting away seconds as he walked, thinking Garth would want to know how long it took the burning to start under the layer of sunscreen.

Two minutes later, he could feel something like heat but wasn't burning.

Rav abruptly pulled the hood from his face.

Bright light stabbed his eyes.

He ducked his head harshly to one side.

Memories or nightmares of being thrust into the sun flashed near enough to throw his heart into his throat, but he managed to hold his reaction to a single step back, pulling the overzealous grad student who held his arm only slightly off balance.

Stay. You are fine. Escape is easily possible and not necessary. Breathe and stay. He fought down the need to flee and heard Garth step up next to them breathing faster than the walk warranted.

Ethan slit his eyes open to assess the situation. They were in a courtyard that abutted a small college gallery. People were gathered mostly on the other side of the brick lined space near the sliding glass doors. The sun glared in a clear sky near the edge of the tall building above.

At that moment he chose to overpower Rav's grip to bend his left arm upwards and set his hat onto his head. With a slight head tilt, it at least blocked the rays from stabbing his eyes, which were not benefiting from the sunscreen application to the rest of his body, so he was able to watch Moraine's resident Alena and PhD student Abby lead her to a space next to him and remove her hood. Moraine looked uncomfortable, but not afraid, and eyed the gathered crowd suspiciously.

"Welcome, everyone, to congratulate Dr. Miller, Dr. Dalton, and Dr. Qualls for their being awarded the Smith Grant!" The chairman's voice boomed over the courtyard.

After a smattering of applause, Carol added, "They work so hard we had to capture them in order to steal some time for celebration. Congratulations Miller Lab! Now, everyone come on inside where the champagne won't freeze!"

Released by his so-called captor, Ethan gratefully followed Carol's gray spikey hair through the glass doors into the shade of the window lined room. Plenty of daylight radiated through the room, but at least it was indirect, so he could see without wanting to cower.

"How are we doing?" Garth's whisper was overly excited.

Flexing his bare hands that had only just started to feel slightly tight, Ethan answered, "I don't think it would stand up terribly long under direct sun, but it's slightly better than nothing. Especially under clothing or in here."

"Yes." Garth gave a fist pump of victory before dropping his hand and giving Carol an innocent expression.

"I need you both up front for recognition and a photo, please," she told them. "Here, son, that hat and the hood didn't do your hair any favors." She reached up to remove his hat and tousle his hair into some semblance of order.

It took all of Ethan's remaining restraint to not flinch from her hand.

"There we go. Come on now." She strode for the front of the room in her purple pumps.

Garth was wearing a tight smile. "I don't think I would have gotten away with that–"

"Don't try." Ethan obediently moved to the front of the room, which put his back to the wide window behind the table that bore most of the decorations and snacks. The bite of the sun glowing against his back and neck was unnerving until it cooled in the narrow shadow Garth cast as he stepped behind him.

The continued congratulations and mandatory picture taking took up the next ten minutes. When Moraine was forced to say a few words, she used most of them to thank her team. Then that part was finally over, and Ethan found himself next to Moraine at the edge of the room holding a paper plate with a piece of cake and a cannoli on it thanks to Carol.

"You look as uncomfortable as I am," Moraine said to him while smiling and nodding to someone else.

"You must hide it better." It was difficult to resist the urge to rub his eyes. He took a sip of the champagne in his glass and nearly choked on the bubbles.

"Not a fan of champagne?" Moraine spared him her scrutiny and kept her smile aimed forward. When he recovered from the buzzing sensation in his throat and up his nose, he spotted the twitch of her lips that showed amusement on top of her social smile.

"Not my go to," he managed to choke out. Truth be told, he realized he hadn't tried anything carbonated since being back.

After a few more greetings, she said softly, "Thank you for the warning."

"We have Garth to thank for that," he replied.

"Still." She looked him fully in the face for the first time, a meaningful look. Somehow there was no trace of fear or even questions about the last thing he'd said to her that early dark morning.

"I haven't seen that charity dinner appear on my calendar," Ethan said after a moment in which she didn't look away.

"Oh, I…didn't want to hold you to that."

"I told you I'd go. I don't mind." He eyed his champagne. "Much."

She seemed to be debating how honest he was being.

"I may need a better suit though."

"I don't have the right experience for that." She glanced at, and dismissed, Garth and several of the other surrounding men as options to provide a recommendation. "Hmm, you know what, maybe ask Carol."

A shoe squeaked against the tile floor a few paces away. Garth, clearly noticing he was falling down on his promised duty of eating from Ethan's plate, had also noticed Moraine's proximity. "Oh, hey. How's it going? Nice party, for a, you know, forced work party in the middle of the day kind of thing."

Moraine chuckled and turned to greet Carol who had walked over.

Behind their backs, Garth traded his plate holding a single bite of cake for Ethan's full one. When the women turned toward them only an instant later, threatening their subterfuge, for some reason they both decided shoving a fork into their mouths was the best cover—Garth with a bite half the size of the whole piece and Ethan the empty one that had been on Garth's plate.

Garth still managed to speak around his mouthful better than Ethan covered gagging on the icing that had remained on the edges of the fork. "You're devious, Carol."

"Well, you can't just make such an achievement without a little recognition. I'm sorry for the paltry menu. I did have to accommodate the chairman's schedule. Perhaps you all can have some drinks and steaks later, on me?"

"If we do that, you're definitely invited," Garth said.

"I would enjoy that—hello dear, did you get the…" She drifted away with another professor, scattering the group.

"You going to make it?" Garth asked and handed Ethan a napkin.

Ethan used it to wipe off his tongue. "Who knew icing could taste so terrible." He shook his head and dropped the fork back onto the plate.

"Water?"

Ethan nodded and traded his champagne for Garth's bottle of water. He washed down the taste but hopefully not enough sugar to make him sick.

"I didn't have enough time there to give you a clean fork. Did you eat enough to…?"

"Don't think so." He realized what he'd handed Garth. "Sorry."

"Huh? Oh, don't worry about it. I didn't like this stuff even when I did drink. We should probably just find a secluded trash can at some point, though. The cake is good–to me–but I'm going to go into a sugar coma before my lecture in an hour. There's actually some fruit over there." Garth nodded to a table that sat squarely in a sunbeam. "Erm," he noticed, "I'll just go grab some."

"Grab an orange."

Garth choked on nothing.

"I'm kidding. And thank you."

Garth just grinned. "What are friends for?"

PART IV
WORLDS COLLIDE

58

Ethan perched on the metal railing of the brownstone's stoop next to Garth who'd stopped at the front door. Stalling, Ethan checked his phone's clock and then the street while Garth discussed upcoming university holiday events that Ethan had no intention of attending.

Jon's voice rose above the street noise, "What are you doing out here in the snow?"

Ethan pivoted to watch him trudge up the broad front steps.

"Waiting for you," Garth answered. "Although we did just get here a few minutes ago. How was the first day?"

Jon had been right about being able to get his old EMT job back faster than his residency program could figure out their issues. According to what Jon had told them, his old boss had been eager to put him into a recently vacated EMT position on an ambulance that responded to calls in Harlem and North Manhattan. It seemed an EMT impatient to start the week before Christmas was a rarity.

"Were you worried about me?" Jon teased.

A little, Ethan thought to himself. If there was anything odder sounding than a vampire working in a hematology lab, it would have been one working with bleeding patients.

"I was only third man today, while they were orienting me to everything again since I've been out for several months. Didn't actually do much other than watch and hand people a few things. Before I left, I met the paramedic I'll work with tomorrow night. I don't think she has any idea what to do with a half-doctor working as an EMT, but…" Jon shrugged.

"How was it different for you from working there before?" Garth was taking over the questions.

"The siren is really loud." Jon plopped onto the top step, brushing away flurries. "Everyone smells, a lot, but nothing smells worse than the cleaning wipes." He wrinkled his nose into a disgusted grimace. "Those things smell like they're cleaning my brain. But it was ok. I was…fine."

"That sounds good."

"The stretcher is easier to lift…"

Jon continued, but his voice faded as though moving down a tunnel.

A high pitched clicking echoed off the building across the street…Like it had off cave walls.

Panic shot through Ethan's chest, stopping vital functions that should have been keeping him alive. The world twisted and blurred, and he pitched forward, catching himself with a hand on cool metal.

"Ay, what's wrong?"

It took an eternity to inhale again, to bring the man in front of him into focus.

Ethan knew him.

Jon. It was Jon, standing on the top step in front of Ethan's position on the railing, staring him in the face.

Ethan's breath got stuck in his throat, keeping him gagged. He was at his apartment, in New York City, with Garth. And Jon.

But he could still hear the clicking.

"What's going on?" Jon stepped closer, concern in his dark eyes that flicked to the side for a moment before settling back on Ethan.

He could hear it too.

No.

The curse that finally escaped Ethan's lips was in Romanian. Crouched on the railing, he spun around on the ball of one foot and dropped down onto the sidewalk. It rushed up too quickly, but his body knew how to land lightly on soft feet and legs whether or not he told it to.

It could be any vampire. You know there are others here now.

But he would know *her* voice in any form.

It emerged from the side alley darkness, a darker hole in the shadow, and coalesced slowly into solid form.

Ringing like a scream filled his mind's ear.

Moving more quietly than silence, the form morphed into that of a woman. A vampiress. Her pale face came into focus, framed by black hair hanging loose.

Time itself stopped.

"Hello, Etan."

Ethan's lips curled back at the sound of the name on those lips. His head slowly shook side to side. *"No. You don't belong here,"* he hissed at the apparition.

"I came for you, for you belong with me."

"I don't belong to you." It was a whispered gasp.

"I created you. You are mine to form."

"No!" Ethan dropped his center of gravity and slid a foot back, ready to move but directionless, for the world had collapsed in on itself, obscuring all direction.

"Why did you leave us for this place?"

"I have a choice here. Get out." *I escaped you.*

Her glance behind him pierced the veil and reminded him where he stood. Jon still existed, there above him, and Garth. If he knew nothing else, he knew the exquisite danger she posed in any world in which she existed.

"Get inside, both of you, now!" he yelled without taking his eyes off her.

Caterina looked up fully, to study what stood above, and her eyes narrowed in confusion. Such an unfamiliar expression in them.

Yet the change from dark to blue was not.

Ethan leaped backward up to the railing between her and the front door, which the others had opened but not entered. Smooth metal materialized in his palm from its hiding place and flashed silver in the streetlight.

Her blue gaze had followed him, calm as always. *"You protest, and yet you kept it."* She twirled her own knife through her fingers that had a moment ago been empty.

Ethan bared his fangs wide and hissed vehemently down at her.

Garth pulled Jon through the door.

She bared her own fangs and shrieked back, long and high and loud enough to echo across the buildings down the block and the cave corridor still hovering at the edges of his mind.

༏

Garth's heart pounded in his chest. Was it possible that amid all the observing and researching and discovering that he'd never actually *believed* deep down that Ethan was a *vampire?*

He did now. Ethan had never looked so like a vampire as when he'd hissed just now. It wasn't the teeth or the eyes themselves, it was how he moved, the fierceness in the action. Even so, Garth's fleeing hadn't been so much because he was frightened of Ethan, but because he was frightened of what would prompt such a response from Ethan.

He retreated half way up the staircase toward his apartment, but Jon remained by the front door, one hand against the thick wood.

"What is that?" His eyes were black coals when he turned to Garth.

"Vampire. Pretty sure," Garth gasped.

"You've seen her before?"

"Nope, definitely not."

"Could you understand them?"

"No…" Neither of them had been speaking English. It was that old Romanian Ethan muttered when he was stressed or talking about Romania. She spoke the same thing! *How is that possible? And that look in Ethan's eyes before he turned around…* "Oh man. Oh man oh man!"

Jon flinched, one hand going to his ear.

"What?" Garth squeaked.

"Another screech, loud. You couldn't hear it?"

Garth shook his head.

The door burst inward, leaving empty darkness and snowflakes to waft inward.

A pale hand grasped the edge of the door.

Blue eyes peered out from the hood that followed.

She spewed a repugnant sounding word at Jon.

Jon snarled back, but faster than Garth could see her do it, she slashed at him with a glinting dagger. Jon staggered back with a gasp, while Garth could only stare.

A shadow hit her from the side, from outside the door. Or perhaps she hadn't been hit at all, she spun aside so quickly, but her left hand went to splint her side for a moment before rising again in a jab toward her attacker. The shadow grasped the overhead door frame with a leap and launched a kick at her that she avoided by bending backwards, which prompted the dark figure to let go, twist while flying over her face, and land on his feet with his back to the stairs, Jon, and Garth.

"Get up the stairs!" Ethan's voice finally made Garth's feet move, but Jon only backed up to the base of the stairs, and Garth got stuck again at the door to the apartment at the top, watching.

She spun and swung out at Ethan while he dropped into a crouch and jabbed with something shiny of his own before she kicked off the wall into a downward strike, and he pushed up into a flip that spun him away to land in front of Jon again.

"Go!" Ethan shrieked.

As soon as Jon cleared the stairs, Ethan used the rail and the opposite wall as foot holds to leap upwards and launch a new barrage at her from above, but she, impossibly, was faster than he was and drove him up the staircase. They moved more quickly than Garth's unblinking eyes could follow, leaping, ducking, swiping, flipping as if a choreographed acrobatic dance, with distinct movements but with more happening simultaneously than could all be seen at once.

The whole battle was nearly silent—no thunks, clangs, or grunts to attract attention from the other tenants. The loudest sound was a hiss, until Ethan collided with the wood railing with a crack.

Garth hadn't seen the blow that put him there. His grimace was still silent, and he ducked and twisted again, launching himself backward up to the second-floor landing with one kick against a stair. He pushed Jon and Garth the rest of the way into the apartment and stopped in the open doorway, chest heaving.

The vampiress took the few steps up to the doorway slowly, deliberately, staring Ethan down with calm dark eyes. She said something in Romanian.

א

"Come with me. Or move."

"No," Ethan hissed.

What of it? Her calm eyes asked him. *Will you obey now, or later?*

Not here. Ethan dared to raise his chin. *"I'm not moving. Do what you want to me, but I know you won't kill me."*

"I don't need to kill you to get to them." Caterina's irises reignited blue with her final step toward him. She eyed the blood on her knife, dropped it to the ground, and reached for the one in his hand.

Ethan parried with all his accumulated skill and strength and a dread that knew he couldn't possibly win.

When he drew her blood with a surprise jab in the middle of a turn, it was barely a scratch on her arm, and she used it to her advantage, feinting a flinch but hitting his wrist only two moves later with enough force to remove the knife from his numb hand.

His only retreat was through the apartment doorway in a backward tuck rolling to his feet. A kick off the chair to gain height allowed him to connect with her side again, but at the cost of taking a slamming blow to the head. The other side of his head connected with the table, which he turned to roll over.

He could only try to block her next slash of the knife, his knife, and her strength prevailed, flicking the blade to cut deep into the muscle of his left shoulder. His shriek of pain covered Garth's yell, and again he rolled away from her, but she was done playing now. She kicked him in the chest and took his jab at her face with her teeth, drawing blood from his hand.

She ended it by slamming his left arm against the counter corner, cracking both, and poised the end of her knife at his throat. Her leer at the others was more threatening than the knife point, but he was of no more use to stand between them. Not like this.

Meaningless…

Jon stepped forward with a rumbling growl.

Caterina's hiss in return held fierce danger.

Ethan had only one move. *"What do you want?"*

She turned back to him, drifted closer. He could taste her breath. *"Come with me."*

No!

"Talk with me."

And if she didn't like what he had to say? Then what?

She studied him, her gaze lingering at his eyes only inches from her. It was his only play. *"Fine. I will."*

Released from her hand, his blade clanged against the floor.

Straightening up caused a stab of pain that stole his breath, but he cradled his left arm against his body, wiped at blood dripping into his eye, and held his breath to splint his ribs.

"Ethan, no!" What had Garth guessed? He cringed behind Jon who held his own bloody arm.

"Go to the basement," Ethan ordered them, "Lock the door. And check his arm."

"Don't go with her," Garth still argued, but Ethan followed her retreat, pulled the door closed behind him, and stumbled down the stairs.

59

Garth's heart pounded like a jackhammer in his chest. It made his hands and voice shake. "Oh, God, what is he doing?"

"I'll go after them—" Jon started.

"And do what against…that?" Garth interrupted incredulously.

It was enough to make Jon pause.

"No, come on. We don't have a clue what just happened—we do what he said. Downstairs." Garth cracked the door open and peered down the stairs to see if they were gone. Jon gasped from behind him.

Whirling back around, he watched Jon drop the knife he had retrieved from the floor with a grimace that showed his teeth.

"What happened?"

"Careful," Jon warned as Garth hurried back to him. "The knife just burned my hand. Where did it come from?"

"Huh?"

Jon turned his right palm, the arm that hadn't been injured, toward Garth, showing an angry red mark on his palm. Unable to stifle the curiosity, Garth reached a single finger to touch the hilt of the knife lying on the floor.

Nothing.

He grasped the hilt, then picked it up, and looked back at Jon with a baffled expression.

Jon returned it.

"Ok, uh, weird. Let's just get downstairs. I'll carry this. Go."

Ethan hadn't needed to lead her to the fire escape that clung to the outside wall of building at the end of the block. When she'd predictably leaped upward, landed on the iron rail two stories above, and leaped twice more along the platforms to the roof, Ethan leaned against the brick wall and took a moment to steel himself before jumping up to follow.

He stumbled at the roof's edge and hissed at the pain of catching himself with his torn hand.

"You are out of practice." Caterina watched with little concern, undoubtedly certain her actions had been necessary.

"Is that what you want to talk about?" He spit blood from a cut in his mouth onto the roof.

It was and it wasn't. He knew by the way she stood, the way she watched, the way she breathed.

He knew her.

He hated her.

And something else.

She flinched at a car horn from below, breaking the spell.

He had left to escape her.

"This was your world?" A tender question, and yet her tone left her opinion of it clear.

"It is my world." And not yours. *"Why are you here?"*

Although her expression was calm, the intensity in her dark eyes remained. *"You left."*

"I belong here. Not there."

"You belong with me."

No, anywhere but there. *"You have Stefan, and everyone else. You don't need me. Let me go."* He meant to defiantly shout the words, but they came out more like a plea.

"I need…you are mine. This place is for humans. I made you greater—strigoi. And you leave to live with a human and a—" she bared her fangs. *"I should have run the demon through."*

"I never wanted to be…You should go back, where you belong, and leave me alone." He wanted to scream that she might as well kill him now if she thought he'd go back with her, but the words got stuck in his throat.

Old rules still reigned.

Pointless…

"You are strigoi. And I cannot leave you until I have formed you into a full vampire worthy of your name, even if it means I must follow you to this monstrous place and beyond. You must know it cannot be your home."

"It is my home." A whisper.

She floated closer, eyes blue and lingering at his. *"Were you never content with me?"*

Anger and fear and shame twisted in his gut, nauseating him. *"You didn't give me a choice. How could I be?"*

She flew at him. Stopped a fraction of an inch from his face as he froze to stay as still as stone. *"Not all your choices were mine."*

By the time she turned away, a tremble had stolen into his fingers.

"How can you tolerate this world? Loud and bright, and your vampire lord is a fool," she spat.

Who?

"I have no lord here. I don't follow anyone."

"Then you are truly lost. Fear not, Etan, I will not leave you so." Without further pretense, she stepped off the roof.

Ethan dropped to his knees and vomited.

When there was nothing left and his ribs screamed at him, he held his breath and strained to listen for any sounds from the brownstone below.

Traffic. Muted conversations. A distant siren. Nothing unusual.

Rooftops stacked against each other stretched out to the water and the sparkling lights of the buildings in Manhattan beyond. Had he been a fool to think he could escape back home?

He feared he had only whetted her anger with his answers. She had just promised to not leave him alone, and if she could find the people who mattered to him at any time she pleased, they were all in incredible danger.

He rolled over the edge of the roof and sucked a breath at the pain of landing. As much as he wanted to remain alone and away from anyone remotely related to vampires, he was no match for her alone. So. He studied the dark sky. No time to waste.

The basement door was locked as he'd instructed, so he knocked and called, "It's me."

Garth answered with a stifled cry. "What happened?"

"She had questions. She wasn't satisfied with my answers. You need to stay here and bar the door. And window." Ethan walked to the refrigerator, opened it with a grunt, and pulled out a thermos of blood. "Do you have more?" he asked Jon.

"No, but there's some meat, and I can go get more in the morning. Ay, if she just wanted to talk, why did we not try to lead with that?"

The dull taste worsened the churn in his gut but he didn't stop swallowing until he'd emptied the thermos. "There are worse fates than this."

"What do you mean 'you stay here'? Where are you going?" Garth interjected.

"She's not done. I need to find someone before the sun comes up."

"You need to let me examine you. She cut you up good." Jon hovered.

"I'll be fine. It will heal. Don't worry about it." Ethan looked down at the bloody torn shirt. *I should probably change if I don't want to attract attention on the subway though.*

"Your shoulder is fileted open, I'm fairly certain she broke your wrist, and that's just looking at your left arm. Where are you getting your prognosis from?" Jon persisted.

"It healed in a week last time."

"Last time?"

Ethan gave up trying to undo his shirt buttons with his injured hands and just popped them off with a quick pull of the already ripped fabric. The sudden pain from the movement he made to pull his arms from it stopped him with a small gasp.

Jon reached for him. "Let me."

Clamping his mouth shut stopped any sound from escaping as Jon eased the shirt off over his back and left arm, but he couldn't keep his breathing even.

Jon cursed. Ethan's left shoulder bore a deep gash, and dark bruises already bloomed over his left forearm, ribs, and flank. And that wasn't counting what probably discolored his forehead where it had slammed into the table.

"It'll be fine," Ethan trudged to the bathroom.

Jon followed. "The bruising over your flank—you may have internal bleeding."

The cold sink water pulled a grunt from him when it hit the bite wound on his right hand. "What are you worried about? Where?"

Jon leaned into the room and pointed to the red and purple covering his lower left side.

"That's been twice as bad and healed with no problem. It's fine."

Jon's dismayed look met his gaze in the mirror. His face looked worse than he'd imagined, with blood smeared down the right side. He splashed water from the tap and gave up pretending it didn't hurt to wash the gash in his forehead but again refused Jon's offer of help. It was his fault, his problem, and he needed to move now if he had a chance of protecting Jon and Garth from her. If he paused to stop and feel his wounds, he'd never get there.

A quick rub with a towel removed most of the blood from his hair, and he didn't bother with the rest of himself but turned back to the bedroom.

Garth was already standing by the bed holding a shirt and an anguished expression. Ethan accepted the shirt and tried to ignore the latter but was slowed by the struggle of trying to get his injured arm into the shirt sleeve.

"Wait," Jon insisted. "Sit." He pointed to the bed.

Ethan complied mostly because he couldn't completely shake the light-headedness that assaulted him.

"I'm going to at least cover this." With a roll of gauze he had produced from somewhere, Jon quickly wrapped his shoulder, then finished pulling the shirt on while eyeing the teeth Ethan inadvertently bared in a grimace.

Jon already had gauze wrapped around his own forearm. "How's your arm?" Ethan asked.

Jon continued on to button Ethan's shirt front. "It burns. A lot, honestly, but it's just a cut. Not…" He scanned all of Ethan.

"Uh, Ethan, is the knife silver?" Garth asked.

Ethan stood to try to pull away from their ongoing concern. "Silver? Plated, yeah. Why?"

"Jon, show him your hand."

Why does this matter–Oh. The burn on Jon's hand halted him for a moment. *Wolf demons…these were made to fight you, weren't they? Is that why they're silver plated?* Ethan crossed the room to the half-empty dresser and pulled the silver chain from a top drawer. "Hold out your good arm."

Uneasily, Jon did.

"This is pure silver." Ethan held up the delicate chain, wrapped one end around his finger and pressed it against Jon's arm. It only touched skin for a split second–Jon jerked back instantly–but left a thin red line on his skin.

Jon cursed through barred teeth. "What the–"

"You're right," Ethan directed at Garth. "Watch him. It might be different, with the silver. Like burns from the sun are different for us."

"Yeah, ok."

Tossing the chain aside, Ethan deliberately started for the door.

"You should stay," Garth tried again.

"No time." He found his hat on the couch. His knife was on the kitchen table. He picked it up, wiped it on the ruined shirt he'd left discarded on the floor, and slid the knife into the leather loop around his waist which hid the blade inside his pants leg. "Is hers upstairs still?"

"Uh, maybe. Yeah, probably."

"Get it and set the other outside on the stoop. Then stay inside."

"Ethan, thank you. For protecting us." Garth's voice was small.

"You wouldn't have been in danger if not for me." Ethan slammed the front door behind him.

60

Ethan settled into a seat in the back of the subway car, fine with taking on the part of a semiconscious homeless man all the way to North Manhattan. He exited onto the street to skirt the emergency room and entered the research building near the desk where he'd last met the security guard.

Gaining entrance with the university ID still in his pants pocket, he found the hallway empty. There was still too much to be done before the sun came up, so he abandoned subterfuge and chirped a high note. When there was no answer, he descended a level and tried again.

A single sharp chirp came from around the corner—an answer. Breathing a painful sigh of relief that his efforts hadn't yet been proved a fool's errand, he started down the hall toward the sound.

"Are you looking for me?" Seeley rounded a corner. "Woah. What happened to you?"

"You know how to find Caspian." Ethan was direct and emotionless.

"I told you I'm not in his trust. I'm a loner. You said the same. What do you want with him?"

"He has some amount of power here. She even admitted it, calling him lord of this land. At least, I assume it was him. He can either help, or they're as good as dead anyway. You know where to find him." It wasn't a question.

Seeley scowled and reached into his pocket. "Who's she?" Then, "Back to no chatting, are we? Did 'she' do this to you? Avoiding her is starting to sound like a good idea." He handed Ethan a black business card from his wallet. "This address. Go into the club. Silver door in the

357

back. Knock. If they want an invite, hand them this. If they ask for ID," he tapped his face next to his eyes.

Ethan took it and spun away.

"You're welcome," Seeley called to his back.

The address was in lower Manhattan, disarmingly closer to all the common tourist attractions and around the block from the Flatiron building, so Ethan trudged back to the subway to ride it downtown.

Feet away from an enormous subway station that was at least half mall, the designated building was probably connected by some underground passage, but it was not worth the search in the wee hours of the morning. The outside entrance was a bland windowless door tucked between other street level entrances. Despite the hour, the door was manned by a thick-necked man who would have proven difficult to move by most people. When Ethan flashed the black business card, he opened the door and motioned up the narrow staircase immediately on the other side.

Music with a low driving beat pulsed through the walls. The door at the top of the dark staircase opened into a dimly lit room with a bar on one side, grouped lounges on the other, and a floor full of the all-night club crowd in between. Somehow the music was enveloping without becoming ear-splitting. The crowd, mostly packed close together and moving to the music, was varied in many aspects that did not include species. They were all human.

Ethan began to question whether or not he was at all in the right place but then saw a figure in the back corner. He was groping a young blond woman, drawing her behind a curtained door. His eyes met Ethan's for a single instant before lighting blue and disappearing through the doorway.

Alarm flared through him at the thought of what might happen to the woman, before reality settled back down on his shoulders. Even if he had been in any shape to challenge another vampire, he was acutely aware that this was yet another world he did not know the rules to. Another world in which he had no power to save young girls from vampires. At least that one hadn't been screaming.

There was a silver door beside the bar. That was where Seeley had told him to go to find Caspian. He needed to follow the instructions if he had hope of completing the mission he'd set out on. When he knocked on the door, the metal shutter slid open from the inside of a narrow window at eye level. Dark eyes studied him through it. "ID?"

Ethan stared back and let anger and fear turn his irises blue.

The window slammed shut. A series of latches clicked heavily before the door swung open to another staircase slanting upwards. A tight wariness in his chest now, Ethan watched the vampire at the base of the stairs close the door behind him and turned to slowly climb the staircase toward the open doorway above. The ride from the research building had been long enough to temper the urgency fueled adrenalin, letting pain tighten his chest and side and pound loudly in his head. Each step took exacting effort.

As he ascended, he realized he could no longer hear the music from the room below, or even the sounds of traffic from outside. The music in the room at the top of the stairs was lower and softer, and there was a comfortable darkness only broken with indirect lighting from the room's edges and behind the bar. There were fewer people in that room—a female draped across the velvet couch, a male leaned against the bar. Zero quick heartbeats behind the haze of music and smoke.

And—his eyes flicked to a glass carried by the female who crossed the room in front of him—alcohol wasn't the only beverage in the glasses. He smelled blood, and some of it was human.

Eyes followed him silently from the shadows as he stepped gingerly to the bar. Without looking directly, he warily took note of how many hovered in the drape lined room.

"What can I serve you tonight?" the greasy-haired bartender asked him.

The language of this world was still English, he acknowledged before answering. "Caspian."

"He's not down tonight, but I can offer you—"

"I came only to speak to Caspian. Get him for me or tell me where I can find him." Ethan's voice was low and calm, but it was a demand that he spoke.

Another vampire sauntered up to Ethan on his side of the bar and waved the stammering bartender aside. "As he said," he spoke with an airy tone of superiority, "Caspian is not seeing anyone tonight. I can see that you've had a rough night, but rest assured, you can address me with your concerns."

Turning his flat gaze to the slippery looking male with carefully styled hair and a dark maroon dress shirt with several top buttons undone, Ethan repeated steadily, "No, you cannot. My concern is with Caspian. I will speak to him."

He reached his hand for Ethan's shoulder, perhaps to reassure him or steer him aside or subdue him—Ethan didn't wait to find out. He used his wounded but unbroken right hand to draw the short blade at his waist. Once he held it uncontested at the vampire's throat, he considered the possibility that not every vampire had been trained by as vigorous a hand as his former mistress.

At the edges of the room, two others rose to their feet. Ethan pressed the blade a measure more, pricking the air with the scent of vampire blood. "Take me to him. He will want to hear what I have to say."

"I see you won't be persuaded." The vampire's attempt to maintain his careless demeanor was betrayed by his nervous swallow and slight wave of his fingers at the others. "Very well. His wrath can be on your head."

"Fine." Ethan left the blade against his throat until he motioned toward the door next to the bar, prompting Ethan to drop the point to the floor and allow him to approach it.

That door had to be unlocked by an old key taken from the vampire's pocket, and the stairwell ended in another door that he knocked on before speaking to the doorkeeper on the other side.

The room beyond the door was even quieter than the others. Thick curtains covered wood-paneled walls—there had been no windows in the entire building so far. It was much smaller than the other two areas he'd passed through and held only two vampires, neither of which was Caspian.

Ethan turned blue eyes to the vampire who had claimed some measure of authority.

"He's not just standing in here," he defended with a slip of a step back away from Ethan. "And your threats are no good here. They will incapacitate you and end your suffering if you so much as suggest following me into his quarters." He motioned the vampires who stepped into the center of the room. These felt more dangerous; one held a large naked blade, and the other rested his hand inside his jacket. "Sit. I'm going to get him."

After a quick glance at the plush couch, Ethan remained standing and turned his glare back to the watchful eyes of the guards. The other disappeared into a door that blended into the wall. It took concentration to avoid swaying on his feet, but he would not show weakness now.

His endurance was tested as minutes ticked by, but finally the paneled door swung silently open again. A tall slender vampire exited, dressed in a tailored black suit that he wore fashionably without a tie. His collar length hair was styled back without a hair out of place. The smile on his lips managed to sneer slightly at the edges, just showing his elongated canines.

Caspian. Leader of the strange world that lived beneath the sight of millions of humans in one of the most famous cities in the world.

"Dr. Dalton. I did wonder when I would see you again." His eyes traveled the length of Ethan with a hint of interest. "Clearly you have had a bad night. Tell me, what is it that only I can help you with?"

"By your admission, you're lord of the city, of all the vampires in your dominion. Including Caterina." Ethan watched for his reaction.

"Ah, yes."

They *had* met.

"It's you she was looking for," Caspian concluded. "That answers all the questions. She sired you in the old country, then you returned. Well, that's one interesting conundrum solved. Is this her doing then?" He waved a hand glittering with rings at Ethan.

It seemed too much to hope that Caspian could control her, but surely he did hold some measure of power. It was evident that many deferred to him. Perhaps he was more than he appeared to be. Or perhaps the rules were different in New York and would not hold the likes of Caterina. Regardless, as he'd told Seeley, Ethan didn't see another option. She hadn't killed them yet because it didn't yet serve her purpose, but she had promised to return. And he was clearly useless against her by himself.

"Just keep her away from me."

"Dr. Dalton—May I call you Ethan?" Caspian continued without waiting for an answer, "Whatever this is between the two of you is not my concern. If I remember correctly, you requested in no uncertain terms to have nothing to do with me or mine. And now you come demanding a service?"

The soft stirring of another entering the room interrupted them, or, more accurately, what she carried did. The crystal goblet in her hand held human blood—not packed red blood cells or even previously refrigerated whole blood, but blood fresh enough to still have some warmth to it. Ethan was unable to stop his glance of surprise toward it, but with every thread of strength left, he was just able to squash his desire for it enough to keep his eyes from turning.

Diamond cufflinks sparkled at Caspian's wrists as he gestured at the goblet. "Come. You look terrible. Refresh yourself while we discuss this further."

While most of his concentration went to ignoring the cup and Caspian's offer of respite, Ethan also noticed the gold chain at Caspian's neck and the rings on his other hand. The most powerful vampire in New York had a clear affinity for shiny precious adornments. That, as well as the girl downstairs, and the fresh blood, made him reconsider his previous assumption. Perhaps the rules weren't so different after all. The different surroundings, the clothes, the modern conveniences, it was all just a nicer facade. Too much was feeling familiar.

If he did know the rules, then he also knew it wasn't about him. It was about the group Caspian held power over, and, more so, about its sovereign. For Caspian to care about something, it had to be his problem.

And what is important to you?

"No." Ethan remained rooted to his spot on the floor. "It doesn't matter what happens to me. This is your problem because if you don't contain her, there will be at least two slaughtered in my apartment building, or in the street or at their places of work, and I'll either be dead alongside them or won't be around to contain any part of it. I am not strong enough to stop her, and if you aren't either, then at some point in the not so distant future there will be public evidence of the latest 'interesting conundrum' splattered across the news. Considering your instructions to me to avoid exposure, it seemed like a matter that should be brought to your attention. I came to warn you, not to ask for anything."

Every cell in his body cried out for the blood a few feet away, but, if he knew the rules, then he knew that the cup would come at too high a price, even if he didn't know for certain what that was. So, without further word, he turned away from the Lord of New York City.

The trip down the three stories of stairs was nearly enough to send him to his knees on the dirty pavement outside, but he made it back into the subway. He had done everything he could tonight. It was time to go home.

61

The building Caterina crouched atop was rows of buildings away from Etan's, and directly above the entrance to a train tunnel, but she could see his dwelling. She could have entered it again, if she'd desired, but finding her knife on the doorstep was enough for the time being. If she killed his companions, she would drive him further away, and he would be more difficult to find once more. Better they stayed as they were and where they were for later use.

She ran a single finger down the cut Etan had inflicted on her forearm. Tasted the blood.

It was bitter in her mouth.

Her duty to her vampire was not done. As she'd suspected, he was not complete. Instead of embracing all that she had made him, he was playing at being human again. He was ill equipped, deluded, and petulant. He still did not comprehend all he was, who he could be, with her.

As she had told him, come what would, she could not leave him as he was, lost and alone.

If she had to start over, she would train him again, but she doubted it would take so much. Perhaps only a reminder and a completion of a trial he never quite accepted.

In time he would be great, as she always knew he would be.

The edges of the sky were blushing pink when Ethan fell through the front door of his basement apartment. Because he'd done so silently, he made it in and to the chair before Jon stumbled to his feet and turned on the light that left Ethan cringing.

At least he turned it back off after discovering him and turned on the one in the bedroom instead. "You look…worse. What happened? Where did you go?"

"To tell the vampire who thinks he rules the city to do his job and keep better track of her."

Jon gaped at him.

"I don't know if he will. Or can. You need to watch yourself. And Garth, when I'm not around."

"You think she'll be back?"

"Did you put the knife outside like I said?"

"Yea—Garth did."

"Then she already has."

As Jon rushed to the door, Ethan dropped his head into his hand. His hands were starting to shake with fatigue and pain.

Curses announced Jon's findings before he came back in and slammed the door closed. "She took it?"

His intensity only made Ethan more weary. "Yes."

"That's why you had us put the knife outside."

Yes.

"Who is she?"

An old despair threatened to crush him. He was in his city, not her cave. She wasn't supposed to be here. How could she be? She was part of that cave. He had almost become able to pretend, at times, that the cave didn't exist. That it hadn't been him there. That this person, here, was the real Ethan.

He should have known better.

"Caterina," he answered. "Daughter of the Lord of the *strigoi* of Romania and my…sire." Cliche or not, it was the word Caspian had used. "She made me a vampire. She bit me. She beat me into the vampire she wanted. I watched her kill at least ten people with her own hand during the two years I was there. Because I'm here, because I defied her, you may be next. I'm sorry." He grimaced harshly.

"How…" Jon dropped to the floor beside his chair. "How is that possible?"

"I don't know. I wouldn't have imagined she could leave…" But she had been around a very long time, and he'd only known her for two years. There was no telling what she was really capable of.

"What happens next?"

Ethan shook his head, wincing as it throbbed. "I don't know. But she will kill you without a thought, maybe even regardless of me. There were stories of…" he looked down at Jon, "your kind killing vampires. If they're true, she killed scores of you to get revenge for someone killing her…clan member. And Garth–" Pain stabbed as he tried to shift back against the chair.

"Hey, take it easy. Can I check you out now?" Jon reached for him. "It'll heal–"

"I know you said it will heal eventually, but maybe there's something I can do to make it heal more quickly, or be less painful."

"There's only one thing that can do that," Ethan breathed with a wince.

"We can start with that then." Jon followed Ethan's glance to the kitchen and started for the refrigerator. "Then let me try some splinting and maybe some pain killers. I'll get more blood as soon as the sun's up, but meanwhile Garth had this upstairs." He handed Ethan a thermos. "Drink it and let me look at your arm."

That's not it.

Thermos in his torn right hand, Ethan made himself let Jon unbutton his shirt and ease his left arm out of the sleeve. When he took a sip, the thick liquid gagged him. He managed to chug it anyway but by the end was breathing hard and scowling.

Jon was watching. "Is something wrong with it?"

Ethan heaved another slow breath before answering. "It tastes worse when…we crave something else."

"You mean…human?"

He was holding Ethan's fractured arm; he could feel it tremble.

"But…you said it's not necessary."

He had. But he didn't know it, not today.

Jon pressed against a bone in his forearm which stabbed like a dagger and pulled a gasp from him.

"Sorry. I think it may be broken. Is that–does that seem possible?"

"With enough force, yes."

"Have you broken a bone before?"

"Yes."

"It healed?"

"Yes."

"Did you splint it or anything?"

"No."

Pain flared again when Jon touched his ribs. Without much remaining energy for restraint, his vision sharpened in response.

"Sorry, again. Do you think you broke those too?"

"Don't know." Shrugging hurt. "But that heals too."

Jon cursed. "How many times have you been beat up? Er, when you said she 'beat' you into a vampire, did you mean that literally?"

Memory barely had the teeth to stab more harshly than reality, today. "Not only…but yes."

Jon stopped probing his bruises. "When you fought her last night, did you think you could best her?"

"No. But I couldn't just let her hurt someone else on my account either."

Without an answer to that, Jon moved to unwrap the bloody gauze from his shoulder. "How did she get here? Do you think she followed you? From Romania?"

"I don't know how. She's lived there for centuries…" He gave up trying to stop from shaking, and Jon sucked air through his teeth as he examined the gash in his shoulder and upper arm.

"Warn me before you pass out, please." He reached for another roll of gauze without completely letting go of Ethan.

"That takes more…" he hissed faintly.

Jon cursed again. "How old is she? Has she ever lived anywhere else?"

"I don't know exactly. They count time differently…"

"New York City is quite the change from a cave."

"Cate is as strong as she is cruel."

Jon's hands stilled. He repeated Ethan's name for her, the one that few others dared to use. "'Cate'…?"

Did Ethan hate her? Or did he hate who she had made him? A cold hand clenched tightly over his heart and bent him over until he was slipping from the chair. Jon caught him, able to take all of his weight before easing him onto the floor.

Quiet except for muttered curses, Jon did something with tape that secured the bandage on his shoulder and examined the wound on his head with a light from his phone. "I can wrap your other hand so the cuts don't open every time you move it, if you want," interrupted the swirling in Ethan's mind.

His stomach cramped as tightly as his chest, and he couldn't find which way was up in a fog that had little to do with the bump on his head, so he didn't fight or move when Jon gradually pried the empty thermos from his hand and pulled his shaking fingers open.

He almost didn't hear the footfalls on the steps outside.

When he couldn't shove away the first thought that came to mind, panic stabbed. "Don't let Garth in," he blurted urgently.

Jon froze. "Why?"

If Jon couldn't read his expression, he must be blind.

His quiet curse said he could. "You said we didn't need it."

"I've healed from this before," he rasped. "But never without it." Pain that pierced deeper than any of his wounds nearly pulled a groan from his open mouth. "This is a test I never passed."

Jon bolted for the door. Residual horror still painted his furrowed brow when he opened the door and held up a hand. "Hey, er," his step out the door pushed Garth further back on the stoop, "he says not to let you in just now."

"Is he ok?" Garth's voice asked.

Jon's hesitation was too long.

"Ethan?" Garth called through the open door.

A stomach cramp made Ethan hunch over and struggle to breathe through it. "Don't, Garth."

"How is he?" Garth's voice was more insistent.

"He's not worse–"

"Not worse? I don't know how he was standing up before! I should hope it's not worse! Where did he go?"

"He didn't say exactly. Something about seeing the top vampire to tell him what happened."

"He–what? Why? Who is she?"

"To maybe keep her from killing us, or something. She–she bit him, he said."

"*She* bit him? She…! She's the one…Did she kill Jack?"

Ethan clenched his eyes closed. After the last two years, Jack sometimes became just another in the stack of bodies at her feet. "Yes," he croaked.

Garth's heart was beating enormously loudly. "Will she…will she kill you?"

"She won't kill me…" Ethan's whisper faded. *But I'll kill myself before she could take me back. Surely I will…*

"But–" Garth leaned past Jon.

Ethan gripped the smooth floor as though to anchor himself to it. "Leave, Garth!"

"Ok, ok," Garth backed up, but stayed in front of the door, heart hammering. "Did he go back to the lab? Or say anything about getting…food?" he dropped his voice to ask Jon.

"I d'nno–no. I don't think so. I gave him the thermos you left here, and I'm going out to get more soon."

There was a pause. Still curled down over himself, Ethan let his eyes open and tried to bring a small detail on the floor into focus.

"Is he going to be ok with that?" Garth asked.

Jon was looking at something on the kitchen floor. Ethan's wallet and ID badge lay where they'd fallen with his graceless entrance. "Depends on what all I get…"

"Shoot! Ethan? I'm not coming in, ok?" Besides being an octave higher than normal, Garth's voice was steady. "But talk to me. What do you need?"

There was no answer that he could give that Garth would find acceptable.

Garth took a few deep breaths during the silence. "Ok, no, that's not a good plan. Stay here. I'll get it. No, I don't need the ID. Pretty sure I can get it honestly."

His brain must be further into madness than he'd thought. Ethan raised his head and looked toward the door. Still well outside the threshold, Garth met his eyes. "Hey, look, if I was that injured and needed…What if it's necessary…? Maybe I've had this a little wrong. I know you keep saying I don't know what I'm talking about. Maybe you're right…" He trailed off. "I'm sorry. I'll get back as soon as I can. Just hang in there for a couple hours."

62

Twelve hours later, Garth spoke at the closed basement door rather than bothering to knock, "Everybody ok in there? You need anything?"

To his surprise, it opened promptly to Jon's unshaven face. "Hiya," he combed his fingers through his tangled hair. "Good timing. I need to leave for a shift."

Garth looked beyond him into the empty front room wondering if that meant he was allowed in now or what. "How is he?"

"Better than this morning. I think." Jon stood on one foot to shove the other into a heavy black boot. "He took the blood bags you brought and the cow stuff I convinced the butcher to source and has been in there for the rest of the day." He nodded at the closed bedroom door.

Garth held up the plastic bag in his hand. "I raided Chinatown."

"Brilliant." Jon took it and left the door open while he turned to the kitchen counter.

"Is it ok if I come in, now? Jon?" Garth started to feel forgotten on the doorstep.

"Yea–Sorry, I thought you could hear him. Come on in here, just leave him be in there. I'll take one of those to pass through." He pulled one plastic container out of the bag and took it to the bedroom door, calling, "Takeaway delivery."

After leaving it inside the bedroom door that cracked open enough to receive it, he carried the other container Garth had brought to the counter where he had the blender set up.

"That was all she had right now," Garth added.

Jon nodded. "I won't use much." He paused in the middle of

reaching for the package of meat on the counter and looked back at Garth. "This does feel odder with you watching."

Sitting down on a stool, Garth gave him a "really" side eye. "I just bought it, already." He considered the blender. "It's only weird if you don't clean up after yourself and I find it in the sink later."

After Jon had finished blending some of the raw meat with the blood–bloody Mary smoothies, Garth fleetingly decided to name them—and pouring it all into two thermoses, he headed for the door.

"Am I supposed to stay and hang out, or…?" Garth asked hesitantly.

"You can stay out there. If you don't mind."

He could hear Ethan's voice from the bedroom and waved Jon away when he started to repeat the message. Hearing his voice, flat but clear and even in full sentences did a lot to calm Garth's anxiety. "Ok, will do." He nodded and settled onto his stool with his elbows propped on the table. "Have a good shift."

Once Jon had gone, Garth ran upstairs to retrieve his computer before settling back down at Ethan's table. Not quite sure what he was doing, but eager to help in any way he could, he shifted around on his stool and logged into World of Warcraft and started playing with the sound muted.

When he hit a stage that required listening to his teammates, he paused with the cursor hovering over the volume. Ethan would be able to hear it, even from the bedroom, so he ventured, "Hey, uh, would you mind if I turned on the sound? Quietly? It won't be loud."

"No, that's fine," came from the other side of the door.

He entered a game just as Ethan said, "Garth?"

"Yeah?" He ejected himself and waited, but the silence stretched so long that he'd almost pushed play again before Ethan's voice restarted.

"I…I don't quite know…"

"It's ok," Garth replied. "You just heal up in there. We can talk later. You need anything?"

"No."

He'd finished two quests when Ethan spoke again. "I didn't mean for you to do something you weren't comfortable with."

Garth gave that some consideration. "It was fine. I didn't have to steal it. I just walked up and asked the tech. I told her who I was, who I work with, and that I needed some blood for something urgently. 'Do you have any expired, or unmatched that you could spare?' or something like that. Turns out, she did. Handed the two units right over. I didn't even have to lie, so, integrity is pretty intact. Anyway, don't think I didn't hear what you told Jon about it working better when it counts, and you looked like you should have been in an emergency room, so..."

Maybe it was enabling an addict, but it hadn't seemed that way when he'd seen Ethan bleeding and in absolute torment on the floor earlier. God forgive him if he was wrong, but it had seemed like mercy. The calm voice behind the door was evidence that he had been right about it helping, at least.

After a moment, "You have such a sense of right and wrong. I can't even remember what I used to..." His voice sounded so tired.

"I can show you where it comes from, if you want." Because it certainly wasn't himself.

Predictably, Ethan didn't ask for more in the moment, but that was ok. Garth leaned forward and clicked back to the game.

ꓘ

"You ready for a night shift, Doc?"

Jon met Ellie the paramedic, his partner for the near future, at the back of their ambulance. She was a young pretty ginger with eyes the color of the sky—or the color the sky would have been with less smog.

"It's just us tonight?" he asked.

"Yes, indeed."

Right. All in then.

Ellie didn't seem to know what to do with an EMT with his strange set of credentials, so he deliberately let her take the clear lead. She received the report from the team handing off to them and he followed her requests for restocking.

The cut on his arm wasn't deep, but it still stung and bled if disturbed, so he'd wrapped it tightly underneath his dark uniform shirt. Fortunately, the contact burns, or whatever he was going to call the reaction he'd had to touching the silver knife, was little worse than a sunburn and pretty easy to ignore. At least, it was until he used the hand sanitizer for the first time and had to hold his breath until the stinging had worn off. The small place on his arm where Ethan had touched him with that chain hurt worse, but it was covered too.

All in all, he was in quite a state for a first real shift, but there was nothing for it. He'd eaten everything in the apartment that he hadn't needed to leave for Ethan, and had two thermoses in his bag even though he felt fine. Overthinking it more would just make it worse. Time to get a move on.

Their first call was for a pedestrian hit by a car.

What would be the point of easing in anyway? he thought as Ellie drove the ambulance through the evening traffic to the piercing cry of their siren. *Might as well see if I can do this straight away.*

The intersection they pulled up to was already blocked by a fire engine, and dark FDNY jackets and NYPD hats swarmed around a silver sedan that rested half-over the curb. In the copious city lights and the red and blue strobes from the emergency vehicles, he glimpsed what might have been a body under the front of the car.

"Bags and go." Ellie slammed the ambulance into park and threw her door open.

Snapping his second glove on, Jon followed her to the rear of the ambulance where he took a black bag from her and jogged across the intersection while an officer held the traffic at bay.

Smells. He always noticed the smells first now. The ever-present fog of car exhaust, the hot dog vendor down the block, the rubbish bin down the alley, and, cutting through it all, human blood.

Such a strange thing that it automatically had that qualifier now.

As he approached the front of the car, a horn shouted over the sounds of car engines and clamoring voices, and a baby squalled.

A baby?

He dropped to his knees next to the front bumper and peered around several pairs of boots under the front of it. A woman's legs, and the source of the blood, but no baby.

Breathing again, Jon looked up and around him to spot a female NYPD officer holding a screaming toddler next to an overturned pram.

A fire department EMT was giving Ellie a list of vital signs that sounded high but stable. She nodded and addressed the woman who lay with her legs pinned under the front of the car, "Hey, I'm Ellie. What's your name?"

The woman was crying, in obvious pain and distress, but managed to sob, "Ann—is my baby ok?"

Jon leaned forward to scan Ann for sources of obvious trauma while noting that she was breathing, obviously, and moving her arms and head freely. Under the smell of blood that he was trying to ignore, something else about her smelled wrong, but that wasn't enough to go on to know what it was. Deciding she was in trouble but not imminently dying, he followed her worried look to the baby in the officer's arms.

"I'll check the baby." He bounced back to his feet and held a hand out to the officer. "How's the little guy?"

She handed him the toddler, who was possibly somewhere between one and two and screaming a throaty squall with tears running down his round cheeks. "He was still strapped into the stroller. I don't think he hit the ground," she reported.

"Ok, lad, you're all right," Jon held the boy with one arm and looked him over as he felt along his smooth, nearly bald head. He paused with his hand on his chest, feeling his rapid heartbeat beneath. There was no odor of blood from him, and he was clearly moving his arms and legs while straining against Jon's hold. "You look good. Here, let's go let mum know you're all good, yea?"

Cradling the boy against his chest, he stepped back to the car and knelt next to Ann. "Ann. Here we are. He's all right."

Sobbing even harder, she reached for him. "Nate!"

He extended the boy to her, shielding him from the sight of her blood on her leg with one hand, and held him against her cheek while she clutched him to her. Nate's little dimpled hands wrapped around her neck, so Jon supported him there, letting them hold each other. Gradually the "wrong" smell eased from both of them as their cries softened, comforted by each other's presence.

Ellie met his eyes over them and mouthed, "Is he ok?"

When Jon nodded, Ellie stood to talk to the officer.

After a moment, the officer knelt down behind them and told Ann that she would take care of Nate for a little while and meet them at the hospital.

Prying the little hands from around her neck was difficult, but Jon pulled Nate back into his chest and nodded at Ann, reassuring her again, "He's just fine. Let's get you out so we can all meet at the hospital, yea?"

Once he had handed Nate off to the officer, he knelt back beside Ellie. "What do you need?" he asked, scooting a bag closer within reach.

"This car off of her leg." Ellie eyed the cluster of firemen who were currently working on that.

Without stopping to think, Jon crouched and threw his weight against the dented bumper. It creaked back a couple inches, surprising the straining firemen and making Ellie look at him.

Don't draw attention—Rather than answer Ellie's look, he looked up at the firemen appreciatively, as if they had moved it, and back at Ann, who moaned as they pulled her leg out from under the car. Her foot was folded down at an unnatural angle, and blood rapidly pooled under her leg.

Grabbing several bulky dressings from the bag next to them, Jon quickly leaned forward and pressed them against the opening in her skin where bone protruded through.

A sudden twinge of hunger and the desire to take a bite out of her bloody leg blindsided him.

Aghast at the thought, he pulled back a fraction, dropped one hand down to the ground and stared down at the concrete under his fingers.

That's ridiculous and foul and how can I even think that?

But it wasn't easy to shove the thought aside.

"You good?" Ellie asked, reaching over him to apply more pressure to the bleeding wound.

"Yea," he answered quickly but didn't look up. Suddenly unable to remember what the world had looked like a moment ago, he worried his eyes had changed without him noticing, so he kept his head down.

Feel it. Then feel something else.

Bloody terrible directions.

The best he could do was focus on his own hands. He made them hold the now-bloody gauze tighter against her leg and lift it off the ground so Ellie could wrap tightly around it to hold everything, including her foot, in place.

Only when she had finished and he could back out of the puddle of blood and pull his bloody gloves off and inhale another whiff of fire engine exhaust did he look up again. Refusing to think about it all right now, he pulled on new gloves and helped maneuver their patient onto the backboard, focused on getting her there safely.

The voice behind him was low and quiet. "Keep your eyes down when it's dark and there's light shining straight at them."

What?

They were already lifting the backboard to the stretcher, so he forgot to think about how much he was lifting as he twisted to try to see who had said it.

Behind him there were only officers and firefighters and some bystanders straining to see.

He had to turn back and help get their patient situated on the stretcher and into the ambulance.

Her hand full of IV supplies, Ellie dropped into the bucket seat at the head of the stretcher and called to Jon, "Avoid the bumps!"

He shut the back doors on her and jogged to the driver's side, thinking, as he got in, that he truly had no idea what he was doing. Nothing felt quite right.

63

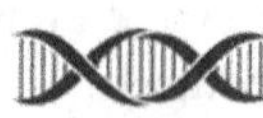

The world was all pain and blood and memory.

Ethan's phone didn't know that. Stubbornly holding on to a 7% charge, it beeped to announce a calendar invitation.

From Carol.

The current world came into focus again, strangely interweaved with the one he'd fled.

He sat up, gaze flitting to empty blood bags, empty thermoses, bloodstained clothes, and eventually returning to his phone.

Carol was requesting a meeting. Today. Soon.

As if nothing had happened at all.

If he didn't go, it was admitting that something had. Admitting he didn't belong. That he belonged with her?

No.

He belonged here.

So.

He would go.

When he walked out of his bedroom dressed for work, Garth gaped at him from the couch. "You were almost dead like 36 hours ago. What on earth could you possibly need to go in for the week of Christmas?"

"Carol scheduled a meeting at 9:30."

With no comeback to that, Garth wilted.

"And Moraine sent an email. Jon was back?" Ethan pulled the refrigerator open with his right hand.

"He was. He just left for a run, so I came back down. But now it looks like I need to get ready to go. You're sure about going in? I could call Carol…"

375

Ethan swallowed the pig blood. "I can do it." It was the world he'd chosen. *Should I have left some of that for Jon?* Too late now. He set down the mostly empty container and moved to the coffee maker.

"I know you heal quickly, or so you keep saying, but there's no way you're just fine now."

The coffee burned a little hotter than he had expected down his throat, making him clear it before speaking. "Not completely, but good enough to ride a subway and sit in a meeting. I was going to have Jon cover my shoulder again. It rubs on the shirt."

Garth looked at the door. "I…can't catch him. But I can help."

Ethan eyed him over his coffee cup.

"The gauze and stuff is still right there." Garth shrugged and picked up a stack of gauze and some tape. "I'm not saying it'll be pretty, but probably easier than doing it yourself?"

"If you insist." Ethan swallowed the last of the coffee and started undoing some buttons on his gray dress shirt.

Garth's lean forward was a little more tentative once he had the shirt sleeve off. "Oh. Well, that is a little better."

It had gone from a gash down to the bone to a long cut along the top of his shoulder. It still pinched when he moved, but he could at least raise his arm again, if he'd wanted to. He didn't, because it hurt his side and his wrist to do so, but he could have.

After several minutes of Garth gingerly laying gauze and tape on his shoulder, Ethan advised, "The idea is to not have this be obvious. Please don't use all the gauze." He'd turned his head away, so he couldn't see what Garth was doing, but too much of the gauze pile was missing now.

"Right. Well. This is probably ok then. Sorry, not up to doctor, or EMT, par."

"It's fine. Thank you," Ethan replied stoically. At least his arm still fit in the sleeve, and he proceeded to button the shirt back.

"How's your head?" Garth asked.

The scalp laceration had been one of his more obvious injuries, but what was left was hidden by his hair, as long as he didn't brush it straight back. The lingering headache was minimal; although, he hadn't been faced with much light yet. "Better."

Garth was still looking at him like he was broken.

Ignoring the fact that he did feel as if he were barely balanced on the edge of a precipice, he dumped the remnants of the coffee carafe and the plastic container into a thermos. "You were going to get ready?"

꜊

It wasn't so hard to walk at Garth's pace to the subway, stand leaning against the back door of the train, or walk through the bowels of the hospital while holding his breath past the ER. The fluorescent lights were more annoying than usual, but Ethan made the trek across the glass overpass to Hammer building before the sun crested the next building over.

Carol greeted him, "Come in, Ethan. How are you this morning? You look a little down."

"I'm well, Carol," he lied through his teeth and sat carefully on the edge of the leather chair across from her large desk covered in neat piles of paperwork. "How's the chaos over here going?"

"Never ending herding of cats, that's the truth of it." She adjusted her purple glasses and picked up a folder.

Most of what they went through was paperwork related to the job, stuff that had only just been finalized. He did his best to nod and sign what she gestured to and be present enough to answer a couple questions.

When he walked out of her office an hour later, Garth found him, clearly keeping tabs on him. Whether it was as his injured friend or the potentially unstable vampire, Ethan wasn't sure. He'd seen enough now, surely, to recognize the threat either way.

As they started down the stairs, Garth noted, "I was about to say that you look pretty back to normal, but now we're taking the stairs one at a time."

Ethan grunted slightly, finding that hard to dispute at the moment, given the deliberation it was taking to take the stairs even at the slow pace. His side and back had tightened throughout the morning's activities, making the jarring motion of each step down uncomfortable.

As the fluorescent lights gave way to daylight, he found himself hesitating.

"What we need," Garth speculated too brightly, "Is an umbrella." Ethan's sigh nearly turned into a groan and drew a more serious look from Garth. "We ok?"

We? With a vague grunt, Ethan pulled his hat down further and kept walking, closing his eyes when the sunbeams stabbed at them and reignited his headache.

He left Garth out in the lab and retreated to the dimness of his office until Moraine approached his door sometime later. He hadn't gotten much done in the interim, he realized, if his dark computer screen was any indicator. It felt abruptly important to not be in the tight space with her, so he stood and headed for the door before she could walk in and gave some bland greeting.

"Good morning," she returned. "Sorry to interrupt. Did you see what I sent you this morning?"

"Yeah…"

"Here's part of it." She laid some printed charts on the nearest table and, when he stepped forward to read the one on top, leaned over them next to him. "Dr. Bianchi was talking to…"

It would have been easier to focus on her words if the sound of her heart beating hadn't been so loud. It might have been possible to read the page in his hand if the warmth of her skin hadn't been so close to his. Looking over at her was a mistake, so he pulled his face away from her to focus down on the page. He should have been thinking about anything other than her blood right now.

"Shoot."

Garth was still behind him sitting at the other table, wasn't he? It was his exclamation that broke the dangerous route his thoughts had started down, his heartbeat he'd just heard speed up. Ethan should have been annoyed at his constant watching, but somehow, right now, it gave something like accountability to know he was there and aware of what could happen.

"Alena," Moraine greeted her resident, whose research they were supposedly discussing, as she walked in and joined them at the table on Ethan's other side. The women started talking to each other over him.

It was made more difficult, now, by the noise on either side, but Ethan found the sound of Garth's heart beating, even faster than before, and listened to it, reminding himself he was there watching. The ache in his arm spasmed—making it harder to hold on to the paper— and he leaned forward slightly as it spread into his side and chest. When his stomach got involved, he gave up even trying to understand what the two researchers were clamoring about on either side of him and thought only that he should leave, immediately.

"But I'll get with you later," Moraine was dismissing her resident. "Ethan you can take that, get back with me later or check out the workspace."

Once Dr. Bianchi moved away from his side, he inhaled for the first time in a while.

Moraine paused and asked quietly, "Are you all right?"

He should never have let her get close enough to notice. "Yeah," he tried to dismiss her concern anyway. "I'll get back to you."

As soon as the door closed behind her, he gave it up and bent over the table. He tried to convince his mind and stomach to follow the rhetoric he repeated, but it slipped from him like sand through his fingers.

He wanted to be fine. Had willed himself to be fine. But the thought of it had poured in so suddenly and so fully, he couldn't push it away with any amount of effort, and now his mind was consumed with one thing, and he couldn't focus on anything else. The need pulled so deeply, he had abruptly forgotten how to deny it.

Garth stopped just out of reach. "Talk to me."

And say what? That he was a hopeless, monstrous addict consumed by one hunger? He closed his eyes against the visions that danced in his mind's eye.

"What do you need?"

Ethan gripped the table and shook his head. "I shouldn't…"

Garth took a breath. "And what happens if you don't."

He knew his eyes were blue when he looked up.

Without moving, Garth swallowed slowly. "Ok."

The vestige of his facade crumpled, leaving him scowling in disgust at himself while his eyes filled with tears of hopeless despair. Cate had left him bleeding and broken, again. What was he supposed to do? Maybe it was physiologically necessary.

"Let's just get through today, right now, ok?" Garth's voice was too high, but he still didn't seem afraid. "We'll address the rest later, on a day that's not two days after getting almost killed by…Yeah." He heaved a sigh. "This is different, isn't it?"

"Yes." *Because I don't have to go find it. It's sitting in front of me, everywhere. All I'd have to do is take it.*

He hadn't said it aloud, he knew he hadn't, but Garth's expression said he'd read it on his face. "Ok. Let's make a plan. Knowing there's a plan to get it makes it easier."

He wasn't wrong.

"I'll go ask again. Or maybe take your ID in case they're on break or something. You can wait here?"

For someone else to walk in? "Basement," he breathed out through his teeth.

"What if…for the first time, someone actually is walking around down there, alone…"

He tried to hide the thought of piercing someone's skin with his teeth to find the blood pulsing underneath.

"Ok." If Garth's voice had gone higher, it would have been falsetto. "Come with me it is then. Is that better?"

It shouldn't have made a difference, but for some reason Ethan couldn't fathom, it was. He nodded.

"Then let's go."

Garth's movement was simultaneously sudden and too slow all at once, because deciding to give up on constraint had been the hard part. What followed couldn't happen fast enough. He found himself at the first-floor stairwell landing, pain flaring through his chest and running through his burning stomach while Garth clamored down the stairs behind him.

They were in the hall nearly in view of the blood bank when another option presented itself.

The scent of warm fresh blood yanked him toward it. He spun and rounded two corners before slowing himself with a twisting grip on the handrail with his injured left arm. It produced enough pain to make him take a breath and shorten his steps.

By the time Garth caught up, with real fear in his eyes, the source was visible.

There was a blood drive going on in the cafeteria.

Not taking what someone else needed seemed immaterial when contrasted with the option of killing someone. If they were giving to save a life, his taking some wouldn't even undermine their purpose.

Ethan pulled his white coat closed, strode into the milling crowd, and darted behind the curtains erected for the drive. The bags of recently collected whole blood were easy to find, and he was away with two of them before anyone looked up from their tasks.

Then he did retreat to the dark of the basement, breaking the seal on one of the bags before his feet silently leaped the first broken wheelchair, falling to his knees in relief.

It was the taste, the real complete taste of human blood. While he consumed the first as if dying of thirst, he relished the second bag perched on the edge of a stretcher in a secluded room.

Finally he felt full, sated completely, without even the ball of tension that had threatened to choke him since she had appeared again. There were still problems, but they were less important, solvable, now that he felt whole.

64

"Hey, Rav, what's going on? Shouldn't you be on break?" Garth asked from his stool at the edge of the lab table where he had been watching the few comings and goings of the lab members like a guard on duty for the last two hours.

"No, I've got a meeting with Dr. Dalton again, because I still don't have a thesis."

"Uh, he's—"

"Rav." Before Garth had barely started the excuse, Ethan swept in like there were no cares in the world. "You can set up right there. Let me grab my laptop."

Garth settled his chin onto his fist so he wouldn't gape and watched silently as the scene from normal lab life played out in front of him. Ethan looked so completely different from the cowed, hurting, frankly frightened man who'd nearly begged for help two hours earlier. Physically he was moving easier—no winces or stiffness as he sat down on a stool and rolled it toward Rav. He held his laptop with his unfractured right arm, but otherwise there were no signs of discomfort.

But that wasn't the most profound change. Not only was he not hiding from human interaction or holding on to the table like his life depended on it, neither was he withdrawn and distracted as was often his normal. He was engaged, animated even, and interested in what Rav was showing him.

What did that blood have in it?

Garth knew what was in it, biologically. Although he'd heard Ethan describe it as nutritionally dense, it wasn't really, as far as human consumption went. It was mostly water, proteins, cells which were mostly proteins, maybe a decent amount of cholesterol, depending on whose it was, and some electrolytes. It didn't have many calories, and there were far more nutritionally dense foods, even better choices among the few things he'd seen Ethan eat. But something in it certainly seemed to make an immense difference.

You work in a hematology lab, Qualls. Maybe you can figure it out one of these days.

⟨

Garth didn't follow Ethan into his basement apartment, but Ethan hesitated just inside the threshold. "Garth…"

"No, let's not do the regret and shame part tonight, ok?" Garth protested gently from the bottom step. "Just rest up and finish healing."

The rest of the day had seemed to go relatively normally, except that Ethan had actually let Garth hover nearby the whole time, but now Ethan's expression was dismally vulnerable.

Garth understood. Or at least he understood that previously he had not understood, as Ethan had tried repeatedly to tell him. Garth had seen addiction result in the death of others, although his own had only ever threatened his own life. It was a different thing for the object of one's addiction to be the lifeblood of another. For taking it to mean killing the other.

Perhaps he had now seen enough to realize how easy it would have been for Ethan to take it that way. Witnessing brief demonstrations of strength and speed had meant nothing compared to the display of his skill in the fight with *her*.

In the moment in the hall by the cafeteria, when he'd lost sight of Ethan, when he'd prayed harder and faster than any other single moment in his lifetime, except one, he'd had to admit to himself what else he'd come to understand. Ethan *had* killed to take it.

The look on Ethan's face said he knew what he'd given away.

But he hadn't killed today. Today, an alternative had been unknowingly offered and providentially placed.

"I'll check in tomorrow morning, but you know where to find me. Ok?"

65

"Did you have a good Christmas? I mean, you know, between night shifts?"

Jon handed his partner her coffee and slid into the driver's seat of the ambulance. "Er, yea, I…went to a bar with my flatmate–roommate."

"Not so bad. No family in town?" She peeked under the plastic lid into her latte.

"No…" His mum had sent a box of shortbread. Not eager to revisit the experience he'd had after trying a bagel last week, he'd given it to Garth, who had been the one of their odd trio to come up with gifts. The steaks Garth had given Jon had actually been really good, and he'd given Ethan some apparently really fancy roast coffee. Ethan was very Ethan about it–couldn't tell if he'd been happy or not–but the bag was almost half empty by the end of the day, so apparently it was agreeable. "You?"

"No family in town either, but I went over to a friend's for a couple hours. You ready for this one?" She pointed at the computer screen to the call details.

"Yea, why not?"

After fighting traffic for three blocks, Jon double parked in front of an apartment building with a broken streetlight outside, eyed the two police cruisers in front of them, and waited while Ellie picked up the radio to clarify the situation with the dispatcher. A week into the job, sometimes it felt almost natural again. And then the flimsy glove he was putting on would snag on his fingernail that he'd had the audacity to not file for two days and rip into pieces.

Garth and his spreadsheet had already noted that his hair and beard grew so fast he needed to shave twice a day if he didn't want a beard. He would probably be interested to hear it was the same with his nails. Garth found most things "interesting."

Whispering a curse, he reached for another glove.

Once dispatch had verified that the call was primarily a medical call, Ellie guessed, "They must have sent more officers just because of the location."

"Maybe." It wasn't a block with the best reputation. As he eased his hand carefully and frustratingly slowly into the nitrile glove, he checked the side mirror and got out into the street.

They both shouldered bulky black bags and approached the front of the soot-stained building. The front door stuck and squeaked in protest to Jon pushing it open. The hall was narrow and dim and smelled of cigarette smoke and something sour.

"EMS!" he called.

Ellie pointed to the stairwell at the end of the hall. "Try the second floor?"

Since that's where he heard stomping and the screech of a police radio, Jon nodded. Stepping around something sticky on the top stair, he spotted a door ajar midway down the hall. There was movement audible behind the other doors, but nothing else was open. He started for the door, and Ellie followed him as he repeated loudly, "EMS! Anybody need help?"

They entered the apartment door to find that it opened to a strange maze of smaller rooms. It smelled of humans. Lots of them.

"Anybody need help?" Ellie called again as she opened the first door on the left to reveal a closet.

The air split with a crack loud enough to knock Jon off balance with just the sound. He managed to push Ellie down and forward into the closet. "Get down!"

Another shot rang out loudly in the small space, spurring him to drop lower himself. There wasn't enough room in the closet for two, and he wasn't eager to pull Ellie out into the potential path of flying bullets, so he yelled over the ringing in his ears, "Stay put!" and ducked his shoulder into the door opposite the hall from hers.

It flew open, and he landed hard on the stained wood floor.

Shouts erupted from the hall and deeper into the apartment, several including the word, "Police!"

Ellie's wide blue eyes peered across the hall from her hiding place. He motioned for her to stay where she was and turned to look behind him. He was in a small square room that contained only a bare mattress and some clothes strewn about. A dirty window stood ajar. No people. Realizing that details were standing out even more clearly than they typically did now, Jon leaned against a wall, slid down to a crouch, and took a deep breath as he rubbed his ringing ears.

Staying calm while bullets were flying was counterintuitive.

Sirens screamed outside, indicating the arrival of more police cars. It would have been nice if one of them had warned them to stay outside a bit longer.

Steps clanged—on the fire escape outside the window to his room.

Still crouched, Jon spun to face it in time to watch a dark blue uniformed arm and the distinct shape of an NYPD hat lead a tight squeeze through the window. As soon as the officer stumbled to his feet on the wood floor, his hand went to his gun.

Jon held his palms up and spit out, "Medic!"

The officer froze where he stood, looked Jon over, and then scanned the room. Jon didn't know the officer, but he looked familiar, perhaps from another call. The officer strode two steps to the closet, nudged the one-hinged door open, and, eyes on the hall, stepped closer to where Jon was still crouched obliquely next to the door.

Two blood drops splattered on the scarred wooden boards next to Jon's shoes. He looked up to see a rivulet of blood dripping down the officer's hand.

"You're bleeding."

Odd. He hadn't smelled the blood.

No, he could smell it. But it wasn't right. It smelled like...

"Bloody—"

It smells like mine.

The officer took a step back. The muscles in his jaw tightened before he looked down at Jon. "Took you long enough."

Jon opened his mouth. Closed it. *Is this possible?* Tried again, "I haven't met anyone...else."

The officer's eyes narrowed. "How—" But when more yelling broke out, his attention snapped back to the hall. "Get back." He gripped Jon's shoulder and pushed him behind him. "Where's your partner?"

"The closet across the hall."

"Out of the line of fire?"

"I think so. What's going on? We got sent in here for a medical call."

Irritation flickered across his face. "It started that way until someone across the hall realized there were drugs sitting unclaimed on the table." The officer's radio squawked, and his reach for it stopped short as he flinched and looked at his bloody left arm.

Jon stood. "Let me."

"It's fine." He dropped his voice, "It'll be gone in a day. Not worth drawing attention to."

Just like Ethan said. How is this possible?

I'm still an EMT. "Yea, then maybe I should stop it bleeding everywhere."

He pursed his lips and looked again at the blood running down his hand before stiffly holding his arm out. "Quickly. Our partners are out there."

Jon ran his gloved fingers up the uniform sleeve until he found the cut in the tough blue fabric over the officer's bicep. "Assuming you don't want me to cut the sleeve open, arm out." He reached into the bag behind him for a packet of gauze as the officer undid his shirt buttons and pulled the left sleeve off his arm.

The blood dripped from a wound in his upper arm. Jon pressed a handful of gauze straight onto it, which made the officer suck in a breath and bunch his lips over his teeth. It looked like a natural response, but considering what Jon thought was true about the officer, he suddenly wondered if it was a practiced response to avoid grimacing with his lips back. The feeling of his own teeth on his lips had stopped him from a wide expression more than once in the last few days.

Jon leaned in to examine the wound–a deep gash sliced cleanly through skin into the muscle of his bicep. "This will heal in a day?"

The officer looked down at his arm and swore quietly. "Deeper than I figured. Maybe two. Or three."

"Because that makes more sense." But it did seem that it had stopped bleeding already.

"How old are you?" The officer's voice dropped lower as he cautiously watched the door.

"Er, 28."

"No, I mean, when were you bitten?"

Jon stopped mid-reach for more gauze and followed the officer's eyes to the empty doorway. It was real. He was truly asking him that question.

"Almost two months ago." He had to stop and add the one he couldn't remember.

The officer's eyes narrowed again as he looked back at Jon. "Seriously? And you just, what, came back to work?"

Jon shrugged. "Actually, I'm here because my residency coordinator is dragging his feet, but what else was I supposed to do?"

Jon started wrapping a roll of gauze around his upper arm, and the officer paused for a moment to clench his jaw before continuing the whispered exchange. "Have you figured out what to eat?"

"Found a good butcher near where I'm staying." Jon secured the bandage.

His exhale seemed relieved. "Our blood needs to be disposed of. Contact the wrong way by another person could be deadly." He eyed the bloody gauze Jon had dropped to the floor with a couple discarded wrappers.

Jon grunted, thinking of Ethan and his tests. "Yea, I wasn't getting out of the apartment without knowing that one." After a second look at the officer's uninjured but bloodstained forearm and hand, Jon popped open a plastic vial of saline and wet the rest of the gauze he had out. "Here."

He took it and started wiping his hand off. "I thought you hadn't met anyone else. Who gave you advice?"

"I didn't say he's like me." Jon gave a tight-lipped grin.

"At least you know to watch your mouth," he muttered. Eying the white bandage on his arm, he reached to pull the sleeve of his dark T-shirt as far down as it would go.

"Did you get who cut you?"

"She was scared. Trying to get away. I wasn't who she was trying to hit."

"You let her go?"

"I didn't try very hard to stop her," he admitted. "Doesn't matter if I'm not saying that she assaulted me, anyway. And neither are you." After a glance to make sure Jon understood, he clenched his jaw again and reached his left hand back into the uniform sleeve. A voice somewhere in the apartment yelling "Sanderson!" had him glancing back at the hall.

"Is that you?"

He nodded. "My partner just noticed I'm missing."

"Should you answer?"

"If you're going to do this, you need to remember that if they can't hear or smell it, you shouldn't either." He buttoned his uniform shirt. "It hasn't been that long for you. You should be able to remember how much they can hear. Hearing more won't make sense to anyone."

Considering that, Jon rotely gathered up bloody gauze and discarded wrappers off the floor and grimy mattress to tuck inside a biohazard bag. The body camera on the officer's chest only registered when he adjusted it back into place over his uniform. "Er, is that on?"

"Muted and pointed at the doorway the whole time," he replied evenly. "You need to be more careful."

"Sanderson!" The voice was in the hall outside.

Snapping upright, as though back into character, the officer tapped his camera, answered, "Smitty," and stepped into the hall. "A couple of them got out the fire escape. They were down before I could follow."

The older officer shook his head and grumbled something about his foolhardy kid of a partner.

Jon heard Ellie call his name, but he paused before answering and instead called back, "Ellie! You all right?"

She yelled, "I've got a guy bleeding over here!"

He grabbed the bag at his feet and moved to cross the hall. "Sorry, had to check someone over there. You all right?"

She nodded quickly, focused on holding pressure on a man's bleeding thigh wound.

Assaulted by the familiar smell of human blood, Jon bent over the man on the floor. Officer Sanderson watched, eyeing the blood, the man, then Jon, and, after a quick shake of his head, turned back to his partner.

Once they had stabilized the man with a bullet hole in his leg and had him strapped onto the stretcher, Ellie rode down the tiny creaking lift while Jon ran down the stairs to meet her at the front entrance. Sanderson was there, talking with a sergeant, but he didn't acknowledge Jon in any way.

I guess that was all the information I get?

After spending most of the following day in the empty basement apartment alone, going for a run, and pacing around the empty space for a couple hours into the evening, Jon found himself upstairs knocking on Garth's apartment. It wasn't typical for him to be socially needy, but Ethan wasn't around despite it being a holiday and the late hour, and he was concerned. Or so he told himself.

"Hey." Garth looked relieved when he opened the door, but that quickly switched to apprehension. "What's going on?"

"Nothing, I don't think. Do you know where Ethan is?"

Garth closed the door behind him. "I think possibly the roof across the alley, but maybe you can see better if he's actually there right now."

Jon crossed the room to lean out the open window over the fire escape. "The roof? Why is he up there?" There was a faint outline of a silhouette against the sky on the edge of the higher building's roof, but it was shrouded in shadow.

Garth shrugged, looking uncharacteristically disheartened. "Watching out, maybe."

The fire escape creaked in the wind, drawing Jon to look back out the window—to find a figure on the railing in front of him.

With a snarl, Jon jerked back and reached a hand out to block Garth.

Before his clearer vision registered the familiar face.

Ethan just nodded at his protective posture and let his gaze wander back out toward the street, while he remained crouched on top of the rail, apparently as comfortable on the three-centimeter-wide ledge above the two-floor drop as Jon had been leaning against the window sill.

Jon craned to look out at the roof of the neighboring building four floors above. "Did you just jump down here from the roof?"

Ethan nodded as though it was nothing.

That jump looked impossible. Could he do anything like that? He'd nearly carried a large patient down the stairs alone last night, and it had him wondering. The few tests Garth had put him through during the first week hadn't been extensive on that front.

"If you don't weigh less, how come it doesn't sound as though you're taking the building down when you do that?"

"I absorb the force. The rail doesn't take it."

That almost made sense.

"Something wrong?" Ethan asked.

"No, I…" He ran out of excuses. "Are you on guard up there or something?"

"To call me a guard would be to imply I could do something about it if she returned," Ethan answered dully.

Jon didn't have an answer to that. She had been impossibly fast and silent and seemed just as deadly. "Do you think that Caspian bloke can stop her?"

Ethan stepped from the railing to the window sill and into the room as smoothly as descending stairs. "I don't know. I've never seen anyone who can match her strength, but he must hold some sway here to be *stapan*. He would have to be strong to be respected—this world can't be utterly different—but there is more to his control. Loyalty, power over resources…Whether whatever it is will hold Caterina, I–" he shook his head and stopped. "To be a ruler," he restated.

"That one I figured out in the context," Garth said from the couch, his posture somewhat deflated.

"Why hasn't she come back already?" Jon asked. "It's been a week."

"She's patient. Time isn't the same for someone who has lived hundreds of years."

It followed, in the way that something completely illogical could. The idea that his life might stretch beyond a normal lifespan still hovered in an area of Jon's brain labeled "unfathomable." "How are you healing up?"

"Just some residual soreness. Is your arm healed?" Ethan returned.

"Almost. Just a scratch now. Doesn't hurt anymore."

"You reacted more strongly to the pure silver. It would seem higher concentrations and longer exposures would be something to avoid."

It was such a random thing to react to, silver. "Do you think that's the only thing that I'm…that will burn like that?"

"We could trial some things, maybe," Garth proposed, naturally.

"Hey, er, I wanted to talk to you about something, also…" Jon addressed Ethan, who had perched on the arm of Garth's couch, then hesitated, unsure how to go on. "I met someone. Else."

"Are we breaking up?" Garth asked, with at least a bit of his usual lightness.

Jon gave an uneasy laugh. "I mean, like me."

He had Ethan's attention. "Are you sure?"

"I couldn't tell by looking at him, but his blood smelled the same."

"Blood?" Garth asked.

"He's a copper. He was on the scene I got called to. Got cut by somebody. When I looked at him, all…surprised, he just looks at me like, well, yea, why are you just now noticing?'"

"He's actually a cop?" Ethan clarified.

"For sure. His partner was looking for him."

"What did you tell him? What did he do?" Ethan prodded.

"I bandaged his arm. It was a deep cut, but he didn't seem to think anything of it and just wanted to keep anyone else from noticing. He seemed, I d'nno, surprised that I hadn't met anyone else. Told me to be careful disposing of his blood—not in as much detail as you did—and to not act as though I can hear or smell better than others," he recounted to an intent Ethan. "Then just went back to his job like nothing had happened."

"There are others, just out there, working, being…" Garth mused.

"What did he look like?" Ethan asked.

"A cop. No, I know what you mean. He's tall, white, 20s maybe, red-brown hair, but he does a better job of keeping it cut." He waved at his own mane. "Brown eyes, I think. He really looked normal. He didn't open his mouth very wide, so I never saw," Jon flashed his teeth. "As I said, I wouldn't have known if his blood didn't smell off, and if he hadn't said those few things to me."

"Did he say anything about who he is or what happened to him or anything about his history?" Ethan asked.

"No, nothing. All I got is that he seemed surprised that I was so surprised and…clueless. But he seems to know exactly what he's doing. I did hear another cop call him Sanderson. That's it. Ay," he abruptly realized where he had seen him before. "Except I think he said something to me at a different scene a few days ago. It was on the street at night, and there were all the usual emergency lights. Someone behind me told me to keep the light out of my eyes. I checked it out later–Did you know our eyes reflect light? I mean, mine do, I don't know about yours–"

"Oh, they do!" Garth broke in. "Remember that time with the microscope, when I turned the light way up? Man, I'd forgotten about that."

"Let me know if you run into him again?" Ethan asked after a pause of staring off into space.

"Yea. If I can find you."

"You know where to find me." He stood, stepped back out the window, and disappeared with a silent leap upward.

Jon sighed and dropped onto the couch next to Garth.

He just wasn't getting a lot to go on.

66

"Oh, hey."

Bent over a microscope on the back table in their lab, Ethan moved only his eyes to look up at Garth before focusing back on the magnified slide of blood cells.

"Are these more viral test slides?"

"It's not virulent or persistent enough to be a danger in here in this quantity," Ethan rationalized. "And the viral lab was overrun with students."

"Rude," Garth quipped while still hovering. "Want another set of eyes on these?"

Ethan slid the stack of slides toward him by an inch or so. He'd been grateful to get back after the forced hiatus of the holiday, and working in the lab today had given him a stable context to continue interacting with others despite the pit of dread in his stomach, but he had no more energy to pretend everything was normal with Garth. Especially not with tonight coming.

Garth took that answer happily anyway and settled onto a stool next to him with a little hum to himself, turned on the microscope in front of him, and reached for a slide.

Content that his slide showed another example of complete cell death after exposure to the virus, Ethan made a note on the sheet on the table and removed the slide to set in a precariously full pile on his right.

"Hey," Garth started again after only a minute had gone by. "I think these cells are intact."

The one Ethan was studying appeared to have lysed, but he kept scanning to finish and make sure. "Is it a W viral exposure?" He'd found three samples now that appeared to accept the virus Jon carried without immediately lysing.

"Uh, no. V."

That had Ethan looking up. He practically pushed Garth out of the way to examine the label on the slide. He'd run 237 of these tests now, and only his own cells hadn't lysed in response to his virus.

"Hold on," Garth sputtered and reached to spin the brightness knob down as Ethan leaned down in front of him to see for himself.

He maneuvered the slide around until he had seen the whole thing twice. "You're right," he breathed.

"Is that the first one?" Garth was flipping through a file.

"Other than mine."

"Where did these samples come from?"

Ethan hesitated. "Unidentified, possibly. I'll look it up." He took the slide with him back to his computer.

"Do you have any accompanying data?"

"Genotypes. I didn't print all those off, but I have the file." A few clicks later, he had the initial summary pulled up, complete with graphic circles above lists of code-like gene designations. Behind him, Garth bobbed up and down, looking for an angle from which he could see the dim screen. Ethan clicked again. "Printer."

When it had finished whirring from the other side of the room, Garth scampered back with a stack of papers, tripping over his stool as he laid them down on the table. "Ok, let's see…" He flipped for a few moments, while Ethan glanced back and forth between the papers and his screen. "Well," Garth started summarizing some of the genetic findings, "We've got probably mostly Eastern European descent." He pointed at another section. "That should mean Caucasian, and dark hair and eyes. So, he—oh she, actually—probably looks a bit like you."

"Like all of us."

Garth glanced at him. "Ok, yeah. I mean that's the interesting stuff that we already guessed. The rest of this…"

"Two sets of data to compare isn't much to go on."

"No, but it can't hurt."

"I'll go back and see if I've got enough of the sample to run a sequence." He thought he knew how to get the original identifiers for the batch of samples. It might give more context to know who they had come from.

"Even more data." Garth leaned back.

It was a ridiculous task for two people.

"Hoo boy," Garth sighed. "Welp, on to the next one. That was a pretty good find for my first slide of the afternoon. When do you leave for the charity dinner?"

Ethan exhaled slowly. "I'm supposed to escort Moraine over there at six."

Garth grinned. "Got your suit in your office?"

Like a good New Yorker, he'd carried it with him on the subway that morning. He grunted an affirmative and turned back to his microscope.

⟩

At 5:50 p.m. Ethan stood in the bathroom staring in the mirror. He unbuttoned his suit coat, then re-buttoned it and assessed the hair he'd actually attempted to style.

He was regretting his promise. Two weeks ago, he could have endured the party, the small talk, the juggling uneaten hors d'oeuvres and unanswerable questions with relatively mild discomfort. But his past had come in the flesh to haunt who he'd tried to become. To remind him who he was and what he'd done. To dangle dread of what might still happen to him and those around him.

Still, the party was part of the life he was trying to live, who he wanted to be. And he had promised. So, regardless of the rest, he would go.

He ran his hands down his coat. It wasn't much the worse for the commute, he didn't think, but he wasn't positive of the best way to wear a three piece suit. Carol's recommendation had taken him to a polished place that didn't just *sell* suits. The tailor had told him exactly what it was he should be wearing and picked out the pale shirt and black tie to go with the charcoal material for the pants, jacket, and vest. Ethan had made sure the cuff links weren't silver, at least. The small gesture had felt important, considering his roommate.

After deciding he was approximately as good as it got, he walked back across the hall toward the lab where he was supposed to meet Moraine. Maybe he shouldn't have, but he had offered to escort her to the museum despite her needing to arrive early.

It was all worth it for the second look Moraine gave him when she walked into the lab a few minutes later. He shouldn't have cared, but there it was. The way her eyes lit up made him momentarily forget the rest.

"Ethan—whoever you asked about the suit steered you right. You

395

look great."

He managed to find his tongue, "Forgettable next to you, I'm sure, but I couldn't drag you down at least." Her blue-silver dress draped her figure in a way that a lab coat definitely did not, and her golden hair was in loose polished waves that kissed the tops of her shoulders.

She smiled. "No risk of that."

Maybe it was good Garth had opted not to be his wingman, present to observe and try to encourage things that shouldn't be. Or had his absence been designed to have the same effect? *You kind-hearted fool.*

"Could I trouble you to help me with something?" She held out a necklace. "The clasp is giving me a hard time."

He took it from her and paused to examine the intricate network of flowers and vines intertwined with small gems. He ran his fingers along its length, admiring it. "Hand worked silver."

"It is." The edges of her eyes lifted in surprise. "It was my grandmother's."

"It's beautiful."

"Thank you." She lifted her hair from her neck.

Ethan stepped behind her and realized the necklace was not long enough to allow him to do the clasp without touching her skin. "I'm sorry—my hands are cold."

Once she insisted, "You're fine!" he draped it over her neck and quickly fastened the clasp. She turned. "What do you think?"

The gems caught the light and were matched by her earrings. "Perfect."

She waited a moment looking back at him before saying, "I've called a car downstairs. If you're ready."

"Yes. I am." He grabbed his coat and wallet and ruefully left his hat on his desk while she retrieved her own coat from her office. They met in the hall and started for the elevator.

Ethan shortened his stride to keep from rushing her, but as they waited for the old elevator to arrive, she scrutinized her strappy shimmering heels. "You know what? I was overambitious. There's a long night ahead." She smiled sheepishly over at him. "Do you mind waiting a moment?"

"No, of course."

She pulled a pair of folded lightweight shoes from her coat pocket. "At least I always carry emergency flats, like a good New York lady."

After dropping the flats to the floor, she crouched gracefully to undo the straps at her ankles and caught her balance with a grip on his arm as she removed her heels. His arm tensed in his suit sleeve, but he kept it steady until she straightened, a couple inches shorter and holding her heels. She noticed his straighter posture and let go. "I'm sorry. I should have asked first."

Not sure what to do with any of his feelings or her reactions, he gave a dismissive shake of his head and led the way into the elevator.

Outside, Moraine waved to the driver of her hired car and slipped in through the car door Ethan held open. "We need the north entrance of the Met."

Ethan joined her through the opposite door, and the driver snaked out into the streets.

"It's kind of you to come early with me," Moraine said.

"I can't escort the host and bring her late." Ethan ducked his eyes away from the flashing headlights. The evening sun was hidden behind the skyscraper-edges of the Manhattan canyons, and the city lights were all lit.

"Getting there only an hour and a half early–this is the part where I trust all the people I delegated to!"

Given that she spent the majority of their remaining ride time on the phone with the caterer, Ethan figured that wasn't entirely an accurate description of her role for the night.

Once there, he followed her into a side entrance and let her whisk off to answer someone's questions while he found the coat check. And remembered all the reasons he didn't do this kind of thing. Moraine had warned their grad students not to pry into his missing two years– he could hear their conversations through his thin office door–and he controlled what he answered during a lecture, but tonight promised to be more difficult.

67

When Ethan found Moraine again, she was in a side hall directing the chaos like a maestro. He hung at the fringes and watched her answer questions and make polite corrections until even that felt like an imposition, and then he wandered away.

The main room they were using was empty with all the tables already set up and the lights turned low. The entire wall on the other side was a bank of windows, but due to the hour, it was all dark glass reflecting an image of the interior. The main dais was surrounded by channels of still water that reflected the candle light. If he ignored what was to come, the atmosphere was calming.

The central attraction in the room was an ancient Egyptian temple. The whole rectangular mass of stone, flanked by engraved pillars, was housed there. After leaping the channel of water to land with more of a slapping sound than was necessary, thanks to his polished dress shoe, he surveyed the carved gray stone more closely. It was an interesting dichotomy, to hold an event discussing future research breakthroughs in a room with an object of such ancient history. As he scanned lines of hieroglyphs, one in the center drew his focus. The top portion of the pictograph resembled a wolf. What if there were one alive who could remember history even half as ancient? What legends and myths could they tell? Sometimes future mysteries were solved by looking at history. Perhaps Moraine's selection of the setting had been intentional.

The pop of her heels on the tile announced her presence. Ethan moved to a more visible location before he spoke. "Everything looks nice."

She relaxed and looked at him as if finding what she was searching for. "I think it does. We're nearly ready."

"Do you need help with anything?" He took the bridge over the canal and weaved around the high-topped tables to her.

"I think all I have left to do is find the person in charge of the lights and then tell them to open the doors to let people in. And then hide quietly for a few moments to remember what I'm supposed to say during my welcome speech. Which will be short. Oh, and find the musicians."

"They're back there somewhere. Maybe that entrance."

"You saw them?"

"I heard a stringed instrument…a minute ago." He led the way toward the sound of turning instruments that she couldn't hear until she could. While she spoke to them, he found someone in a museum uniform to ask about the lights, so they were on by the time she walked back in. The green and gold lighting was strategically placed to enhance the ambiance of the room rather than brightly lighting the space, which Ethan appreciated.

He let her go instruct someone to open the doors and find her quiet space alone. From an unconsciously chosen shadow behind a pillar, Ethan watched the space gradually fill until it buzzed with conversation from dozens of well-dressed guests.

"I should have known to find you hiding in the corner."

Ethan looked into almond eyes that found his from the other side of the pillar. "Evening, Lee. I didn't know you would be here."

"I, on the other hand, heard you were escorting our host?" A smile played on her red lips.

"Yes…"

"Well, you certainly look the part." She gestured appreciatively at his suit. "I don't think you had that when we were dating. Or if you did, you made a mistake not getting it out."

"You didn't let me take you anywhere fancy enough for it," Ethan found some old banter.

"That's true. Fair enough," she responded in kind.

"Are you here with your fiancé? I just realized I don't know his name."

"Ben—yes, he is. And before you think I'm a bad date for abandoning a finance guy in a room full of science professors, let me just tell you that he can hold his own in any conversation." She held up a finger to make the point, "Case in point: me. I think it's why we work. I don't know anything about finance, and he doesn't know genetics, at least more than the basics, so we talk about everything else. If you and I had…I mean, we would just talk about work all the time–couldn't escape it. I like all the new things I think about when I talk with Ben."

"Good. I'm happy for you." It was genuine. It was a strange miracle he'd ever gone out with her to begin with, as obsessed as he'd always been with work.

She hesitated. "I do feel bad about–"

"Don't," Ethan interrupted firmly. "There's no reason. He's better for you. We would have figured it out eventually, but it would have taken longer, and, who knows, maybe even been a mess, and one of us would have had to move offices anyway, and–"

"Ok, ok," she interrupted what had degenerated into bad teasing.

"But I'm serious," Ethan added. "Don't feel bad. I couldn't have picked a relationship back up, and he sounds perfect for you. Ok?"

"All right. And anyway, you have quite the date tonight. Dr. Miller is very accomplished."

"She is an impressive woman."

"And beautiful."

She was right, but Ethan turned away with a shake of his head. "I'm just her escort. I'm better alone right now. You know I was always basically married to work anyway."

"Maybe so." Her coy smile didn't look convinced. "Would you come meet Ben? I think he would like to meet you, if you're ok with it."

Ethan nodded and followed her. Once he had exchanged a cold handshake and some pleasantries and admitted to himself that Ben really did seem good for Lee, he excused himself to search for his "date" as he'd promised.

He found her uncharacteristically nervous heartbeat behind a bathroom door and tapped lightly. "Moraine?"

"Yes," she answered brightly. "Ethan, come in. Is it looking busier out there?" She stood before the mirror, but he couldn't imagine what part of her appearance she could be touching up.

"It is." He glanced at himself in the mirror for something to do and re-buttoned his jacket. Not sure how to reassure her, he managed, "You're very good at this. Nothing to be nervous about."

Her smile was one that seemed to warm the room. "And it's for a good cause," she declared, preaching to herself perhaps.

"That too." He gave her a careful version of his lopsided smile in return.

"Then let's do this." She gave a readying nod at herself and turned to him.

Placing his hand at his waist, Ethan offered her his arm.

"Are you sure?" she asked, eyes on his.

He nodded. He'd decided to be. To be present where he was, with her. Not others. Not the ghosts.

"Then thank you." She placed her arm over the crook of his elbow, where the suit layers hid the temperature differences in their skin, and let him escort her to the temple room. After a quick glance to see that she was ready, he took a short but confident stride to enter it. She ignited her professional smile, greeted a couple standing nearby, and waved at another as they approached the preordained front of the room where a lectern stood. She released him as she stepped behind it, which allowed him to shift to a less central place at a nearby table.

She welcomed the growing crowd and thanked them for their time and presence. She thanked others who had contributed to the event, including, for some reason, Ethan. If it had been only to remind some of his presence, it was with permission, he mused. Her short speech about the night's goal was full of hope rather than the fear often associated with the word "leukemia." It was a reminder of the need without the guilt trip or a long daydream-inciting speech. Other fundraisers should have been taking notes.

Her last word still echoed against the temple's stone wall as waiters with trays of drinks and food stirred the waiting guests, prompting renewed interaction among them. Ethan didn't try to rejoin her once she was done but only gave a nod and half-smile of assurance when she looked his way before joining a conversation with some others standing nearby. He would better serve her by having his own discussions with potential donors.

All the defined hard edges in the room proved advantageous, funneling sound in ways that allowed him to have no doubt as to what was behind him or out of sight and helped reduce the jumpiness that usually came with being in the center of a changing environment. The wine a waiter purposefully served him was a sharp red, clearly indicating Moraine's taste was better than she had advertised and her memory as good as Carol's, and he ultimately picked up a random hors d'oeuvre and held it to keep from continually being offered others.

It wasn't so uncomfortable to discuss the research he accompanied Dr. Miller in doing. It was the other questions, the predictable ones that followed the mystery of his reappearing existence in the genetics field, that had him resisting the urge to disappear back into the shadows behind the stone temple. He remained because the mystery is what he'd effectively given Moraine permission to use. And if he stayed in a group of at least three people, he could maneuver to be more of a net in the conversation tennis match.

"Dr. Ethan Dalton. You're that researcher who was dead for a while, right? How are you here now?"

Slight nod and hesitation.

To the mustached man across the pub table with the flickering candle: "It's been a few months now, hasn't it? I saw your name in the recent article—"

"Ah yes, it accompanied my article, you may have seen it…"

A nod to appear engaged.

After some self-preening about his own research, Dr. Mustache continued, "But where were you really, all that time?"

Vague glance across the room and half a shrug.

The man with glasses and a nose reminiscent of a beak followed his look across the room and answered distractedly, "Not dead, obviously—hello there Dr. Deeks! How are you…"

He managed it for an entire hour before Moraine reappeared like an angel at his side with a sleek-stemmed glass of red liquid. "Don't think I don't realize the effort you're giving this tonight," she said quietly while still nodding at someone else.

"The wine is good." He took a long sip.

"If I didn't know you better, I'd almost say you were having a good time."

She smiled at his prolonged swallow.

"I know they pressured you into taking me on, but I still appreciate you sticking your neck out for me. It may not be equal in value, but," he shrugged a shoulder, "I owe you some effort."

"Consider us even, Ethan. But know I'd appreciate your company anytime it wouldn't make you miserable."

His reply died on his lips.

People still trickled in and out, and among those entering the room sauntered a man in a fitted dark patterned suit, white shirt, and maroon tie. It was the kind of outfit you knew instantly was fashionable, simply because he was the one wearing it. His hair was styled, his jaw wore just the right amount of stubble, his posture was sure. Hanging on his arm was a woman who must have been pretty, given the amount of skin she flaunted in her blood red dress. There was an air of superiority in the way he looked around the room, as if, despite his physical position, he was a king on a throne surveying his subjects.

His black eyes found Ethan's from across the room.

Ethan jerked his face away from Moraine.

It had been too unexpected. Surprise mixed with any emotion was infinitely more difficult to conceal. But the reasons he had to blink the blue from his eyes didn't matter as much as doing it quickly and calmly, as Moraine was querying his name in a concerned tone.

"Sorry, fine." The words were paltry when he turned back, but he was more focused on finding him again. There. Lips sneering in a smile that threatened to reveal too much, except they wouldn't, because he was much too sure of himself.

Moraine must have followed his gaze. "Wow, Mr. Barnes actually came."

Barnes?

"Do you know him?" she asked.

By a different name. He bunched his own lips to avoid returning the sneer.

"You…don't approve?"

He had the ability to hide his distaste much better. Maybe he *was* out of practice. "Why is he here?" Ethan still hadn't taken his eyes from the other vampire but watched him move through the crowd, playing those who interacted with him like an instrument.

"He heads up a significant financial firm downtown. I was given his contact information some time ago. He's sent representatives to functions before, but never come in person. I've never met him, actually, but I'm sure it's him. It must have been your name this time." She smiled in jest.

It probably was my name.

"You do know him?"

Ethan couldn't figure out how to answer and ended up parting his lips twice to try but coming up short. "It's complicated." The woman with him was human. He could tell easily. *What are you playing at?*

"Why does it look like you hate him?"

It's not just him. Closing his eyes, he pulled in a slow breath. *Calm, stay calm.*

"Ethan?"

He finally looked over at her. "Don't ever let yourself be alone with him."

Her eyes widened and blinked at his sudden warning. "Ok. I doubt I'll have to worry about that, but ok, Ethan."

Ethan turned back toward Caspian and his escort. Surely if he was at the gala, milling about with a room full of known and rich people, as that persona, he wasn't going to try anything, right? *He's doing a better job than you are, right now,* he scolded himself.

By the time "Mr. Barnes" positioned himself to approach Moraine, Ethan had fitted an old mask of indifference carefully back into place. Moving quickly and lithely around the people who had maneuvered between them, he slid into place at Moraine's elbow as she took his hand in greeting. "Thank you so much for coming, Mr. Barnes."

"Thank you for the invitation, Dr. Miller, Dr. Dalton," his words flowed like silk.

"Mr.….Barnes," Ethan took his surprisingly warmer hand stoically but on guard.

Caspian's eyes taunted with hidden mirth even as his words glided on flawlessly. "This is my guest, Miss Robins."

Do you know? Ethan nodded at the slender dark-haired girl without offering his hand. She was likely the one in the most danger. She would leave willingly with him, to be taken anywhere. Of all the things to wear on a date with a vampire—if you were going to bare that much skin, at least avoid wearing that color.

He could not repeat the rest of the conversation, but the words didn't matter. Ethan's attention was on Caspian's posture, his hands, mouth, the way he breathed. He was possessive of the girl, sickeningly professional with Moraine, taunting to Ethan, and ever so smugly sure of himself.

"He's cordial enough," Moraine observed, as he glided away to the next mark in an expensive suit. She'd missed the gibe in his last glance at Ethan. "Although quite sure of himself, isn't he?"

Ethan grunted in agreement.

Trapped at her side, he found himself greeting a few more guests, most with similar amounts of self-confidence. At least the conversations were easier, with Moraine fielding most questions and even redirecting one unnecessary one about his past.

By the time the numbers of people had dwindled and the line of those approaching Moraine had petered out, Ethan felt a tightness not far from that of being trapped under a sunlit sky.

"I'm not leaving, but I'm going to step outside for a minute," he told Moraine.

She gave him another smile. "Thank you, Ethan."

68

The darkly glowing night sky in front of the stately Metropolitan Museum of Art held only relief tonight. Breathing freely for the first time in untold minutes, Ethan took his time wandering along the street toward the bare trees that lined Central Park.

The sound of their branches creaking and scraping against each other was just audible under the noise of the cars and horns and distant voices. Bike wheels whirred. Feathers fluttered. A dog growled. Leaves whispered.

And there, against that rock, lingered a shadow deeper than darkness.

His eyes lightened on purpose.

"Hello, Etan."

Somehow, in an old way, it didn't surprise him to see her there. *Are you here for me, or are you following Caspian now?* He met her eyes, waiting with a coil in his chest and a flat mask on his face.

"You are a shadow of what you could be." She floated down off the rock she had been standing on.

"What if this is what I want to be, right here?"

"Is it? Are you really content now?"

The sound of Moraine's shoes on the sidewalk behind him cracked his mask. *No!*

"Who is this?"

Aching to stop her, he stepped back and to the side to put himself between them with his palm held back at Moraine. *"She's no one."*

"Is it her you are content with?"

"No. I barely know her. She's not a part of this." But he feared Cate saw

through him.

Moraine naively interrupted, "Hey, I think it's nearly time–"

"Moraine, stop."

Her footfalls and words did stop, only steps behind him, and Cate glided closer to him over the thin layer of snow, studying her with interest. Ethan's breath caught on something sharp in his chest. There was so little he could do if she chose to attack.

"You do like this kind, don't you? Is it the hair, or the eyes?"

Air hissed through his teeth at her knowing jab.

"You will…kill her also?" The English words were wrong in her mouth–the first he had ever heard from her. Of course they were these. They weren't spoken for him, but for Moraine.

"*No!* Moraine, get back inside. Now!"

"You will kill her as you did your first."

"You killed Iulia. You just used me to do it."

"Still denying your own choices, Etan?" Her gaze turned back to caress Moraine, who had only moved a couple steps back, heart beating quickly in her chest.

There was only one move to keep her alive. "Go!" Ethan shouted at the woman behind him, putting command and fear and almost a shriek into the word.

He didn't face her, not completely. He didn't know what all she saw. But he could see the fear in her eyes an instant before she turned to run.

When he turned back, Cate was still watching, still standing in the shadow the tree cast in front of the streetlight. With Moraine further away, he could hope to slow Cate down at least, if she thought to pursue her.

"You do care for her."

"No." If he didn't convince her, would she find her later anyway?

"Then why fight so hard?"

"I fought for others I didn't know. They're people, the ones you kill, not just subjects to be used for your pleasure."

He had her full attention again. She stepped silently to him, leaned close to look into him. Gut twisting, he stood and let her.

"Yes." Her blue eyes searched his. *"Understanding you completely has ever eluded me."*

And then she was gone. Without stirring a leaf, she whispered away, leaving the quiet sounds of the park and the softest foot impressions on the snow.

Ethan almost collapsed with relief.

Then he sprinted back to the museum and spotted Moraine on the steps. She was walking more slowly now, while still casting glances behind her. Others trickled down the stairs as they left, including Caspian—

No. It could still end so badly. If she had seen enough–if she told him or he guessed–she could be in the same danger. He sprinted down the street and leaped the edge of a few stairs out of view of the others.

Moraine's farewell greeting was audible. Caspian, the woman still on his arm, lifted a waving hand to her.

Ethan clicked twice in his throat.

An inconspicuous tilt of his head betrayed Caspian's perception but did not interrupt his conversation. Only after completing his words and sultry smile to her and another nearby, did he turn vaguely toward Ethan. After handing the girl's arm to the man behind him, who Ethan should have realized was with him as well, he descended the steps to stand two above Ethan. Without speaking, he raised a brow with an irritated quirk of his head.

Ethan kept his voice flat and kept his gaze on the park rather than on Caspian. "She's prowling in the park. Threatened someone walking by. In case you're interested."

A sharp glance at the greenspace betrayed that he may actually be interested. "Hardly worth an interruption, but thank you for the information. If you'll excuse me." He stalked off to the man and the girl and a waiting car.

That left Moraine to walk back inside uninterrupted.

As he closed his eyes to fight off the world's spinning, Ethan breathed again.

Cate hadn't killed Moraine. Caspian hadn't spoken to her. But what had he done?

꒷

Caterina hovered along the edge of the neatly demarcated little forest and watched Ethan retreat up the stone steps.

Then it is you who tries to wield the young lord against me, Etan. You who claim to have no allegiance.

At their first meeting, Caspian had left her with a warning and an invitation she had not accepted. When he approached her the second time, after she had found Etan with the human and the wolf demon, he had been much more courteous. Claiming he had not recognized her for who she was, a princess of the old world, he attempted to welcome her properly and led her to the center of his domain amid the ravines of metal and stone and glass.

In the first truly quiet place she had experienced in the city, she was given a small room lined with rich fabrics and furs, which had been enjoyable. She had been offered clothing to replace hers, which she had not initially accepted, as well as fruit, wine, and blood in abundance. When she had rested and enjoyed his gifts for long enough, she had found vampires positioned outside her room to keep her where she was.

Rather than dispose of them immediately, she had used them to discover more regarding her situation and their leader. While Caspian seemed to have no true respect for her, her calm persistence with her guards unearthed him again.

He returned with a vampire who spoke Romanian to aid communication and educate her in the ways of his world. Rather than fear, he employed other methods of living with the enormous human population. Those with power in their world must never suspect vampires existed. When interacting with them, one must appear completely similar. By doing so, there were ways of gaining wealth and power within their ranks. With the peasants there was a different way. Some of them came willingly to play with vampires, fancying them legends and enjoying pretend rituals. Caspian's domain held a room, rife with bodies and music and food, for amusements for humans. Still others came for something else, offering their own blood for some recompense.

She was told that the taking of a human in public was not acceptable, especially if you were observed. However, there were innumerous other ways to obtain their blood. She was then offered all of them. It was gluttonous how much was available. Perhaps living in the midst of so many had given these vampires less bridled appetites.

Once she had allowed him to show her the advantages of his realm, she thought to test the boundaries of it. Feigning her own respect in great measure, she gained "permission" to leave the fortress and venture out into the city. Despite the new supposed freedom of movement, she found herself watched and tracked by the most able vampire she had thus far seen.

She let him test himself against her, and tested herself, as she became accustomed to movement amid the lights and sounds that still cowed her. For the time being she would watch and listen and partake of the offered nourishment. When the time came, she would leave him.

Tonight, she wished to be alone, so she avoided her vampire

watcher at the edge of the forest and instead traversed easily through the shadows to the most beautiful building in a land crowded with them. The arches and towers of carved gray stone were only a copy of the ancient buildings in her own land, but still it had drawn her in with its familiarity and cold grandeur. With a hand on the thick wood of the door, her gaze followed the curve of the arched doorway to the carved crucifix at its point.

She had retreated to the cathedral before and had not been followed inside, as if the legend persisted even far from its origins, but as in all churches except one, the heavy lacquered wood of the door pushed easily inward under her hand. After stealing silently through the knave, she leaped upward to a balcony that held pipes of the huge organ and plenty of shadows to hide her from anyone's eyes. Before her, pillars stood guard at the room's walls which arched to a tile roof high above.

In the quiet candlelight she considered Etan.

He who made her feel complete sought to hate her. He couldn't utterly, she saw it, but his conviction to do so seemed unbridled despite his previous actions in her realm. It left her feeling betrayed and empty, but that was all but irrelevant.

The problem she would address now, which would pull her mind from the other, was that Etan still clung to his place in his old world, amongst its people. Perhaps it was possible to live among them, as Caspian did, but Etan sought to *be* one.

Had she never succeeded in teaching him who he was and what he was capable of? Perhaps not, if he claimed his decisions and actions were hers instead of his own. She had failed in her training of him.

Etan needed to make a choice he could not deny. If she could ensure that he did so, he would fully become a vampire. If he accepted his choices, he would have to see who he was. But once he was a true *strigoi*, would she have to accept his choices? If he chose not to return, would she force him back? Set guards upon him to ensure he did not escape again? Would she limit his potential by coercing a single response?

Those of her realm who completely understood the truth of their life lived there willingly. Over the ages, some had traveled to other realms, perhaps even this one. Not all had been compelled to stay.

Without her, Etan would not reach his full potential, but when she was finished creating the *strigoi* he should be, at least he would no longer flounder in the dark.

69

Ethan had texted Garth back. It had seemed prudent to avoid a significant level of panic when he hadn't returned home after the charity dinner. The text had been enough at least to keep Garth at bay over the three-day holiday weekend, but now he was vibrating with concern at the doorway to Ethan's office.

"Hey. How was the fundraiser?"

Ethan didn't look up. "Moraine knows how to throw them. I expect a good amount was raised."

"What happened? Why are you still here?"

"Working over a holiday has its advantages."

"Yeah, right. But you haven't stayed away this long since–?"

"Changed my mind. Keeping a distance is probably better for you."

"In what way, exactly?"

The lab door opened to admit the first of the sparse morning meeting attendees. Garth backed off, and Ethan waited until everyone who wasn't on winter break was present before easing out of his office into a seat at the back. He kept his eyes down, as if that would enable him to avoid notice. Still, amid the chatter and few other heartbeats, he heard Moraine's speed up.

"Good morning! How was the benefit dinner, Dr. Miller?" Garth tried a new tactic.

"Great. It was a fantastic turnout and a great venue. I hope it will help fund ongoing research via the Leukemia Foundation." Her reply was upbeat, but surely even Garth could hear the forced quality to her voice. Maintaining the businesslike demeanor, she efficiently proceeded through the standard meeting agenda. By the time she concluded, Garth shot him another curious stare but couldn't linger long due to some other commitment.

Moraine let the room empty.

At the end of the party, Ethan had gone back in to make sure she was safe but let her leave without seeing him. He had scared her purposefully to keep her from harm, and now it was time to face her reaction.

"Do you spend a lot of time here when everyone else is gone?" she asked him carefully.

As he still wore the same clothes she had last seen him in, sans the suit coat and tie, it was fairly evident he hadn't spent much time at home. The question was a parry that displayed her lack of ignorance but a diversion from the real issue.

"Moraine." He stood and looked at her.

She matched his step forward with a step back.

"I'm sorry. She…" The explanation, any explanation, fell from his lips as he watched that same fear enter her eyes again.

They invariably ended up looking at him with fear. It was the way it always ended. He knew, and he'd been a fool to imagine otherwise. He retreated a step and looked away, trying to not let any of the emotions flicker into his eyes.

"What happened to you over there?" she asked with only a little waver in her voice.

"A lot."

She scoffed at his vague answer.

"I can't give you specifics," he said softly.

It gave her pause, time to take a breath. "Who is she?"

"She's dangerous. If you ever see her again, get away, as fast as possible."

Moraine was undeterred. "You've given me a lot of warnings about who to avoid. Barnes. Her. What about you? It seemed she was trying to warn me too."

"I won't hurt you…"

Under any circumstances? Can you really promise that? his thoughts accused.

"But there's the possibility that you might? You've been dangerous to others?"

Lying seemed too deep an insult. And pointless. "Yes."

She backed up further before asking the next question. "The woman you said I reminded you of. The one you… 'hurt.' Is she dead?"

As though under some compulsion to tell the truth, he answered again, "Yes. She's dead." He opened his mouth again to give assurances, but the look in her eyes said it was moot. It was just as well; it couldn't have been completely truthful anyway.

The shake of her head gradually increased in volume as she took another step back. "Don't ever touch me."

Resigned, he nodded.

"Or anyone else in my lab. If I ever have reason to think…"

"I won't." His voice was a tight whisper.

"No." She agreed sternly, and strode quickly and stiffly out the door.

No part of Ethan wanted to address Garth's questions, but there he was, entering his basement apartment with his doggedly persistent landlord at his heels. If he hadn't been out of animal blood and in need of a shower, he might not have come home, or so he told the part of his mind that argued that he owed Garth something. He was the only human who had ever not run from him after seeing so much of the truth.

"Did you blow her off?"

"No," Ethan rebutted his new theory. "I went. I escorted her. I told you it was a good party."

Garth threw up his hands. "Then what happened? She was flirty with you for weeks–I saw it even if you didn't. Today it's all weird. What happened?" His voice dropped, as it still did occasionally, even when they were in private, when transitioning to particular topics. "Did something happen?"

"No." *Yes.* "I mean, not like that…"

"Like what? Something did happen?"

"Caspian came."

"The–the top vam–to the charity–" Garth's eyes bugged.

"He's a finance person in this world, apparently–forget him. He's not the problem."

His squeak held a question mark.

"I walked out, to the park, toward the end. Cate was there."

Garth's face froze, eyes wide, mouth crooked in a half-started question.

"Moraine followed me out."

By the sound, Garth's mouth closed, but Ethan had looked away.

"She…threatened Moraine. I had to get her to run back inside…"

"And?" Garth's prod squealed out when he didn't continue.

"I yelled at her to go back in."

"But, it was ok then? She left and then…what is she mad at you for yelling? That doesn't make sense."

Ethan whirled around at him, eyes blue and teeth showing, and knocked him back into the kitchen cabinet without moving a step.

It took a moment–Garth had to start breathing again–but he got it. "Like–like that? You're saying you looked like that?" He paused, "Of course you did, you were facing Cate. "

Ethan sneered.

"Am I not allowed to call her that? It's just what you were calling her."

If she heard you…

"How much did Moraine see, exactly? Did you go after her?"

"No! I don't know, exactly. Enough."

"To figure it out?"

"Not enough for that, not all of it, just enough to be frightened."

"You're saying she's just scared of you now?"

"It's the normal response, Garth," Ethan glared. "The response every human who even guesses what I might be gives–except for you. *Why don't you run?*"

"So just explain it to her," Garth glossed over his Romanian words and replied as if it were obvious. "She's a scientist. We show her the facts, the science. The–"

"You will do no such thing," Ethan snapped. "Seeing enough to be scared is one thing. If she knows, if we tell her, what do you think happens? Remember the rules? Remember who *else* was there last night? It could be a death sentence."

"They can't just kill someone for finding out."

"Why not! Will you stop them?" he bellowed before his voice flattened out to continue, "Because I cannot."

Garth cowered, if only slightly. "Ok, but what if she asks? She's not just going to be like, 'he's scary' but not ask why, is she?"

"Not everyone chooses to investigate the monster under the bed. Even scientists believe what they want sometimes. You know that."

"One look at what, blue eyes, and she's just going to avoid and scowl at you until the end of time? And that's it? I don't get why this would scare Moraine like that."

"She saw enough. She heard enough."

"Heard what? You said something? Or Ca–her? Does she speak English?"

"Apparently enough. To tell her I should do it."

"What?"

"Kill her. *Like I killed Iulia!*" *Because Caterina is apparently destined to kill me. Doing it in her world wasn't enough. I can't exist here either.* It felt like she had him by the throat.

"I–I didn't catch that last part, but that's fine." Garth's voice had gained a tremble.

"Moraine knows enough to be afraid," the words hissed between his teeth. "And she's been through enough to be done with dangerous monsters. You will tell her nothing."

Garth wasn't arguing anymore. He knew, or had guessed, things about Ethan's past that he'd never said out loud.

Did it matter? Ethan Dalton had died in that cave. Perhaps Cate was here to remind him of that. Ethan snatched the nearest small object–a spoon from the table–and hurled it at the wall.

Garth dropped to the floor with his hand out defensively.

The spoon vibrated handle-side first in the drywall above the stove. *Not him.*

Ethan spun away, out the door, leaving it to sway open in the cool drizzle.

70

Ethan went back to the lab, because where else would he go?

He badged in through the door of the research building and wandered through the ground floor.

"What are you up to tonight, Professor?"

It was the security guard following him, calling him back before he could round the next corner. Irritated, Ethan glared at Seeley. He usually got ignored in the quiet halls at the late hour, not chased down.

Seeley's next statement did not clarify things. "Just so everyone knows, we all belong here."

Ethan sighed, confused and annoyed at his coy words, then further confused by his cautious posture. He turned toward the other end of the hall to see a man wearing an NYPD jacket.

The tall young officer looked back, apparently also confused for a beat, but then there was a subtle change in his stance. "And you said you were alone here," the officer accused Seeley, without taking his eyes from Ethan, and slid back a step while bringing his hands up slightly in a move that definitely rang as defensive.

"Yeah, well, he doesn't work with me," Seeley answered. "He just works upstairs—one of the lab rats—professors. Just a coincidence."

Coincidence? Do you know what I am? Ethan stepped silently closer to the officer, who dropped his center of gravity and flicked his gaze between Ethan's hands and eyes, as if watching for an attack. And knowing where to look for the first signs.

What are you? His hands were open and ready. Lips pursed closed over his teeth. An ear that cocked toward Ethan. A name badge that read "Sanderson." *NYPD*—"You're the cop."

"'The cop'? What do—" the officer's eyes narrowed.

"Jon said there was another. A cop named Sanderson."

He straightened slightly. "Jon… *You're* the one who raised him?"

"And where were you?" Ethan was not in the mood for subtlety. "If there are more of you here, why didn't someone find him? I was under the impression it would be frowned upon to be found out by an emergency room doctor."

The officer resumed his defensive posture. "'More of us'? Obviously, there are others in the city, but we're not as pervasive as you. If he were bitten here, it would have been taken care of, but he clearly wasn't, and I had no idea he existed before two weeks ago. He must have come into the city after he was turned, but if you found a lycan in the emergency room…"

Ethan was momentarily distracted by the word "lycan." Was that really the accepted term for what Jon was?

Sanderson continued, "You're right, he would have been found, but if he made it to the ER, it probably would have been by someone who would have just killed him to cover it. You saved him."

"Wait, wait—you saved a lycan?" Seeley broke in incredulously. "You have no idea how the world works."

"You want to tell me?" Ethan turned to glare at the vampire. "Who is this guy?" He jabbed a thumb at Sanderson.

"Sanderson? No idea. Met him a few weeks ago. Apparently he bought some more land somewhere recently he's got to pay for and likes this off duty assignment for some reason. He really does seem to be a legit cop though. How did you end up saving a new lycan?"

"And who are you?" Sanderson interrupted. "Is Caspian into science now?"

When Ethan snapped a threatening blue gaze to him, the cop's pupils expanded to fill his irises with blackness. Like Jon's.

"Woah!" Seeley jumped forward but stayed out of the immediate reach of either of them. "Professor, he didn't mean anything by it. Just suspicious by nature. Asked me the same thing actually. But this is not the place for a confrontation. Please."

Ethan watched Sanderson ease back a step with his hand on his flashlight. There was no point in running from it anymore. If his old world was going to follow him across the ocean, then he needed to know about this one. Outmaneuvering Cate was his only chance to survive, and possibly Jon's as well. If these two were doing so well, he needed answers from them. "If I don't know how the world works, then tell me."

Sanderson shifted under his gaze, shot a glance at Seeley behind Ethan, and took a step to the side to get his back off the wall and give himself an avenue of escape down the intersecting hall. "Historically, lycans," with a single finger, Sanderson slowly pointed to his own chest then to Ethan, "and vampires don't like each other. So you saving one is a little radical. But I have no quarrel with you. I'm here as a cop, just doing my job."

It was the same story as he'd gotten in the cave, in new wrappings, about some historical feud between them. "How do you know Caspian?"

"I'm a lycan in a vampire dominated city. Of course I know who's at the top. It seems you share my sentiment of not liking him much, so we're in agreement there."

"Who would have killed Jon in the hospital?" Ethan continued.

"Why am I the one answering his questions?" Sanderson asked Seeley, who, from the sound of it, shrugged.

"Who would have killed him?" Ethan repeated.

After a press of his lips, Sanderson answered, "There are humans who know, who consider themselves keepers of the peace. The current vernacular for them is 'Warden.' Most of them tend to prioritize threat reduction, which means they probably would have just killed him because it's simpler."

The world got bigger and bigger at every turn. When Ethan glanced back at Seeley for verification, he just nodded.

"Some people do know? How does everyone not know?"

"Mostly because there aren't very many of us," Sanderson answered.

Such a simple answer. *And yet I managed to find three in the span of a few months.*

Seeley had followed his skeptical glance between them. "Yes, you found us, but this is the most densely populated area anywhere. We're still talking around 100, give or take, in a city of millions. You're the brain, you can make that an accurate ratio–"

"One to 80,000."

"–yeah…"

"Vampires," Sanderson clarified quietly.

"Right," Seeley conceded. "Fewer lycans. Doesn't much make sense that there are any at all, but I guess history is steep. Something about the gang wars–I'm too young for all that though. Anyway, we also tend to live together in groups. Loners," he spread his hands to acknowledge himself, "Are the exception, not the rule. It only really works out in specific circumstances, but this city is one of them." He looked at Sanderson. "I think it's fairly similar…"

Sanderson just nodded.

"Although you're going to find them," Seeley waved at Sanderson, "in absurd places like middle of nowhere Texas. How was it for you? You were brought back to a group when you were turned?"

It seemed a stretch to think he'd get away without giving up anything if he wanted answers. After a flicker of his upper lip, Ethan answered, "Yes."

"In Romania?" Seeley asked.

Right. He'd looked him up. Fine. "Yes."

"Seriously?" Sanderson breathed.

"A secluded one?" Seeley continued.

"Yes. But surrounding villages knew. Or certain members did. They—we raided them. Somehow some of them still managed to not believe or remember."

Seeley nodded, as though it made perfect sense. "Did you believe the legends when you first heard them? Given casual contact with the unexplainable, most people will choose to remember something that fits better into their world view."

"It wasn't casual contact."

"It's an old congregation?" Sanderson asked.

"Yes," Ethan understated.

"It may be known. To a few in authority. In some places there are Wardens high up in government. There are different methods of dealing with the issue. One is to protect old, self-secluded clans. It's often easier and less exposing than eradicating the truly entrenched ones."

It still didn't make sense. "How does word not get out?"

"The world hasn't always been so connected." Another simple answer to a complex question that seemed somehow to explain more than it should have. "And we don't spread the word."

The rules. "You have a leader who makes the rules too then?"

"Erek," Seeley said, prompting a twitchy glance from Sanderson. "What? I know stuff too."

Something else didn't make sense. "You look at me like I'm so weird for finding Jon, yet here you two are, friends."

As if choreographed, Seeley and Sanderson both took a simultaneous step further apart. "That's not—"

"We're not friends."

"This happened by accident. We have work covers to keep. It's not as easy to get or keep a job if you're not part of a group," Seeley defended.

Unconvinced, Ethan kept his objections to himself and continued watching them as closely as listening to their answers. "And if you are part of a group? You live outside society?"

"Sometimes. Or sometimes in a group with society. Caspian has a whole network. I don't even know what all they do. Jobs. Food source. New ID papers when you age out."

Age out? But of course. If he didn't age, one day his face wouldn't match the age on his birth certificate. A problem he hadn't even thought to broach yet.

"As I said, probably the biggest collection of vampires in one place." Seeley kept glancing at Sanderson, but the lycan stayed quiet.

So Ethan turned back to the cop. "Then why didn't you say more to Jon? Help him out some. Do anything except ignore him?"

Sanderson bristled and contended back without raising his voice, "Did you hear what we just said about living alone? Keeping a job? Avoiding questions? Without care, he raises those questions and draws attention. I appreciate what you've done for him, but you don't get to judge what I have or haven't done."

Having lost the tentative comfort level he'd started the conversation with, Ethan eased back a step with a wry observation. "I get it. If you're not the one who infects him, he's not your responsibility."

"Infects?" Seeley interrupted, as Sanderson narrowed his eyes.

Just like that, Ethan felt the dynamic shift. He stopped mid-turn away and watched the confusion in the other's expressions, the glance at each other to see if the other one knew what Ethan had just referred to.

Was it possible that they didn't know the scientific basics?

"What do you mean, 'infects?' You mean 'turns' or something more…specific?" Seeley asked the question, but Sanderson was also watching closely for the answer.

Ethan hesitated. The understanding that stood to be gained from the conversation had been worth a few admissions about himself, but the information about the virus was deeper. He'd been careless to hint at his discoveries because he'd thought it would be common knowledge. If it wasn't…but it was a little too late to simply walk away. And now he was curious about what they did and didn't know. "What did you think caused the physical changes?"

"Are you saying you know?" Sanderson had gone calm and intent.

Ethan faced them again. "Not entirely. I found a previously unidentified virus and DNA changes. It's a hypothesis that one caused the other."

"You're saying this is caused by a virus that changes DNA?" Seeley stared.

"You think you found the cause of vampirism?" Sanderson asked.

"Not just—Jon carries a different virus. Similar, but with some differences."

Sanderson's study of Ethan had become even more intent. "How did you find this?"

"I'm a geneticist. It's what I do."

"Why? Why are you looking at yourself?"

The question seemed absurd. "'Why?' Haven't you ever wondered how this works? How does a human body change physically, and so quickly? Why does it turn some and kill others?"

The others stood frozen, with similar expressions of shock.

Sanderson snapped his focus back first. "'How does it work,' 'why some?' What if someone else got their hands on what you're doing? Do you have any idea how dangerous that could be? Have you even considered—?"

"I can't be the only one who has figured it out." Until a few seconds ago, Ethan had thought at least some of it would be common knowledge.

"Maybe not, but what if you are? There are Wardens with positions in the government, in three letter agencies. What if they knew everything you're trying to figure out? Forget the why's, what about knowing *how* to more effectively kill us? Or—" he took an uneven breath, "if you figure out the answer to 'why some' and it becomes a way to kill everyone who could turn. Or worse."

"Worse?" Seeley blurted.

Worse: "If someone could purposefully turn certain people." Better understanding the threat couldn't squash Ethan's need to understand everything else. "I get it, but I'm being careful. I'll be even more careful. But I need to know how it works—"

"What if—"

"What if I can figure out exactly how it changes the DNA? How to stop it? What if there's a way to reverse it?"

He'd never spoken that question—wish—aloud. *But what if there is? What if there's a way to reverse what they've done? Could I go back?* It was the question buried deepest in his drive to know.

It stopped the others as sure as a slap to the face.

What if?

What would it change? He saw a glimpse of regret mirrored in the lycan's eyes before he opened his mouth to argue again.

The click of a door echoed down the hall and stole their attention. As if following the cue of a play, they changed their roles. Sanderson moved toward the nearest outside door as though to take up a post. Seeley dropped a hand to his belt and angled himself to put his desk in his view. Ethan simply started strolling down the hall as though he had been all along.

The distracted man in scrubs and a surgical hat barely glanced at any of them as he passed except to acknowledge Seeley's nod.

As soon as he was gone, the curtain on their play dropped, and everyone abandoned their act to stop where they were and turn vaguely back to each other. After eyeing the others again, Ethan decided that he'd had enough. He'd learned a lot, revealed more than he'd realized, and wasn't taking anyone else's orders again.

Ignoring Sanderson's mumbled, "He's going to get someone killed," Ethan turned away.

Before he could get around Seeley's end of the hall, he reached toward Ethan. "Hey, you were gone too fast the other night. I found this over a month ago. You didn't by any chance break into the microbiology lab last month did you?"

It was his university ID in Seeley's hand.

No, it was his old university ID.

The last time he'd seen it...

It had been in his wallet when he'd been hauled into the cave. In the wallet he'd never seen again.

A chill washed through his chest, sharpening his view of the small innocuous card.

Caterina had his wallet. It was how she'd found him. She'd followed the addresses on the ID's.

Seeley slid back a pace. "Did you?"

"No."

"It is yours?"

Ethan took it but continued studying at it as though it were a foreign thing. "It was...How long ago did you find this–That night of the break in–November?" She hadn't just found him at home, she knew he was at the university.

"You know who it was?" Sanderson leaned forward.

So long ago. A month before she'd confronted him.

Who knew how much she had found out.

He ignored their questions and walked away.

71

"You got a lot more out of him than I did!" Jon paced in the vestiges of the morning light that made it through the apartment's window covering.

"An abandoned hall could be a better place for a conversation than a crime scene," Garth offered from his seat on the couch.

"Keeping the secret and their 'cover' or whatever seemed very important," Ethan reported from his perch on the arm of the same couch. It was understandable but not encouraging that it seemed keeping such secrets would only get more difficult.

"But seriously—how does the whole world not know?" Jon repeated.

"I just told you everything they said."

"What about the people who know, the 'Wardens'? The ones who should have killed me? Why don't they tell everyone?"

"I don't know."

"Maybe they know how people would react." Garth's brain was on. "Maybe, if there's really so few of you, it is actually protective that the world at large doesn't know."

Ethan tended to agree with Jon's snarl.

"They really didn't know about the virus?" It was Garth's turn to repeat a question.

Ethan shook his head.

"Now what?" Jon paced back again. "How does this change what we're doing?"

"It doesn't," Ethan replied. "I'm not stopping research. And I'm not joining a group."

"And if…*she* comes back?"

"I'm working on it."

"Do you know what she wants?" Garth asked quietly.

The old sour dread filled Ethan's stomach. The answer to that question was obvious. She wanted the vampire she thought she'd made. The real question was this: how long could he keep her from getting it. Or how long could he *afford* to? Because he knew in his gut what lengths she might go to get what she wanted. How far would he let her go to save himself?

"Not entirely," was the answer he gave.

"Do you think Sanderson might actually talk to me?" Jon had returned to the kitchen.

"I don't know. He seemed to prefer being alone."

"That's very helpful–" Jon stopped mid-sentence and pointed to the wall above the stove. "Why is there a spoon in the wall? I didn't do that," he defended to Garth.

"I know," Garth replied.

"Then how did it get there?"

"I did it."

Jon spun to look at Ethan. "You…how did you get a spoon halfway into the wall?"

Garth pantomimed throwing before stopping short halfway through the motion.

"You don't corner the market on arguments," Ethan replied sullenly.

"Argument–and it wasn't with me, so you're throwing spoons at Garth now? What happened to 'not him'?"

Ethan sneered. "If I had been throwing it at him, it wouldn't be in the wall."

Jon paced back. "You can jump in a window from a roof, tumble and spin all over the place, have wicked knife skills. Can I–No, I have a real question. I get that you don't know exactly what I can do, so how is that you can do stuff like that? Did you just realize you could do it or learn it or what?"

Ethan earnestly tried to take a slow deep breath. "It's not straightforward. I know the increased strength and agility was innately different after the genetic changes."

"What about things like throwing a spoon handle first, apparently where you were aiming?"

"Learned. Easier because of the innate changes."

"You were taught to throw spoons?"

"It was a knife."

"Can you teach me some stuff?"

"No."

"Because I'm different? Maybe I could figure things out better if I knew what I'm actually capable of." Jon's huff ended with a growl.

"It's not that. I don't know how."

"What do you mean—"

"I only know one way to learn it, and I won't repeat it." The words snapped in the air as Ethan drew his lips back almost with a hiss.

"Hey! Guys! Take a breath! We're all on edge, but snapping at each other isn't going to help, ok?" Garth interrupted.

Ethan curled tighter into the ball he was crouched into on the arm of the couch as Jon kept pacing and waved at him. "I appreciate what you've done, but you disappeared for a week now, and the only other…lycan," he said the word as if it were an illicit term, "I know pretends I don't exist. What am I to do?"

When Ethan didn't reply, Garth jumped in again, "I'm going to ask for your patience, which I get is hard right now. His reticence hasn't been because of you."

"Could have fooled me."

"I didn't say he wasn't upset, just that you don't have anything to do with it. There's a relationship thing and of course—well, never mind."

"What relationship?"

"There was no relationship." Ethan's voice was low as he stood silently. "But for the record, they're not a good idea. Best case, you lie to them. Good case you scare them. Worst case you kill them."

He walked out, slammed the front door behind him, and took a breath of air that tasted like snow and dread and regret.

72

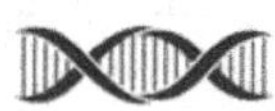

Before Cate had attacked, really attacked, that night two and a half weeks ago, she had dropped her knife. Her movements were always efficient and purposeful. Even if she had been toying with Ethan, it wasn't like her to drop a weapon needlessly. Had she dropped it because of the blood on it–Jon's blood?

Another blink brought the microscope back into focus. There were cells on the slide. Dead, broken cells. They were Ethan's. Exposed to Jon's virus. They had lysed within hours, twice as fast as the human samples that didn't accept either virus.

Had she known that exposing Ethan to Jon's virus would be deadly?

Another memory floated in front of Ethan's eyes. It wasn't his, not first hand, but the story had been clear. In the battles against the wolf demons, or lycans, a theme that was apparently not limited to Romania, the story of one death was told more than the others. One warrior from Caterina's clan, Dorin, had been bitten while protecting Caterina. Not knowing what he did now, Ethan had always assumed he'd died from the wounds, but maybe there had been more to it. Maybe there was a reason she had been sure to keep Ethan from contact with Jon's blood.

He turned to scan the file he'd pulled up on his laptop. The list confirmed his memory. Of the samples he had tested, those who accepted the V virus lysed with exposure to the W virus, and vice versa. Having only tested Jon after he was exposed to the W virus, he couldn't be sure if he would have followed the trend before infection, but Jon's current cells also lysed quickly when exposed to the V virus.

It made sense that if a relatively specific genome or set of other factors had to be perfect for someone to be changed rather than killed by the virus, that it wouldn't be common for a person to be receptive to both. But maybe there was more to it. The more rapid death of his cells was a deviation from the pattern of the other non-compatible samples. It seemed possible that the virus altered his cells to become incompatible with the other virus.

Perhaps the reportedly ancient feud between vampires and lycans was literally written into their DNA.

Moraine walked into the lab room, followed by Garth, retightening the coil in Ethan's chest that had been coaxed gradually loose by methodical lab work. Her discussion with Garth trailed off and her posture stiffened.

"I submitted those overdue grad student evals," Ethan told her, because he was supposed to, and because Garth's sudden look of constipation was too much.

Unwilling to revisit the distrust that hovered in her eyes whenever she looked at him now, he avoided her gaze as she thanked him perfunctorily.

"And Rav finally has a working thesis statement."

"What did he settle on?"

Ignoring Garth's wince at the light-toned falseness in her voice, Ethan told her.

After a couple more lines of stilted interaction, she left Ethan focused on his microscope and Garth standing awkwardly in the middle of the room.

Once the door closed behind, her, Garth started, "What are you—"

"I'm done for now," Ethan interrupted and quickly slotted slides back into racks.

"Ok. Do you mind if I take the walk about with you?"

Since Seeley had given him his old ID five days ago, Ethan had started taking a lap over to the research building and outside at the edge of campus in the evenings, maybe as a sort of patrol, just to feel out the area. It might be futile, but he wanted any kind of warning he could get if Cate was going to come after him here.

Garth must have picked up on his new habit.

"No, fine." He gathered things to take back into his office before leaving.

Remarkably, Garth let him walk for ten minutes before he tried again. "Have you found anything else recently?"

"Nothing new. Although…"

"Yeah?" Garth jumped on that.

"I think the viruses are incompatible. Cell death is accelerated when an already infected cell is exposed to the other virus."

Garth squinted one eye in thought. "You're saying if Jon bit you, that's it. You die. No chance of turning vampire to lycan—I guess that makes sense. As much as anything."

Ethan shrugged. *As much as anything…*

The streetlight came on as she jogged under it. It was a little dark for a jog, but how else could she fit in a workout in the dark months of winter? At least there wasn't much snow on the ground right now, even if the cold air was stinging her lungs.

She dodged some slower pedestrians and sped up across a crosswalk. That corner of the park seemed darker. The bushes held more shadows, and that street light wasn't on. She felt eyes watching, sending a prickling sensation up her neck.

It was enough that she stopped and looked behind her.

But there was no one.

If you're going to freak yourself out, you're going to have to stick to daytime runs, she instructed herself and started jogging again. A little faster around the corner.

A bus lumbered by, and its breeze stirred the branches of the hedge next to her. There was an underpass ahead, dark underneath. Completely dark. She took a right down a path to skirt it but found herself watching the darkness, as though something was waiting just inside it.

You seriously need to—

Someone was standing in front of her.

She stopped, her feet skidding for a pace on a patch of ice.

The person was dressed in dark clothing that billowed in the breeze and left the edges indistinct in the twilight.

Gasping a breath of icy air, she started to jog past, but a hand shot out at her and grabbed her arm before she could jerk away.

"Hey! Stop!" she yelled and pulled against the grip. It wasn't a secluded park. She wouldn't go quietly.

Unfazed, the figure grabbed her other arm and started forcing her back toward the underpass, lifting her so that her sneakers only grazed the concrete path.

The breath she'd meant to scream was punched out of her lungs with a face full of stone under the underpass.

No, no, no, this isn't happening. She twisted, but the person holding her only leaned closer until the piercing blue eyes were even with hers and a gentle hissing breath sent chills down her neck.

Garth considered Ethan's new theory and shivered as they traipsed down the sidewalk around the research building into a wind gust. "I need to find my scarf. How come you're less bothered by the cold? A one-degree lower body temperature shouldn't make that big a difference."

Ethan halted suddenly next to him and jerked to look somewhere to the distant right. Unlike whatever the sounds were that Garth frequently observed Ethan notice and dismiss, something had his full attention.

"What is it?"

"Screams…" Ethan's voice sounded far away.

"Is that weird for the city? What kind of screams?" Garth dropped his voice as though he might be able to hear too if he were quiet enough.

"Terrified…"

Oh.

Ethan bolted into the street.

What—shoot! Garth had no idea how he had just deftly avoided the two-way traffic across the street, but not one to be content at being left behind and fairly certain which way he'd gone, Garth started running down the sidewalk to sprint across the nearest crosswalk with a red 2 flashing to 1 in its countdown.

Two or so blocks of running later, he stopped, hands on his knees to catch his breath, and sought for clues to where Ethan had gone.

Was that a scream? He wasn't sure he had really heard it, like it was almost beyond hearing, and hadn't sounded human at all—*that way!* Garth took off again down the narrow street that ended at the edge of a park. He slowed, letting his legs jog out the momentum, and looked around.

There was a tunnel-like underpass at the corner of the park.

Under it—A figure leaning over something on the ground.

Fear, like a warning, trickled up his spine.

On the ground beneath the figure, was that a person? A woman. A pool of something under her head.

When the crouched figure turned blue eyes to Garth, the fear shot to his legs and made him stumble back a step.

A vampire was killing a woman right in front of him.

"I didn't–" the vampire croaked.

Wait. He knew that voice. And hat, and–

"Ethan?" He started forward again, still stumbling on the fear that he was unnerved to admit hadn't vanished at the sound of Ethan's voice.

"Ethan…help…" The faint voice drew Garth to the woman on the ground, her dark hair splayed across the dirty concrete specked with blood.

It was Lee.

Garth gasped.

"…grabbed me–" Her voice gargled on something wet.

No. No. No. No. pounded like a siren through his head.

"It's me. Don't talk." Ethan's voice caught in his throat.

"What happened?" Garth's eyes followed the blood to her neck where Ethan's hand pressed against it, nearly over her throat. Blood oozed through the shaking fingers. Actually, all of him was shaking.

"Call 911."

"911–Are you sure?" Garth was having trouble piecing together what had happened, and Ethan was blue-eyed and covered in blood. *Surely he didn't–* no assumptions. *Go with what you see.*

There was no blood on his mouth or anywhere but the hand he held her neck with.

"Yes! Now! She's bleeding out!" Ethan's free hand grasped at the pavement next to her, fingers digging at the damp dirty ground, and he ducked his head as far away as he could while maintaining his grip on her neck. He hadn't bitten her, but he wasn't ok either.

Garth fumbled his phone as he pulled it from his pocket. It should be easier to dial 911–*why is it taking so many buttons–*

"911, where is your emergency?" a small voice finally asked from the phone.

He knew where they were, didn't he? What road had he just crossed–"Fort Washington and 173rd, the corner of the park. A woman has been–she's bleeding a lot. We need an ambulance." He dropped his phone to clack on the ground and crouched next to Ethan. Seeing blood coming out of an actual person made his knees feel like rubber, but he'd had enough of watching Ethan struggle. "Let me. Move away, I'll do it."

At first, he didn't think Ethan was going to move, but then he grabbed Garth's hand and clamped it firmly against her neck. "Hold tight. Don't let go." And like something snapped, he darted to the edge of the underpass.

Her neck was slippery, and Garth's hand quickly cramped.

"Ethan…" Lee whimpered.

Don't panic. Don't pass out. Don't panic. "It's ok. Help is coming." *Please, God, get them here now!*

"I found her…" Ethan seemed to gag on something. "It left her here…" He wasn't shaking as hard, but his blue eyes were glued to Lee's face.

"What did?"

Ethan looked back at him as if his IQ must have just dropped significantly.

I get it, but this doesn't just happen!

Lee's face was so white. It felt like her life was leaking out through his fingers. Garth closed his eyes and tried to think about breathing, all while pressing even harder against her slick neck. *Does this happen? And we just don't know?*

Hours—or minutes—later, a fire truck pulled up on the street above. Ethan walked to the edge of the overpass where they would see him and simply pointed. Seconds later EMT's swarmed around Garth and started shooting questions at him.

He tried to answer, "I don't know what happened. We just found her. Yeah, I know her—she works with us. Lee Chen. Medical problems…not that I know of. Ethan! Do you know…"

The flap of a dark coat disappeared around the edge of the overpass and denied him an answer.

"Her throat is bleeding so much."

One of the EMT's blue gloved hands removed his bloody hand from her neck, then pressed hard against the still-pouring blood as their terse communication with each other became even more urgent.

73

Ethan stopped by the hedge across the path from the overpass and tried to breathe past the ice pick in his chest.

Lee. Someone had attacked Lee. She was—he squeezed his eyes shut. This wasn't that world. The deaths were supposed to end.

Someone inhaled on the other side of the bushes.

He snapped his eyes open, stabbing the vampire on the other side of the hedge with a blue glare.

Caspian looked calmly back as he swept the edge of his fancy long coat against the snow dusted bushes. "I did warn you to not let your kills become public."

"I didn't attack her," Ethan hissed back. "I found her. And she's not dead."

"In that case." Caspian waved a hand lazily at the skulking shape next to him.

The vampire didn't make it over the hedge before Ethan snapped the end of his knife toward his throat. "Don't. Let them try to save her."

"She's bitten, isn't she? Then she will likely die even if they stop the bleeding. Most do," Caspian replied easily from his side of the hedge.

"I didn't," Ethan breathed without wavering and held his knife blade steady so that when the other vampire leaned forward, it pierced his skin. He may have evidence that supported Caspian's claim, but statistics meant less when it was someone he knew. "Leave her. I work there. If they can keep her alive, I'll get her out either way."

"If you want the responsibility, then by all means you can have it, but with all the risk. Keep me apprised, and I can still dispose of the body, if you get it out," Caspian droned on as if negotiating a deal. "What is she to you?"

"I work with her."

"Ah, well, first kills usually are intimate."

Anger coursed through him at Caspian's blind insistence. Ethan bared his fangs. "You know it wasn't me. This is on your head. I warned you about her." Only one vampiress had ever been so insistent to take out all he had once held dear.

"You think it was your sire?"

It was pain that insisted that it had been her, but had it? Cate had been at the charity dinner, and so had Lee. She could have seen… "She's…jealous. And she threatened another woman I work with. Unless you know otherwise?" Ethan challenged the vampire who was supposed to know everything that went on in the city.

In a single leaping step, Caspian cleared the hedge and paused to consider Ethan more carefully. "You are clearly hers. I suppose you might know." He flicked Ethan's knife edge away from the other vampire's throat and started floating away down the path, leaving a small paper rectangle to blow in the breeze. "I'll see you soon."

Ethan plucked the business card from the air and hissed at their retreating backs. Anger and pain crashed through him, and a shameful hunger he couldn't banish. Only when he turned back and saw Garth in the snow between him and the street did he realize he'd brought his bloody hand nearly to his lips, the blood taunting him even as it dried.

With a curse, he yanked off his blood-soaked coat, dropped it to the ground, and started for the street where blue and red lights flashed. He needed to know what had happened to Lee.

There was a police officer Garth was supposed to talk to. But where had Ethan gone? Was Garth supposed to pretend he hadn't been there or—there he was, coming down a darker looking path from the park. The sleeve of his white dress shirt was red with blood, and his eyes were blue.

"Ethan, eyes." Garth wheezed with the effort of keeping it a whisper. *Man, this is crazy. If my eyes changed colors when I was upset, I'd really have no poker face at all.*

When Ethan stopped and turned around, Garth made for the police officer. He gave a brief account of finding Lee, glossing over how far away they'd been when they heard her scream, and identified the "victim" as Lee Chen, PhD.

"Mr...." the officer turned to Ethan who appeared at Garth's side dark-eyed and stiff.

"Dr. Ethan Dalton." Ethan answered his questions in as few syllables as possible, without quite making eye contact. As soon as the officer indicated that he was finished, Ethan immediately started for the hospital.

Garth rushed to catch up and tried to steer him without touching him. "We should go get cleaned up right? They won't let us in, probably–"

"I need to know if she's alive or dead. I'll need to get the body out if–not." The catch in the rhythm of his sentence was the only sign in his flat voice that he was upset.

That left Garth to follow wordlessly through a side entrance and down a quiet back hall toward the emergency room, but Ethan stopped before they got there and closed his eyes again. Garth took a breath to ask him if he was ok and got abruptly shushed by a quickly raised hand. Realizing Ethan was listening, Garth shuffled back a step and got as quiet as holding his breath.

Without comment or warning, Ethan whirled around and darted into the stairwell, leaving Garth to feel like a cartoon character who couldn't gain his footing to follow. By the time he got into the stairwell, a door above wafting shut was his only clue, but it was enough. He found Ethan in the men's restroom outside their lab.

Knowing his heart had to be pounding out the question as loudly as his mouth, Garth spit out, "Is she alive?"

Ethan nodded.

Adrenalin dropped suddenly, and Garth sagged against the counter. "For now."

"But that's good."

Ethan slid down the tile wall to the floor and whispered, "Maybe we should have let her die..."

Objections got stuck in Garth's throat. Asserting hope that she would live would mean hoping that she would turn, an alternative that, between them, only Ethan had the rights to judge.

Ethan's eyes turned blue again, but rather than fight against it, he dropped his head back against the wall and stared into nothing, moving at last only to rip his bloody shirt off and toss it to the corner of the room.

Needing to do something, anything, Garth took Ethan's discarded shirt, removed his own, and left to shove them deep into a trash can down the hall. Wiping at his eyes, he visited his office to collect a new shirt, a water bottle, and a thermos of blood.

He returned to find Ethan standing stoically at the sink in a damp T-shirt and dress pants, hands dripping but clean. Ethan eyed the thermos he set on the counter with a look Garth had started to understand. Pretending he didn't, he turned on the water at the sink in front of him and started washing his own hands, wilting a little when he discovered how hard it was to get the bloodstains off his skin and fingernails.

By the time he finished rubbing what felt like the last of his skin off his fingertips, Ethan was grimacing and setting down the empty thermos. He looked in the vague direction of the ER. "I need to talk to her as soon as she wakes, if she does."

Garth nodded.

"Let's try the front this time."

Garth nodded again. The night wasn't about to get easier.

74

Night had faded into early morning by the time a nurse woke Garth in his waiting room chair. His jolt awake put an instant crick in his neck.

Lee was out of surgery and had asked for Ethan.

Garth barely had Ethan's name out of his mouth when he reappeared nearby, and before the nurse could finish repeating herself to him, Ethan interrupted, "Let's go."

She led them up two floors and through the hospital maze to a room that was all glass on one side.

"How is she?" Garth asked hesitantly.

The nurse answered, "We were able to extubate, surprisingly, since there wasn't much swelling, but she needs to keep movement and speaking to a minimum, ok? And we'll keep the visits brief."

Feeling the discomfort of someone in an environment in which he held no expertise or power, Garth stopped watching Ethan until he paused at the entrance to the room. The tension was visible in his bare pale arms, every muscle tight as he looked down, then over at Garth with a question in his eyes. It took Garth a moment to realize that the question was about his eyes. He usually seemed to know when they were blue and when they weren't–he'd said something about his vision getting sharper. But he was blinking against the bright fluorescent lights, and with all the emotions of the night, maybe he couldn't tell anymore right now. Since they were his normal dark gray, Garth nodded reassuringly and followed him through the doorway.

Lee lay on a bed in the center of the room, surrounded by small machines with bright screens displaying numbers or bouncing lines, each connected to her by a tube or wire. A clean bandage covered the left side of her neck and throat. Garth stopped uneasily at the foot of her bed, very unsure what to do next. Her dark eyes opened and landed on Ethan who had frozen at the side of the bed.

He whispered, "I'm sorry, Lee."

Her eyes widened and she tried to turn her head to look around the room, scared. Terrified.

Ethan leaned closer. "It's ok. You're in the hospital. It can't get you anymore. You're safe—" His voice broke on the last word. After another moment, he said, "Garth, I need to talk to Lee."

You're going to tell her. Garth inhaled sharply and backed up. "I'll watch the door." Pulling it mostly shut, Garth leaned against the wall just outside and focused on holding it up rather than on the impossible conversation going on inside the room.

Until an urgent sounding beep at the desk made one of the nurses move his way.

"Ethan, nurse coming." Garth aimed his whisper through the crack in the door.

The door opened under the nurse's hand to reveal Lee sitting up a little and gaping at Ethan on the other side of the room.

"Sir, it may be best for you to step out for a little while, please," the nurse said. She checked a screen and then leaned over her obviously upset patient.

"I'm sorry," Ethan had his eyes to the floor. "You should have them call Ben." He left quickly, picking up speed as he passed Garth, who prepared himself for another Ethan-search only to find him in the stairwell as soon as he entered. "Oh. Thanks."

Ethan started plodding up the stairs.

Realizing it was pointless to ask how that conversation had gone, Garth tried, "What's next?"

Ethan's answer was a palm full of small tubes of blood.

Garth's tired brain spun hard to try to reason that out. "Wha…why did you—are those Lee's?"

"From the nurse, yes. They shouldn't be testing her now, if we can prevent it."

"What do you think they'd find?" Garth panted as he took the stairs two at a time.

"I'm going to find out."

Oh.

"What time is it?" Ethan asked.

The spot of dried blood on his phone case made him misstep half way down the hall. "7:47." He recovered and jogged the rest of the way to their lab door.

Ethan cursed.

"But it's Saturday."

"Can you still help me?"

"Of course. What am I doing?"

"Start prepping a sample for genotyping. Two if there's extra." He disappeared into his office.

Garth had two samples in the small centrifuge by the time Ethan reappeared at the table next to him with some clear plates from the viral tests he'd been running. Garth reached for a pipette while simultaneously handing Ethan one of the tubes he had opened. When his offering was left hanging in his hand, he stopped to look up. Rather than taking the tube of blood, Ethan had leaned both hands against the table edge and ducked his head away. Garth wilted as he listened to the muttered Romanian curses.

"I'm sorry…" In their current form, the blood samples had enabled Garth to engage in the routine of work, but he couldn't recognize the smell of a person's blood. He set the tube down and rubbed his gloved hands over his head. "I'm sorry it's Lee. It's not fair."

Why is it Lee? Did Cate find out somehow that she had been important to him? What is she after?

"Do you want me to–"

Shaking his head hard, Ethan sat down and reached for the tube of blood, cursing again but taking it firmly all the same. Deciding staring at him wasn't going to help, Garth went back to finishing his procedure.

They worked for an hour before Ethan disappeared to a viral lab somewhere and Garth re-labeled a remaining tube with some fake anonymous study numbers to send for some regular electrolyte and blood count labs they could do a lot faster downstairs. Then, left without anything else to do, he sat in the middle of the empty lab and considered trying to find Ethan. Or going down to the ICU to see how Lee was doing. Or having a breakdown right there alone. He considered a lot of things but got stuck where he was until Ethan walked back in. Glad that he'd come back, Garth got to his feet. "Do we know anything?"

"I don't know if I'll get any results on the viral test by the time…we know anyway. I sent the genotype. You did a smear?"

"Yeah, but it looks normal."

"Why don't you go home for a little while?"

Considering that Garth felt like falling over where he stood, it seemed like a reasonable suggestion, but, "How long? Until you can tell what will happen?"

"I'm not sure," Ethan answered after a moment. "Maybe tomorrow morning."

"Ok, I'll be back before then."

75

Garth's thudding heart announced his entrance into the outside lab, but he didn't turn on the light. Ethan watched him bump into a chair while crossing the lab and stop outside his office door. He didn't look especially well-rested.

"Any change?" Garth blindly blurted as he dropped a bag into the mouth of Ethan's office.

"She started running a fever," Ethan answered. "They think she has an infection…" They weren't wrong, they just had no clue how bad it was.

There was a change of clothes and a thermos in the duffle. He left the thermos, but took the clothes and changed where he was. Once he had finished, he crossed the lab to the microscope. "You can turn the light on."

Garth did. "Should we check on her again?"

"After shift change. I'm going to recheck this first."

But the slide Ethan apprehensively placed under the microscope lens didn't tell him what he wanted to know. A few of the cells, Lee's cells, were broken, which sent a new spike of dread through him, but most were still whole, dangling hope in front of him.

Snatching the useless slide from the microscope deck, he hurled it across the room to shatter against a wall.

Garth, having belatedly ducked, looked at him anxiously. "What does that mean?"

"Nothing. I don't know. Some of the cells have lysed, but not all, and it could be a positive or still too early." He leaned back. "I don't know anything."

Garth breathed again. "While that's not true, let's just leave this for now, huh? Go check on Lee again? I can go in alone this time, if you want."

When he didn't immediately answer, Garth started cleaning up the broken slide and some other things left strewn about. "Don't worry about it," Garth interrupted him standing. "It's actually nice to feel useful for a second."

After some uncomfortable waiting for the clock to tick to 7:00, they arrived back at the doors to the ICU to meet a familiar face. "Ben," Ethan addressed Lee's fiancé.

"Ethan!" The man looked nearly as haggard as Garth. "They said you were the one who found her–I can't even–thank you."

There was no answer to that. "How is she doing this morning?"

"I'm not sure. I think maybe not great, like there's something they're not telling me. But they said I could come back now."

Garth put his hand on Ben's shoulder.

"Do you mind if we come with you?" Ethan asked.

"No, of course."

The double doors opened to a sterile hall.

Moaning.

Lee was moaning in pain, and it crescendoed as Ethan woodenly followed the others to her room. Ben pushed into her room to join the nurse inside, but Ethan stood rooted outside the window watching her cry and clutch her stomach.

She vomited across the bed, splashing those reaching to help her. A nurse jerked back and yelled for help.

Blood glistened all over the sheets. Crimson splashes and flecks on the stark white.

Ethan's heart dropped into free fall. All he could see was Jack in that basement hall in the little Romanian town. Vomiting blood all over the floor.

He fled.

Pain twisted his gut, but he pushed into a supply closet before doubling over and caught himself with his hands on the smooth floor, unable to see it for the tears blinding him.

He had killed her. Just like all the others. Like every woman he had ever spared a thought for other than *her*. He was cursed. He was a curse. A cry tore from his throat, crescendoed to the top reaches of his hearing. High up on a shelf above him, something glass shattered.

He barely heard the closet door open, barely saw Garth stumble in and fall to the floor next to him. "No-no-no, what does it mean?

Ethan!" The fear in Garth's voice said he could see it in Ethan's face, but still he asked.

"Jack," Ethan's whisper broke over the name, "vomited blood…He was dying, before…"

"He was dying like that?"

"Until she ended it." Whole body shaking, Ethan bent over and buried his face in his knees.

"You're sure?"

Ethan couldn't answer. Pain grew like a bubble inside until it burst out in a sob that shook him.

Why? Why must everyone I dare to care about die?

He shrieked, at Caterina, at a world where people could die like this, at himself, until he ran out of breath and dropped limply to the floor.

The pain seeped from him into the cool tile, taking all his feelings with it, until he was left empty. Without feeling.

Numb.

He sat up. Pulled the black business card from his pocket and looked at it. There were things that needed to be done.

"Ethan–" Garth caught his breath.

Ethan watched the blue fade from his own eyes. Numbness was better. "Go," he told Garth. "Leave. Or say goodbye and then leave. I'll handle it."

"What are you going to–"

"She's dead."

Garth choked.

"The body needs to be taken." Ethan pulled out his phone. "I'll handle it."

76

It was a terrible Monday morning meeting. Everyone was drooping in their chairs or staring wide eyed at nothing in particular. Dr. Miller had given a somber recounting of the official statement regarding the death of Dr. Lee Chen.

Then the questions started. They were not directed at Garth, but into the room in general, without expectation of an answer. Still, the answers marched in front of Garth's mind's eye, covered in blood and screams.

Ethan sat behind him in the corner of the room, his expression as stoic as it had become in that ICU supply closet, a plastic mask compared to the pain it had held when Garth had found him crouched on the floor. It made him feel cold.

Dr. Miller went silent, letting the others murmur their grief, but her gaze found Ethan and morphed gradually into something like horrified discovery.

Garth's heart dropped. He shook his head, his tongue for once stuck in his dry mouth, while Ethan's blank expression somehow hardened a degree further.

No, none of this is right...

Ethan remained seated and motionless under her suspicion until the meeting broke up.

Garth moved too slowly to follow him to his office, and Dr. Miller caught his arm. "Garth, wait. You don't know what he's—"

"I know better than you do, I'd bet," Garth shot back reactively, before stopping to consider her. He softened his voice, "You don't have it right. He tried to save her. Her death broke him."

There was fear in her eyes as she looked into his face, doubting his words.

"I was there, Moraine."

"Were you there for the whole time? Did you see everything?"

"I saw enough." Garth blinked away tears and waited until she left to go to Ethan's closed office door, which would not have been thick enough to keep him from hearing their exchange.

It was a risk to enter uninvited, but he took it and slipped inside the dark room and shut the door. "Don't worry about her. She's upset too, but she'll realize she's wrong about you–"

"She's right." Ethan's voice came from the darkness.

It startled him. "What do you mean–"

"I killed her. I didn't start it, but I ended it."

Garth backed into the door. "Ben said she died in the ICU a few hours after we saw her."

"She was in too much pain, and I couldn't hand her over to Caspian alive. I didn't know what they might do."

Time stopped for a moment as the reality of what he was saying settled into Garth, then sped forward to catch up again. "How…?"

"Quickly. Bloodlessly." A pause. "With her permission."

Garth searched the darkness for answers. Surely killing her still wasn't right, but it was much easier to rationalize if he'd done it to end her suffering that was going to result in certain death. "But the one that bit her…it's still not your fault that she was dying. So she's still wrong."

"She's still right. I am one of those things. It's safer for her that she hate me."

"She doesn't know you if she thinks–"

"She does." His emotionless tone slapped Garth in the face more than the words. "You've seen enough by now. How do you still refuse to see what I've done? What I am? The good you see isn't there, anymore. If it was ever."

Maybe he needed to see if he was right; Garth's hand mindlessly found the light switch.

Ethan sat at his desk, blinking at the light but otherwise not moving. Too calm, too quiet, but still Ethan.

It wasn't that Garth was blind–he'd been there. He'd seen the fight in his face. He'd seen the pain that was part memory. He just chose to see more. "I didn't say you were good. You are human–"

"I'm not."

"Never mind the DNA changes, all right! You are. Still. A person. You aren't good, none of us are. But you aren't irredeemable either."

Ethan stared back, not accepting his words but not arguing.

How was he so calm? It reminded Garth of his sudden change after he'd taken the blood from the cafeteria. "You said you…killed her without…blood."

"Yes. It turned sour at the end anyway."

"Then did you get some from somewhere else?"

Ethan's eyes hardened.

"You know you're different when–"

"No one else is dead. Leave it at that. Or run away. It would be smarter."

A pause. "Well, only a couple people have ever accused me of that, so it seems you're stuck with me. I'll talk to Moraine–"

"Don't. She'll do what she needs to. I have reports to file. Please close the door on your way out."

Unable to get anything past the lump in his throat, Garth did as he was told.

The lab was empty. Nothing was right. He sank onto a stool and started wishing for some old habits to make it all hurt less.

77

Moraine's confrontation came only a day later. Even with his back to the door and attention on the woman beside him, Ethan could tell it was her walking in by the sound of her steps, by her sniff, and the way her heart rate jumped at the sight of him and the new grad student seated alone in the lab.

"Yeah, you've got it," Ethan pointed to the screen. He was giving Ann an orientation of sorts. She was joining their lab at the beginning of the new semester after deciding on her dissertation's focus, and no one else had helped her get settled despite her technically being assigned to Moraine. When Ann had asked him for help, he'd consented. Their lab was not the most functional at the moment.

"Dr. Dalton."

Moraine's tone was more accusatory than friendly, but he forced a semblance of a cordial sound to his, "Dr. Miller. Ann, you met her yesterday, correct?"

"Yes, I–"

"What are you two up to late, alone?" Moraine was better at subtlety than that; she must not be trying.

It was barely after five, and they were in the lab, not his office. He answered, "I started a brief orientation. If you'd like to continue it–"

"Ann, do you mind if I speak to Dr. Dalton?"

"Oh, sure." She stood and reached for her bag with an unsure glance at Ethan.

"You have access to the calendar now, so you can see the scheduled meetings. Stop by tomorrow when your schedule allows. Have a good evening." Although his words were correct, his delivery was a little flat.

Regardless, Ann smiled and left with a wave.

Once the door closed behind her, he let the vestiges of forced life fade from his demeanor and waited for Moraine to speak.

"I don't want you meeting with the women alone." Her voice was tight.

His answer was detached rather than defensive. "Why do you think we were in here instead of my office? Rav left only a few minutes ago." She inhaled but didn't reply, so he finished, "She asked me directly for help, so I gave it."

She sat in the chair Ann had left and studied him.

With nothing else to say, he let the quiet ring and his gaze drift slowly, unfocused, across the blinking lights of the lab equipment.

Eventually she asked, "Did you hurt Lee?"

It was convenient that she'd phrased it in a way he could answer. "No. I found her."

"Garth was with you?"

"Yes."

"You tried to save her?"

"Yes." He met her eyes and held her gaze until a trickle of feeling threatened his pit of emptiness, making him blink.

"Have you hurt anyone since being back, here?"

"No."

"But you did. In Romania?"

More feelings threatened. He closed his eyes against it.

Her standing sent the chair rolling across the floor, but her steps paced rather than leaving. "It's strange that trauma is not only felt by the victim. Still, I regret pitying you."

"I never asked for your pity."

Her shoes slapped the floor. "Do you intend harm to anyone here?"

It was never my intent. "No."

She swallowed. "You can remain here, but know that I can get you removed at any time if I have any hint of impropriety."

"Yes."

"Including following guidelines as I deem necessary. Starting with you being required to avoid one on one meetings with the students. They must be taken in public places. As must meetings including me."

It was petty of her to announce a rule he had already followed. "Yes."

"Does Garth...know?"

There was a simple answer and a much more complicated one. "Yes."

"Fine, his choice then." She reached for the lab door. "And if you surprise me in this lab ever again…" She left without finishing the threat.

The emotions retreated with her, and he returned to his office but left the door open to the lab.

It was his domain at night.

Sometime later, six hours according to the computer's clock, Ethan sat staring at his screen.

He'd completed a rough map of the RNA from the W virus he'd isolated from Jon while he was still in the early stages of turning. It was far from a full sequence, but it was still a singular achievement. He was probably the only person who had mapped that viral genome.

He had samples of Lee's blood and had tried to start a sequence of the virus in them, but it was contaminated and was going to take a while to sort through to see if he had managed to actually get a sample of the V virus from her. He was still unable to separate the DNA of his virus from his own samples.

So many more answers than he had started with, and so many more questions.

The virus may be the cause, but he still didn't understand how. Or why. Or why he had lived and others hadn't. His viral experiments didn't mean anything without confirmation. Even if he worked tirelessly until he somehow found those answers, would it still change nothing?

Was it all meaningless?

He leaned back from the screen to stare at the blank wall beyond. What did it all matter if he could change nothing?

Lee was still dead. Jack was still dead. Ethan Dalton was still…this.

The dead would not rise. He would still be banished to the darkness.

He couldn't even keep his own darkness hidden from those around him.

He launched the cordless mouse in his hand at the blank wall, where it shattered.

How could I be certain?

The broken pieces held no answers, so he left.

The hall outside the lab was dark.

By slipping carefully through the door and letting it close slowly, he could avoid the motion-activated lights in the hall. It had taken a little while to learn where they all were, but now he could get to the stairwell without interrupting the darkness.

The basement held places in his mind where he didn't want to go, so, on a whim, he went up instead. The bottom half of the ladder to the roof was blocked off by a locked covering, but he got up faster by leaping to the top, and the hatchlike door took only a shove to open.

Gravel scraped under his first step until he adapted how he took the next one. He walked to the short ledge at the edge of the roof and crouched there, staring out at the other rooftops and windows of taller buildings. None were close enough to notice him perched above the world. Life went on below, but he was separate. Alone.

It was as if he had never left the cave. Still fear reigned. Still she controlled who he dared have contact with. Still the need for blood made him a demon. And there was ever the truth of the sun keeping him in the dark.

He was a fool to imagine it differently.

Before the cave, he'd never taken much time to contemplate good and evil, but since living in a hell inhabited by devils, it seemed impossible to escape. Every time he tried to do good, to protect someone, evil befell them anyway.

Leaned out over the empty space, he mused the distance to the ground. The light made distances more exact. That drop lacked the mystery and possibilities the utterly dark abysses granted. In the light, it was clear that a fall from the ledge would not be enough to grant death. It might sting his legs if he didn't roll when he landed, but it wouldn't even be enough to risk injury.

The darkness promised more, empty or not as the promises were.

The numbness threatened to immobilize him. There was no sense of accomplishment, no burning curiosity prodding him onward, only emptiness. Nothing he did changed what he had become. Not even escaping halfway around the world.

He screamed a shrill screech into the endless sea of lights and sounds. With a leap up, he pulled away from the squeeze of despair and started walking along the edge of the roof.

Running.

The ledge ended in empty space, but there was another roof beyond it.

With trust in his legs and months of judging distances in buried canyons, he leaped. The rush of air filled his ears and nose as he drew his legs inward in time to land feet first on the lip of the next building.

As if the momentum had disappeared, he pulled into a crouch that didn't move once his feet and hands touched down.

He inhaled the coolness of the wind and he felt…something.

Afraid to remain still lest he sink again, he found another rooftop within his range and jumped up into a sprint along the precipice. His leap propelled him upward until his hands grasped the ledge and pulled him up into a tucked roll to his feet next to a looming rooftop water tower. Before him, the city stretched out, built of black sparkling building blocks, light and darkness.

As if answering his earlier call, a piercing shriek came from somewhere in those rooftops.

A familiar voice. Still she stalked him.

She would come again soon.

It seemed he couldn't escape evil, but he wouldn't go back to her hell.

He drew his blade and approached the water tower ladder. The time for feeling and pretending had passed. It wouldn't do to be out of practice the next time.

He leaped upwards, danced across footholds, and parried at shadows. Because she would keep her promise, and he needed to be ready.

78

The micropipette spun over Garth's fingers and landed against the inside of his thumb. Again. And again, over his knuckles, to his palm. Around and around.

Like his thoughts.

Garth didn't know what to do. Not about the samples in front of him—he knew what he was supposed to be doing with them. He had no idea what to do with Ethan, who had drawn even further inward over the past few days, remained at the lab continually, as far as he could tell, and scarcely spoke to him at all.

"I tried," he whispered upward, toward the ceiling, despite the fact that God could have heard him speak in any direction. "I've stuck close, like a friend closer than a brother, since he got back. But he's not letting me anymore. What do I do now? Back off? Keep pushing? None of it seems to be making a difference." He missed the catch on the pipette, and it dropped to the table with a clack. "Yeah, pretty sure I've fumbled this one," he sighed.

His phone vibrated in his pocket, and he pulled it out to answer with a distracted, "Hello?"

It was Carol. She needed something to do with paperwork for their new doctoral student, and she hadn't gotten an answer from Dr. Miller or from Ethan.

"I can help," Garth told her. He wasn't getting anything done anyway, and it was already after hours. "Why don't I just walk over now before you leave? No, it's no trouble. I'll see you shortly."

Seeley's chair creaked as he leaned back to prop one heel on the desk. There was a singing competition show on in the waiting room down the hall, and someone was completely murdering "Music of the Night."

"No, don't scream that note—"

Half his bank of monitors went dark.

He dropped his feet to the floor and leaned forward in time to watch the second bank blink out, along with the lights above his head, leaving him in disarmingly quiet darkness.

Keying his radio only brought the crackle of static.

No power, no radio, no monitors. He pulled his phone out, an old-style flip phone, and saw the one bar of service he typically got in the building. He held off calling his supervisor, as he figured he would be busy with his own calls at the moment, and eased out from behind his desk to listen and search the hall.

It wasn't late enough at 6:28 p.m. for everyone to be gone from the building, but the area was at least momentarily empty. He opened the nearest exterior door, looked out into the twilight, and searched for a nearby streetlight.

It was illuminated.

The power wasn't out to the whole block, but just the building?

As he considered what might cause that, Seeley closed the door and walked around the corner to the stairwell. Inside there was only more darkness and quiet. He hesitated. Without communications, he should probably remain at his post, but the breaker boxes were only one level down. When another glance at the hall showed continued stillness, he eased into the stairwell, let the door close behind him, and descended lightly to the basement.

The darkness was absolute. As was the silence.

Except…something was emitting a high pitched clicking.

Seeley stepped into the basement hall and closed the stairwell door behind him. He pulled the Maglite from his belt and stepped forward on his toes in the direction of the breaker boxes. If whoever was making the clicking knew how to navigate using the sound, they had the advantage. He knew the basic basement layout, but he was walking blind now.

And they were up ahead somewhere.

"Professor?" Seeley risked asking the darkness, since he seemed the most likely candidate. "What are you up to down here?" He was an odd one, and liked his dark corners, but Seeley couldn't imagine why he would be tampering with the power to the whole building.

The silence didn't change, but something stirred the air directly in front of him.

Seeley froze.

Still silence.

And a single heartbeat to his left.

He turned to follow it. "What are you playing at, Dalton?"

The voice that answered was sultry and heavily accented and not at all Dr. Dalton's. It repeated his question back to him, "What are you 'playing,' Guard?"

Warning surged through Seeley, uselessly turning his eyes in the utter darkness. The vampire was a stranger. One who navigated darkness like the old ones. And like Dalton. Seeley still didn't know who had beat Ethan up that night a couple weeks ago, but he had said something about a "she." Seeley was suddenly sure "she" wasn't someone he wanted to cross. "What are you doing here?" he asked.

"You guard Etan?" Her voice circled him. "The humans? Caspian?"

He turned to follow and fingered the switch on the light in his hand. She seemed about as good at answering his questions as the professor was. Maybe it would be a good move to answer one of hers. "I don't work for Caspian. Or Ethan Dalton. I'm just working, guarding the building. Did you kill the power? Why?"

"Why?" She repeated, her voice advancing and propelling Seeley to slide back in retreat until he reached the wall behind him. "Why guard them?"

Seeley considered the deeper implication of her question. *This is just a job*, he would have answered anyone else. But he stood there, faced with a real threat, with no clue what her end goal was. How far was he willing to go to do his job of security guard? "This would be a lot easier of a conversation if you would just tell me what you're after."

"Stay," she hissed softly in his face.

An order to stay out of her way.

Seeley swallowed. "I can't just let you keep cutting the power. The next building over is the hospital."

A whisper of movement.

Seeley clicked on the flashlight.

Her flinch didn't stop the swing of her glinting blade.

It was too late to block her, so he didn't try, but instead swung his heavy flashlight at her face while she was momentarily disoriented. It connected with some part of her, but her blade cut deep enough into his thigh to make his leg collapse under him.

His one-legged dodge backwards was clumsy and let her wrench the blade deeper before she pulled it clean.

He grabbed for his own utility knife, held it in his fist, and bared his fangs in a full-throated cry as she launched a leaping attack from above.

79

Jon stood in the hall at the edge of the emergency room, having just delivered a red-faced man in a suit who was still staunchly insisting that he wasn't having a heart attack in spite of the EKG that attested the opposite. He was the ER nurses and doctor's problem now. Oddly, instead of wishing he was that doctor, Jon found himself eager to escape the ER, which was exponentially more overwhelming than the ambulance or the street.

The curtains separating the stretchers did nothing to separate the sounds, and it seemed as though at least twenty people were talking at once—not to mention the beeps, yells, and moans. And the smells were worse. There was blood, of course, amid a potpourri of sweat, urine, vomit, alcohol, something that was certainly dead, and a myriad of other things he didn't dare to try to identify.

Can I come back to this? Work here? Doubt ate at him, and kept him self-absorbed and oblivious to his partner's return from the washroom until she was right in front of him.

"Hey, you—well you don't need to look quite that depressed," she said. "It's the end of shift. If we stall just a little, we might escape a last-minute call and make it to sign out on time."

"Yea…" He gave himself a mental shake. "Yea, ready to go?"

⇗

I bet Ethan wouldn't have just run into that doorframe. Garth ruefully rubbed his thigh and fumbled his phone-turned-flashlight. "Carol? You still up here?" He panted from the stair climb. The elevators were out,

463

and there were no lights on the whole floor either. The power had gone out.

The dark hall seemed to suck in his paltry beam of light.

Something chirped. Like a mouse. Or…a bat.

A chill crept down his arms and made his light waver in his hand.

ᚱ

There was too much blood on the floor. There was a pool of it, glistening in the beam of the flashlight that still glowed from its discarded position on the linoleum. A crimson trail smeared the length of the hall from the pool all the way to where Seeley lay heaving slow breaths. He propped himself against the wall so he could reach down to try to mitigate some of the blood trickling from his thigh.

Bleeding, even from a large wound, should have stopped quickly. Her blade must have severed something important. That much was obvious as he searched for the right place to press his hand against the flow. The edges of his vision blurred as bile rose in his stomach.

No, you cannot pass out! He clenched his teeth and hissed in another breath. Someone would be down there soon. They should have been there already, considering that there was a power outage and he was sitting down the hall from the breakers. If he couldn't get away before someone found him in a pool of his own blood, he was as good as dead. Someone would make sure of it before the human doctors were allowed to try to save him.

The problem, besides his leg, was that she had slashed him across the belly. All the way across. If he so much as breathed wrong, more of his guts spilled out into his hand—which was the only thing holding them in as it was.

It had been torture to scoot himself to the stairwell door. There was no way he was making it up the stairs.

He pulled out his phone, flipped it open. No bars.

Groaning, he let go of his leg and braced his back against the wall. With a heave that spilled something else out of his gut, he grabbed the doorknob above him. After panting a breath and closing his eyes against the stars that exploded and threatened his consciousness, he yanked it open and shoved his shoulder into the gap so it wouldn't close back.

Ok. Last chance. He held up the blood smeared flip phone.

One bar.

Hooah.

Now what? Who did he call?

No humans. Obviously.

Call Caspian for help? Although he'd given Caspian's card to Ethan, he'd been raised in the era that had taught him to memorize everyone's phone numbers.

But if he called Caspian for help, he would owe something. Possibly enough to trap him for the foreseeable future, as long as he stayed in the city. That was something he had already taken great strides to avoid. To give it all away…but what choice did he have?

Wait, what if…

Two months ago he would never have considered it. But he had met some strange characters since then. A vampire who had saved a lycan. A lycan who was a public servant. And had left his contact information on the list of off-duties to call for work.

Would you save me again?

80

Ethan scanned the data on the screen. After analyzing hundreds of samples, he had a handful of genomes from people whose cells accepted the W virus and two apart from his own that accepted the V virus. It was a paltry amount of data even if he had been equipped to analyze it properly. And he still had zero reproducible evidence the theoretical tests would match what would happen to a real person.

His eyes flicked to the syringe on his desk.

What are you willing to do to find answers?

The old and new rules were blurred now.

A brief blip of his computer screen drew his eyes back to it. It had switched to battery backup.

And no light from the lab trickled in under his office door.

Ethan stood, stepped over his desk, and pushed the door open to listen to the silence—the hum of the equipment was noticeably absent.

A new whir started somewhere distant, and an emergency light near the floor flickered on, as did the sample refrigerator in the corner of the lab that was plugged into a red emergency outlet.

The power had gone out. But the lab was connected to the hospital's emergency grid, and the generators had kicked in.

The first step to catch a village unawares was to take out the power lines and leave the occupants in the dark.

It was her.

It was too late for any of the students to still be hanging around, but Moraine was sure to be in her office.

He had to move now.

After hastily pulling off his shoes and socks, he kicked them away and tossed his white lab coat under a table. He had to fight her alone, but the odds of someone needing medical care, and not the ER, were too great to ignore, so he punched out a text before shoving his phone back into his pocket and bolting out of the lab.

The outside hall was dim, lit only by the intermittent emergency lights, and quiet. His bare feet made no sound on the linoleum as he ran down the hall.

He had promised not to startle her, so, despite his better judgment, he called out to her as he approached her door. "Moraine!" The door was closed, but he couldn't wait for her to answer it. "Moraine," he pushed it open and caught himself in the doorway.

She looked up suspiciously from her desk, where a lit candle beside her laptop made up for the powerless lights.

"You need to leave. Now."

"There's no storm, I checked the weather. Flurries, but no blizzard. The power will be back soon–"

"It's deliberate. You need to get out–"

"I'm not leaving with you–"

"Not with me!" Ethan twitched with the effort of standing still rather than hoisting her bodily to her feet. "Go. To the hospital downstairs. Don't go home, don't go outside, don't go to the subway. Just stand somewhere in the middle of lights and people."

"Why would I–"

"Moraine!" Ethan closed his eyes and forced himself to calm enough to extinguish the blue that flared in them. *One last chance to protect a woman I care about.* "She is here. I couldn't save anyone else, but I will not let her hurt you. Or make me–I won't hurt you. If you leave. Right now!"

She stood, slowly, but turned to rummage around behind her desk.

"Forget your bag, just go."

Still she delayed. "I don't understand–"

"Moraine, please!"

She turned back around and looked him in the eyes. Seconds ticked by while she considered him. "Fine."

He backed out and led the way to the stairs. "Don't come back tonight. Stay downstairs. No matter what–"

A sharp repetitive click echoed off the hard floor from the direction of the lab.

They hadn't moved fast enough. She'd found them already.

Ethan tried to keep his shove gentle as he pushed Moraine through the stairwell door. "Run."

At last, her footfalls moved quickly down the stairs as he shut the door and turned back toward the lab. The hall came into sharp focus.

He would not be caught defensive tonight. If he was to buy Moraine enough time to get downstairs and disappear into the ever-busy hospital, if he was to have half a chance against Caterina, he would have to attack first. So he ran toward her voice and the section of hall where even the emergency light had gone out.

He didn't need the sound to navigate the familiar stretch of hall, but he clicked in his throat anyway to announce himself. Let her focus on him. Better him than the fading footsteps beyond that door.

Caterina was a darker shadow in the center of the dusky hall, waiting, sure and calm.

But this was *his* home. He knew where the doors were, where he could use the handrail to run along the wall, where he could kick the only incandescent bulb in the ceiling and shatter it, showering her with glass and drawing her attention just enough to roll through the air above her and land on the other side without contestation.

Her blade met his, flashing sparks in the dark.

अ

Emergency. Hospital Basement. Come ASAP. Quietly.

Jon reread Ethan's text, but it didn't answer any of his immediate questions any better than the first time he'd read it fifteen seconds ago.

He reached to the passenger side door handle, even though the ambulance was still moving. "Ellie, I've got to go."

"What?"

"I've got an emergency."

"What do you mean? Where?" Ellie's hand flicked for the siren switch between the seats.

"Back at Presbyterian—no, it's a personal issue. A…friend…in trouble I think." When she braked for a stoplight, he grabbed his bag from behind the seat. "Can you finish signing off alone? I'm sorry."

"You're going to jump out, right here? I can take you back, or—"

"No, just go, finish the shift right. Put any blame needed on me. I'll see you tomorrow."

"We're not back until Saturday."

"Saturday. Sorry." He opened the door and jumped down before the traffic light turned green, slamming the door behind him, and leapt into a flat sprint back the way they had come.

Ethan spun away, escaping by a hair's breadth Caterina's blade that sunk into the drywall where his face had been.

Forced by her barrage back toward the lab and offices, he leaped into a backflip and kicked out at its arc to send a ceiling tile crumbling down in her face.

Dodging the tile brought her swing up short and left Ethan still untouched except a small nick on his left forearm as he landed on bare feet and danced back to the lab door.

Without time to retrieve his ID from his back pocket, he landed a kick next to the handle. It popped it open and sent him to a roll between the tables inside. It wouldn't have been his first choice to risk damage to the equipment in the lab, but there was one that could be useful.

Except the power was out.

Instead of standing back up, he slid silently under a table to the other side, which made Caterina pause at the doorway to look for him. Grateful for any respite, Ethan stayed in a crouch and took the time for a slow deep inhale, knowing that the hum of the refrigerator wouldn't be enough to cover the sounds of his breath and heartbeat for long. He would only get the moment.

The refrigerator was humming. Because it was plugged into the red outlet.

Would the transilluminator's cord reach that far?

Time to find out, because she moved for him again.

He flipped the table in front of him onto its side, sending computers and papers crashing, and launched it at her with a kick so he could roll under the counter at the back of the room. With a yank he had the right cord in his hand, then shoved the refrigerator out of the way and plugged the cord into the red outlet.

She was charging him.

To avoid getting pinned down, he had to jump upward and roll over the top of the refrigerator. His feet landed on sliding papers by the door.

Now to get back to the other side of the room.

Caterina's lips curled in a smile easily seen in the muted emergency lights, a promise to not make that easy.

Ethan grabbed a lab coat off the back of the door as he advanced toward her, leaping over the table to a stool and then a rolling chair to keep himself a more interesting target. At the last second, he twisted to leap parallel to her rather than straight at her. It threw his own knife swipe wide but misdirected hers as well.

Unfortunately, her grab at his leg found its mark and threw him off so that he landed hard on his side rather than his feet and rolled with air knocked from his lungs back under the counter.

Under the plugged in transilluminator.

Already cringing against her knife point that cut straight for him, he reached up onto the counter with his hand still encompassed in the lab coat he'd grabbed, hit the on button on the microwave-shaped transilluminator, and with a shriek of effort and his leg braced against the counter, ripped the door off the front.

He couldn't see if the UV light hit her full in the face because he clamped his eyes shut against the bright white flare, but he didn't think it did. Still, it hit enough of her before the safety mechanism shut the light off that she shrieked and slammed into the overturned table behind her as she fled from it.

Knowing he had to press his advantage while she was still disoriented from the flash, Ethan stood, ignored the sting where her knife had cut him in the side, and leaped at her crouched form. Shifting the knife to his opposite hand, he ducked down into a forward somersault. His knife hit flesh, tinting the air with her blood, and he landed on his feet outside the lab door.

He'd drawn her blood and had gotten himself out of the cornered position. He twirled the knife in his hand to celebrate the small victory. A bad habit he'd picked up from Stefan.

Cate laughed at him, deep and throaty as she stood and turned to face him. *"It is good to know you have not forgotten all your lessons."*

Your approval doesn't matter to me.

She flew at him, speed apparently not hampered by the burns on her neck nor the gash to her thigh, and he parried with all his accumulated skill and perseverance, bouncing from a crouch to the foothold on the hall rail, to several steps along the wall, to a double backflip. They traveled the full length of the hall before she caught his foot with a kick that threw him back against the wall and landed her blade at his throat.

Ethan stilled, breathing heavily, and watched her calmly as she relaxed with her blade on his skin. Even though it ended this way, he had won the round. Moraine was long gone, in the middle of a crowd in the hospital lights, if she had followed his directions, and Cate's goal would not have been to seriously harm him.

She leaned forward and breathed down his neck. *"Why do you fight?"*

"I won't let you kill her too. Not like Lee."

"Who? Have you killed someone, my young vampire?"

He hissed and tried to draw back. *"I've killed no one I wasn't forced to."*

She sighed and pressed closer.

He hated her. And yet some part of him was still tempted by her. Despite the atrocities, he had embraced her, repeatedly, over the two years, because it was the only escape he'd had. Tonight felt so similar.

"I will teach you to embrace your choices, Etan."

Tonight, he wouldn't choose her. *"That would mean allowing me to choose."*

She smiled, lips parting to show the tips of her canines. The surety in her eyes soured his feeling of victory.

What do you know that I don't?

As if reading his thoughts, she answered by pulling a square of cloth, like a handkerchief, from her shirt at her breast and holding it aloft between them.

It was completely unrecognizable.

Until he inhaled.

Blood.

Garth's blood.

Not him.

His stomach plummeted, and she eased back a haughty step as she replaced the cloth with a smile. *"Good. I was hoping you had learned to recognize it."*

"What have you done to him," Ethan hissed.

"I have done nothing. A small nick on the arm. It's up to you to decide his fate."

81

The thin rope around Garth's wrists tightened the harder he pulled against it, digging into his skin and cutting off circulation to his hands. He stopped yanking against the rope that was knotted all too securely to the heavy bank of filing cabinets and started searching his immediate surroundings in the light of Carol's lantern in the corner.

Carol, why do you have to have these things packed so full? Ethan could have dragged these around the room to find the letter opener Carol probably had on her desk, but Garth was left only with what was within his reach in the front room of her office suite. That included a fake plant in a plastic pot, a few papers left on top of the cabinets, and the large leather chair that he could just kick with his foot.

"Can you reach anything?" he asked Carol, who was tied in similar fashion to the opposite end of the filing cabinet wall.

"No, son, I'm caught in quite a bind here." Her mascara was smudged, but she wasn't crying, just stoically sitting on the floor with her hands at shoulder height where they were tied. She had screamed, as had Garth, when the vampiress had grabbed them, each in one hand as if they were toddlers, and tied them down as if their struggles were even less powerful. Cate hadn't bared her teeth or changed her eyes or done anything to hint at what she was, other than the raw overpowering, and Carol still didn't seem to have a clue. As soon as Cate had gone, Carol had immediately tried to see if she could reach any form of communication to call the police, but Garth's phone was broken out in the hall and Carol's office was out of their reach.

Garth eyed the trickle of blood from the cut Cate had calmly inflicted with the tip of her knife and wiped with a handkerchief, and he switched from praying that there was someone else in the building who could hear their cries to praying that it was empty of all others. If she had only wanted to kill them, she could have done it instantly. Instead, she had bound them and cut him, just a little. It had him remembering his vow to leave a blood trail for Ethan to follow if he were ever kidnapped.

There are worse fates than this, Ethan had told them.

The thought made him yank harder, and the drawer he was tied to popped open with a screech.

"Now that's something," Carol encouraged.

Twisting frantically to his knees, Garth started rifling through the drawer. It was all paper, every file, but they were hanging files, maybe…He tried pulling the metal hanger from a folder, but it was dull and flexible and would take years to saw through the rope.

He left it on the smooth floor just in case and edged forward to see if his newfound range put him in reach of anything else. He got to the side of the leather chair before his arms jerked to a stop at the end of the rope. There was nothing under it or in it–

But there was a mug on the coffee table in front of it.

He rolled onto his knees and scooted his feet back until he rested on only his hips with his arms stretched out in front of him. His heel could just reach the edge of the coffee table. If he could kick the table, if he could just knock the mug off, he could break it and have a sharp edge.

His first kick rattled the mug on the glass surface.

C'mon, you have to get it. You have to thwart her plans somehow!

He tried kicking upward, hooking his heel under the edge of the table top.

It jerked toward him an inch.

"Try again," Carol urged.

He did.

It scooted toward him two more inches.

He kicked harder.

The mug fell off the edge.

It was within reach of his foot if he could bring his toes forward–

Carol gasped.

Garth jolted up to see that a shadow once again filled the doorway. A shadow with a pale face and haunting dark eyes.

She wasn't alone.

Just as shrouded in shadow in his black button down and slacks and hair to his collar, just as pale faced, Ethan followed her in.

And whirled to put his back to them.

Garth pulled his knees back under him and scooted closer to the filing cabinets. Tears sprang to his eyes as he watched Ethan hide his face. If Ethan had followed her because of his blood, he wouldn't have expected Carol. Carol, who he respected and had striven to be his old self with more than any other in this office, was now held hostage by the vampire who had started everything.

It was so wrong.

Garth stifled a sob and whispered, "I'm sorry. I'm sorry I couldn't stop her or get Carol free."

When Ethan straightened and turned slowly to look at them, Garth couldn't imagine the effort it took to keep his eyes dark.

In one step, Cate vaulted the chair to land beside Garth's shoulder.

⌐

"Now you will choose."

Cate was on the other side of the room, but she had Ethan by the throat, strangling him all too slowly.

"Tonight you will become a true vampire."

Garth.

"You will embrace it and not lay blame at my feet."

Carol.

"You will choose who you will kill."

Carol!

"Ethan! What is going on? Do you know this woman? Can you run and get help, son?"

Ethan closed his eyes. Carol. The woman synonymous with the Genetics Department in his mind and memory. Cate held a dagger to her throat. And if Ethan was to get her free, what would he reveal? He would kill himself in Carol's mind, and that might be worse.

He shoved that down, deep, begged for numbness, and opened his eyes.

Mind spinning faster than Garth's heartbeat, he stepped forward. *"This isn't your world,"* he kept his argument in Romanian. *"You have to let them go."*

"Must I? Yet here I stand." Her knife, wiped clean of his blood, glistened in the dim light of a lantern. She lifted the knife toward Carol's throat. *"They will die if you do not choose."*

"Ethan?" Carol's inquiry grew unsure.

"Stop! You don't have to do this. I have already killed. More than once."

"And yet you snivel that it was I who did the killing, forcing you, and claim you belong here, with them. You have not accepted your place."

"So I have to be with you to be a—" No he wouldn't say it, the word was too close, even in Romanian. Carol's smudged face pleaded up at him. "It's ok," he lied to her. "You're going to be fine. She won't—"

"She need not fear me. It is time they feared you. Which will you kill?"

Cate's English words hushed the room.

Ethan cursed her, turned his back to Carol as his eyes lit with hatred, and clamped his lips closed over the hiss that whispered through his teeth.

Still Cate watched him with that damnable amusement in her eyes, dropping her knife tip to Garth when he tried to edge between her and the cabinets to get closer to Carol who was starting to tremble.

"See? Still you strive to be human."

"Why would I want to be strigoi?" Ethan yelled. *"You kill without thought. For food. To prove who you are. To haunt me."*

"I do not kill needlessly."

"You went after Moraine. You killed Lee! Why? Because she once meant something to me? Because you're jealous?"

"I do not stoop to such a debased—"

"I know you threatened Nico to keep her from interacting with me outside the forge." Ethan called her bluff, citing history he'd tried to forget and leaned closer to her face. *"You chose Iulia because I spoke to her. Is this not the same? You can have anyone you want. Why must you have me?"*

She gazed back at him and for once did not immediately reply. *"This is not for me. It is for you. Your woman is gone. I killed none other. I do not repeat trials that had no effect the first time. If you show yourself competent and complete and still refuse me, I will not pursue you, Etan."*

He couldn't believe her. Lee's death could not have been a coincidence. And he had no basis to believe she would leave him alone. She was too good at dangling his greatest hope before his eyes.

"The vampires of this world kill for less, for pleasure and gluttony. You should be wary of who you ally yourself with."

"And you wonder why I prefer the company of humans," he spat.

"They are no better, but that is not the point. You are not of them any longer, Etan. If you learn nothing else from me, you will understand this. Choose to kill one and take their blood, or you will continue to believe you are can remain like them. This is not true."

While they argued, Garth had succeeded in getting as close to Carol as his rope allowed and he was trying to reassure her that Ethan would get them out of it and that everything was alright.

False hope.

Caterina made sure he knew it, leaning down toward them to enunciate thickly, "Which would you choose?"

Ethan flicked his blade, aiming for Garth's rope, but Cate caught his hand and muscled him back a step. *"No more tricks or questions or games. Or they will die and you will choose another."*

Any next move was delayed by the struggle to calm himself enough that he could look at Carol.

Cate laid her blade at Carol's throat.

The stately lady started to cry in fear, and Garth pulled uselessly at his bonds, ripping skin at his wrists.

Ethan was frozen by his own fear of what she would do and his failing attempts to keep Carol's fear from being of him. *"Let her go."* It was a plea again.

"You choose him?" she taunted with her English words and moved her blade to Garth.

"No!"

"Ethan! It's ok. Choose me." Garth called out, his voice calm. "It's ok."

It's ok.

It is not *ok.*

He couldn't kill Garth.

And he couldn't kill Carol.

He wouldn't. Surely, he wouldn't. *"This is not a choice!"*

"Then come back with me. Come back now, and we can choose another."

No! His mind screamed, but he didn't.

Kill Garth. Or Carol. Or go back. *I swore I'd die first.* But his wasn't the death she required.

He faltered back a step.

"What?" Garth entreated. "What did she say?"

She answered, "Choose. Kill. Or come."

Garth's heartbeat tripped over itself. "No," he whispered.

No! Ethan's thoughts screamed. He would rather do anything than to go back to the cave with her. But the cost...

Could he kill someone to keep from going back?

But he had killed to stay alive. What was the difference?

Ethan turned his back on Carol as desperation sharpened his vision again. *"This isn't necessary. I have killed."*

"Enough!" She pricked Garth's neck with her blade. *"No more stalling."*

Ice gripped Ethan's heart. He couldn't go back.

What if– "No! Stop!" What if there was another choice? *"Wait. I will choose. But not him. If you're going to let me choose, then give me the whole choice. Let me pick who it will be."* His own blood whooshed in his ears as he willed her to agree. She had to agree.

If she did, there was a chance for no one to die tonight.

A single whisper of a chance.

And he might not have to die either.

Her head tilted, considering him.

Her blade held still in the air in front of Garth, who crouched, hands extended against the ropes, as much in front of Carol as he could manage.

"If I am forced to take one of them, it is still your choice. Let me truly choose," Ethan insisted.

"You only delay."

"I'm not. I will choose someone, here, tonight, but I have to be allowed to go get them. And you can't harm them," he pointed at Garth.

She pulled an object from her tunic and held it up. It was a candle– the same candle that had been sitting on Moraine's desk. He hadn't seen her take it, but the office had been open during their scuffle in the hall. With a harsh crack against the metal corner of the filing cabinets, she broke the glass that contained it, and cut down the wax at the base before setting it on top of the cabinets. *"You have the length of this candle. Then they die, and you will still choose another."*

"If I choose, if I bleed a human in front of you, you will leave me to go my own way?" he pushed. If he was going to do it, he was going for broke. Despite his disbelief in her dangling hope, if he could get a promise out of her, he would believe her word. To his knowledge she had never gone back on something she stated as truth.

She met his eyes. *"You will be complete. I will accept your decision."*

The air was too thick to breathe. He paused before saying the next words, carefully forming them in the English that she clearly understood well enough. "Then you will let them go?"

Her eyes flicked to his mouth, and part of him waited for her to strike him, but if he was going to be free, then that included how he spoke. And he wanted the others to understand her answer. She raised the flint in her hand and lit the candle. "Yes."

He measured the candle with his eyes, guessing from experience that he had less than an hour, but it was not one of the candles he was used to. There was no time to waste.

"Ethan, what are you going to do?" Garth squeaked.

"Just stay with Carol."

Garth stared back with wide eyes.

Ethan spun and sprinted from the room. As he dropped down the stairs two floors at a time, he pulled out his phone and selected the number of their go-to statistician.

The whole plan depended on her.

If she couldn't make it back to her office in time, then someone would certainly die. Did he have it in him to choose someone else to die if it meant saving Garth and Carol?

"Hello?" a lightly accented voice answered the phone.

"Noami, Dr. Dalton here, I have an emergency…" he spoke into the phone as he pushed into the viral lab.

82

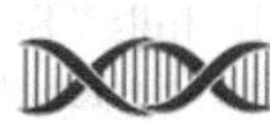

There were stomping boots in the corridor outside the supply closet Seeley had dragged himself into. One set. A pause to inhale.

Seeley chirped a high note from the back of his throat.

The stomping started again, toward his closet, and the door opened.

The lycan balked instantly, jerking back a step and looking back and forth as if expecting an ambush. "What is this?"

"Pretty much what it looks like," Seeley answered from his limp folded position next to a mop bucket.

Sanderson winced at the smell and kept checking the space around him. "Is this a set up?"

"Set up? No, I–"

"I saw the one outside, on the roof across the street. I won't be blamed for this." He ticked his chin at Seeley's bloody self and took another step back.

"Wait, who's across the street? A vampire? One of Caspian's? Do they know what's going on in here?"

That hadn't served to stop Sanderson's retreat away from him.

"No, wait, please. I…need help."

"Call the vamp across the street–"

"I don't–I don't trust them. Why do you think I called you?"

"I have no idea." But he stopped in the middle of the hall.

"I can't move. She sliced my leg half off and gutted me. My coworkers find me, and it's all over. I might die yet, I'm not sure. There's a lot of blood on the floor. On the chance that I don't, I need out of here," he reported stoically. He would have expected more pain out of dying, but then he couldn't feel his leg anymore, so maybe that was it.

"Who did this?"

"I've never seen her before. She's old and strong and fights old style. I assumed she's a new player, but if there's a scout out there, and they know and are letting it play out…I didn't call Caspian because I didn't want to be stuck with him, but he might not have come anyway."

Sanderson stepped toward him again, still as twitchy as a tom cat. "Where am I supposed to take you?"

"Well, uh, I'm still working on that, but we could start with getting off this floor where they're going to be working on the power, eventually. Not sure what's got them distracted to be honest. Radio's still out."

"I should be running for the hills." Sanderson pulled a towel from a shelf above him and tossed it at Seeley. "Keep your blood to yourself and stay quiet."

Seeley used the towel to brace against his gut as Sanderson hesitantly reached under his shoulders and knees.

This isn't a compromised position at all—but pain narrowed his vision to a tunnel.

"Quiet," Sanderson reminded him. "If someone catches me with you like this, it's going to start a war."

"I'll tell them it wasn't you," Seeley wheezed, struggling to breathe through the pain.

"That's going to go over real well if you're dead." Sanderson bumped up the stairs. "Where am I going up here?"

"Turn left, just keep going till I tell you—it would be easier to be quiet if you'd stop bumping me around," he wheezed.

"I'm doing the best I can." Sanderson adjusted his hold on Seeley and backed through the stairwell door into the hall. He grunted a few paces later, "You're bleeding again."

"Sorry," Seeley slurred, finding his head too heavy to hold up.

Sanderson's pace quickened. "Where?"

"Door after the utility closet…there. I have a key somewhere…" He couldn't see anymore.

A jarring crunch later, he found himself lowered onto a forgiving surface. Light stabbed his eyes.

Apparently he could still see. "Hey–"

"I can't see in here," Sanderson retorted as he aimed his flashlight away from Seeley's face and cursed quietly. "You look terrible."

"At least they won't get to kill me…"

Sanderson shifted in the direction of the door.

"What?"

"Someone's coming."

The blood trail ended at an old wooden door with a faded "Gym" etched into a clouded pane of glass.

"Ethan?" Jon pushed the door open, surprised to find that it swung freely–and he was face to face with the only other so-called lycan he'd ever met, Officer Peter Sanderson, in civilian clothes. "You?"

"What are you doing here?" Sanderson whispered harshly, yanked him forward, and closed the door behind him.

Jon didn't see Ethan anywhere, but the trail of vampire blood led to the supine figure on a faded gym mat. "Ethan texted me, said there was an emergency and to meet him in the basement, but when I got here and smelled," he waved at the blood, "I thought it was him–what happened? Why are you here?"

"Neither of us should be. They're apparently fighting," Sanderson pointed at Seeley, "and we shouldn't be caught in the middle."

Jon leaned over the bleeding vampire and pulled gloves from his pocket. Ethan might still need help, but he couldn't ignore the person in front of him. "You're the security guard?"

"Which makes you the professor's lycan," the pale figure rasped faintly. "Name's Seeley."

"Jon." He pulled the trauma shears from his bag and widened the rip in Seeley's pants leg. "Bloody–is someone going to tell me that this is just going to heal?"

"Might," Seeley's words were barely audible. "Not so sure about the rip in my belly though."

"Why is he still bleeding? Ethan stopped bleeding in minutes. Course his femoral artery wasn't severed." Jon answered his own questions and scanned the room until his gaze landed on a roll of athletic tape lying on a weight bench. He jumped up to grab it and dashed back to crouch at the vampire's side. "Hold on, Seeley, this is probably going to hurt."

"Can't feel it anymore..."

But as Jon lifted his leg onto his shoulder so he could reach to wrap the tape tightly around his thigh in repeated loops, Seeley shrieked a piercing cry that made Jon cringe. He kept at it until the blood stopped leaking through the tape and he ran out of the roll. After dropping Seeley's leg back down to the mat, he moved the towel that covered his abdomen.

Froze for a second.

Loops of bowel lay on top of his blood smeared abdomen. "Someone talk to me about vampire bowel injuries."

Seeley seemed to be focusing on breathing.

Sanderson was shedding his bloodstained jacket. "Push it back in. And get out of here."

Jon brushed his hair out of his eyes with his forearm and leaned over Seeley. "Look, this is bad. Even if I 'push it back in,' there's no way you heal fast enough to keep it in there, and then there's infection…" Or maybe there wasn't. If Ethan was right–

"Won't get infected," Seeley grunted. "You a doc?"

"Sort of. But not a trauma surgeon."

"Might heal if you got it closed…"

There might be internal injuries or… "Just close you up and hope for the best?" Jon gaped at Sanderson and wished for an answer for once. "Would that work?"

Sanderson pursed his lips. "It might."

"Then I'm going to need some suture." Seeley was shaking. "And…blood. Right?"

Sanderson was eyeing the hall, so Jon tried Seeley. "Any chance your security ID lets you into the blood bank?"

Seeley's wry chuckle wasn't promising, and Sanderson was making for the door.

Which Jon suddenly realized wasn't closed anymore. There was a shadow in the open space between the door and the jam. His grunt of warning came out in a quick low rumble, but Sanderson was already reaching for his light.

The shadow seemed to simply slide under Sanderson's arm. Halfway across the room it materialized into Ethan, disheveled with the faint scent of his own blood on him, and asking, "What happened?"

"You tell us." Sanderson had adopted a completely different posture that made Jon look twice. He still held his flashlight, but the straight-backed cop was gone. Instead, he had dropped his weight, slid one foot back, and leaned forward with one hand hovering in the air at his side. His eyes drilled into Ethan. "What have you done?"

<h1 style="text-align:center">83</h1>

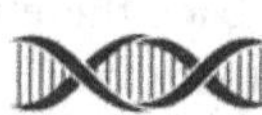

Ethan looked Sanderson in the eye, considered him. How was it that this man, a lycan, who had only met him once, could see so clearly what he was when every single other person he had seen or met since being back saw only the facade–the bookish professor of little physical threat? Even Seeley and Caspian were surprised when he could so much as control his eye color. Only Sanderson had started out presuming that he was the dangerous one.

Nothing yet, he only answered in his mind before turning to Seeley and taking in his broken appearance and Jon's rushed bandage. "Why did she attack you?"

Seeley's eyes slit open. "You are hers, aren't you? She moves the same…" He grimaced before continuing. "I was just doing my job. She didn't like it."

"Someone else came with you from Romania." Sanderson was a coiled spring at the edge of the room.

"I didn't invite her," Ethan replied without looking up.

"Did you kill the woman on campus last week?"

Jon answered, "No, she did," at the same time as Ethan's quiet, "Yes."

Ethan added over Jon's sharp inhale. "When she was bleeding from everywhere and begged for it."

Sanderson's posture softened a measure. "Did the one who came with you bite her?"

Ethan shook his head, finding he might Cate's denial after all. "I'm not sure who did it."

That had Sanderson tense again. "Caspian has a spy outside, at least one, watching the building."

Ethan sneered, hissing, but not at the officer. Perhaps his assumption that Caspian was incompetent was too generous. If he knew Caterina was in the building gambling lives, what could he be playing at by standing idly by? But that wasn't important right now; the candle was burning down. He turned back to Jon.

"Can I nick your ID to get into the blood bank?" Jon jumped ahead of him.

"Keep your face out of there if you want back in your program," Ethan retorted. "There are bags in the fridge under my desk in my office. Take the four bags of O negative to the basement, where I had you. He can have the rest," he nodded at Seeley. "The doors will be unlocked." As soon as he got back there first.

"Should I take him down there, or—"

"I'll leave that to you. Just put the O neg in a different room."

As Ethan retreated to the door, Seeley's radio blurted indistinct static, making them each flinch.

How much noise or other collateral damage had Cate wrought? Would it be enough to distract those who responded to the power outage, or would it lead them straight to her? And him.

Ethan turned back to Sanderson, who hadn't looked away from him since he'd come in. "Keep responders away from Haller level sixteen."

The look on Sanderson's face promised an argument, but Ethan didn't have time. There was no doubt that Cate would keep her word. He picked up the bag he'd left at the door and ran back toward the hospital.

⟩

"What's on the sixteenth floor?" Sanderson asked.

"I d'nno," Jon was focused on Seeley, who may have just passed out. Considering Ethan's response when he was cut up from his first encounter with this Caterina, that didn't seem to be a good sign. "His office is in the medical building. I've never been there but have the number—ay I can't carry Seeley up there and back down to the basement without someone taking notice. Are you going to help or should I come back for him?"

"You know we shouldn't be involved in this."

"I know nothing of the kind, seeing as you've only ever said three sentences to me about anything! I'm not leaving him here to die, and I owe Ethan, so get on out of here if you want, but I'm staying."

There was a pause. "What basement are we talking about?"

"Under the ER. I d'nno know if it's connected to this one."

"I can get you there." Seeley wasn't fully passed out after all, although he sounded close, and still had his eyes closed. "But grab a wheelchair. You're not carrying me like before."

"I'll find a wheelchair. Then I have to go find Ethan's office," Jon said and dashed for the door.

ꓘ

Ethan walked into his open office and considered the small syringe full of milky liquid on his desk. If he was going to do what he had in mind, there were two reasons to use that: to make this decision irreversibly while he was calm, and to get answers from it.

He pocketed it and picked up the half-empty bottle of sunscreen. *One more test for your theory, Garth,* he thought as he quickly smeared it over his body.

His eyes fell to his phone.

It had been twenty-four minutes since Cate had lit the candle.

He stared at the screen, willing it to ring.

Noami Becker needed to hurry.

He opened a drawer and snatched up a portable battery and shoved it into the bag he shouldered before leaving. Ran to the staircase. Dropped down four flights. Jogged through the dark overpass. Pushed into another staircase.

Twenty-six minutes.

He leaped up twelve floors, feet gliding from the top of one railing to another. Upward.

Until he stopped, crouching on the edge of a rail.

Twenty-seven minutes.

He texted her again, asking where she was.

Twenty-eight minutes. The reply: "Walking in now. Meet me at my office. You owe me coffee tomorrow."

I'll owe you much more than that.

Thirty minutes.

How much wax had melted?

He tapped on her office door. "Ms. Becker."

"Dr. Dalton." The dark-haired woman behind the desk answered with a light German accent. "What statistical catastrophe brought me back to my office after seven tonight? I have to admit, I've never been called in for an emergency before."

Ethan closed the office door behind him. "It's hard to explain. I'm afraid it's something I'll just have to show you."

"All right then." Her dark eyes studied him curiously as he walked to the side of her desk.

He paused and shoved down emotion that threatened to interrupt his careful plan. It didn't matter that she would suffer. Cate had Garth and Carol. And him. It was the only *choice* available to him. At least he could get some answers while he was at it.

Ethan leaned down next to her, reached for her computer mouse with his right hand and looked at the computer screen in front of her. His left hand pulled the syringe from his pocket.

She followed his gaze to the screen.

"Here we go…" While she was distracted, he reached around her, hovered the needle over her left shoulder. Jabbed quickly.

"What—" She jumped up.

The syringe dropped to the floor.

Her eyes searched him. Confusion.

He grabbed her by the arms and spun her away from him.

"What—stop! Let go of me!"

The volume of her voice increased with each word. He wrapped one arm around her waist, pulled her tightly to him, and clamped his palm over her mouth. "I'm sorry Ms. Becker. I'll need you to come with me for the next part."

He had the leverage to lift and carry her to the door, but she still had too much fight in her and landed kicks against his shins and while trying to throw her head back into his chin.

Probably he should have thought this part through better. With both hands available, it would be easy enough to carry her upstairs despite her struggles, but she would make a lot of noise, which would be a problem if there was still someone else in the building.

There was a sweater on the back of her chair. That would work.

"Get your hands off—!"

At least you're still mad at me, rather than scared. He shoved the sweater into her open mouth and pulled it behind her head to tie in a knot, careful to avoid covering her nose, then regained control of her hands and pulled them behind her back to hold them together with one hand. With his other arm, he tossed his bag back onto his shoulder and grabbed her legs, slinging her warm body into his arms as if carrying a child.

She arched and kicked, not easy to hold, but neither was his grip in danger of slipping against her struggles.

Stay mad, keep fighting me. Don't go quietly.

He listened over her muffled cries to the empty hall before walking through it to the stairwell.

They had better still be alive.

Cate had better keep her promises.

This had to be worth it.

84

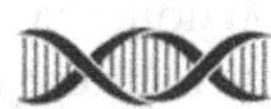

Had the candle just flickered?

Huddled in front of Carol, wrists raw and hands going numb, Garth watched the candle, because Cate was watching the candle.

She was perched on the back of the leather chair, crouched in a posture he had seen from Ethan. She hadn't moved, except to alternate between looking at the door, at him and Carol, and at the candle.

Having only grasped snippets of her argument with Ethan, it had taken him a few minutes to figure out what the candle was for.

But he had.

It was a countdown.

When it went out…what? They died?

Probably something like that.

Whatever it was, no way it was good.

There was nothing he could do. He couldn't protect Carol. He couldn't even get away himself. There was nothing he could do to save them or keep Ethan from being forced to go with her. He was completely helpless.

Even his prayers had degraded to a frazzled, "Help," bouncing around repeatedly in his skull.

So he watched the candle.

From his position kneeling in front of Carol, he couldn't quite see how much wax remained, but it couldn't be much.

And that flame was definitely flickering now.

Her dark eyes moved from the candle to him.

It was death he now stared in the face.

The last time he had faced it, he had been a blathering

incomprehensible fool.

Could he accept it with more courage tonight? More hope?

Her eyes moved to the door.

Nothing.

He waited.

There was something. A muted sound, like–

"Ethan!" He was holding someone. *No!* Who had he–that was Noami Becker, the statistician Garth had been working with for their latest paper. "Noami? What…" She was trying to fight Ethan, and although he adjusted his hold on her arms and legs, she wasn't getting anywhere. She had something in her mouth, gagging her, but she didn't seem hurt. Yet.

"Ethan, son, what have you done?" Carol gasped.

Ethan flinched, as if struck, but kept his eyes on Cate. He made a strange movement and dropped Noami's feet.

The rope connecting Garth's wrists to the cabinets fell slack and something clanged loudly. Garth looked down and realized Carol's rope, an inch below his, had also been severed by the silver knife that now lay at their feet.

They were on the wrong side of the room to simply run out, but he turned, kicked the knife aside as he did, and pushed Carol further back away from Cate. He couldn't get them out but he could get in Carol's face. "Hey, look at me, not them, ok? We're going to be ok. Look at me."

ⴽ

"Let them go." The moment Ethan released Noami's legs to throw his knife, she had lunged away, but he kept a firm grip on her arms which brought her brief moment of escape up short. *"You don't need to hold them anymore. I have chosen. I'll take this one, in front of you, as requested."*

"You know the girl?" Cate questioned.

"You heard him say her name. Yes, we know her."

"She's not your usual type."

"Isn't she?" Ethan held her gaze. Let her see that he had chosen Noami for a reason. She didn't need to know exactly what it was to be convinced.

"Do it in front of them. It is not only about the killing."

But even the facade of Dr. Ethan Dalton would die if he did any such thing in front of Carol. *Bury it.* He had to keep his eyes clear a little longer. *"The woman is too easy to scare. Let her go and keep him. He thinks he does not fear me. Let me change that. But there's no point in keeping her."*

Cate arched an eyebrow.

"You said this was to be my choice. Can I not also choose who will fear me most?" he pressed.

Noami managed to jab her elbow into his wounded side, which knocked the bag from his shoulder and loosened his grip so that she got her gag out and almost pulled away. Keeping hold of her required that he focus back on her and grab both her upper arms, lifting her off the ground as she screamed and kicked back at him.

Maybe it was his handling of her, wrapping his arm back around her waist so he could cover her mouth and stop the screams, that convinced Cate. Whatever her reasoning, she gave a light nod.

As soon as he saw it, Ethan jerked toward Carol and Garth. "Carol, get out, go. Run. Get help."

With a nudge from Garth, who must have understood that he was to remain, Carol stood, cautiously limped around the chair and coffee table, and ran for the door. As her heels popped against the floor of the hall, faster the further she ran away, Ethan loosened his stranglehold on his anger and fear and allowed the faintest bit to touch his eyes.

Cate watched his eyes turn blue with an expression that did not reveal whether she regretted letting Carol go. Regardless, it was too late to change it now. Carol might never look at him the same way, but at least she wouldn't know the whole of it.

Not like Garth.

Ethan kicked the bag toward the corner of the cabinets where he was crouched and wondered how much he was going to have to spell out to him to get his intent across.

Noami eyed the door Carol had fled through and struggled with renewed fight.

His grip on her solid, Ethan let her try.

"No more games. Kill your choice, or I will kill him and chase her down," Cate ended his stalling.

Garth had opened the bag, the one holding a UV lamp, the largest he could find, and the battery pack from his office. But he was eyeing the wrong vampire.

"Not her," Ethan told him. "Even if we get away, she'll come after you again, kill you to spite me, and still make me kill."

Freezing where he crouched with the light in his hand, Garth's face scrunched in confusion.

"It's for me. Stop me before I drain her."

Because Ethan had realized something, while he was on the phone with Noami, contemplating sinking his teeth into her and drinking her blood. If he allowed himself to bite her, to drink from her, he would drink his fill. He did not know if he would be able to stop while she still had enough to live.

He certainly would not be able to do as Caterina had done two and a half years ago, to bite and not drink at all. He had watched her kidnap and terrorize and kill, but he would never be able to accuse her of being out of her own control. Right or wrong in his morality, he could not match her self-control.

He needed Garth. If the woman he held struggling in his arms had any hope, it was because he was not alone.

Garth's eyes bugged. "You can't!"

"If I don't, then your life and Carol's are on my head. And she'll die anyway."

Noami froze in his hands.

"Take *me*," Garth insisted, his eyes begging. "I'm ready to die. I'm secure for eternity. I know what comes next. Ethan, just choose me instead. Don't kill her!"

"It's already done. She's already been exposed."

"What? How?"

Caterina did not make idle threats. In one smooth move she leaped to Garth and pierced his arm with her knife.

Baring his fangs and rage, Ethan shrieked at her.

"No more time," she stated plainly with her knife at Garth's throat.

This was it.

No more time.

He looked down at Noami.

There it was.

Fear.

It filled her eyes and trickled down her cheeks and screamed from her mouth.

As it should be.

He let go of her mouth and grasped her hair to tilt her head to one side. Her blood pulsed just under her skin in rapid strokes.

With her screams and Garth's yell drowning out the wail in his mind, he pierced her smooth skin with his top teeth, released momentarily to allow blood to start pouring from the punctures, and took hold of her flesh with a full bite, latching on and swallowing.

Sweetness filled his mouth and mind, purging him of the doubt and fear and hate.

For a moment.

A single long moment.

Then he could hear again.

"Ethan. Ethan! That's enough, man. Let her go!"

Garth's voice.

His heartbeat.

Ethan seized it in his mind and held on until he could also hear the heartbeat under his grasp. Still beating.

He let go, spilling blood over his chin and across Noami's neck and shoulder as he pushed her limp form from him to the floor.

"Finish it."

Ethan turned to Cate, eyes flashing but voice firm end even. *"What is it to you if I'd have her die slowly? She is mine. It is my choice. You have only to keep your word. I am what you made me! Is it not enough? I have been since the day you used me to kill Iulia. Now leave us alone as you promised."*

With a blink Caterina raised her chin and studied him, as if he had changed into a different person than he had been a moment ago.

Then she nodded.

And swept away.

The metal filing cabinet creaked as Garth collapsed against it.

As Ethan looked down at the blood covered woman at his feet, the world folded in on itself in an almost orderly fashion. This is what he was. The old Ethan was dead. He'd known it, but he'd tried so hard to pretend otherwise.

"Ethan? She's still bleeding."

She was. He knew he should pick her up and carry her to the basement for help, to Jon, but he also wanted to put his mouth back over the blood pouring from her neck, so he stood motionless.

Garth crawled closer, awkwardly dragging the bag and holding on to his arm. He stopped outside the pool of blood, grabbed her discarded sweater from the floor, and leaned over her to press it against her neck.

"I can't carry her." He looked up at Ethan after another moment.

"I know." Ethan crouched to pull a towel and a canister of bleach wipes out of the bag on the floor.

85

Jon pulled one last suture taut and tied it off. A surgeon would have had something to say about the rough line of harried stitches, but at least Seeley's intestines were contained inside his abdomen.

Seeley crumpled back against the stretcher, trembling. Jon had stolen a bottle of lidocaine to go with the sutures only to be told it would have no effect. The vampire's shrieks still rang in his ears.

Sanderson, who had been holding the flashlight and standing a wary watch since warning Jon to avoid Seeley's teeth, pulled him back a step from the stretcher Seeley lay in. "Toss him the last bags and back off."

Once it was clear that Seeley could still raise his head enough to tear into the bag of blood, Jon retreated into the hall with Sanderson, discarded his gloves, and washed up. He didn't know Sanderson, but the expression on his face clearly read that he didn't want to be there, yet he still was. "Thanks."

Sanderson's only acknowledgement was a twitch of his ear.

The hospital must have still been running on generator power, because the basement halls were pitch black and the rooms only lit by dim emergency lights near the floors. Jon had grabbed all the blood that he could find in Ethan's office, and Seeley had just drunk everything except the O negative he had stashed in the room with the thick door where he had woken up to a strange version of the world and himself.

Seeley's security radio squawked again, the voices competing with static.

"What's happening out there?"

Sanderson shook his head. "It's been all aimless searching."

The next report, audible from the radio propped on the rail in the hall, was not aimless at all, but an order for immediate security and police response to the sixteenth floor of Hammer research building where someone had been taken hostage.

Jon's gaze snapped to Sanderson's.

Whatever was going on up there with Ethan and Caterina was only going to result in more casualties if a bunch of people tried to crash it. "Can you do something?"

"Like what?" The cop paced a short distance. "This isn't my normal precinct. I'm not even supposed to be here."

"I d'nno, a diversion or something?" Jon was grasping. "Anything. She's insanely strong and fast. She'll kill as many as go up there if–"

"It's not my fight."

"It's mine! You can't just let them be!"

Roughly rubbing the back of his head, Sanderson pulled out his phone and paced away. A moment later, Jon could hear his side of the call as he gave his name and badge number to someone on the other end. "I'm in the ER with a friend and just heard the call come over. Listen, someone just ran through here with a knife, exited the south end through a side entrance, not the main ER."

Would it be enough to redirect the others?

"I can help if you hand me the radio." Seeley's voice, stronger than it had been minutes ago, called through the door.

"Careful," Sanderson warned Jon as he ducked back into the room.

Jon grabbed the radio from the rail and stepped over the empty blood bags to hand it to Seeley. "You ok?"

"Feels like my gut's on fire," he grunted. "But I'm not holding it shut or looking down a tunnel anymore, so thanks."

"What are you going to say?"

"Same as him. Give 'em more rabbits to chase."

Leaving him to it, Jon paced back into the hall.

Sanderson looked ready to leave. "We should get out of here."

Before Jon could object, the scent of blood drew his, and Sanderson's, attention down the dark hall.

It wasn't the same as the blood in the bags Seeley had just drunk. It was fresh, and there was a lot of it.

And some of it smelled like Garth.

"Garth!" Jon lunged down the hall, aiming the light from his phone in his hand in front of him.

Twin points of light reflected back, startling him before he recognized Ethan. He was carrying someone, a bloody someone, and

Garth, also covered in blood, walked beside him.

"Hey!" He slid to a stop in front of Garth and grabbed him by the shoulders. "What happened? You all right?"

"I'm ok, it's not that bad–you need to help her," he pointed to the woman Ethan carried past the wheelchairs. "She's lost too much blood I think."

The O negative.

Dashing back past Ethan, Jon led the way into the room with the thick door. "In here!" He pulled on gloves from his pocket, leaned over the unconscious woman Ethan laid on the bare hospital bed, and lifted the blood-soaked clothing from her neck.

"What happened?" No one had told him he'd be treating a human trauma victim in the abandoned basement. He had blood and one more pack of sutures from the ER supply closet but nothing else. "Someone find me some supplies! IV, gauze, an airway, something, anything!" He didn't even have a monitor or a blood pressure cuff or–

You don't need it. Listen.

He shut his mouth for a moment and leaned closer, with his left hand holding tightly against her throat and his right over her chest. Her heartbeat was steady but rapid, and her pulse was too soft. Her breath passed easily through her throat and into her chest in shallow but adequate breaths. She was unconscious, but stirred and groaned as he moved her head, perhaps only passed out.

"Is anybody going to tell me what happened? Is this her only wound? What's her name?"

His only answer was a coarse grunt from Sanderson, from the hall.

Jon looked at the puncture marks in her skin under his left hand. *Maybe I know what did it, yea, but,* "This doesn't tell me the whole story."

"Yes, that's the only one." Garth was the one to ultimately answer as he pushed a short rolling cabinet into the room with one hand. "Her name is Noami. And this is the only stuff down here."

"Why are you trying to keep her alive?" Sanderson's voice, still from the hall outside. "She's going to die anyway."

"She won't." The first words from Ethan were flat and terse.

Garth spun to him. "Do you know that?"

Ethan had pulled the neck of her shirt down further and was examining something on her shoulder. "She'll turn." He added more quietly, "If I'm right."

"Are you saying that you tested her?" Garth gaped at him. "One of the standardized samples..."

A new fear distracted Jon from his questions. "Hold on–Garth did she bite you too?"

"No, I'm not–just a cut from the knife."

"Why did she want her?" Jon bent over Noami again to find that the bleeding had mostly stopped. But he needed to get more blood back into her.

"'She' didn't."

Jon looked up to see Sanderson standing at the doorway and followed his eyes toward Ethan. "No, he wouldn't…"

The blood on Ethan wasn't just covering his chest and arms where he'd held her, but stained his chin and neck as well.

He had.

The one who had told him they didn't need the blood. Didn't have to be monsters. He had bitten that woman, drank her blood, undoubtedly infected her with the virus he carried.

Was anything he'd said about Jon true?

Feeling that the floor had fallen out from under him, he grabbed onto the edge of the bed.

"It was her or Garth." Ethan's voice was barely audible under the blood rushing through Jon's ears. "She would have killed him."

Sanderson's eyes went black as Ethan walked past him to the hall. "There are cops heading to the sixteenth floor. Is there anything to find?" Sanderson asked tersely.

"He cleaned up." Garth's voice was pinched and faint.

I've never seen anyone else's eyes do that… Jon's swirling thoughts were still stuck on the other lycan.

Blood. You need to get blood into your patient! Figure the rest out later.

He reached for the cabinet and rifled through the drawers until he came up with an IV catheter and tubing. *That you can work with.*

Finding a vein in her arm was surprisingly easy for someone in shock, and he quickly readied the blood, primed the tubing, connected it to her IV, and squeezed the bag so it would flow quickly.

She moved her head with a moan, and blood started oozing from her neck again.

"I need more supplies than this." Jon spoke to Garth, since he was the only other person left in the room, dropped the emptied blood bag, and pierced a new one onto the IV tubing. "Can you hold this while I get more supplies from upstairs?"

"Yeah." Garth stumbled over, looking pale himself.

Jon cursed and grabbed a rickety stool. "Just sit, hold this, I'll be right back and check you out. Ok?"

Garth nodded woodenly.

Sanderson was still in the hall, watching Jon and scowling. "We shouldn't be here." His voice was low. "This is between vampires and humans. We shouldn't be found with them."

"Then you go," Jon said. "I have to try to save her."

"The odds are against her. She'll die. Terribly."

"I still have to try." He found himself abruptly wanting very much to keep being a doctor, to keep learning how to take care of those who needed help.

Sanderson shook his head and turned away. "I can't do anything else for the human or the vamp. I'll leave out the back."

Never mind Ethan, or Sanderson, or anyone else. You're the only one in the bloody basement taking care of them right now. Who's to say you can't do it upstairs, in the ER? Do it anyway.

After you keep her alive, right now.

Jon took the stairs five at a time, bolted down the hall behind the ER at full speed, and slid to stop to take the next turn to the supply closet at a controlled pace. Counting on the EMT uniform he still wore to keep anyone from questioning him, he piled his arms with more IV supplies, bags of fluids, and rolls of gauze. The packs of suture went into his pocket, as did another handful of gloves and a couple of full syringes that lay on the table behind a curtain.

As he passed it, the automatic door to the ambulance bay opened to no one and let in cool air and something unidentifiable, a scent or a sound that tickled some instinct and raised the hair on his arms and neck. Jon slowed, watching the doorway warily, and backed toward the stairwell door.

There was nothing out there. Nothing but shadows.

Gauze dropped from his arms as he wrestled the stairwell door open. He kicked it down the stairs and quickened his steps down.

A rhythmic ticking echoed through the stairwell.

A chill ran through him and sharpened his view of the shadowed stairs and railings. He jumped down the last flight of stairs, threw the supplies in his arms into the basement hall, and turned to look up, drawn by some need to see the danger before it descended upon him.

A dark figure hovered two stories above him, a black hole in the darkness.

Jon tapped the light on his phone and aimed it upward.

Twin points reflected the light, blue jewels that peered out from a deep cowl.

A thin blade passed in front of them, reflecting the light off its silver surface.

He growled, a low instinctual rumble in his chest.

Ethan flew past him, leaped straight upward, and landed on the railing, becoming a shadow that melded with the other.

86

"Does your word mean nothing?" Ethan hissed.

A seething whisper answered, "I do not come for you."

"You can't have him either." No more. He couldn't save Jack. Lee. Iulia. Or the boy in the cave. But she didn't get to have any more.

"He is monster."

"So am I. And it's my choice who I protect, not yours. It wasn't Jon who killed Dorin. Take your revenge elsewhere."

"Get out of my way."

"No."

A shriek and a string of Romanian curses rained down from above with a whoosh of air.

⅄

Grab the bag!

Garth dropped the nearly empty bag of blood onto the bed next to Noami and stood, clutching the bedrail when the room went fuzzy for a second, and tried to follow the command Ethan had yelled before running out.

The bag. That could only mean the one with the UV light, right? Where was it?

Something thumped down the hall.

Hurry up, Qualls!

He turned around in a circle in the dim room and spotted the canvas bag resting on the floor in the corner. Reaching for it sent a sharp pain jabbing through his left bicep, which stopped him short. He felt like a

503

wimp, all woozy about a wound that was nothing compared to anyone else's. *C'mon, just get it and move already. Pass out later!*

Holding his left arm splinted against his chest, Garth dumped the bag, grabbed the light, paused a step later to reach down for the battery pack, and stumbled out into the hall.

Jon stood in the stairwell doorway, staring up.

Garth nudged him aside and froze with a gasp.

In the beam of Jon's phone light, two figures appeared to fly and dance around each other two floors above, bouncing from the rail, the walls, and the stairs.

"She's back?" Garth gaped upward as Ethan twisted away from the edge of a glinting blade.

"For me," Jon whispered.

Ethan leaped forward, grasped the handrail, and swung around to land a flight of stairs lower. A vampire-shaped shadow followed, lighting on the landing above him with a shriek higher than a whistle. Garth couldn't see her blade hit Ethan, but blood drops splattered the stairs when he leaped upward to grasp the railing above her head.

Instead of following Ethan's flight, Caterina turned to stare down the stairs at them.

Garth aimed the UV light toward her and looked down to orient the battery pack. He hovered the plug an inch from the socket and looked back up.

Ethan's feet swung toward Cate's head, missed when she ducked and spun, and Ethan landed in front of her, one foot on the rail, one against the opposite wall. Her blade flashed at his left leg, and he lost his footing and dropped down, spinning to land on his other foot and a hand on the stairs.

※

Ethan lunged up the stairs toward Cate, swiped at her, and failed to drive her back up the stairwell. "Garth, now!" he yelled.

"I can't!" Garth squeaked. "I'll get you!"

She hit the knife from his hand, metal clanging on metal, and it spiraled downwards to clatter on the concrete floor below.

Ethan couldn't keep her from killing another person. He'd never been able to. Not alone.

"Garth, just do it!"

He would either burn or he wouldn't, but it didn't matter. Enough was enough.

Garth couldn't breathe. His friend, covered in a woman's blood, fighting for another's life, had ordered Garth to irradiate him.

Ethan slammed against the wall in front of Cate's poised knifepoint.

Last chance, Qualls.

Garth plugged in the light.

Cate shrieked and stumbled backward. Her cloak slipped from her face and shoulder, the edge of it gripped in Ethan's fist as he ducked down. With another shrill scream, she disappeared upward to a floor high above in the blackness.

Ethan dropped flat to the concrete stairs.

Jon leaped forward and dropped over Ethan, shielding him and extinguishing the light that had enabled Garth to see.

A door somewhere above slammed.

Garth yanked the cord out of the battery. Pain sliced through his arm again and pulled a yelp from him.

The dropped light cracked against the hard floor.

"Ethan?" Garth stumbled backwards through the stairwell door into the dimly lit hall.

A silver knife came spinning across the floor.

Jon followed the knife, supporting but not carrying Ethan into the hall. He gave the knife hilt another kick with his boot, which guided it back toward the rooms that had become his emergency ward, and switched directions at the last second to take Ethan into the room Seeley occupied.

Garth followed but hesitated in the doorway, remembering he was still bleeding. "I'm sorry. I did what you said." His voice came out wavering.

"You did good," Ethan breathed with a wince. "I think I'm ok. Maybe sunscreen isn't completely useless against UV."

Sunscreen? "Really?"

Jon pulled Ethan's shirt off his bloody arms. "Is she coming back?"

The eyes in the room all shifted to Ethan.

He shook his head slowly as his eyes drifted to the doorway across the hall. "No, I don't think so. Jon, I'm fine. Go save Noami. Her heart rate is dropping."

Jon stopped, head cocking to the side before he burst past Garth. He stooped to gather some supplies from the hall floor on the way into Noami's room.

Ethan's eyes found Garth's. Garth stared back at the man who he had watched lie, kidnap, nearly kill, protect, and self-sacrifice in the span of an hour.

Did his actions and choices make him an evil creature?

Or only human?

"Help Jon, please," Ethan whispered.

Nodding, Garth turned to stagger across the hall.

87

Ethan leaned against the wall and fingered the small glass slide in his hand, pressing it against the tender skin of his palm. His whole body felt sunburned, and he had cuts and gashes across both arms, down his ribs, and a gash in his left thigh. But the sunscreen had prevented deep blisters on his back and neck, and he had Noami's blood in him. It already didn't feel as bad, 48 hours later.

He watched Noami in the hospital bed wince in her sleep. The morphine Jon had stolen wouldn't work on her pain for much longer. She was turning.

He had the proof in his hand.

Cells in the tissue of her shoulder had accepted the virus without lysing. It had been possible to get results from the cells around the concentrated virus he'd injected even before the virus shared by his bite had spread systemically.

His theory was right.

The virus was the cause of the changes in their DNA. His testing model worked—he could expose cells to the virus to determine what a person's response would be.

And he had isolated the viral RNA from Noami's cells before her DNA changed. He had the blueprint of the virus that had turned him and was turning her. It was already clear that it was similar to Jon's but different in several key ways.

He finally had the answer to the years-long questions about what had changed him.

Jon turned from the bedside of the patient he had not left and set down the syringe of morphine to reach for more fluids.

On a chair next to them, his arm sporting Jon's stitchwork, Garth eyed the syringe.

Ethan almost stepped forward to pick it up, but he stopped. Garth had waved off Jon's original offer of pain relief, but if he changed his mind, who was Ethan to intervene? He could no longer even pretend to have the moral standing to return to Garth the accountability he'd attempted to give Ethan.

That farce was over.

At least he could remain in his position at the lab and continue the work of answering questions. Actions taken in the hours after the ordeal had insured it.

Police and security swept the hospital looking for the intruder who destroyed several breaker boxes but found no suspects. A large amount of blood was found in the basement, but it wasn't confirmed to be human. Possibly it had been contaminated by cleaning chemicals from a nearby closet, rendering the usual tests ineffective. Momentarily-missing security guard David Seeley reported for duty long enough to tell them he'd been "knocked around" when he'd investigated the basement but didn't see who did it in the dark. He'd then promptly taken a few days off work to recover.

Carol's report was harder to handle.

Police followed her alarm to the sixteenth-floor administrative suite to find nothing amiss except a broken mug and a burned out candle, but she was not easily deterred. Once Jon had stabilized Noami, Ethan was forced to address her 24 missed calls on his phone and the ongoing police search in the hospital.

"You need to go tell Carol we're fine." Ethan set his phone on the counter next to the chair where Garth sat with his arm cradled in his lap.

Garth gaped up at him. "And tell her what?"

"We all got away. Soon after she left. The…delusional kidnapper left, was chased away, whatever."

"She was there, Ethan. She saw that there was more to it–with you, with Noami–"

"Tell her she's mistaken," Ethan tersely interrupted. "Dismiss her story. Everyone's fine."

"But–" Garth sputtered, "I can't just dismiss Carol. She's–"

"It's necessary."

Garth went silent.

"I'll come up…soon." He was still covered in drying blood. "You might change your shirt."

Garth walked out somewhat unsteadily, leaving Ethan with little confidence in his ability to formulate a believable cover story.

Ethan took advantage of the change of clothes he had long since stowed in his bulky messenger bag and the working plumbing in the abandoned basement and painfully removed the blood—his own, Naomi's, a little of Cate's…And struggled to ignore the accusing voices of the pattering water droplets against the cracked tile of the shower.

The blood in his system was doing too well a job filling the void where he'd stuffed all the feeling. Everything felt…more, which made facing the consequences of his sins more difficult.

By the time he'd limped up the 17 flights of stairs to the hall outside Carol's cordoned-off office, with his hat shading his face, and his hands in his pocket to hide the burns and a gash, Garth looked to be flagging under Carol's questions. Ethan's arrival instantly redirected her attention.

He took the offensive, "We're all fine, Carol."

"Where—"

"Noami left. She's fine."

"That woman! Son, what happened—"

"I had to play to her insanity for a minute, but then we held her off and got away."

"She had a knife! But you did too…"

"Yes, that helped." Ethan handed an interested officer a small knife he'd borrowed from Seeley—the appearance of which would raise far fewer questions than his own.

"That's not the one I remember…" Carol mused.

"The situation was tense."

"There was—what were you speaking to her, Ethan?" She turned her bespectacled gaze up to him.

He couldn't look back, didn't want to know if there was a trace of the fear left. "She was speaking Romanian."

"Did you know her?" the officer asked him.

"No. I just know the language."

"You came in with her." Carol added quietly.

"She forced me to." There was a momentary relief in speaking four words which were not a lie.

"Why did you leave and come back with Ms. Becker?" Carol asked. *Was that a hint of accusation?*

Ethan swallowed. "She was threatening all of us. Demanded I retrieve another hostage or she would kill you and Garth. When I got Ms. Becker, I came back with the knife and got her to release you to go for help. But we got away before you came back," he finished the story he'd arranged all at once.

"I'm going to need more details," the officer told him.

"That's all you're going to get. It happened quickly."

"Do you have anything else to add ma'am?" The officer addressed Carol.

"No," she answered after a pause. "I'm sure Dr. Dalton has given it to you straight."

Ethan turned away. Her use of his title plunged an icy dagger into his back, but he had been the one to hand it to her.

Eyes blue and face slack, he left without a look back.

Noami Becker called in the next morning, when she "heard they were looking for her," and told them she had escaped with Dr. Ethan Dalton and was perfectly safe. If she hadn't said as much, she wouldn't have had the option to return to work after her upcoming leave of absence.

Ethan returned to the Miller Lab in the early morning hours to reset it from the battle ground it had become and leave a check and requisition form for a new transilluminator and two new computer monitors on Dr. Miller's desk. He kept his interactions with her terse, and followed all her previously established guidelines to the letter. Despite the suspicion in her voice, she'd followed suit.

It was necessary.

If he lost access to the lab, all his research was lost. He had proof of what had changed him, but it was only the start.

Maybe he could get further with a good data analyst on his side.

Alone wasn't better, after all, but Garth looked at him differently now, like he was lost. Finally he understood.

As did Ethan.

He wasn't part of this world. He needed it, to do his research, and to live a life that wasn't in the bowels of a mountain, but he wasn't Ethan Dalton, not really.

He despised her for it, but Cate had proved her point.

He doubted her wounds were bad enough to keep her down for long, but she would keep her promise now—he was as sure as he could be that she would. He was hers, made in her image. She would honor his choices. As much as he wished for assurance that she would leave and go back now, he couldn't muster that much faith. Or he knew her too well.

Caspian was another matter. Had he or one of his killed Lee? They had been at the site of her attack nearly instantly. But why? And why stand guard, as it seemed, but not intervene while Cate attacked humans and vampires and lycans inside the university and hospital buildings? Caspian had warned him not to pursue his research. Was that his way of trying to expose or stop him? New hate ignited like a flame in Ethan's gut.

Evil was not confined to a cave in Romania. It had lived here before, always. And he was capable of so much more of it than he'd imagined before.

***

Garth was watching him. Ethan had cleaned up, but Garth would always be able to see the bloodstains on his face now. Garth stood, cradling his wounded arm with his other, and leaned against the wall across from Ethan. "She's turning? She won't die?"

"Yes. She's turning."

Garth's mind spun behind his eyes. "Why did you inject her with virus first, before…what if there had been a way–"

"There was no other way. I had to make sure it was the only decision. And now I have answers."

"But, you said until you were willing to infect someone else, you only had theories. You wanted to try it."

"It was necessary."

"That doesn't sound like you. It sounds like her."

Ethan didn't bother to deny it.

Garth shook his head slowly. "It's wrong."

Wrong. Evil. Of course it was. To save himself, he'd damned Noami to this hell. It didn't matter that he technically hadn't killed anyone. Did it? "How do you know?" he asked Garth.

"Because the One who made me said so."

"The one who made me demanded I give her a death. But Noami isn't dead. This was the only thing I could do that wouldn't result in *someone's* death."

Garth was quiet.

"It may not be right, but no one died. Maybe no one else has to die for me. Now you understand. I did this. It was my choice. It was the best I could do, and if you say it's evil, then you're probably right. *I* am not *good.* She was my sacrifice, the one I was willing to give for myself and my village. I'm no better than Cate or that farmer who sent us to die." He looked away. "It's your turn to leave, now."

After an inhale, Garth answered, "No, I won't leave you alone. I'm not good either, but for the blood of the One who died for me. I can't tell you what you should have done. The world is too broken. Maybe there really wasn't a good answer. But this is my world now too. I'll be here. For you, and for her. But how far do we go with this? The research. When does it end?"

"When I can stand in the light again," Ethan whispered.

Garth breathed quickly, evenly. "Then I guess I'd better stick around to point you to it. But answer this, please: Would you inject someone else? Test someone else? To get answers?"

Ethan looked back at Garth.

He wouldn't, would he? Because he hadn't. Even though there was another chance staring him in the face.

Because it wasn't just Noami's sample that he'd put a name with. He'd gotten identifiers for a whole batch.

He'd identified which sample was Garth's too.

If his theory was correct, and he was now more sure that it was, Garth's genome would accept changes made by the W virus. He was the option to prove that his theory worked for both viruses. He could be turned to a lycan.

But no one else would ever know. Ethan had removed the results from even his private archives.

Not Garth.

This world needed him.

"No."

Garth nodded. "Then I'll help. With the research too."

It didn't make sense.

"That's my choice," Garth concluded, as if the matter was done.

"Ok," Ethan muttered. "Your choice."

The heart is deceitful above all things,
And desperately wicked; Who can know it?
Jeremiah 17:9 (NKJV)

Some sat in darkness and in the shadow of death,
prisoners in affliction and in irons,
For they had rebelled against the words of God,
and spurned the counsel of the Most High.
So he bowed their hearts down with hard labor;
they fell down, with none to help.
Then they cried to the LORD in their trouble,
and he delivered them from their distress.
He brought them out of darkness and the shadow of death,
and burst their bonds apart.
Some were fools through their sinful ways,
and because of their iniquities suffered affliction;
They loathed any kind of food,
and they drew near to the gates of death.
Then they cried to the LORD in their trouble,
and he delivered them from their distress.
He sent out his word and healed them,
and delivered them from their destruction.
Psalm 107: 9-14, 17-20 (ESV)

The light shines in the darkness,
and the darkness has not overcome it.
John 1:5 (ESV)

ACKNOWLEDGEMENTS

THANK YOU to Brad for always being my cheerleader, for putting up with me when I go into a "book hole," for technical support, for science edits, and for last minute proof reading. To Daddy, my eager first reader with helpful plot advice. To Amy, my first friend to read my book-baby and faithful editor who made sure I kept the right mood with my word choices. To Mom, for originally teaching me to read and write, consenting to read a story I wrote, doubting my sanity slightly, and ardently supporting my every endeavor. I didn't kill the goat, just for you. To Brenna, for getting all the inside jokes only a sister could and for keeping me in the right tense. To Emma, for giving me inside knowledge of genetics and academia. To Cala Coffee, my writing home away from home. I went through nursing school, night shifts, grad school, and babies without drinking coffee, but when your iced lattes gave my writing new caffeine-induced focus, I was in. To Candace and Lynn for giving Romania more context, for enough excitement to make me actually consider publishing, for many book conversation and couch dates, and for a cover and art better than my wildest dreams.

If you would like to learn more about writing, may I highly recommend Steven James's books on writing and storytelling. They inspired me to make this the very best story I could.

ABOUT THE AUTHOR

B. W. Green writes honest stories about humanity and our Only Hope. She was raised as a missionary kid in Southeast Asia and has lived in Guam, Singapore, Liberia, and the north and south of the United States. Her time in New York City provided firsthand knowledge of its dynamic atmosphere, which serves as a rich and authentic backdrop for her novel.

She resides in Alabama with her husband, two daughters, and Boppey the cat. She works as a nurse practitioner and enjoys gardening, baking, and the creative process of writing.

www.ingramcontent.com/pod-product-compliance
Lightning Source LLC
Chambersburg PA
CBHW011510010826
48973CB00015B/2897